NINJA
THE MOST DANGEROUS GAME

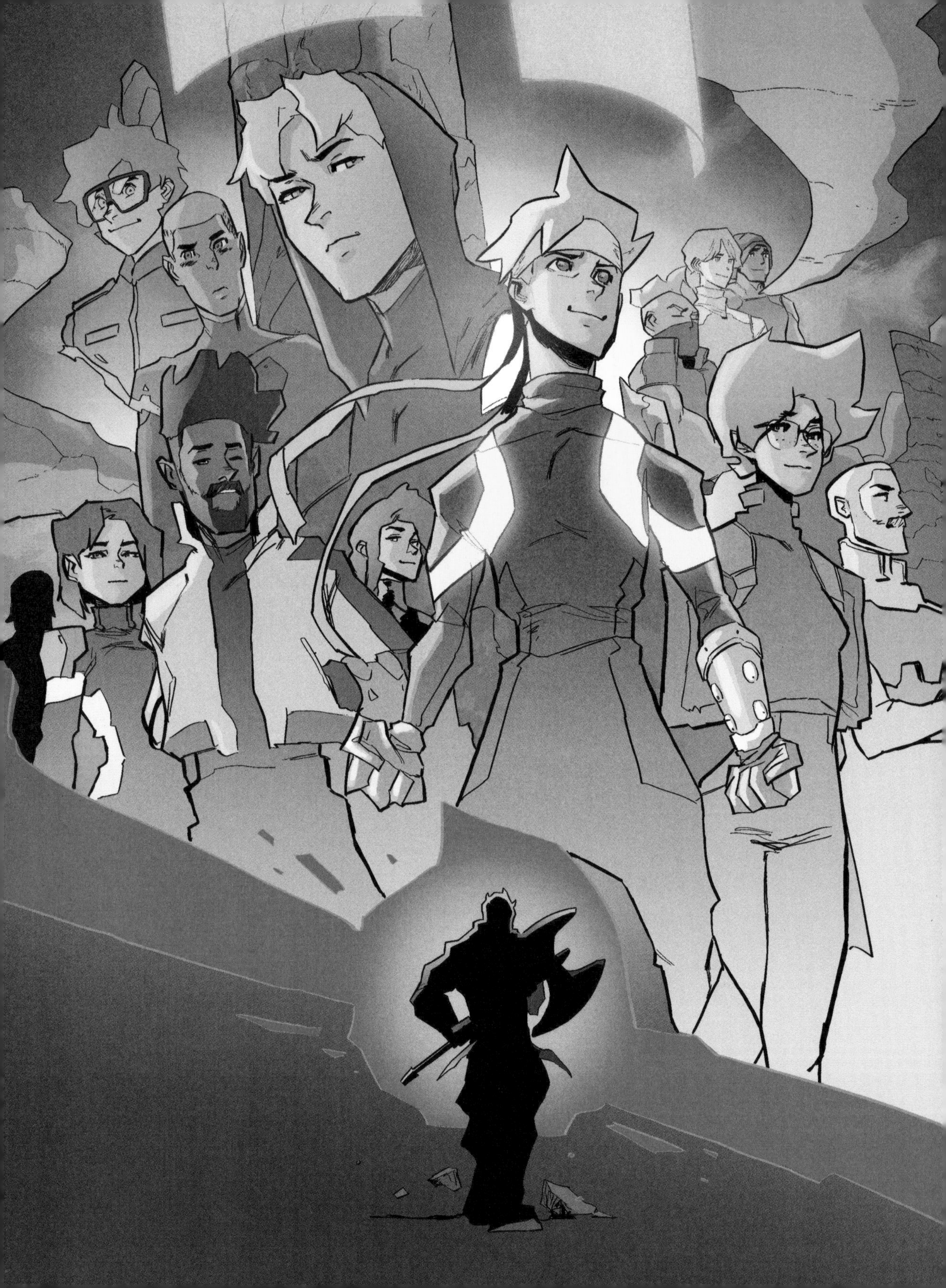

THE MOST DANGEROUS GAME

VOLUME 1

TYLER "NINJA" BLEVINS
AND JUSTIN JORDAN

ART BY FELIPE MAGAÑA

COLORS BY BRAD SIMPSON
LETTERING BY CARLOS M. MANGUAL

TEN SPEED PRESS
California | New York

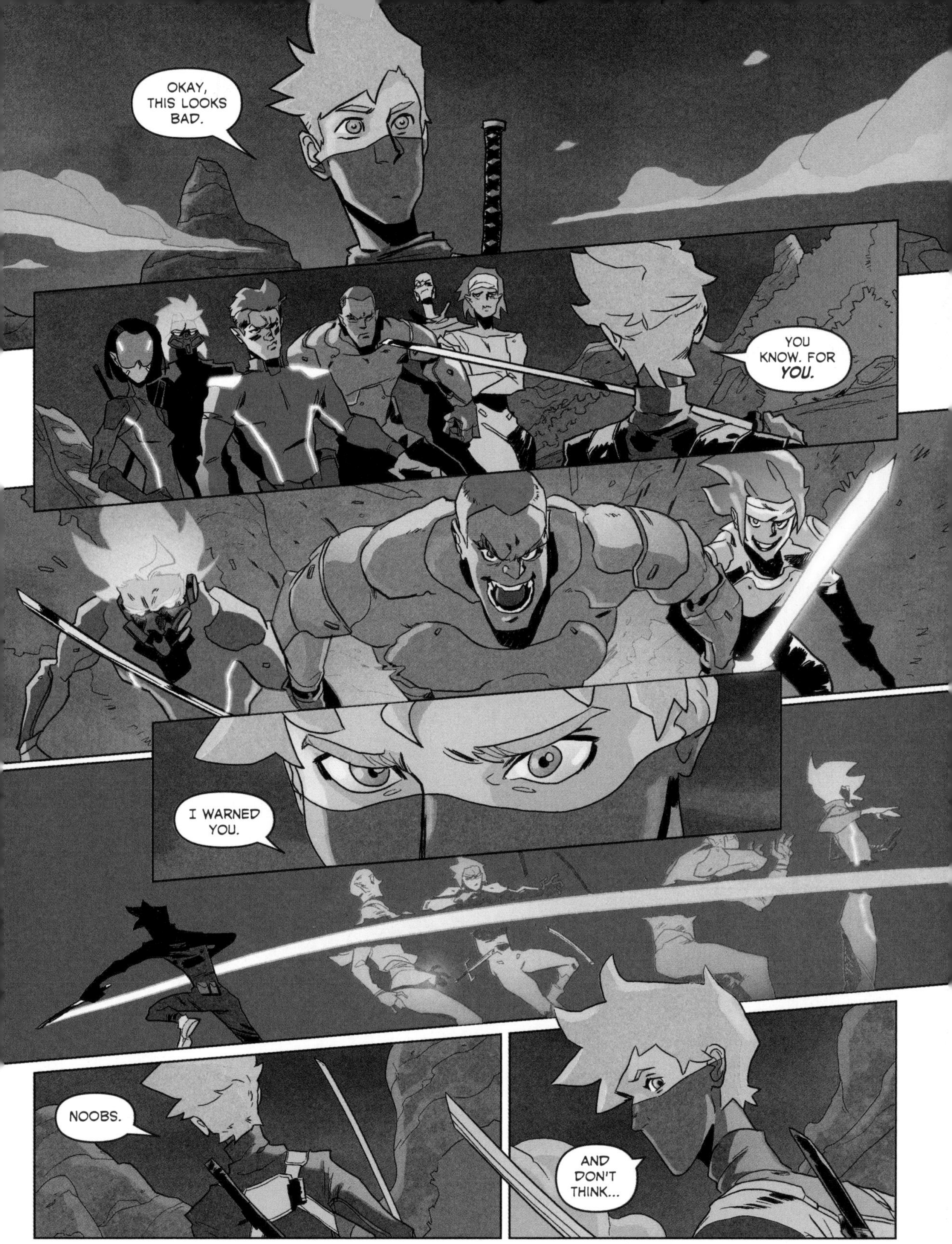
OKAY, THIS LOOKS BAD.
YOU KNOW. FOR YOU.
I WARNED YOU.
NOOBS.
AND DON'T THINK...

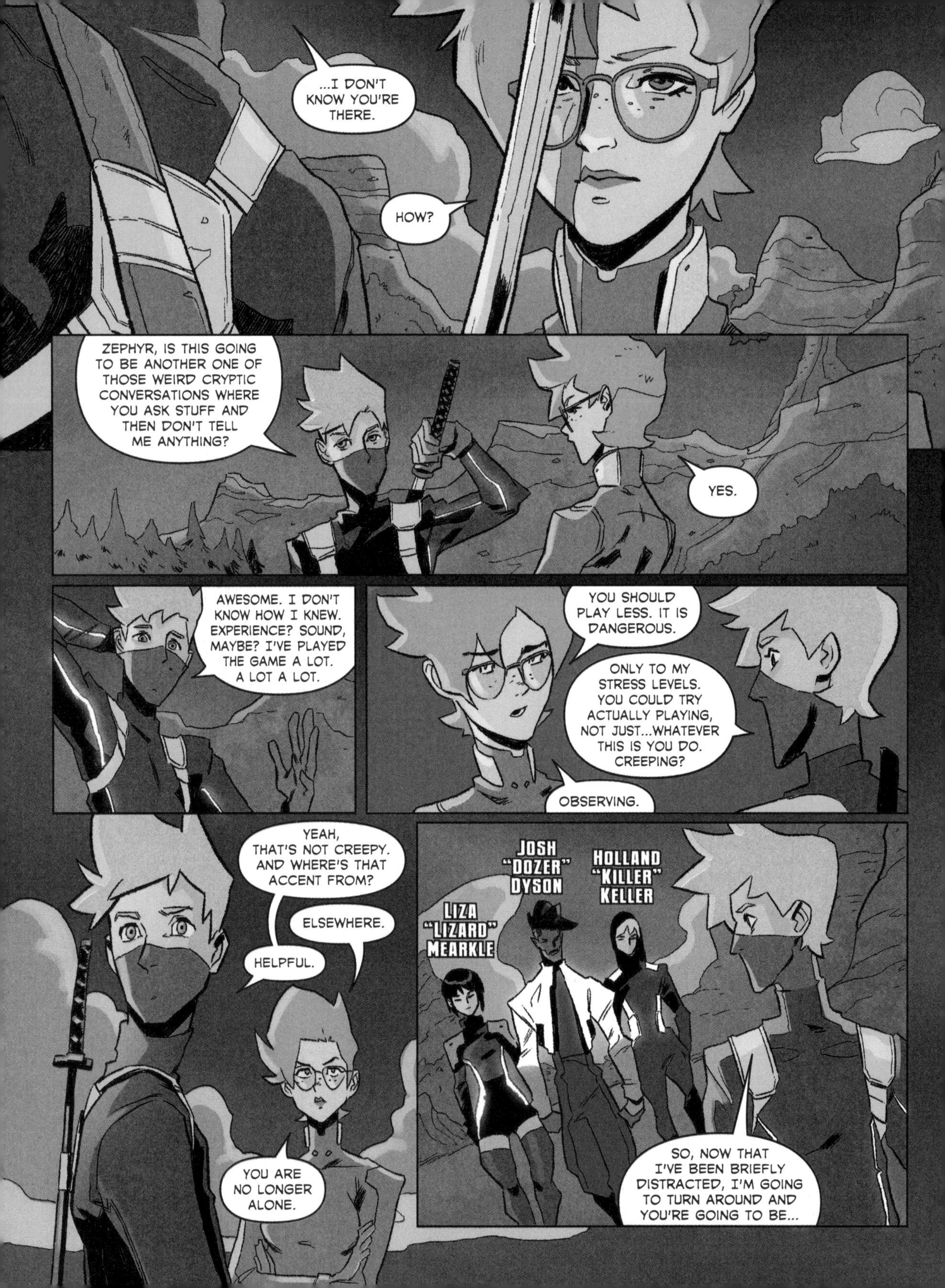
...I DON'T KNOW YOU'RE THERE.
HOW?
ZEPHYR, IS THIS GOING TO BE ANOTHER ONE OF THOSE WEIRD CRYPTIC CONVERSATIONS WHERE YOU ASK STUFF AND THEN DON'T TELL ME ANYTHING?
YES.
AWESOME. I DON'T KNOW HOW I KNEW. EXPERIENCE? SOUND, MAYBE? I'VE PLAYED THE GAME A LOT. A LOT A LOT.
YOU SHOULD PLAY LESS. IT IS DANGEROUS.
ONLY TO MY STRESS LEVELS. YOU COULD TRY ACTUALLY PLAYING, NOT JUST...WHATEVER THIS IS YOU DO. CREEPING?
OBSERVING.
YEAH, THAT'S NOT CREEPY. AND WHERE'S THAT ACCENT FROM?
ELSEWHERE.
HELPFUL.
YOU ARE NO LONGER ALONE.
JOSH "DOZER" DYSON
HOLLAND "KILLER" KELLER
LIZA "LIZARD" MEARKLE
SO, NOW THAT I'VE BEEN BRIEFLY DISTRACTED, I'M GOING TO TURN AROUND AND YOU'RE GOING TO BE...

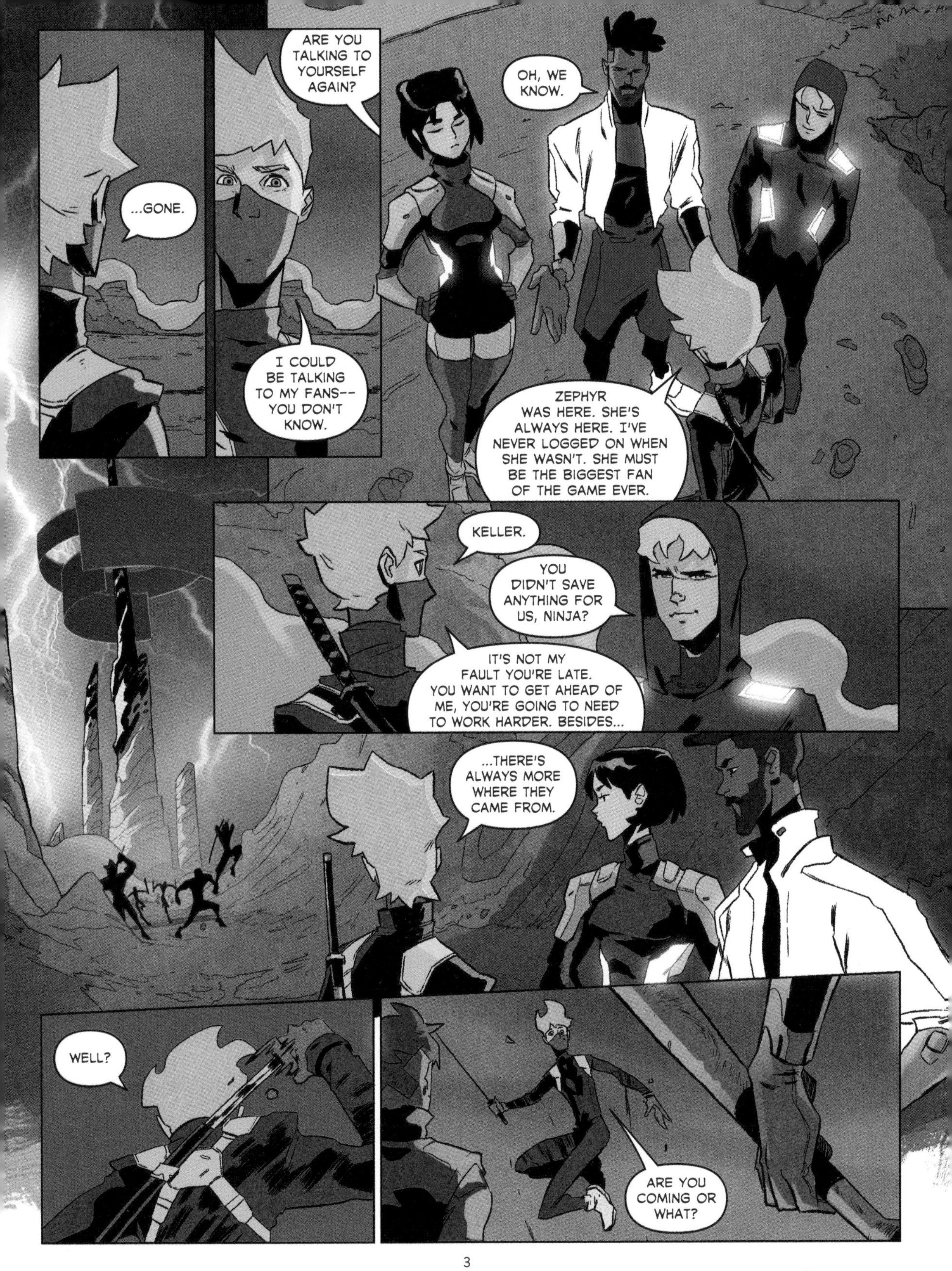
...GONE.
ARE YOU TALKING TO YOURSELF AGAIN?
I COULD BE TALKING TO MY FANS-- YOU DON'T KNOW.
OH, WE KNOW.
ZEPHYR WAS HERE. SHE'S ALWAYS HERE. I'VE NEVER LOGGED ON WHEN SHE WASN'T. SHE MUST BE THE BIGGEST FAN OF THE GAME EVER.
KELLER.
YOU DIDN'T SAVE ANYTHING FOR US, NINJA?
IT'S NOT MY FAULT YOU'RE LATE. YOU WANT TO GET AHEAD OF ME, YOU'RE GOING TO NEED TO WORK HARDER. BESIDES...
...THERE'S ALWAYS MORE WHERE THEY CAME FROM.
WELL?
ARE YOU COMING OR WHAT?

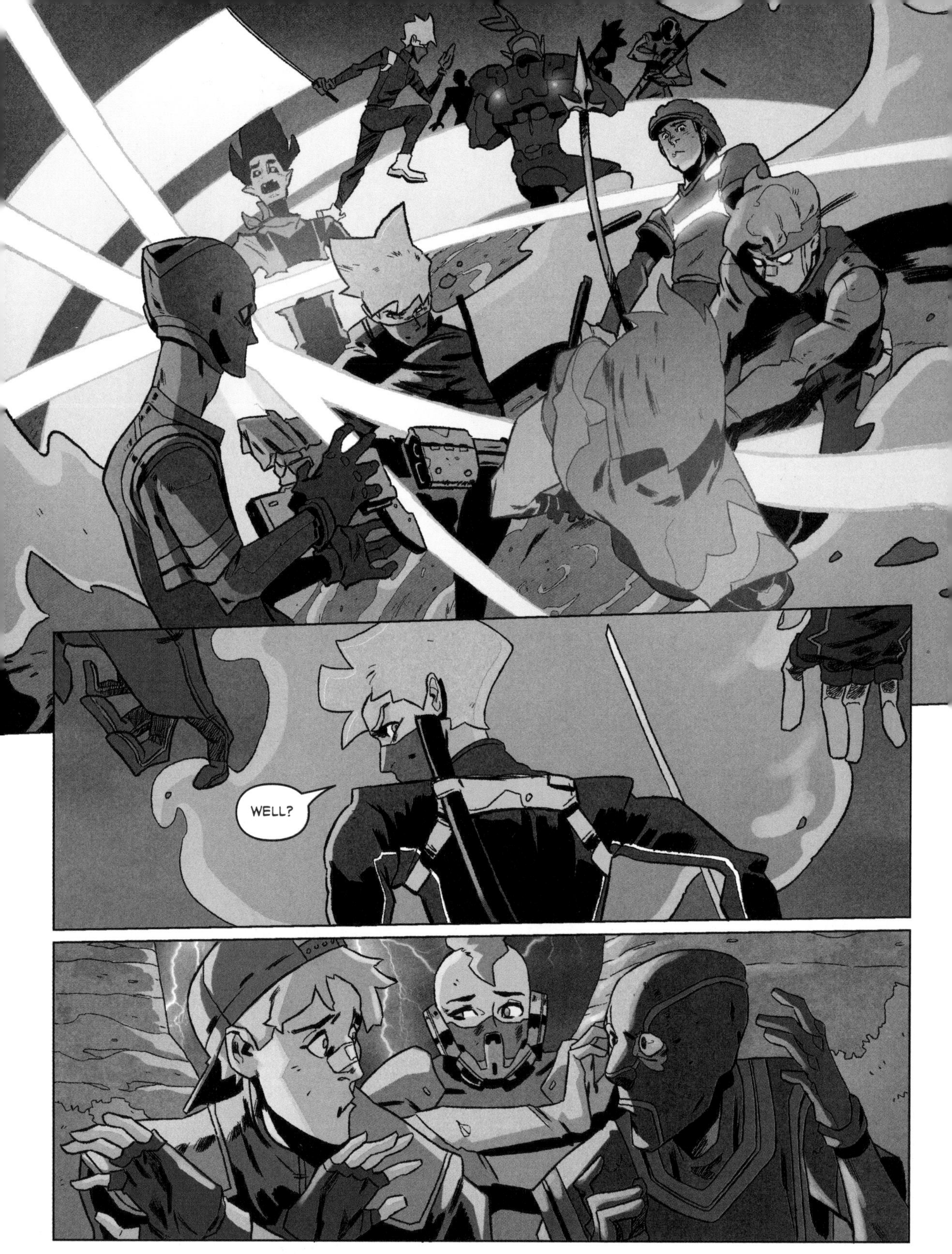
WELL?

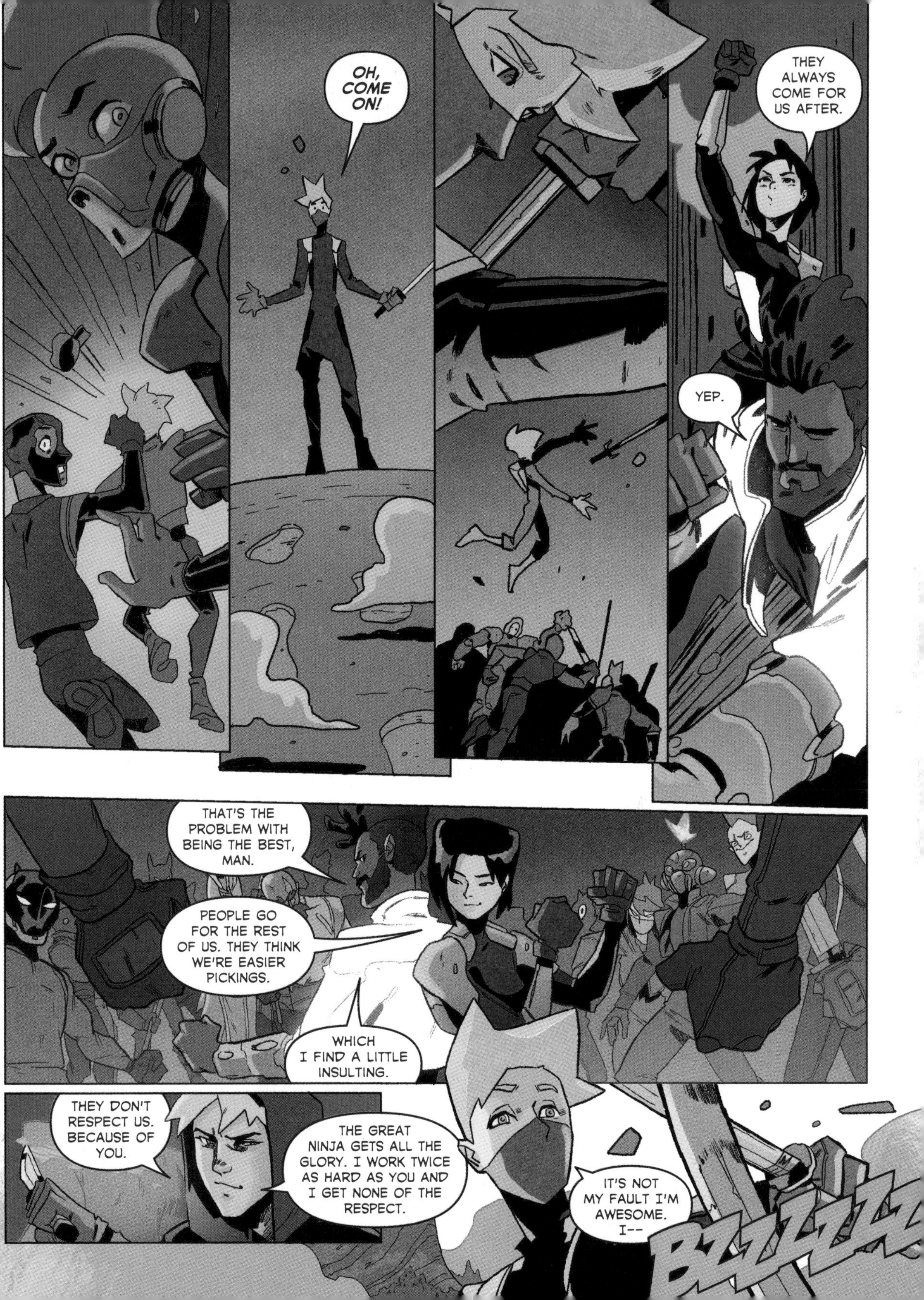
OH, COME ON!
THEY ALWAYS COME FOR US AFTER.
YEP.
THAT'S THE PROBLEM WITH BEING THE BEST, MAN.
PEOPLE GO FOR THE REST OF US. THEY THINK WE'RE EASIER PICKINGS.
WHICH I FIND A LITTLE INSULTING.
THEY DON'T RESPECT US. BECAUSE OF YOU.
THE GREAT NINJA GETS ALL THE GLORY. I WORK TWICE AS HARD AS YOU AND I GET NONE OF THE RESPECT.
IT'S NOT MY FAULT I'M AWESOME. I--

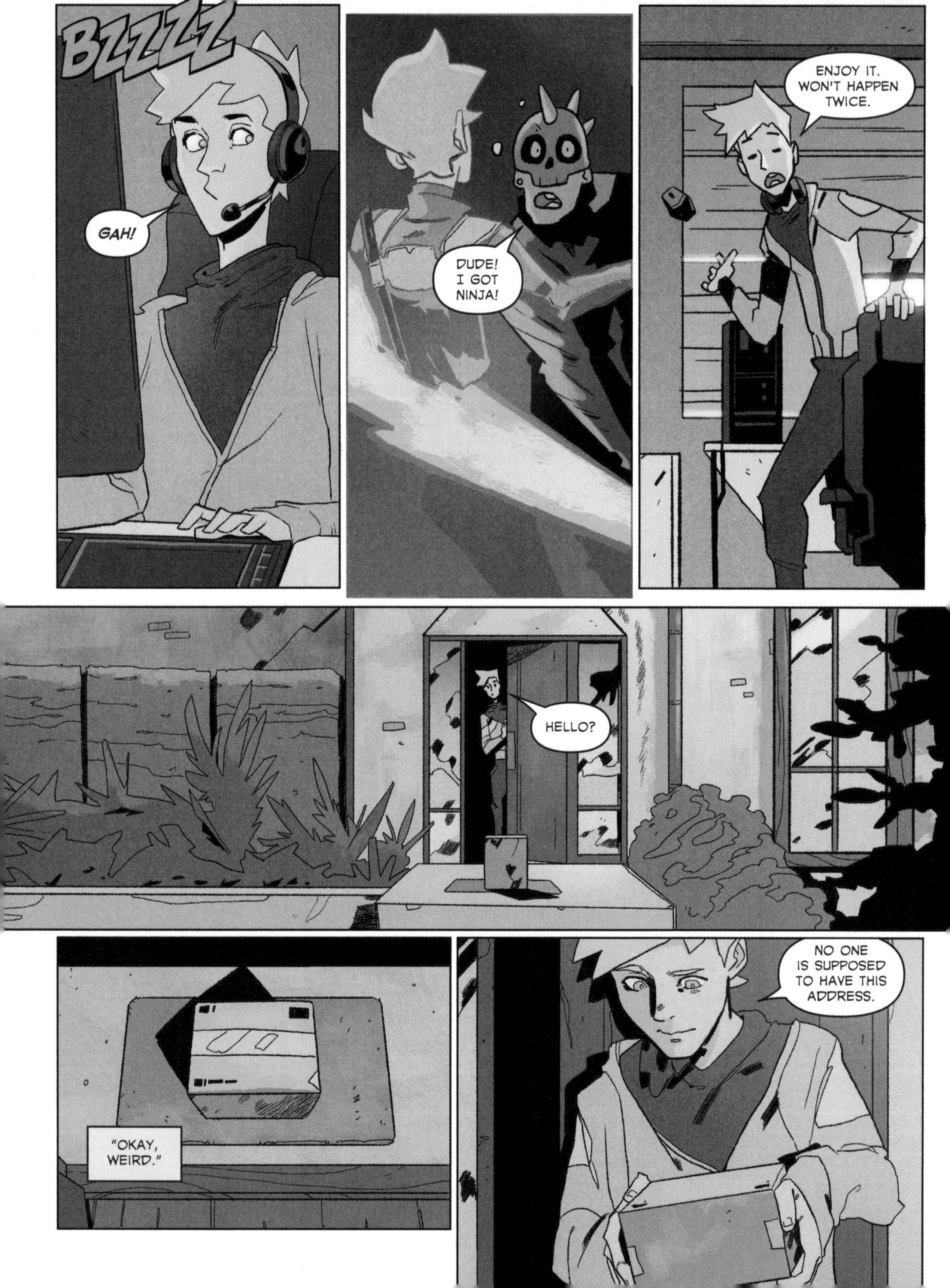
BZZZZ
GAH!
DUDE! I GOT NINJA!
ENJOY IT. WON'T HAPPEN TWICE.
HELLO?
"OKAY, WEIRD."
NO ONE IS SUPPOSED TO HAVE THIS ADDRESS.

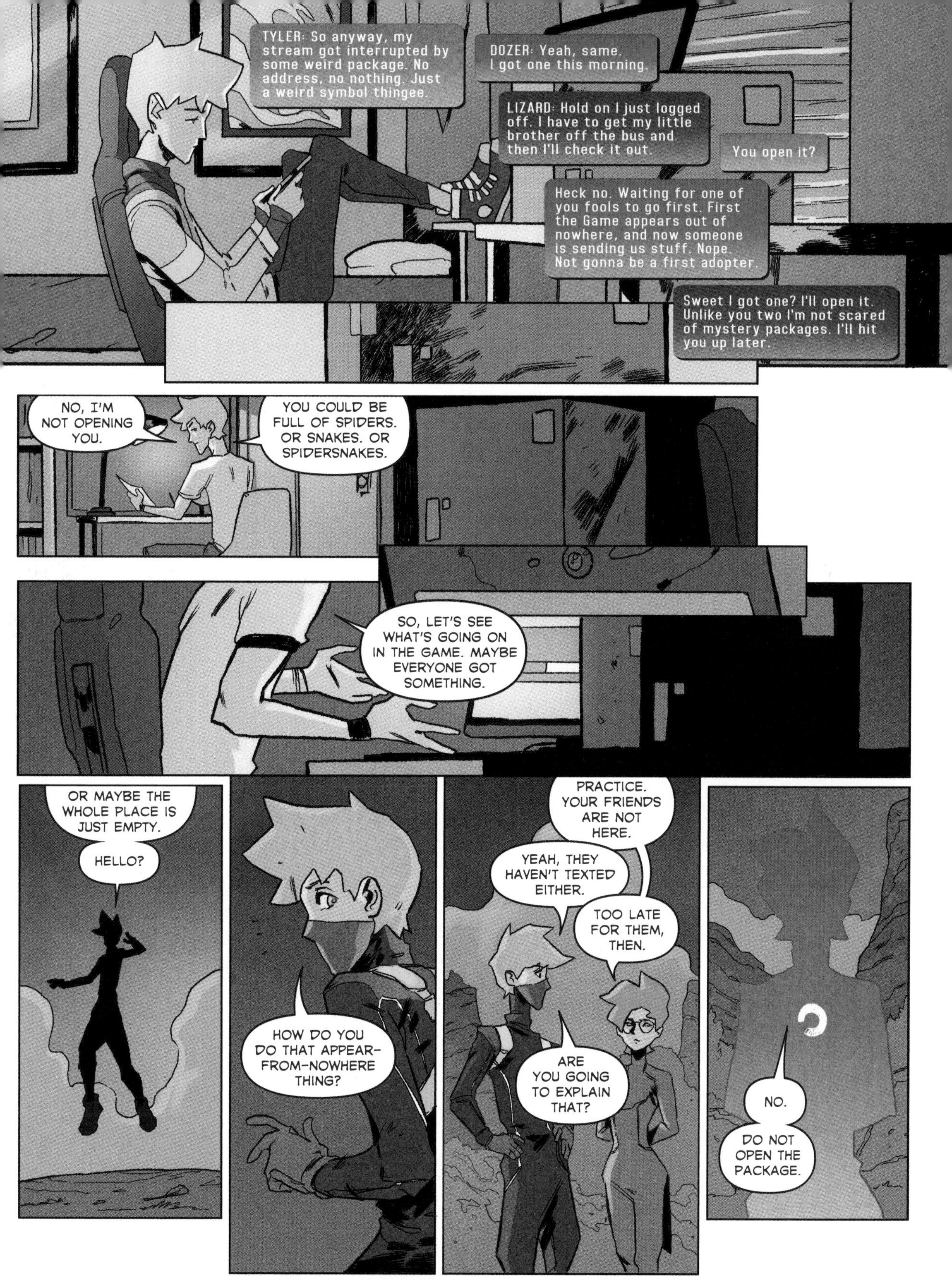
TYLER: So anyway, my stream got interrupted by some weird package. No address, no nothing. Just a weird symbol thingee.
DOZER: Yeah, same. I got one this morning.
LIZARD: Hold on I just logged off. I have to get my little brother off the bus and then I'll check it out.
You open it?
Heck no. Waiting for one of you fools to go first. First the Game appears out of nowhere, and now someone is sending us stuff. Nope. Not gonna be a first adopter.
Sweet I got one? I'll open it. Unlike you two I'm not scared of mystery packages. I'll hit you up later.
NO, I'M NOT OPENING YOU.
YOU COULD BE FULL OF SPIDERS. OR SNAKES. OR SPIDERSNAKES.
SO, LET'S SEE WHAT'S GOING ON IN THE GAME. MAYBE EVERYONE GOT SOMETHING.
OR MAYBE THE WHOLE PLACE IS JUST EMPTY.
HELLO?
HOW DO YOU DO THAT APPEAR-FROM-NOWHERE THING?
PRACTICE. YOUR FRIENDS ARE NOT HERE.
YEAH, THEY HAVEN'T TEXTED EITHER.
TOO LATE FOR THEM, THEN.
ARE YOU GOING TO EXPLAIN THAT?
NO.
DO NOT OPEN THE PACKAGE.

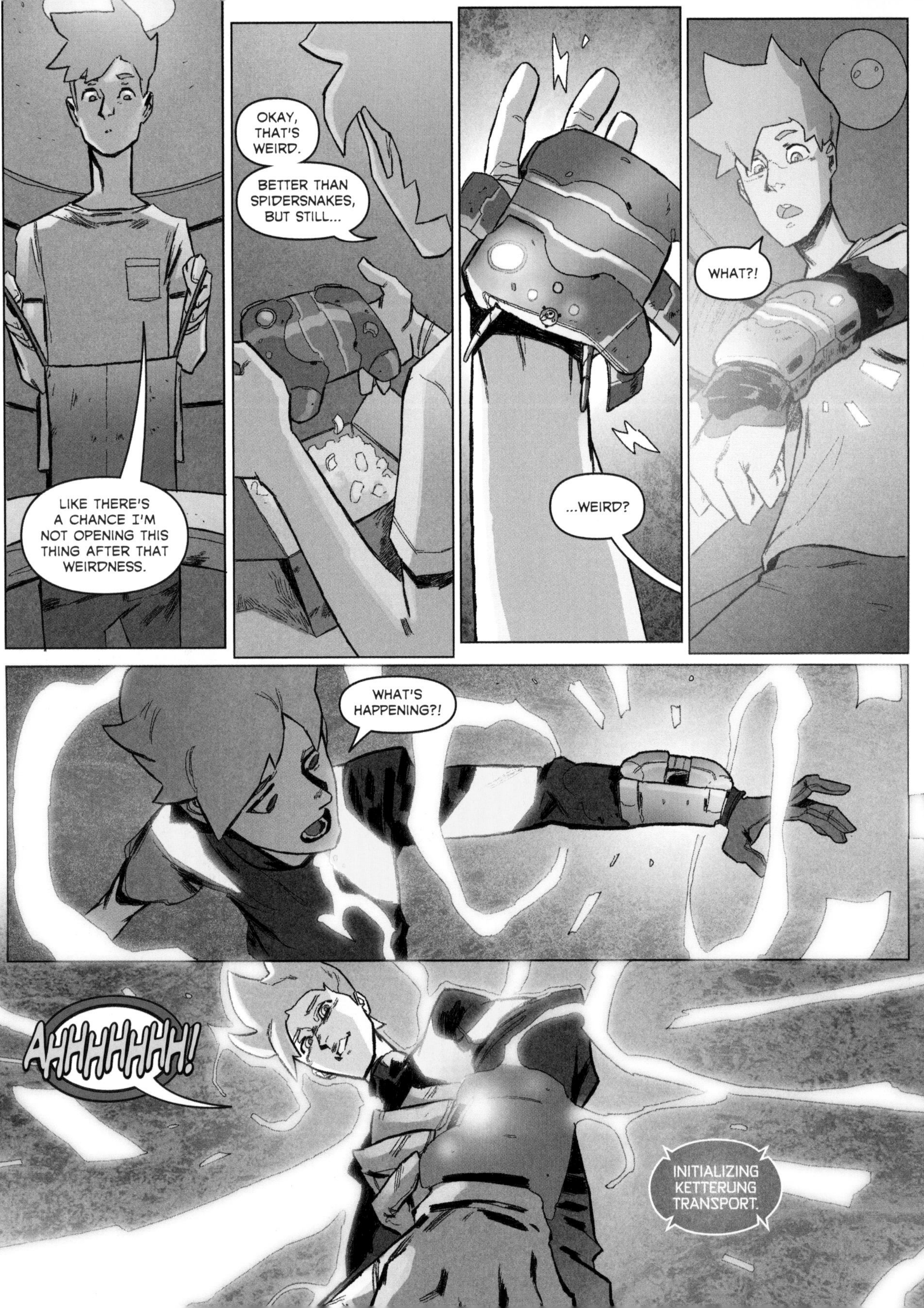
LIKE THERE'S A CHANCE I'M NOT OPENING THIS THING AFTER THAT WEIRDNESS.
OKAY, THAT'S WEIRD.
BETTER THAN SPIDERSNAKES, BUT STILL...
...WEIRD?
WHAT?!
WHAT'S HAPPENING?!
AHHHHHHH!
INITIALIZING KETTERUNG TRANSPORT.

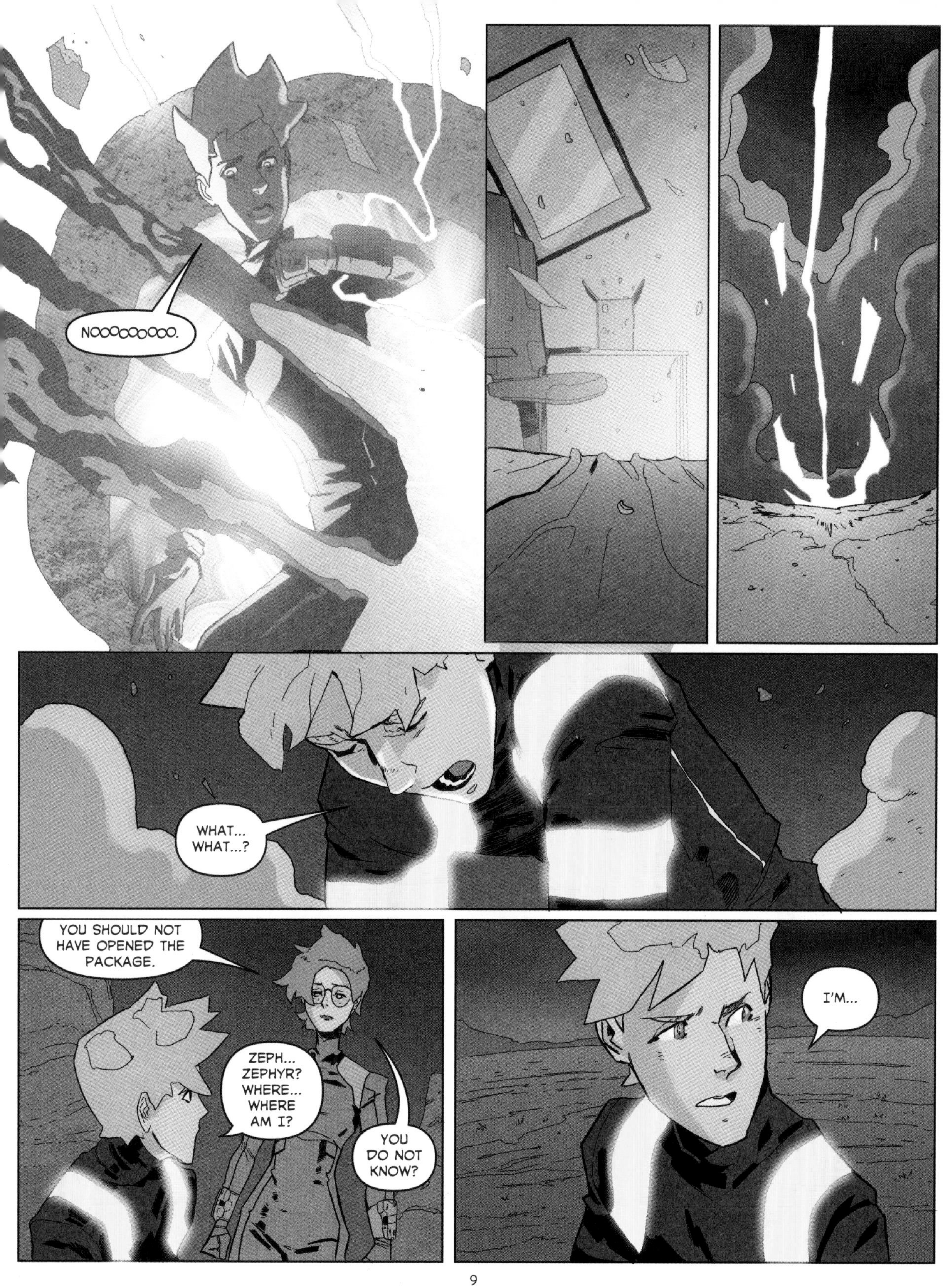
NOOOOOOOOO.
WHAT... WHAT...?
YOU SHOULD NOT HAVE OPENED THE PACKAGE.
ZEPH... ZEPHYR? WHERE... WHERE AM I?
YOU DO NOT KNOW?
I'M...

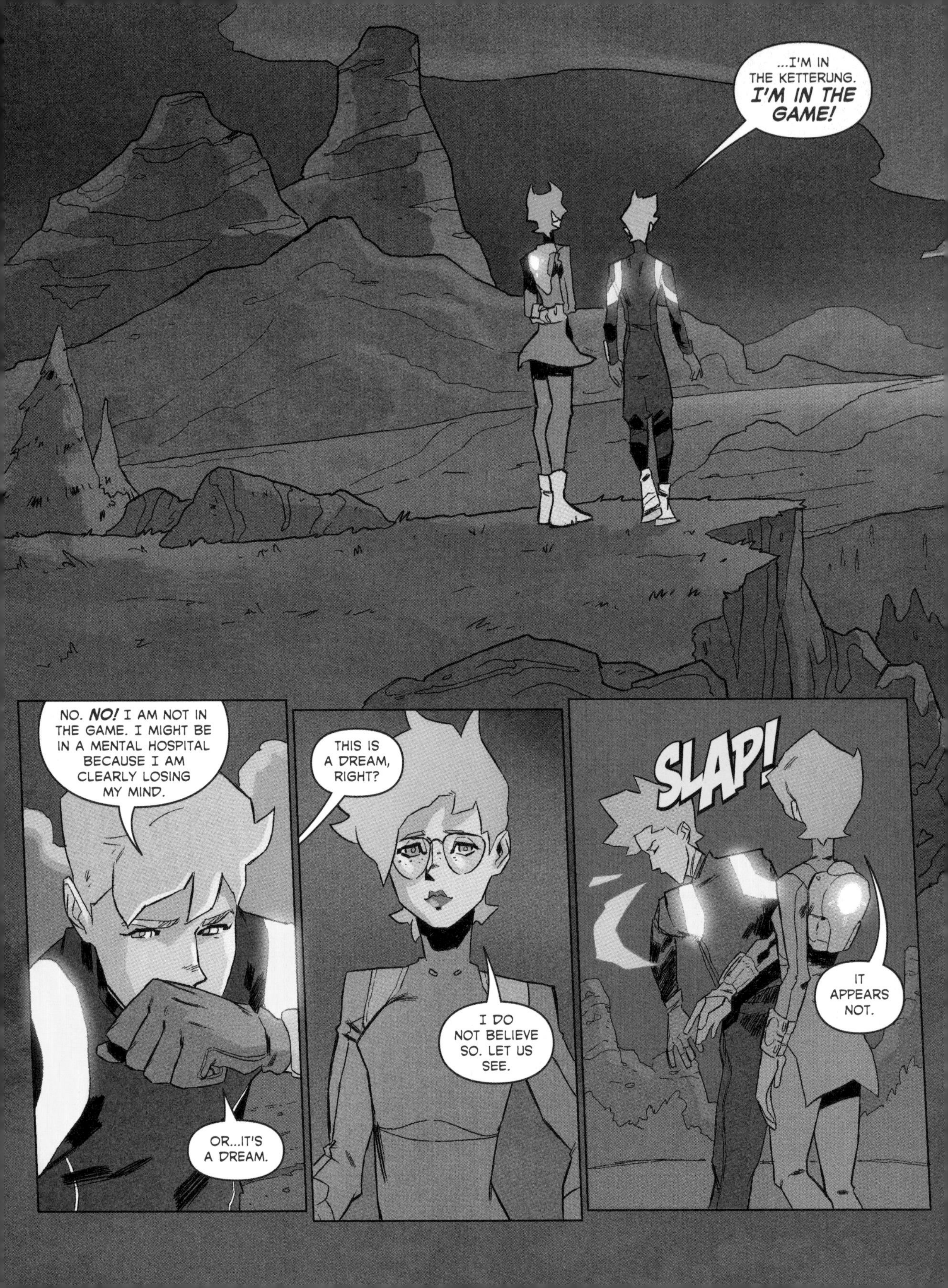
...I'M IN THE KETTERUNG. *I'M IN THE GAME!*
NO. ***NO!*** I AM NOT IN THE GAME. I MIGHT BE IN A MENTAL HOSPITAL BECAUSE I AM CLEARLY LOSING MY MIND.
OR...IT'S A DREAM.
THIS IS A DREAM, RIGHT?
I DO NOT BELIEVE SO. LET US SEE.
SLAP!
IT APPEARS NOT.

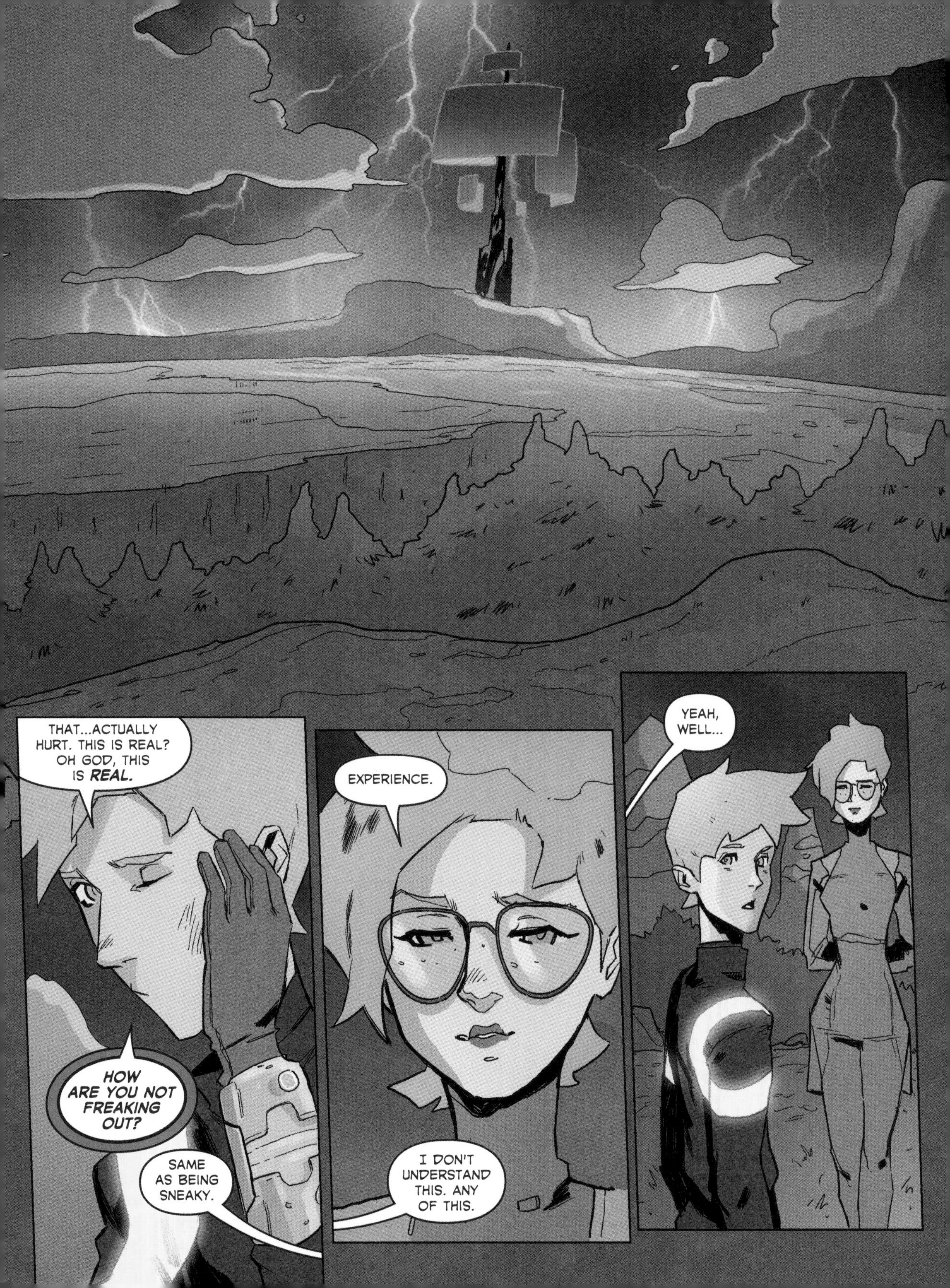

THAT...ACTUALLY HURT. THIS IS REAL? OH GOD, THIS IS REAL.
HOW ARE YOU NOT FREAKING OUT?
SAME AS BEING SNEAKY.
EXPERIENCE.
I DON'T UNDERSTAND THIS. ANY OF THIS.
YEAH, WELL...

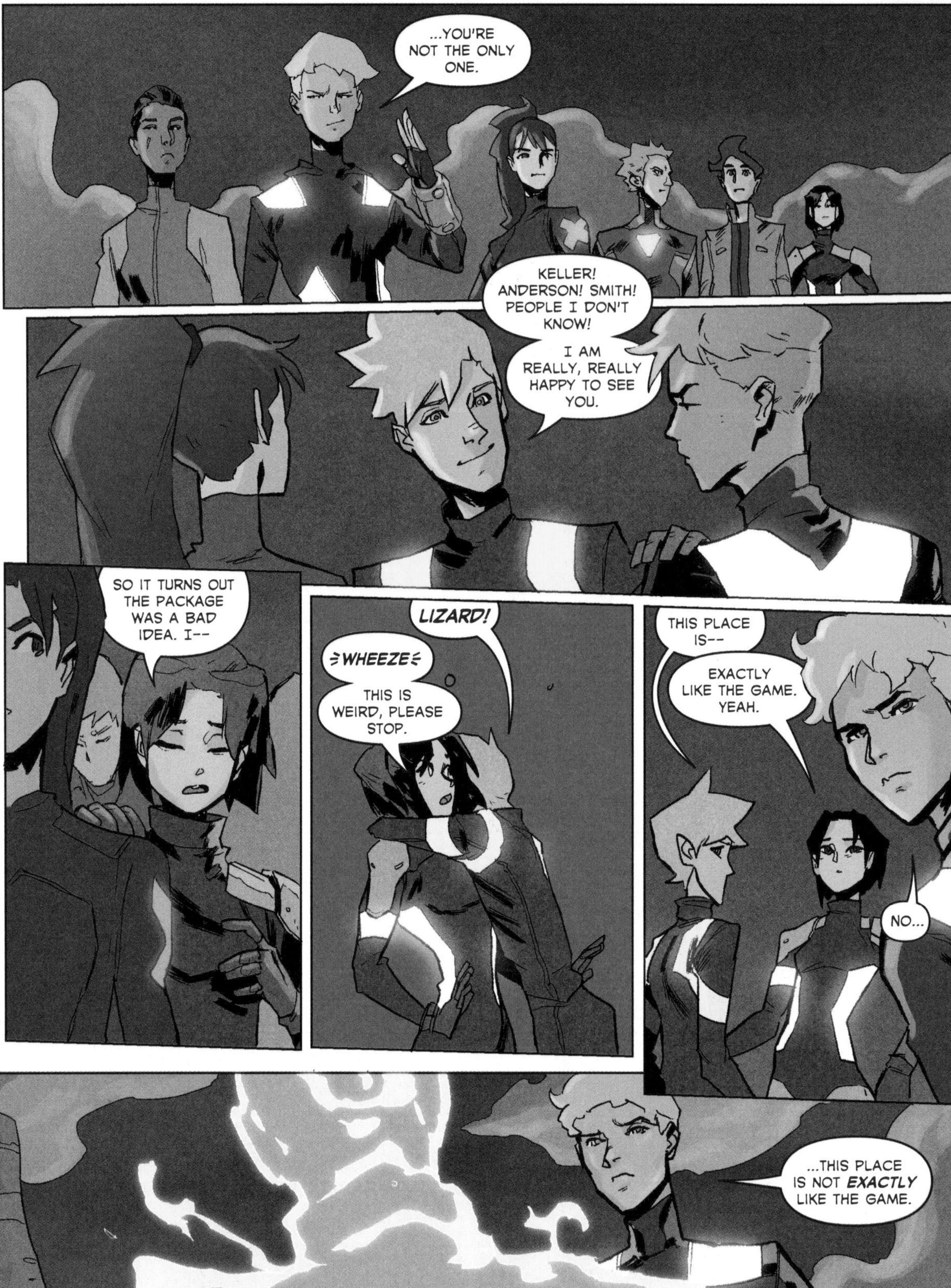
...YOU'RE NOT THE ONLY ONE.
KELLER! ANDERSON! SMITH! PEOPLE I DON'T KNOW!
I AM REALLY, REALLY HAPPY TO SEE YOU.
SO IT TURNS OUT THE PACKAGE WAS A BAD IDEA. I--
LIZARD!
WHEEZE
THIS IS WEIRD, PLEASE STOP.
THIS PLACE IS--
EXACTLY LIKE THE GAME. YEAH.
NO...
...THIS PLACE IS NOT *EXACTLY* LIKE THE GAME.

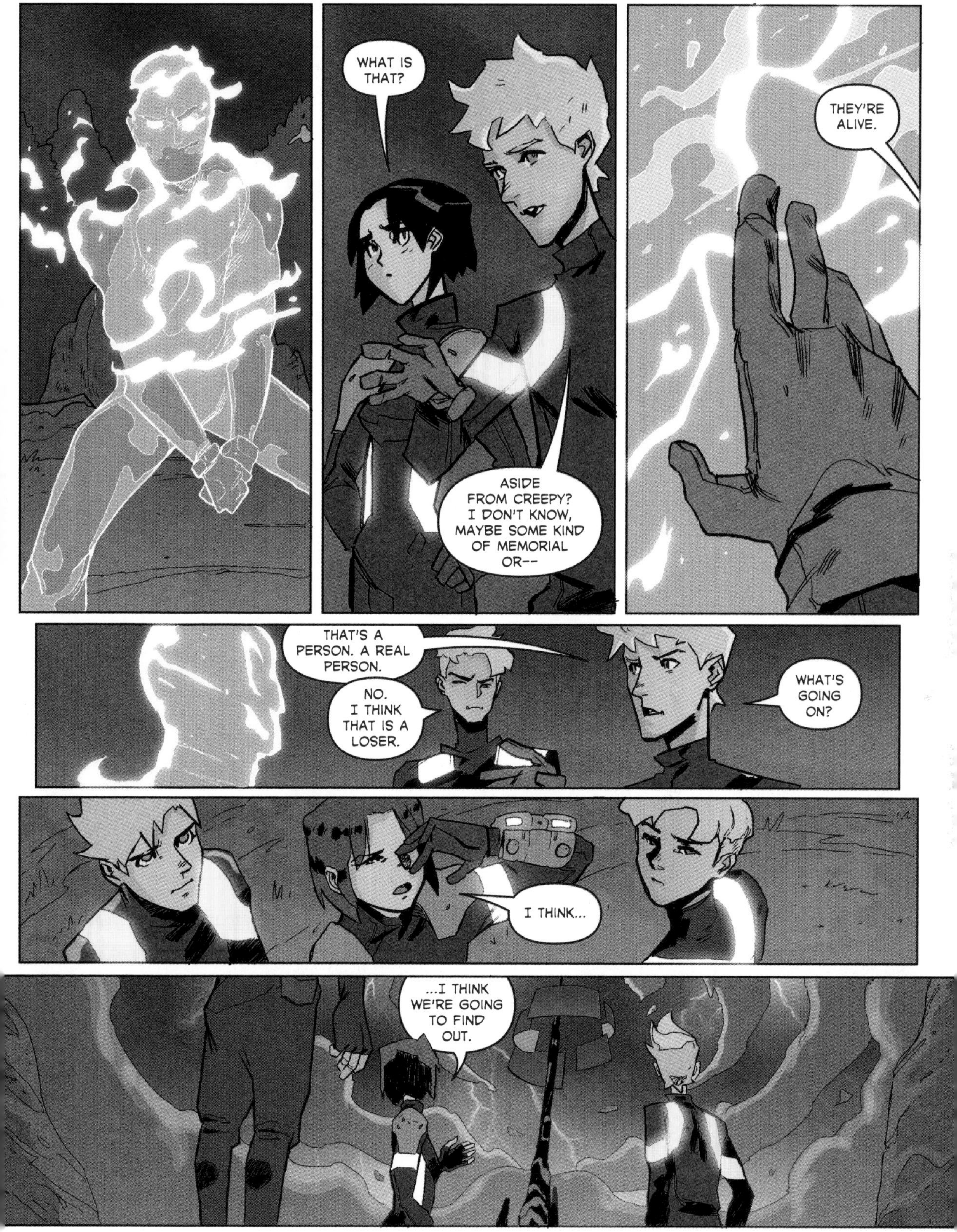
WHAT IS THAT?
ASIDE FROM CREEPY? I DON'T KNOW, MAYBE SOME KIND OF MEMORIAL OR--
THEY'RE ALIVE.
THAT'S A PERSON. A REAL PERSON.
NO. I THINK THAT IS A LOSER.
WHAT'S GOING ON?
I THINK...
...I THINK WE'RE GOING TO FIND OUT.

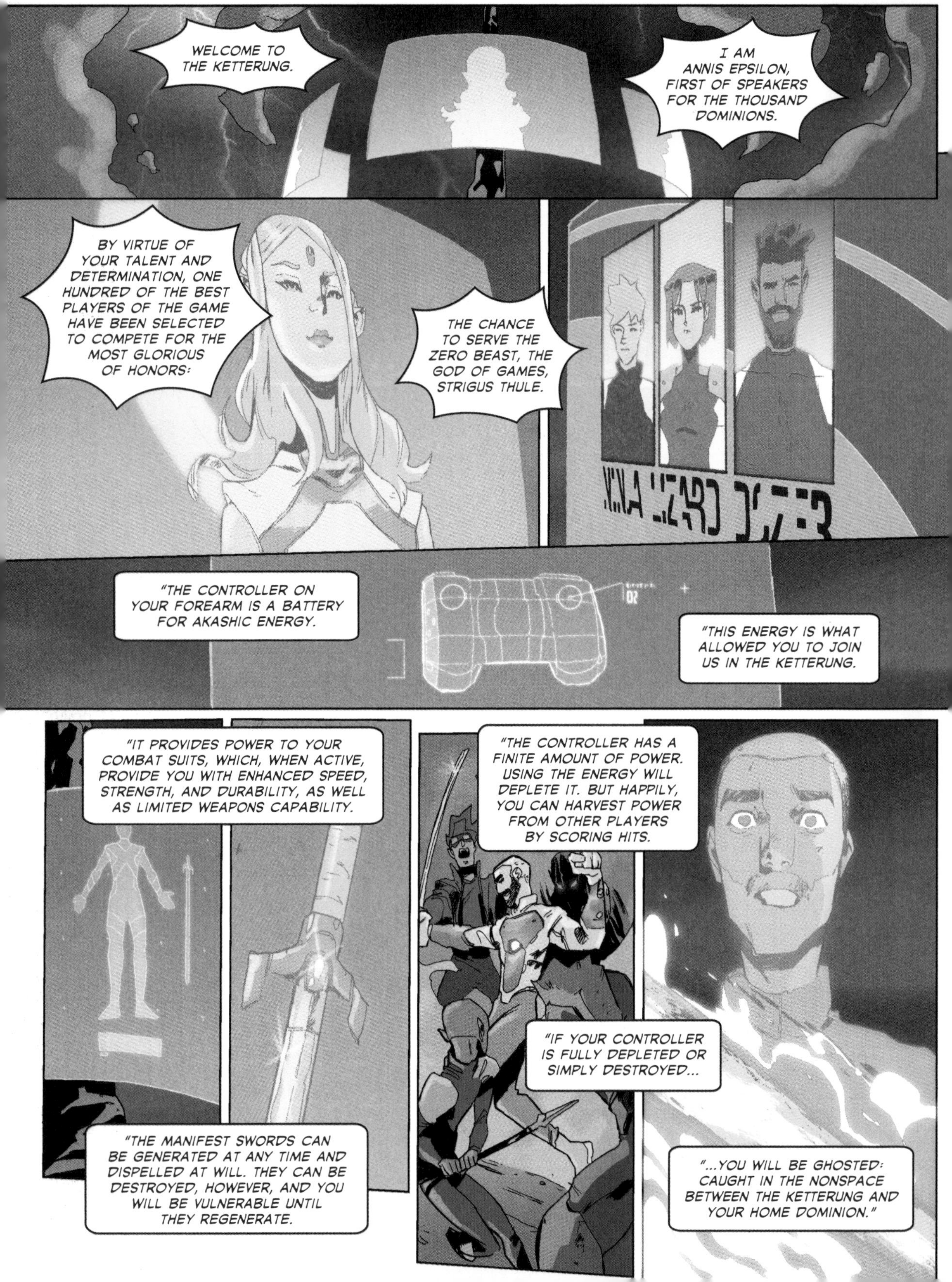
WELCOME TO THE KETTERUNG.
I AM ANNIS EPSILON, FIRST OF SPEAKERS FOR THE THOUSAND DOMINIONS.
BY VIRTUE OF YOUR TALENT AND DETERMINATION, ONE HUNDRED OF THE BEST PLAYERS OF THE GAME HAVE BEEN SELECTED TO COMPETE FOR THE MOST GLORIOUS OF HONORS:
THE CHANCE TO SERVE THE ZERO BEAST, THE GOD OF GAMES, STRIGUS THULE.
"THE CONTROLLER ON YOUR FOREARM IS A BATTERY FOR AKASHIC ENERGY.
"THIS ENERGY IS WHAT ALLOWED YOU TO JOIN US IN THE KETTERUNG.
"IT PROVIDES POWER TO YOUR COMBAT SUITS, WHICH, WHEN ACTIVE, PROVIDE YOU WITH ENHANCED SPEED, STRENGTH, AND DURABILITY, AS WELL AS LIMITED WEAPONS CAPABILITY.
"THE MANIFEST SWORDS CAN BE GENERATED AT ANY TIME AND DISPELLED AT WILL. THEY CAN BE DESTROYED, HOWEVER, AND YOU WILL BE VULNERABLE UNTIL THEY REGENERATE.
"THE CONTROLLER HAS A FINITE AMOUNT OF POWER. USING THE ENERGY WILL DEPLETE IT. BUT HAPPILY, YOU CAN HARVEST POWER FROM OTHER PLAYERS BY SCORING HITS.
"IF YOUR CONTROLLER IS FULLY DEPLETED OR SIMPLY DESTROYED...
"...YOU WILL BE GHOSTED: CAUGHT IN THE NONSPACE BETWEEN THE KETTERUNG AND YOUR HOME DOMINION."

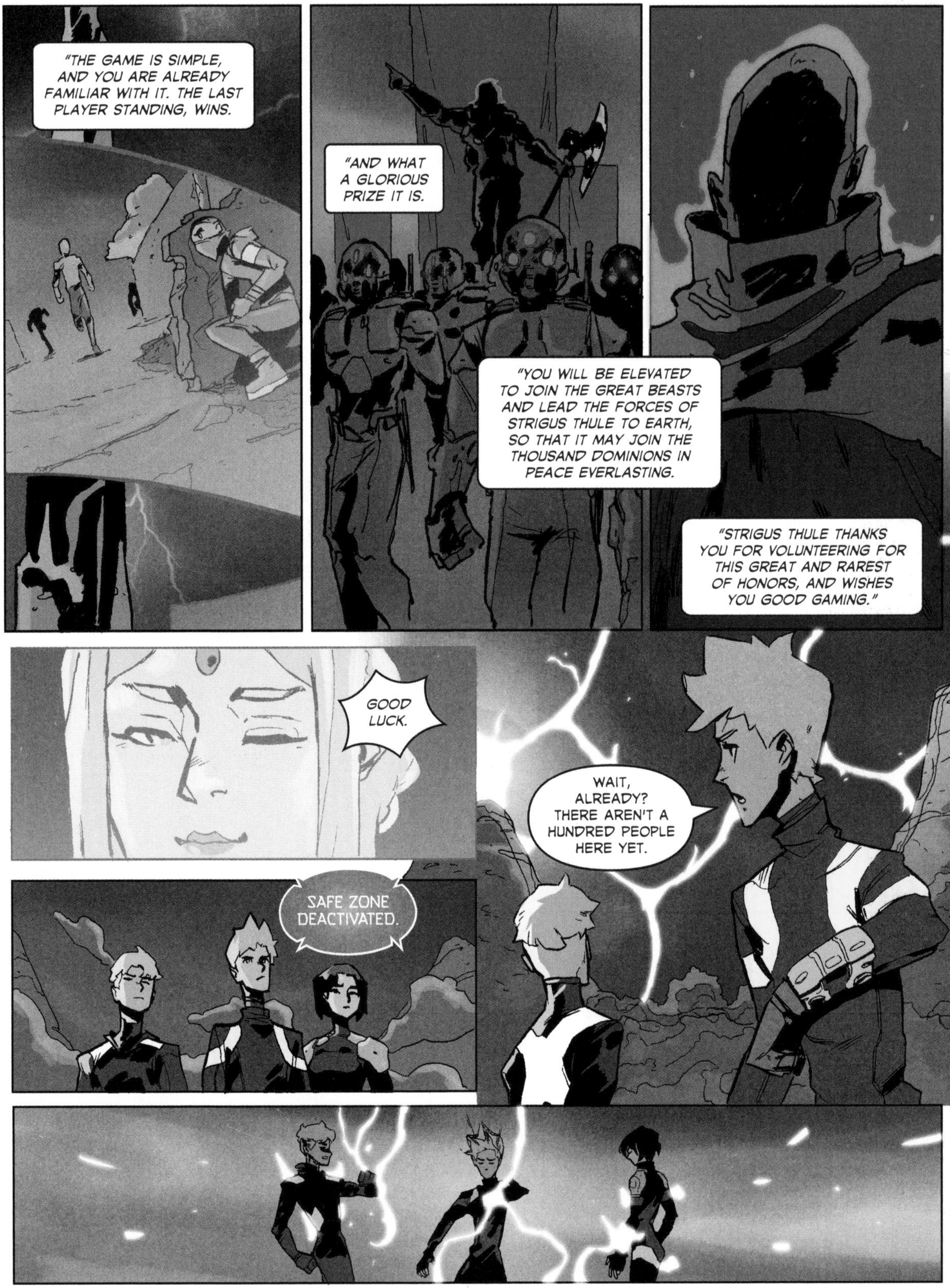
"THE GAME IS SIMPLE, AND YOU ARE ALREADY FAMILIAR WITH IT. THE LAST PLAYER STANDING, WINS.
"AND WHAT A GLORIOUS PRIZE IT IS.
"YOU WILL BE ELEVATED TO JOIN THE GREAT BEASTS AND LEAD THE FORCES OF STRIGUS THULE TO EARTH, SO THAT IT MAY JOIN THE THOUSAND DOMINIONS IN PEACE EVERLASTING.
"STRIGUS THULE THANKS YOU FOR VOLUNTEERING FOR THIS GREAT AND RAREST OF HONORS, AND WISHES YOU GOOD GAMING."
GOOD LUCK.
SAFE ZONE DEACTIVATED.
WAIT, ALREADY? THERE AREN'T A HUNDRED PEOPLE HERE YET.

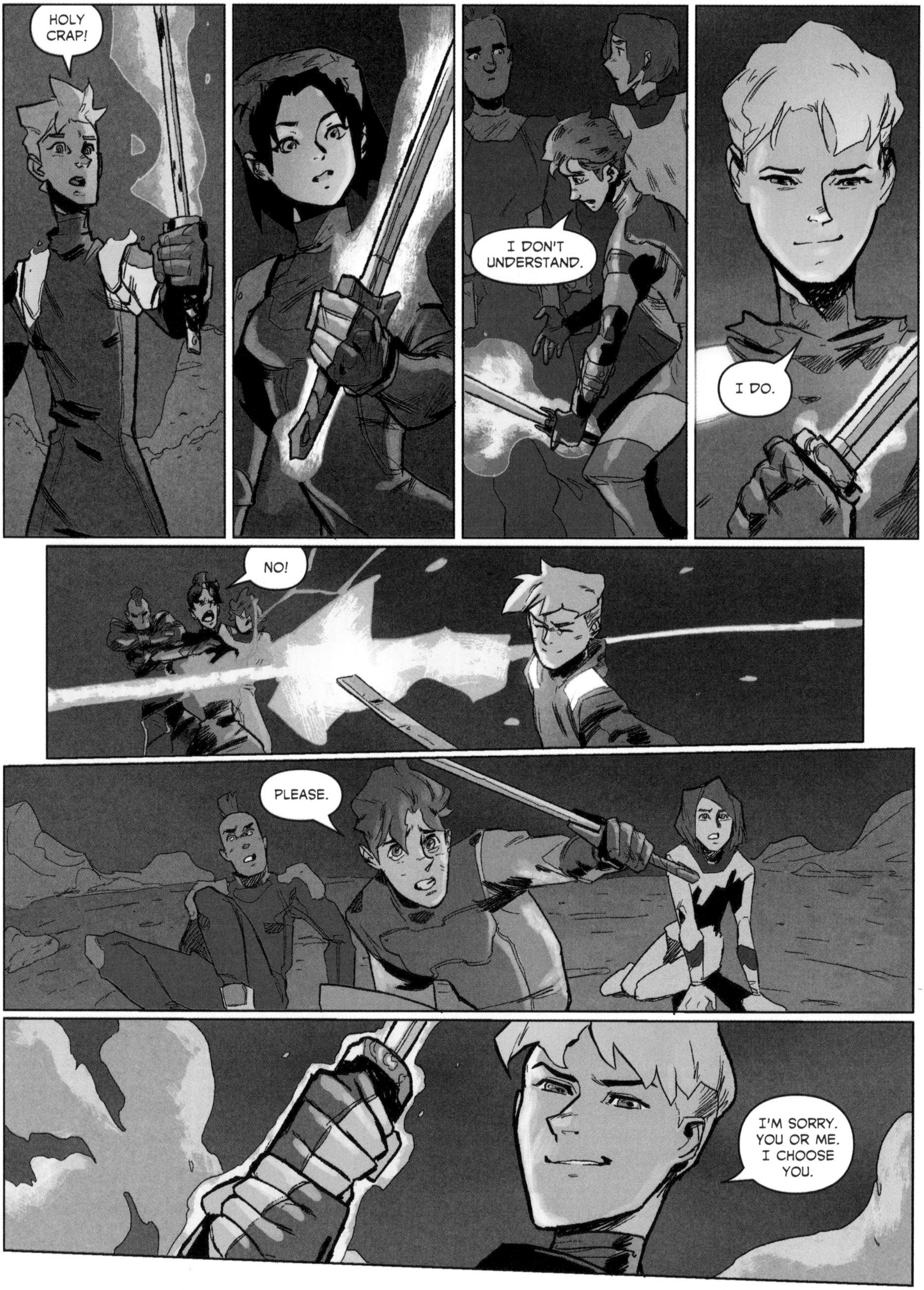
HOLY CRAP!
I DON'T UNDERSTAND.
I DO.
NO!
PLEASE.
I'M SORRY. YOU OR ME. I CHOOSE YOU.

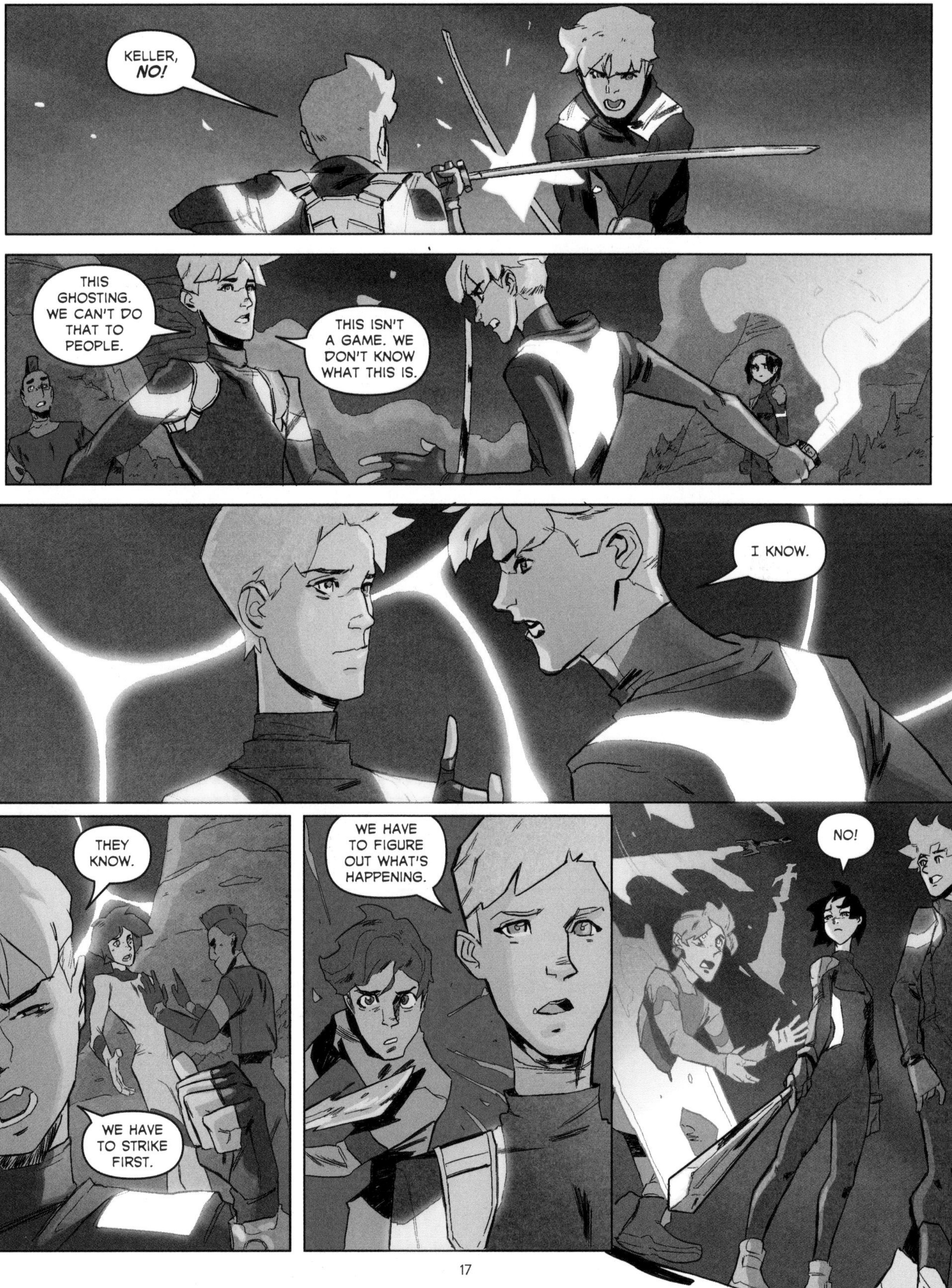
KELLER, NO!
THIS GHOSTING. WE CAN'T DO THAT TO PEOPLE.
THIS ISN'T A GAME. WE DON'T KNOW WHAT THIS IS.
I KNOW.
THEY KNOW.
WE HAVE TO STRIKE FIRST.
WE HAVE TO FIGURE OUT WHAT'S HAPPENING.
NO!

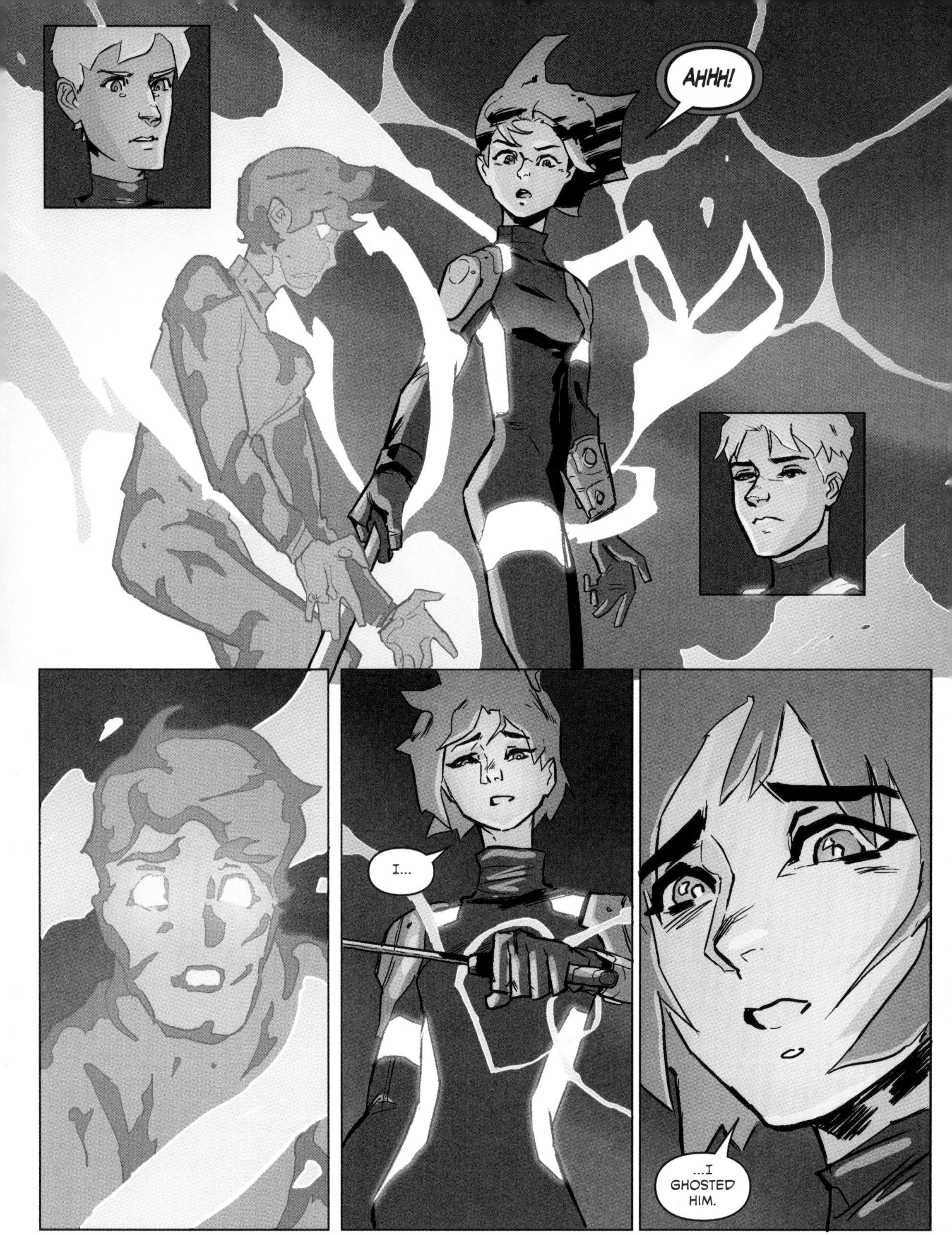
AHHH!
I...
...I GHOSTED HIM.

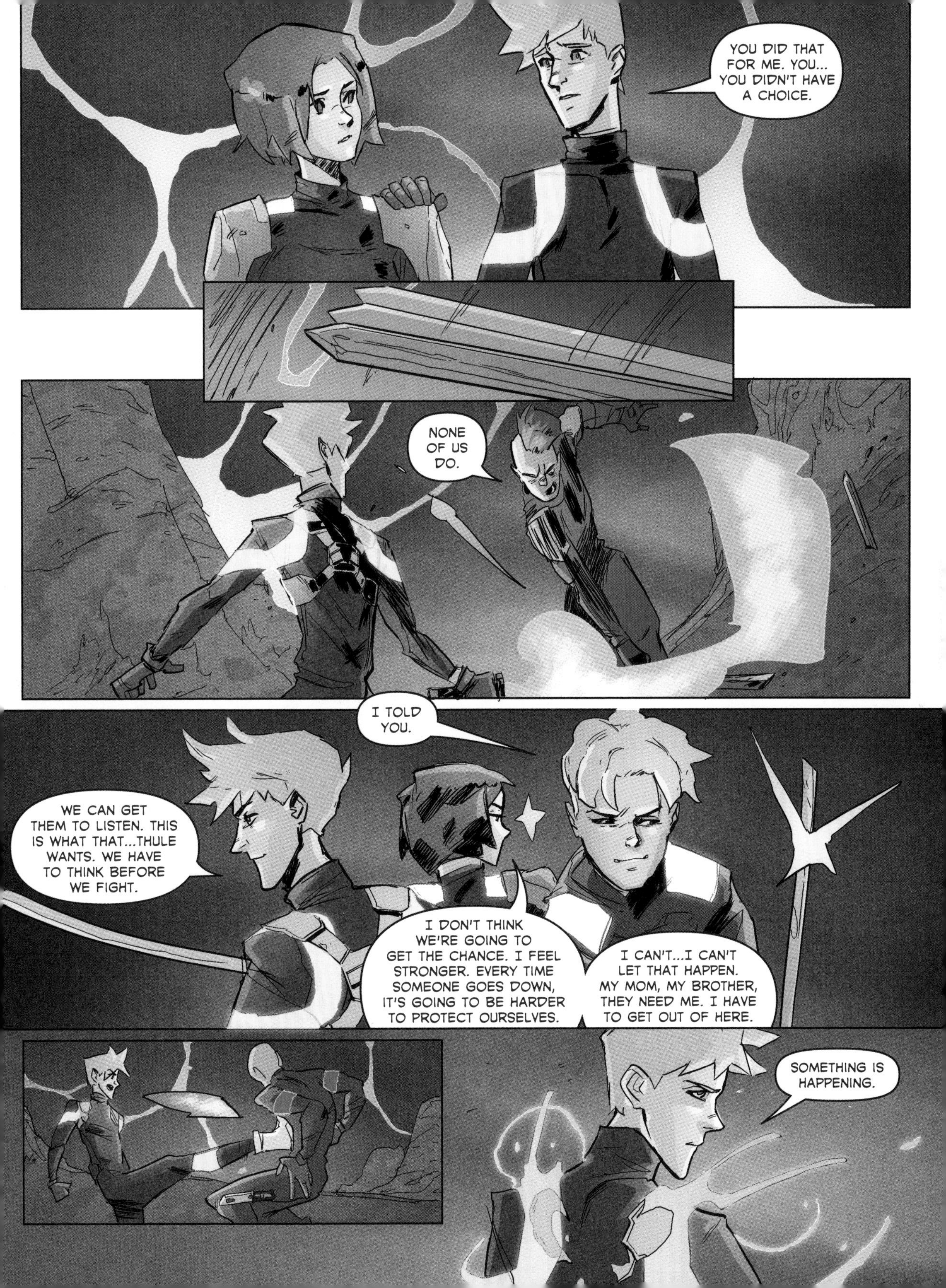
YOU DID THAT FOR ME. YOU... YOU DIDN'T HAVE A CHOICE.
NONE OF US DO.
I TOLD YOU.
WE CAN GET THEM TO LISTEN. THIS IS WHAT THAT...THULE WANTS. WE HAVE TO THINK BEFORE WE FIGHT.
I DON'T THINK WE'RE GOING TO GET THE CHANCE. I FEEL STRONGER. EVERY TIME SOMEONE GOES DOWN, IT'S GOING TO BE HARDER TO PROTECT OURSELVES.
I CAN'T...I CAN'T LET THAT HAPPEN. MY MOM, MY BROTHER, THEY NEED ME. I HAVE TO GET OUT OF HERE.
SOMETHING IS HAPPENING.

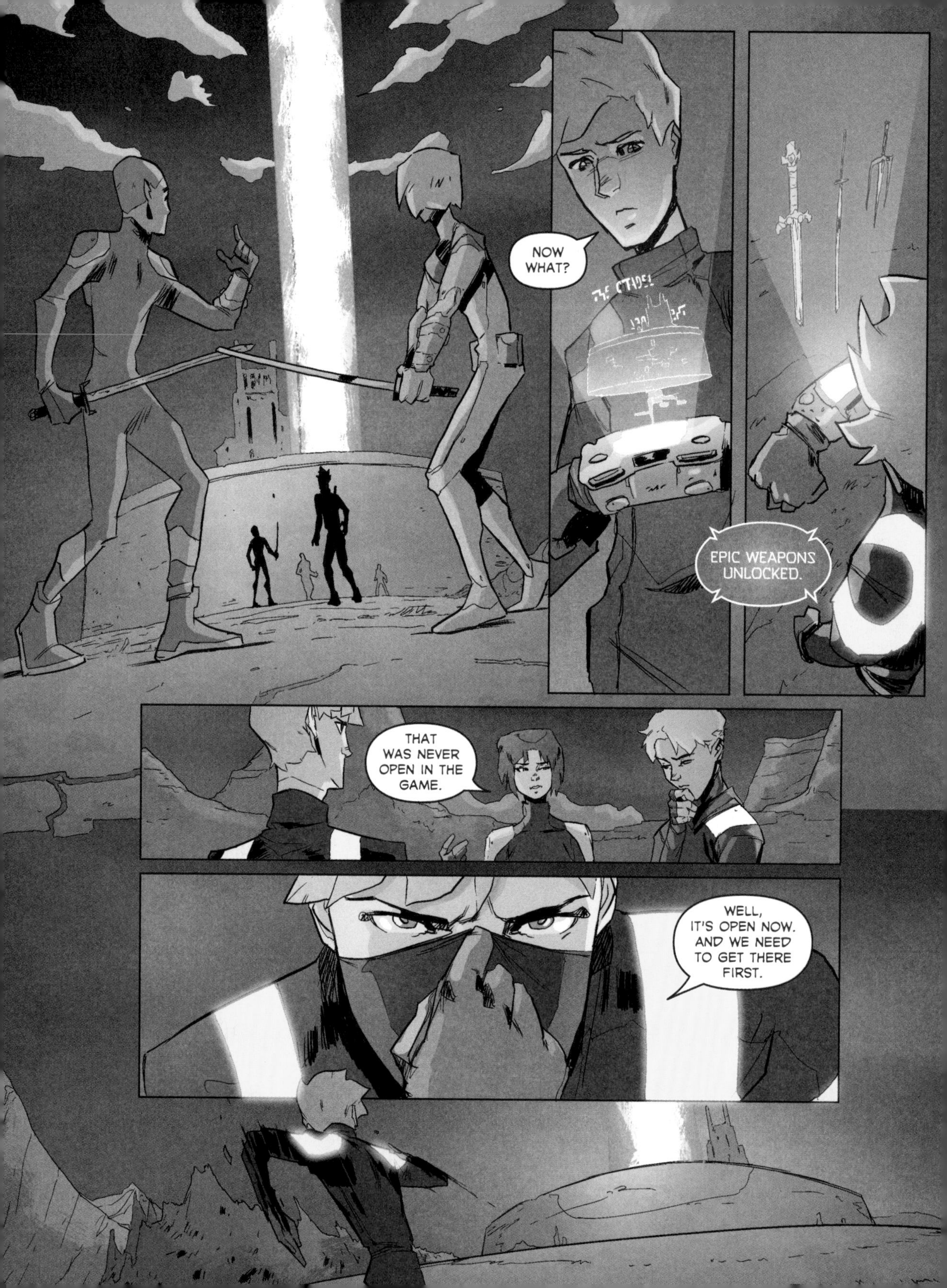
NOW WHAT?
THE CITADEL
EPIC WEAPONS UNLOCKED.
THAT WAS NEVER OPEN IN THE GAME.
WELL, IT'S OPEN NOW. AND WE NEED TO GET THERE FIRST.

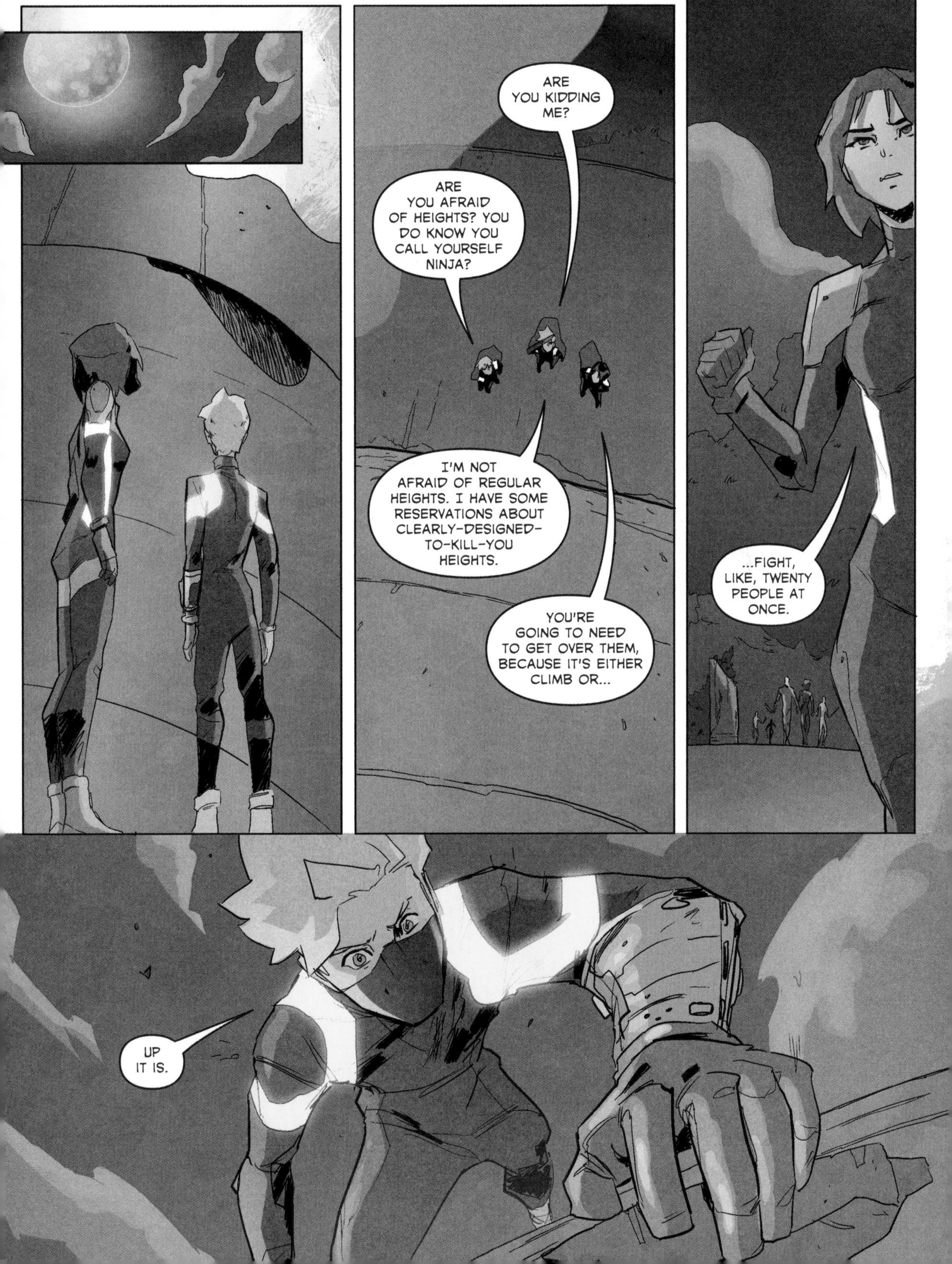
ARE YOU KIDDING ME?
ARE YOU AFRAID OF HEIGHTS? YOU DO KNOW YOU CALL YOURSELF NINJA?
I'M NOT AFRAID OF REGULAR HEIGHTS. I HAVE SOME RESERVATIONS ABOUT CLEARLY-DESIGNED-TO-KILL-YOU HEIGHTS.
YOU'RE GOING TO NEED TO GET OVER THEM, BECAUSE IT'S EITHER CLIMB OR...
...FIGHT, LIKE, TWENTY PEOPLE AT ONCE.
UP IT IS.

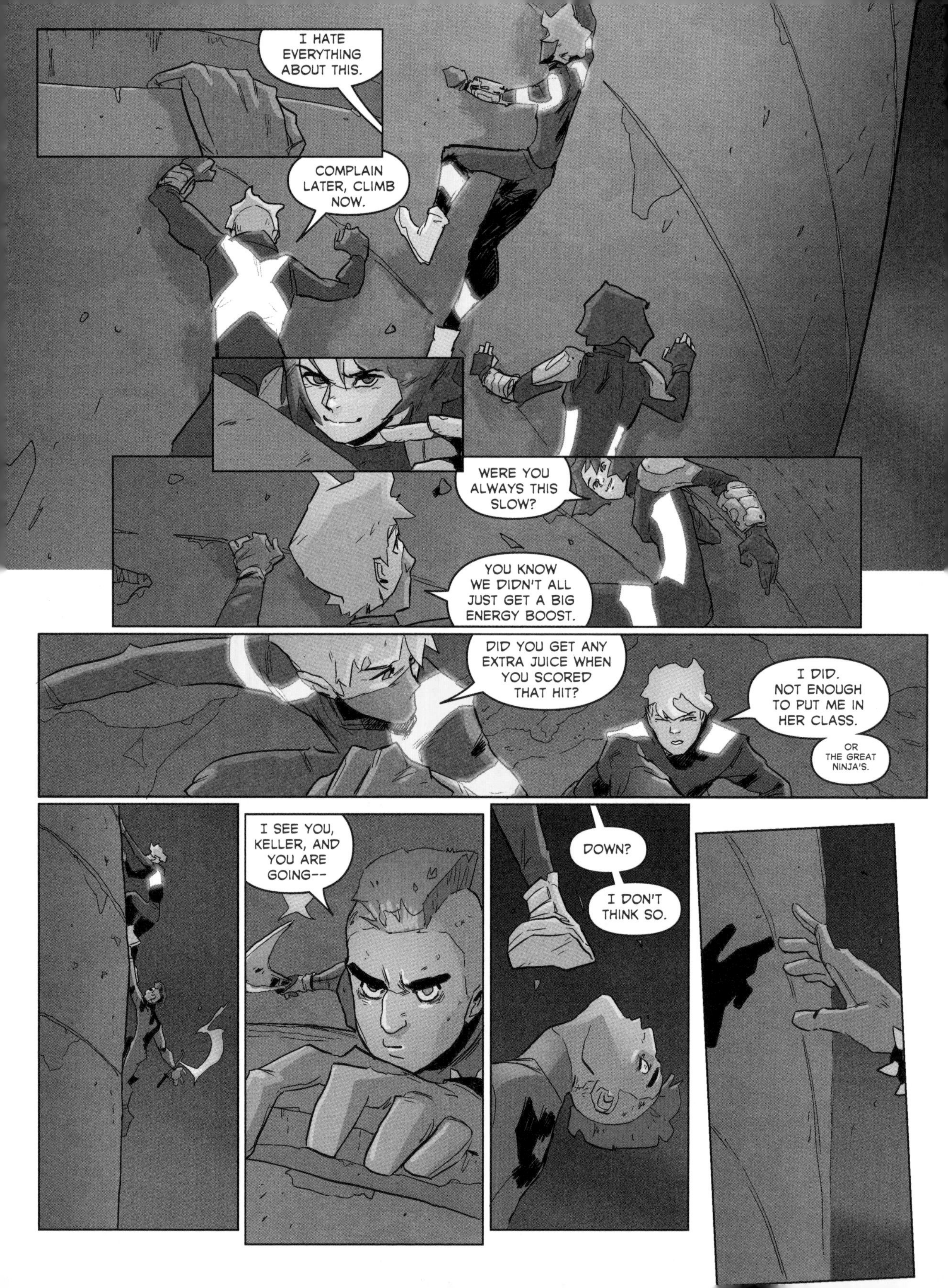
I HATE EVERYTHING ABOUT THIS.
COMPLAIN LATER, CLIMB NOW.
WERE YOU ALWAYS THIS SLOW?
YOU KNOW WE DIDN'T ALL JUST GET A BIG ENERGY BOOST.
DID YOU GET ANY EXTRA JUICE WHEN YOU SCORED THAT HIT?
I DID. NOT ENOUGH TO PUT ME IN HER CLASS.
OR THE GREAT NINJA'S.
I SEE YOU, KELLER, AND YOU ARE GOING--
DOWN?
I DON'T THINK SO.

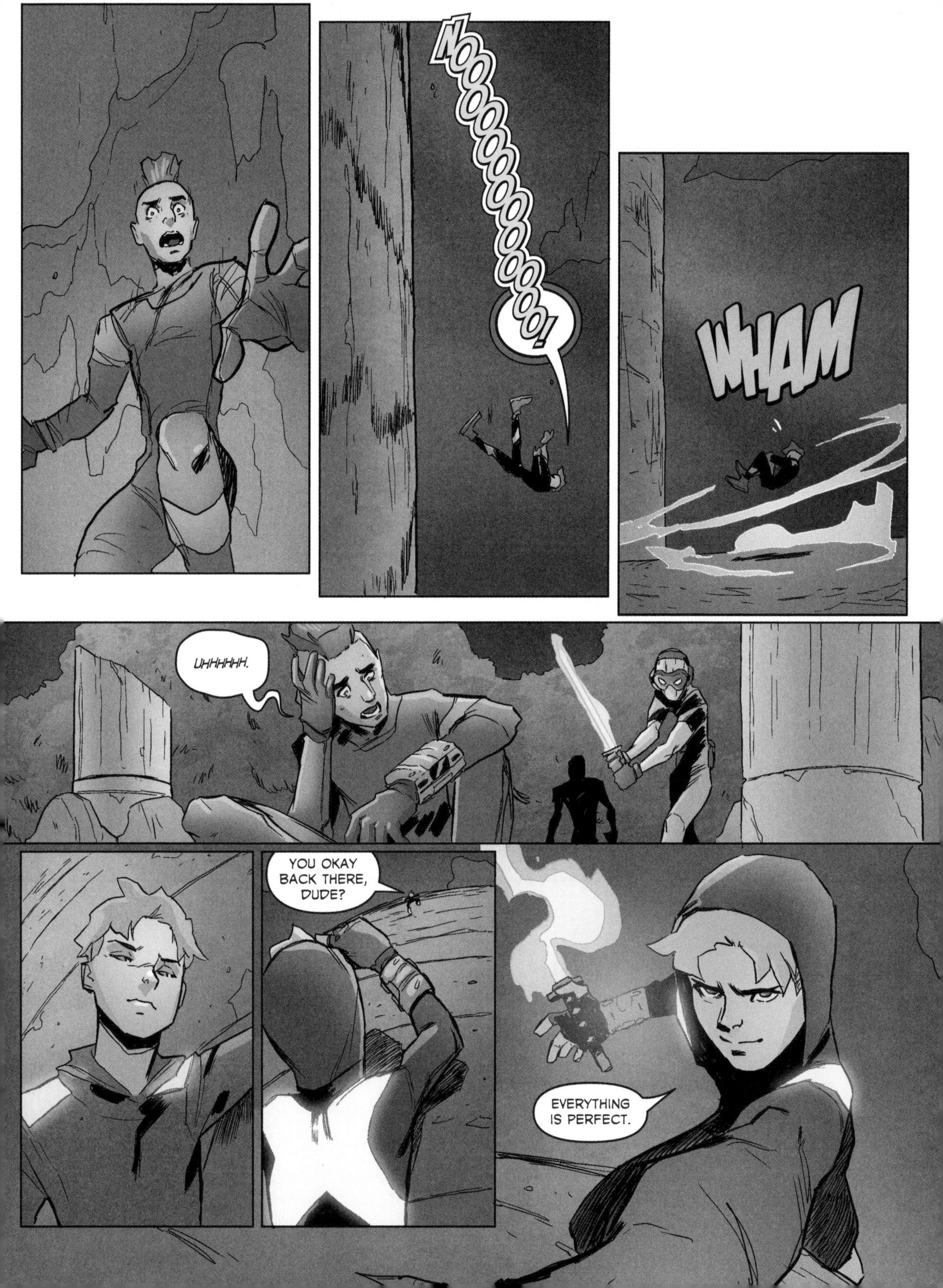
NOOOOOOOOOOOOOOOO!
WHAM
UHHHHHH.
YOU OKAY BACK THERE, DUDE?
EVERYTHING IS PERFECT.

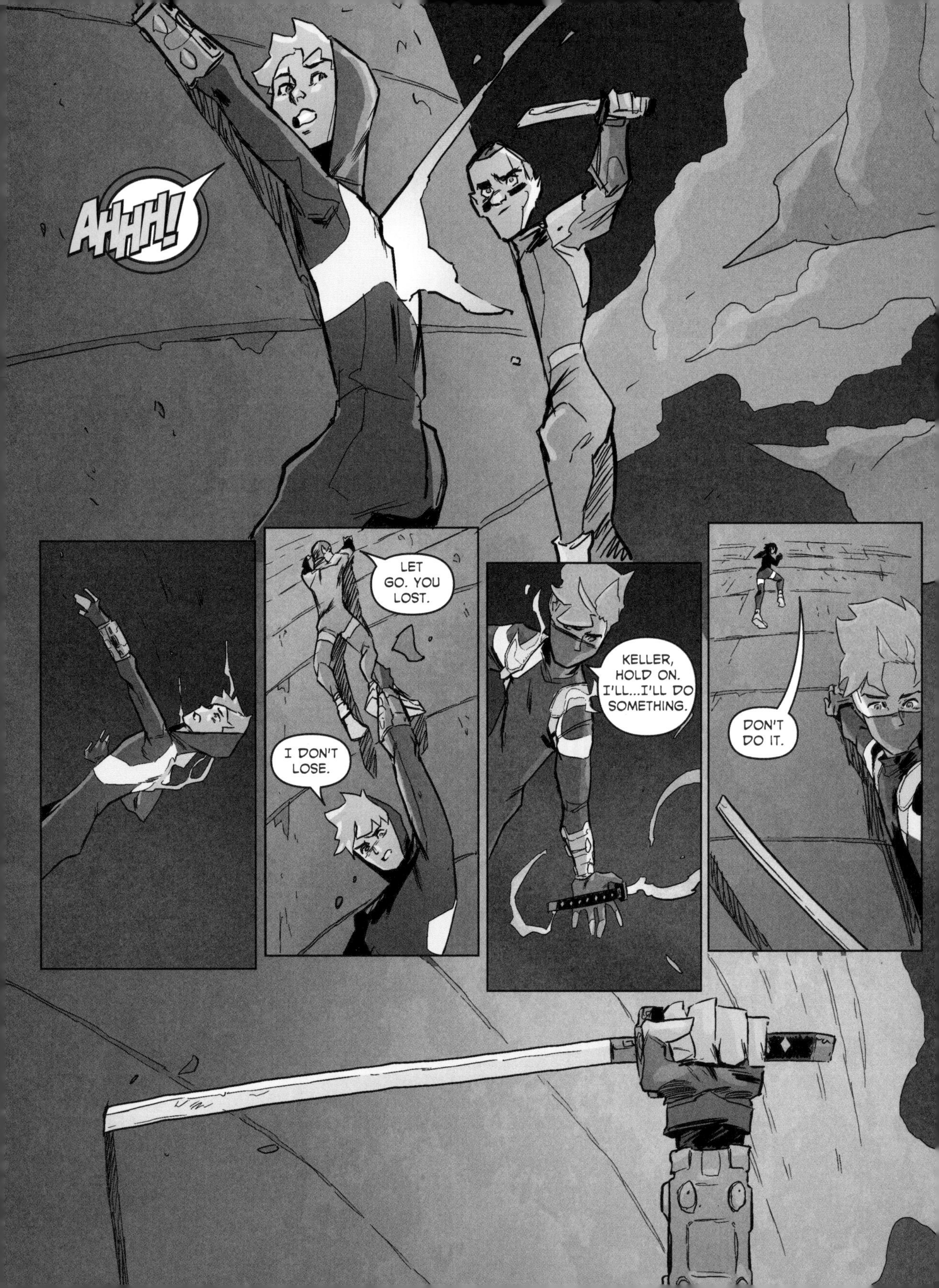
AHHH!
LET GO. YOU LOST.
I DON'T LOSE.
KELLER, HOLD ON. I'LL...I'LL DO SOMETHING.
DON'T DO IT.

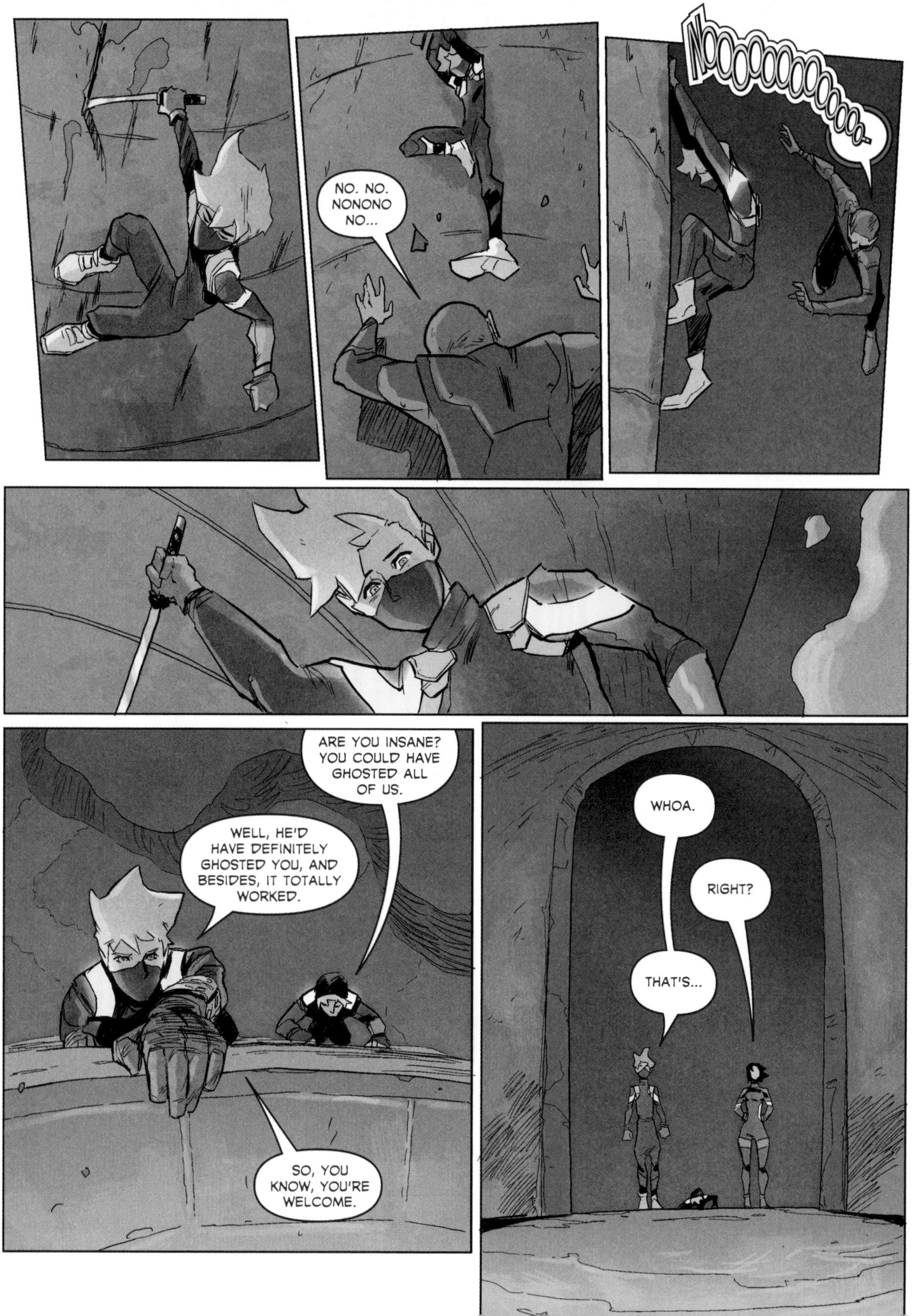
NO. NO. NONONO NO...
NOOOOOOOOOOOOO-
ARE YOU INSANE? YOU COULD HAVE GHOSTED ALL OF US.
WELL, HE'D HAVE DEFINITELY GHOSTED YOU, AND BESIDES, IT TOTALLY WORKED.
SO, YOU KNOW, YOU'RE WELCOME.
WHOA.
RIGHT?
THAT'S...

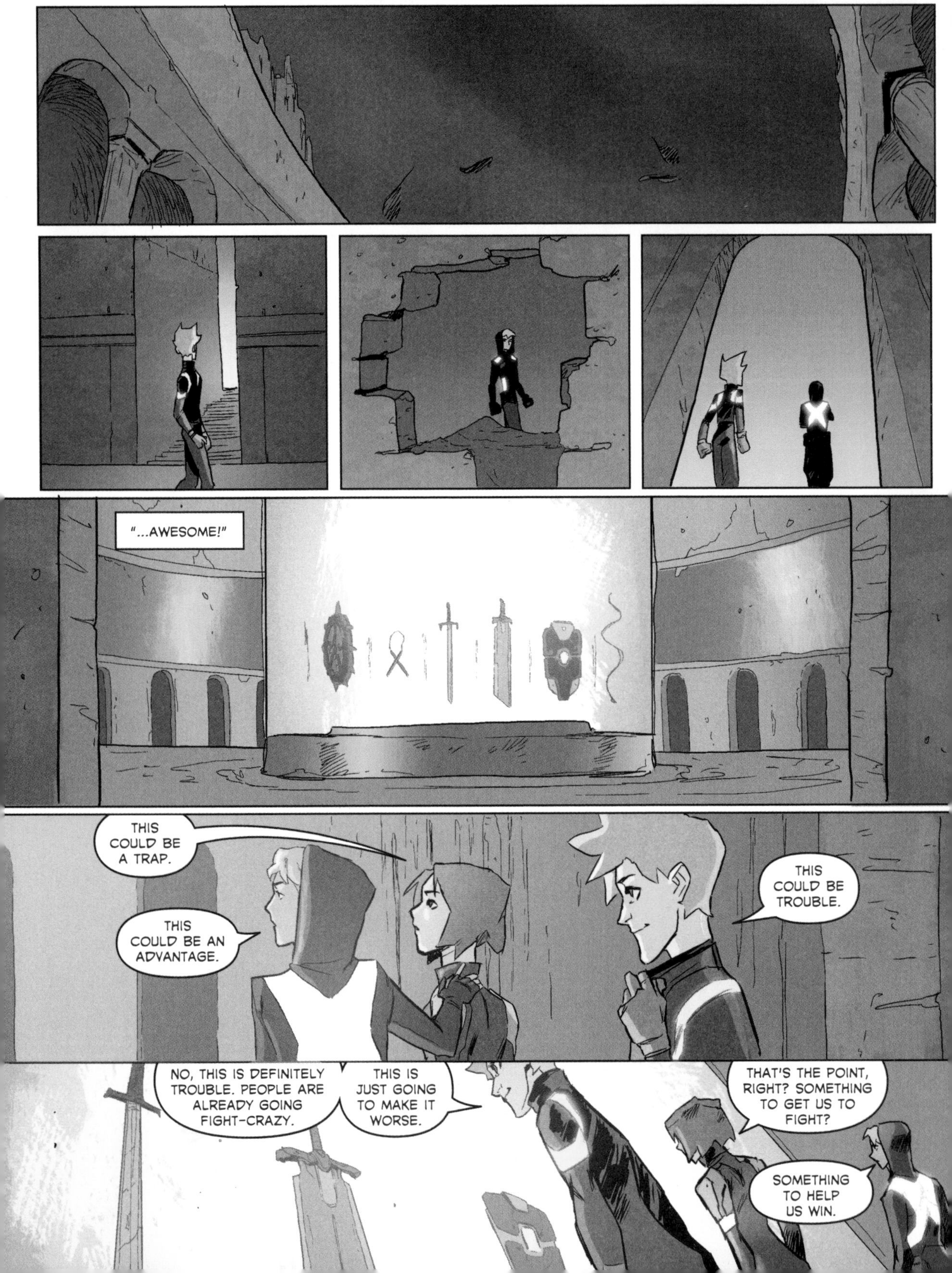
"...AWESOME!"
THIS COULD BE A TRAP.
THIS COULD BE AN ADVANTAGE.
THIS COULD BE TROUBLE.
NO, THIS IS DEFINITELY TROUBLE. PEOPLE ARE ALREADY GOING FIGHT-CRAZY.
THIS IS JUST GOING TO MAKE IT WORSE.
THAT'S THE POINT, RIGHT? SOMETHING TO GET US TO FIGHT?
SOMETHING TO HELP US WIN.

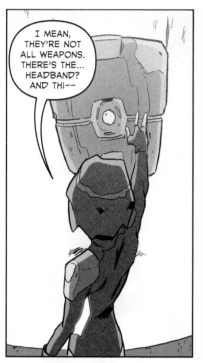

I MEAN, THEY'RE NOT ALL WEAPONS. THERE'S THE... HEADBAND? AND THI--

HOLY CRAP!

LIZA?

IT...OKAY, LOOK, I REALIZE THE BAR FOR CRAZY HAS BEEN SET PRETTY HIGH TODAY...

...BUT WHEN I TOUCHED THE SHIELD IT...SPOKE TO ME.

LIKE ON A SPIRITUAL LEVEL?

LIKE ON "A VOICE IN MY HEAD" LEVEL.

SO THESE THINGS ARE ALIVE. OR AT LEAST...SMART? ARE WE SUPPOSED TO CHOOSE THEM OR DO THEY...

...CHOOSE US?

PLEASE TELL ME IT'S SAYING SOMETHING TOO.

IT'S SAYING... WATCH OUT?

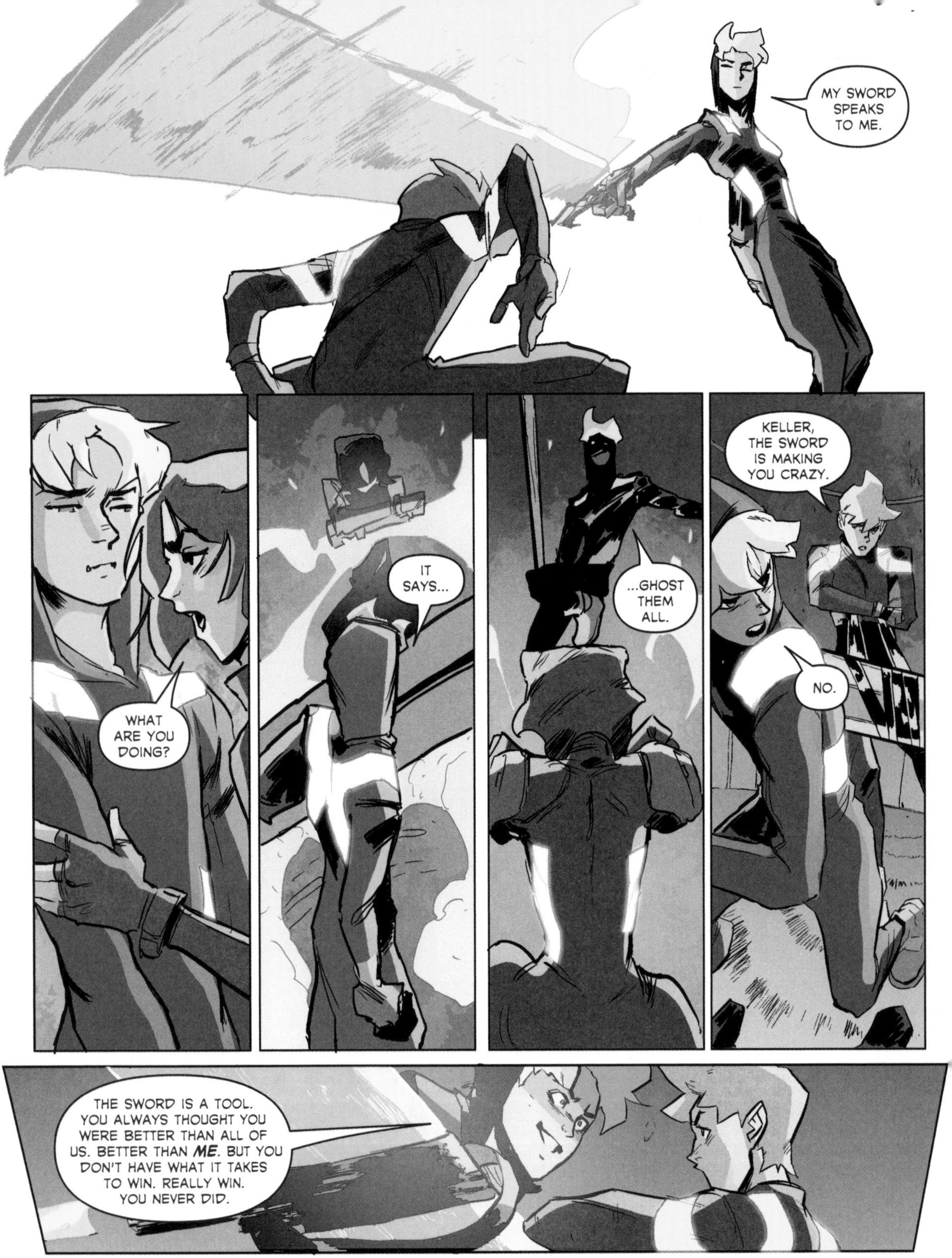
MY SWORD SPEAKS TO ME.
WHAT ARE YOU DOING?
IT SAYS...
...GHOST THEM ALL.
KELLER, THE SWORD IS MAKING YOU CRAZY.
NO.
THE SWORD IS A TOOL. YOU ALWAYS THOUGHT YOU WERE BETTER THAN ALL OF US. BETTER THAN *ME*. BUT YOU DON'T HAVE WHAT IT TAKES TO WIN. REALLY WIN. YOU NEVER DID.

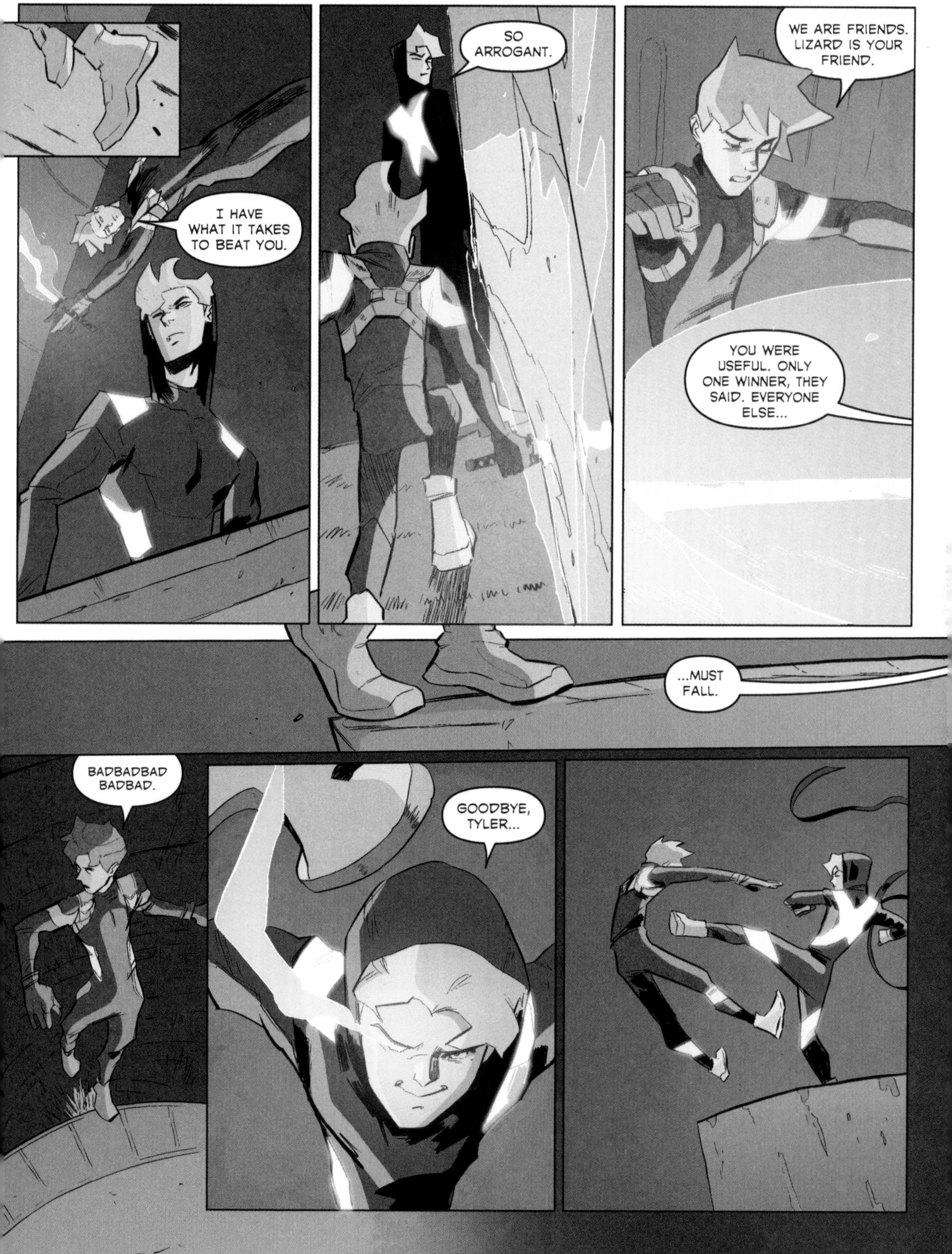
I HAVE WHAT IT TAKES TO BEAT YOU.
SO ARROGANT.
WE ARE FRIENDS. LIZARD IS YOUR FRIEND.
YOU WERE USEFUL. ONLY ONE WINNER, THEY SAID. EVERYONE ELSE...
...MUST FALL.
BADBADBAD BADBAD.
GOODBYE, TYLER...

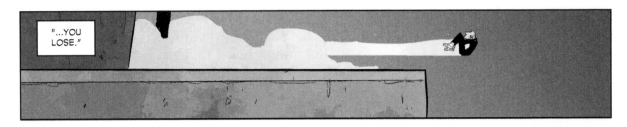

"...YOU LOSE."

"BETRAYAL IN THE GAME!

SO EXCITING. SO ILLUSTRATIVE.

THIS IS WHY THE GREAT BEAST SHOWS YOU THIS.

"NOT FOR ENTERTAINMENT.

"FOR ENLIGHTENMENT."

BECAUSE THERE IS ONE CERTAINTY IN ALL DOMINIONS.

THAT LEFT UNCHECKED, ALL WILL FIGHT AGAINST EACH OTHER.

FRIENDS WILL BETRAY FRIENDS. CHAOS. DESTRUCTION. DESPAIR.

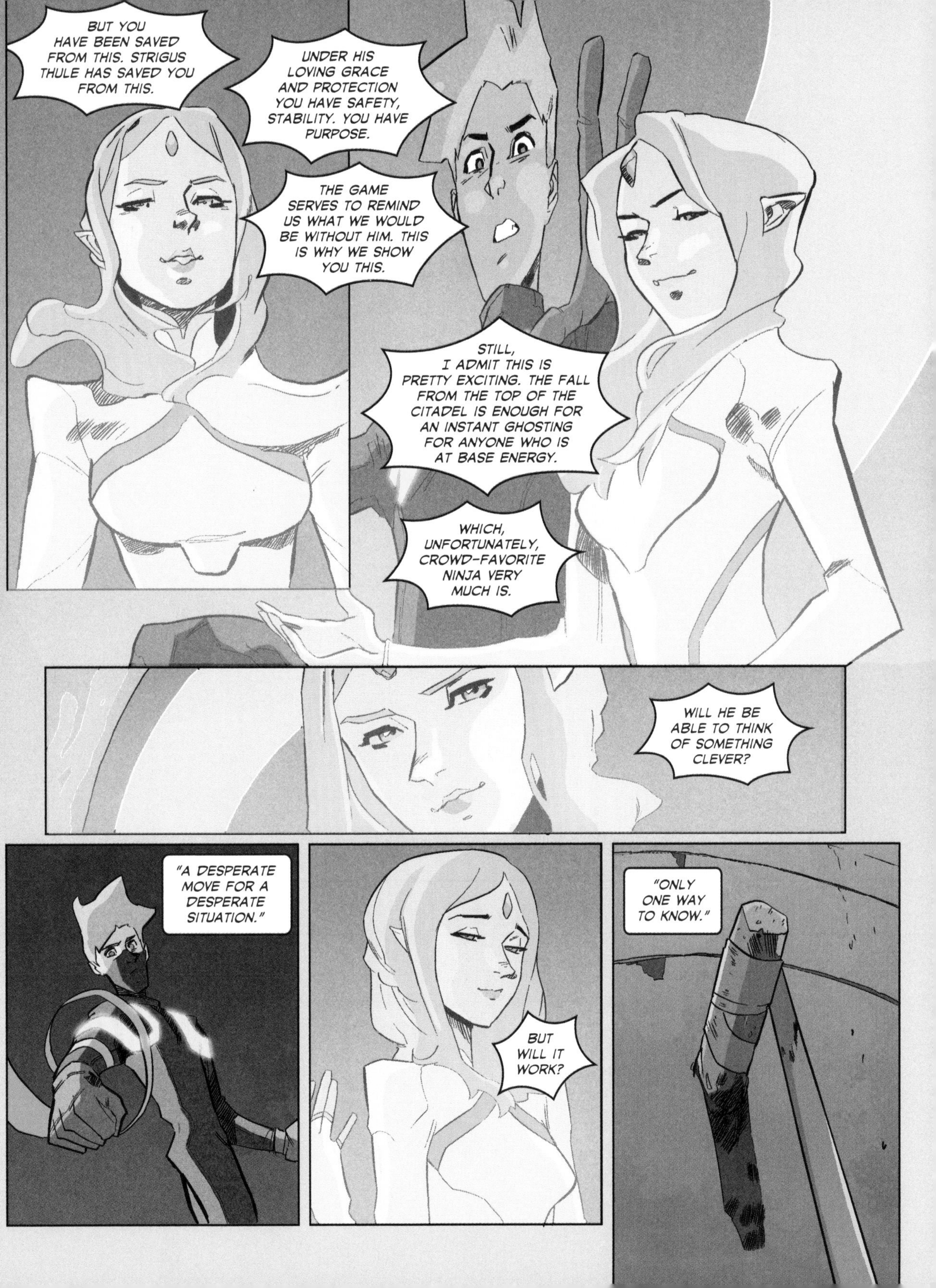
BUT YOU HAVE BEEN SAVED FROM THIS. STRIGUS THULE HAS SAVED YOU FROM THIS.
UNDER HIS LOVING GRACE AND PROTECTION YOU HAVE SAFETY, STABILITY. YOU HAVE PURPOSE.
THE GAME SERVES TO REMIND US WHAT WE WOULD BE WITHOUT HIM. THIS IS WHY WE SHOW YOU THIS.
STILL, I ADMIT THIS IS PRETTY EXCITING. THE FALL FROM THE TOP OF THE CITADEL IS ENOUGH FOR AN INSTANT GHOSTING FOR ANYONE WHO IS AT BASE ENERGY.
WHICH, UNFORTUNATELY, CROWD-FAVORITE NINJA VERY MUCH IS.
WILL HE BE ABLE TO THINK OF SOMETHING CLEVER?
"A DESPERATE MOVE FOR A DESPERATE SITUATION."
BUT WILL IT WORK?
"ONLY ONE WAY TO KNOW."

OOFFF!

SMACK

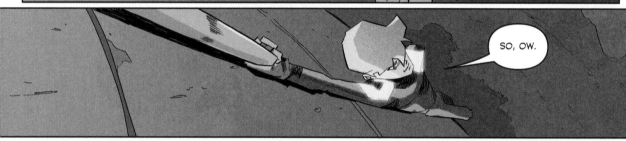

SO, OW.

YES, I DON'T IMAGINE IT FELT GOOD FOR YOU, EITHER. BUT... *UH*...THANKS?

DO YOU HAVE A NAME?

REALLY? HB? FOR HEADBAND?

NO, NO, THAT'S GREAT.

MAKES PERFECT SENSE.

I DON'T SUPPOSE YOU HAVE ANY SUGGESTIONS ABOUT WHAT TO DO NOW?

ARE YOU GOING TO FINISH THIS, OR DO YOU WANT TO GLOAT ABOUT STABBING US IN THE BACK?

NEITHER.

NINJA WAS A LIABILITY. LOOK AT YOU, PROTECTING HIM. YOU GHOSTED SOMEONE. NEARLY GOT GHOSTED YOURSELF. I HAD TO DO THIS.

BUT I DON'T WANT TO PLAY THIS GAME ALONE. BECAUSE RIGHT NOW...

"...EVERYONE ELSE IS COMING."

YOU WANT *ME* TO HELP YOU.

I DO.

HE WAS MY FRIEND.

AND WHAT ABOUT YOUR FAMILY? YOU WANT TO GET BACK TO THEM, DON'T YOU? THEN YOU NEED TO LEARN THIS LESSON.

THERE ARE NO FRIENDS HERE. ONLY ALLIES...

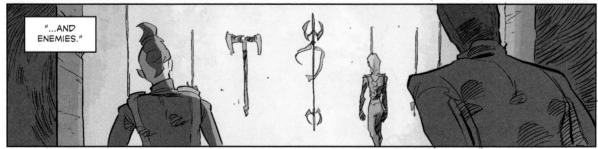

"...AND ENEMIES."

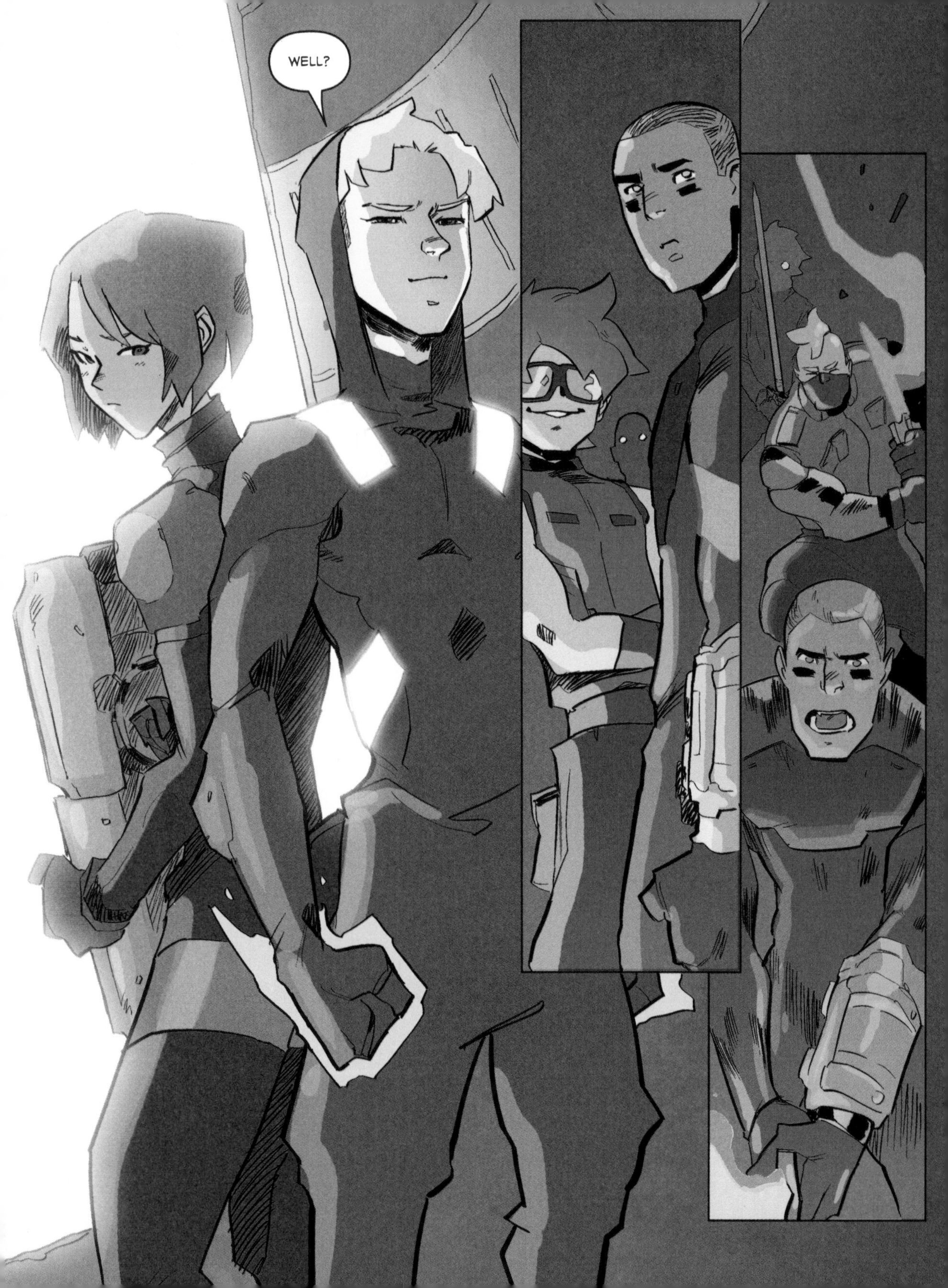
WELL?

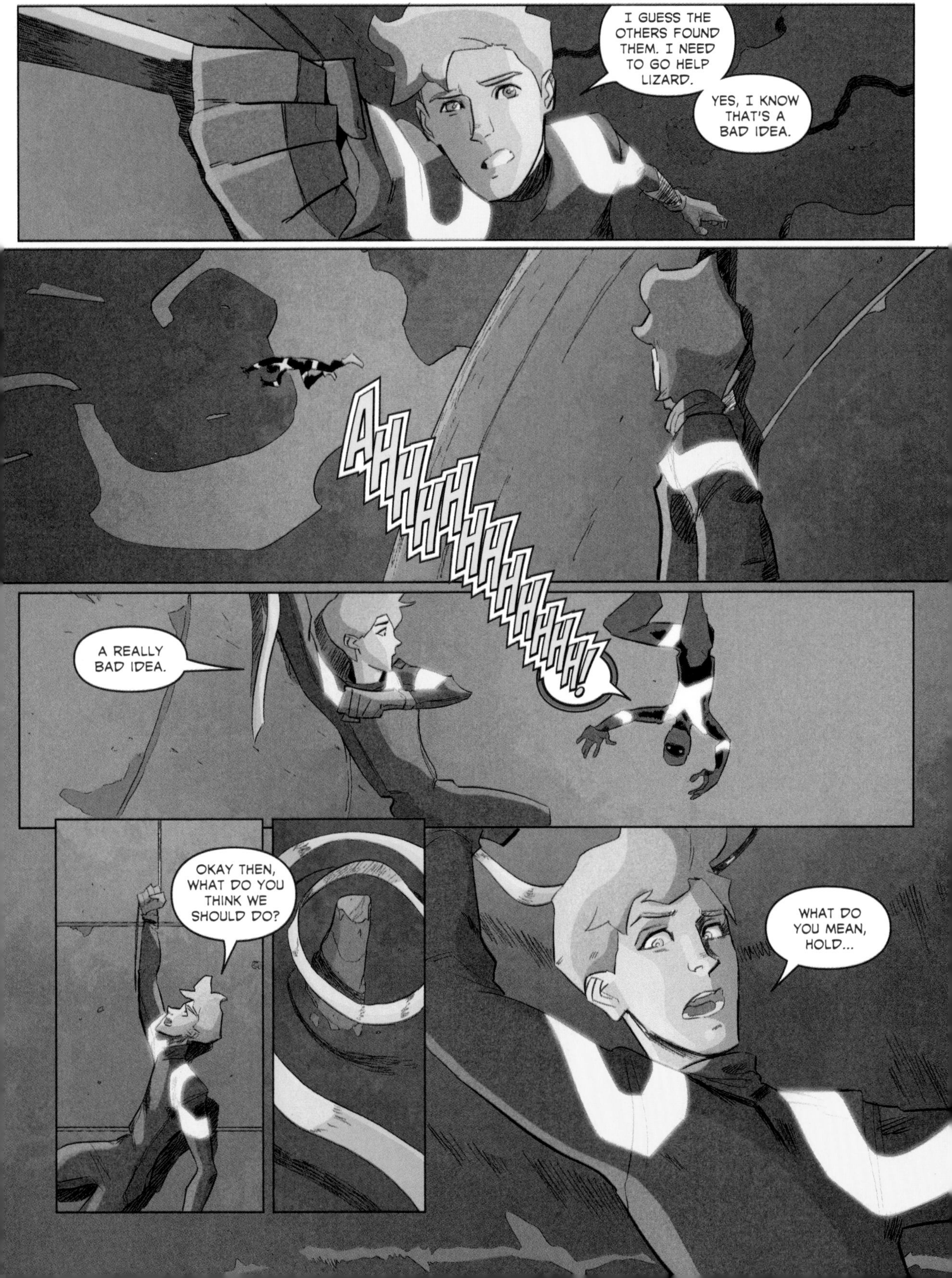
I GUESS THE OTHERS FOUND THEM. I NEED TO GO HELP LIZARD.
YES, I KNOW THAT'S A BAD IDEA.
AHHHHHHHHHHHHHH!
A REALLY BAD IDEA.
OKAY THEN, WHAT DO YOU THINK WE SHOULD DO?
WHAT DO YOU MEAN, HOLD...

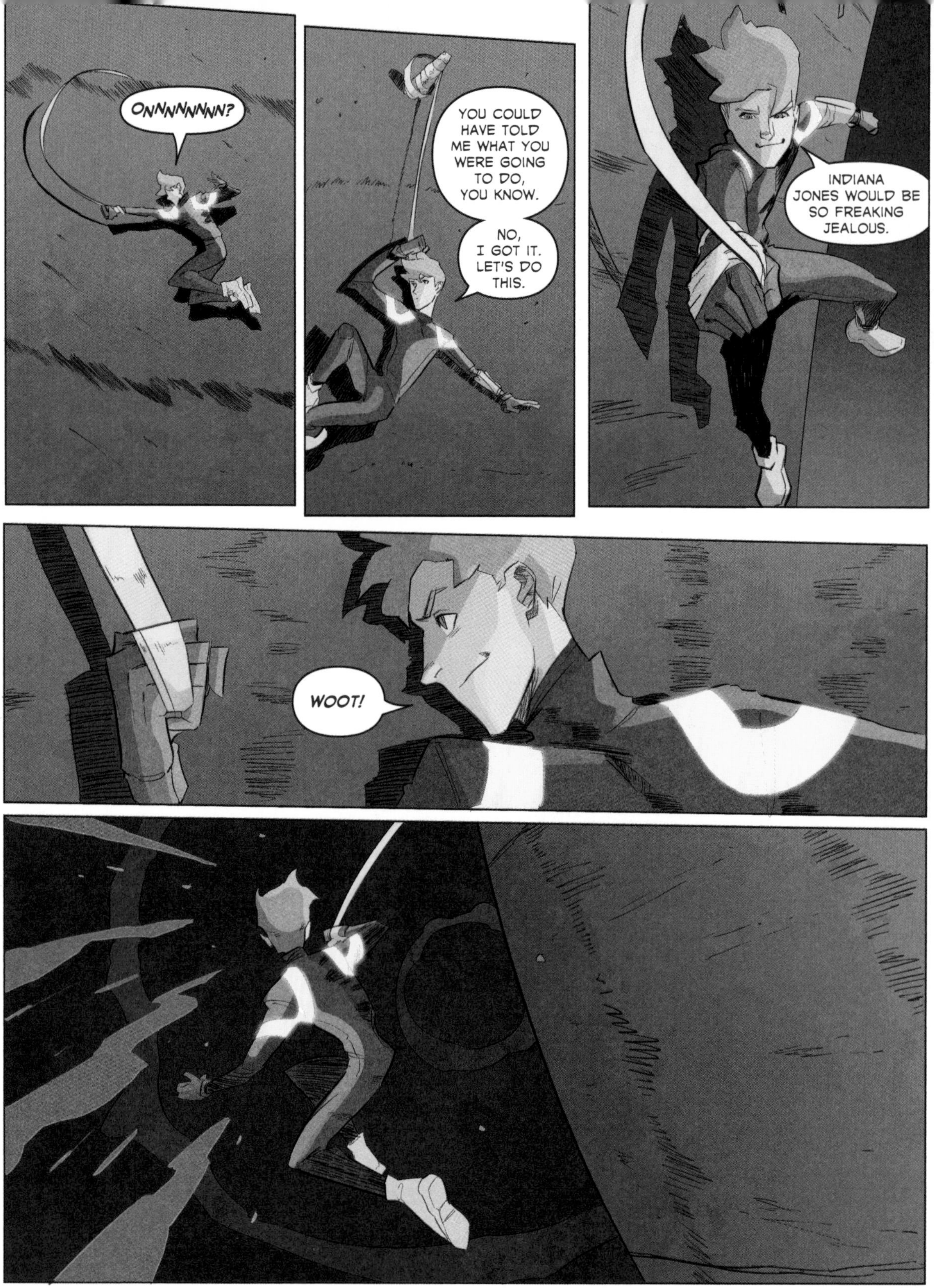

ONNNNNNNN?
YOU COULD HAVE TOLD ME WHAT YOU WERE GOING TO DO, YOU KNOW.
NO, I GOT IT. LET'S DO THIS.
INDIANA JONES WOULD BE SO FREAKING JEALOUS.
WOOT!

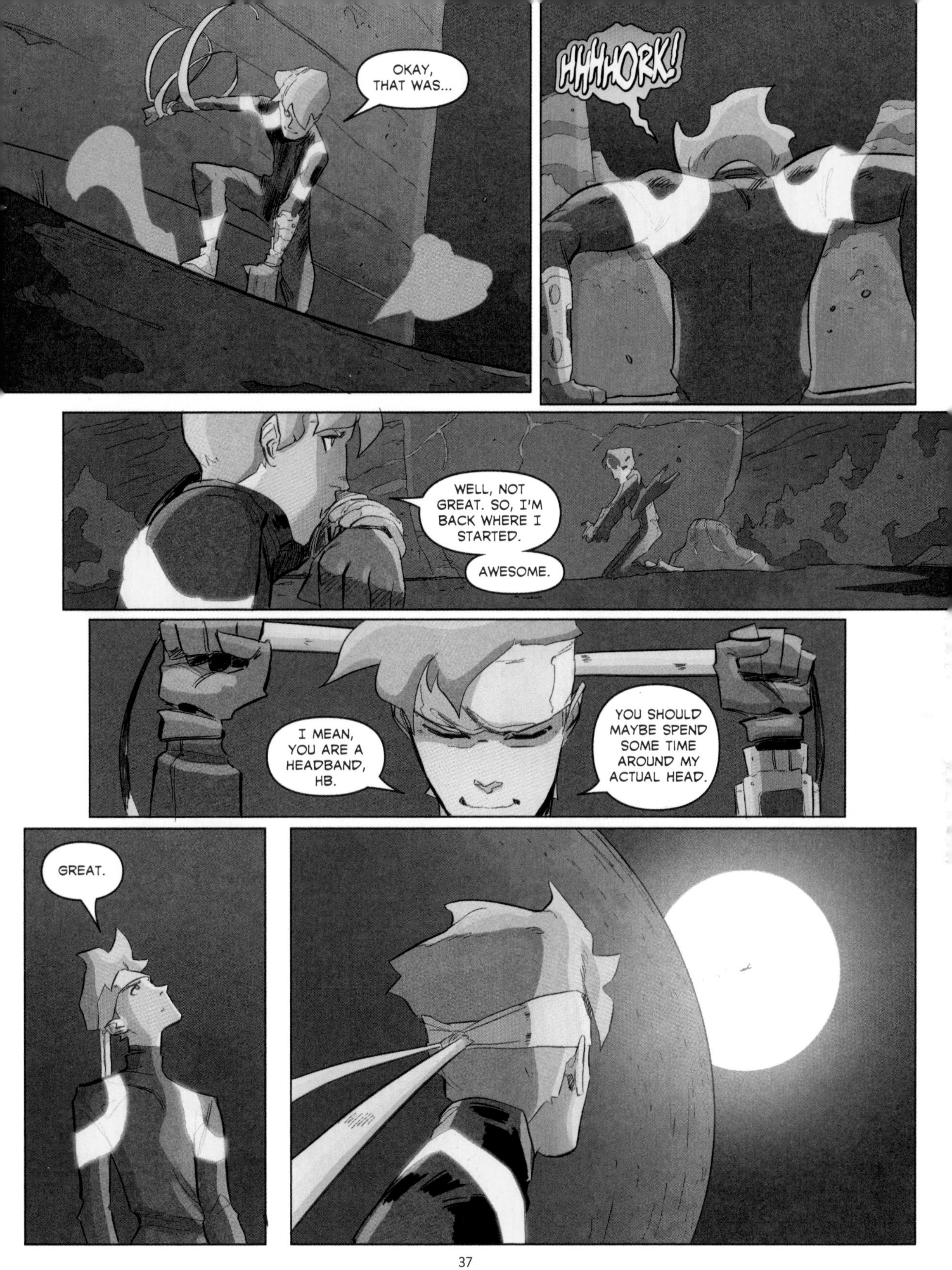
OKAY, THAT WAS...
HHHHORK!
WELL, NOT GREAT. SO, I'M BACK WHERE I STARTED.
AWESOME.
I MEAN, YOU ARE A HEADBAND, HB.
YOU SHOULD MAYBE SPEND SOME TIME AROUND MY ACTUAL HEAD.
GREAT.

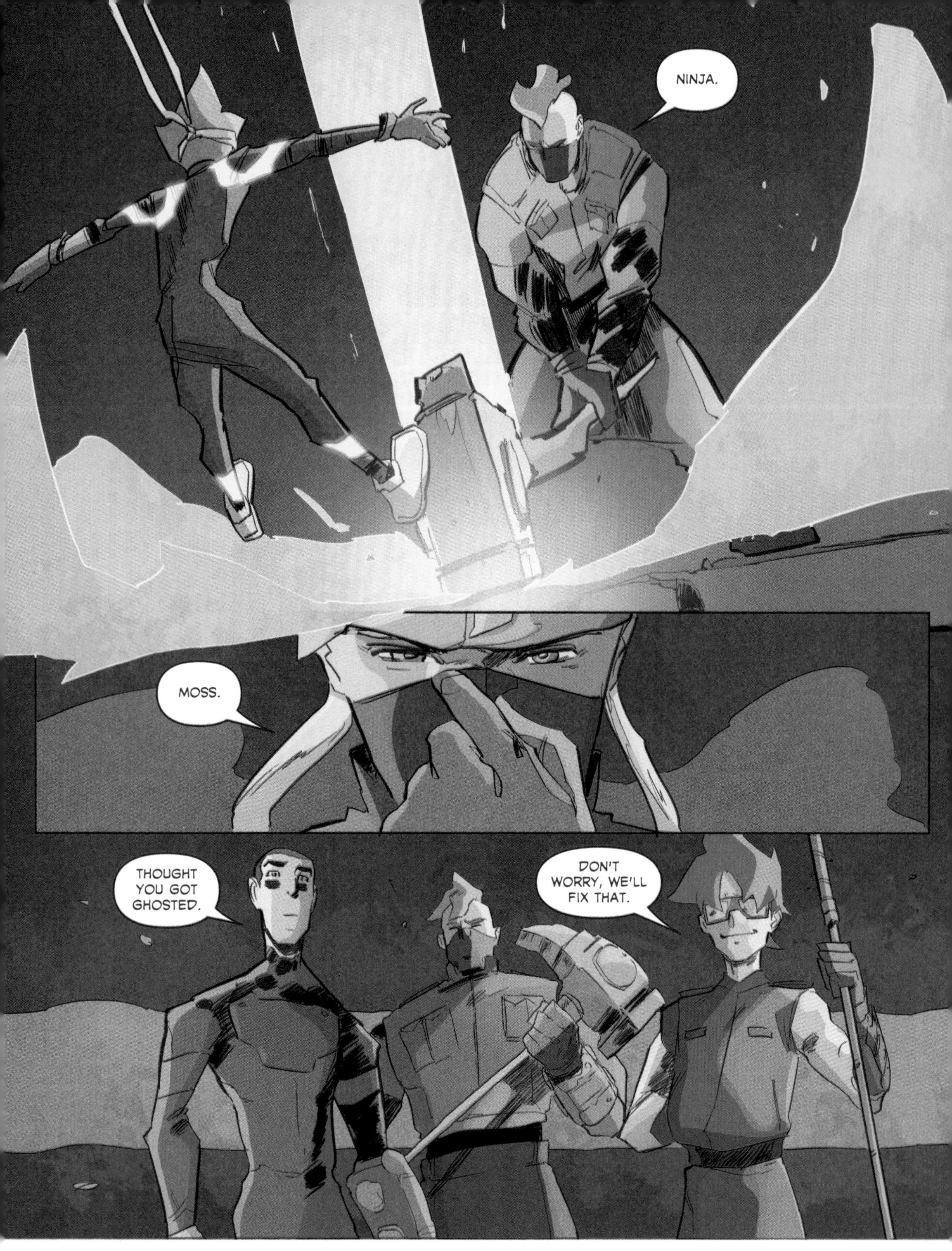
NINJA.
MOSS.
THOUGHT YOU GOT GHOSTED.
DON'T WORRY, WE'LL FIX THAT.

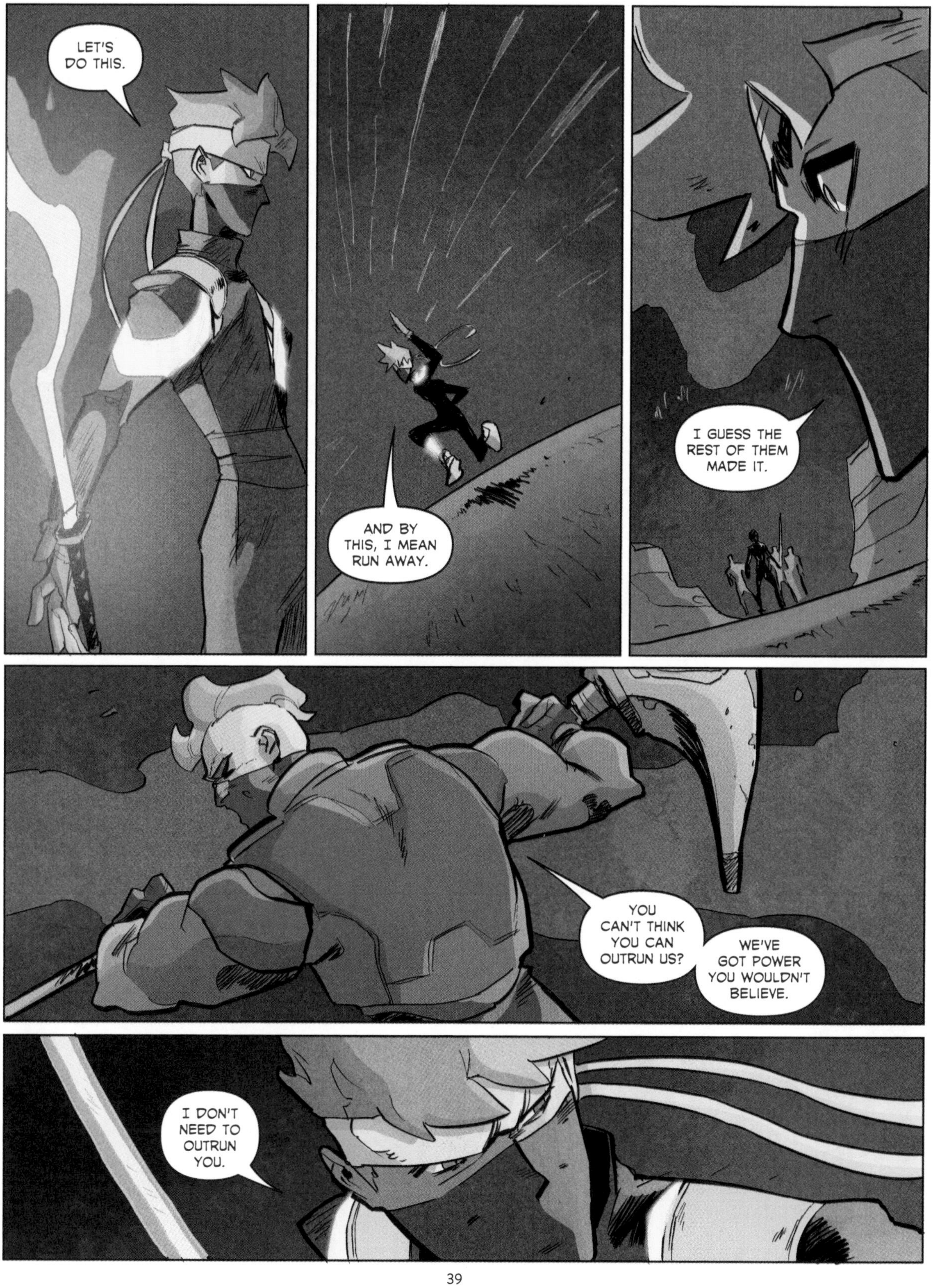
LET'S DO THIS.
AND BY THIS, I MEAN RUN AWAY.
I GUESS THE REST OF THEM MADE IT.
YOU CAN'T THINK YOU CAN OUTRUN US?
WE'VE GOT POWER YOU WOULDN'T BELIEVE.
I DON'T NEED TO OUTRUN YOU.

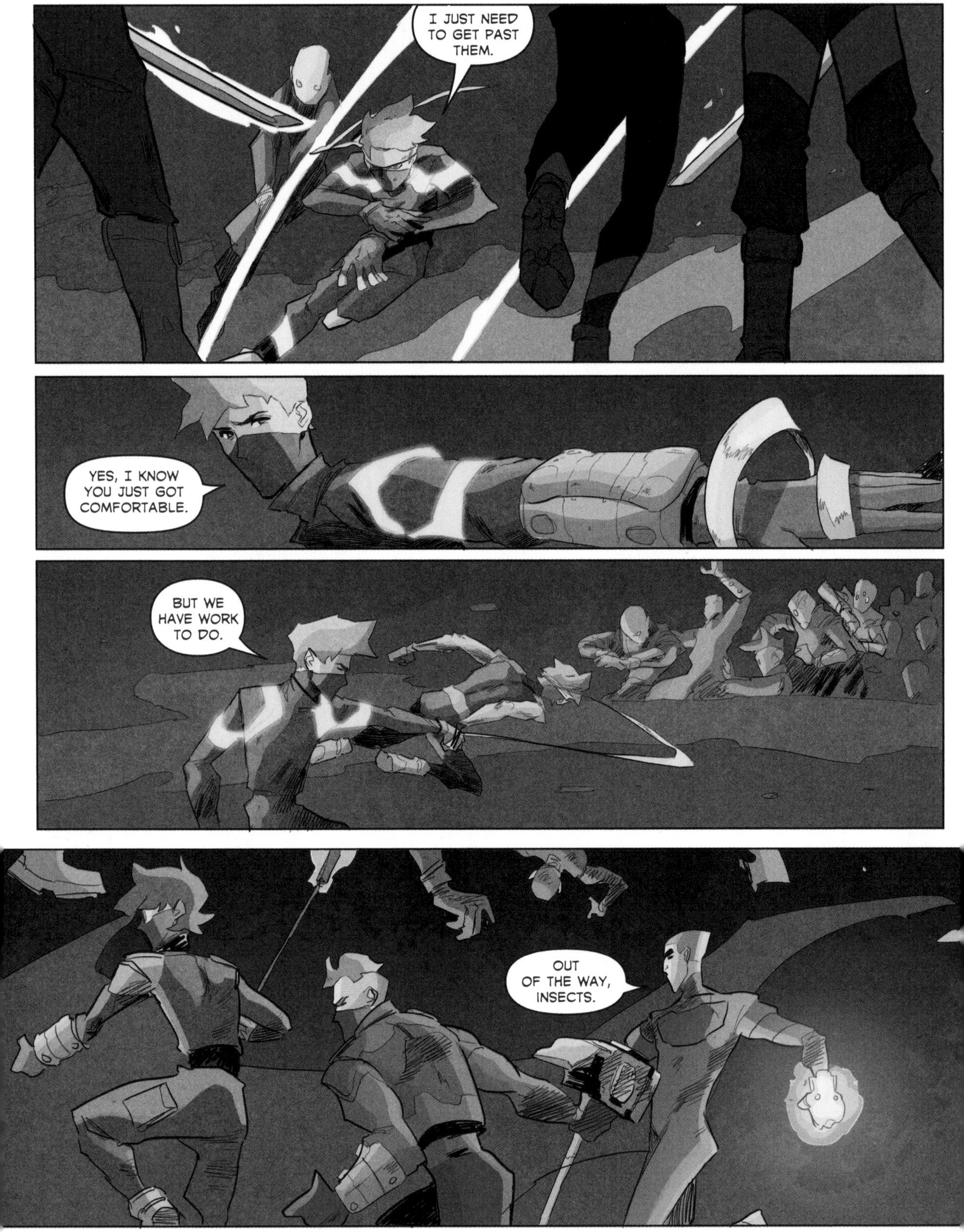

I JUST NEED TO GET PAST THEM.
YES, I KNOW YOU JUST GOT COMFORTABLE.
BUT WE HAVE WORK TO DO.
OUT OF THE WAY, INSECTS.

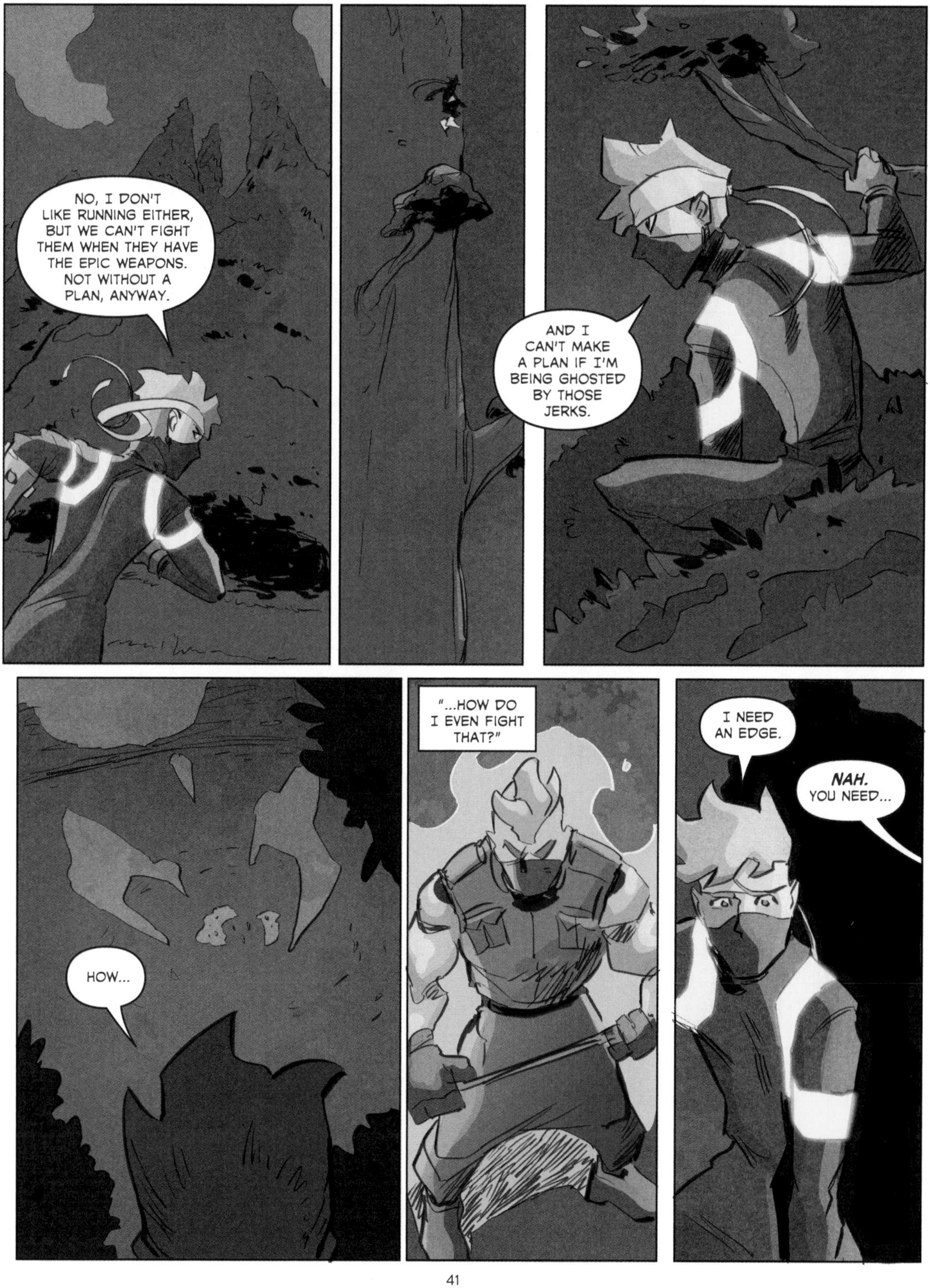
NO, I DON'T LIKE RUNNING EITHER, BUT WE CAN'T FIGHT THEM WHEN THEY HAVE THE EPIC WEAPONS. NOT WITHOUT A PLAN, ANYWAY.
AND I CAN'T MAKE A PLAN IF I'M BEING GHOSTED BY THOSE JERKS.
HOW...
"...HOW DO I EVEN FIGHT THAT?"
I NEED AN EDGE.
NAH. YOU NEED...

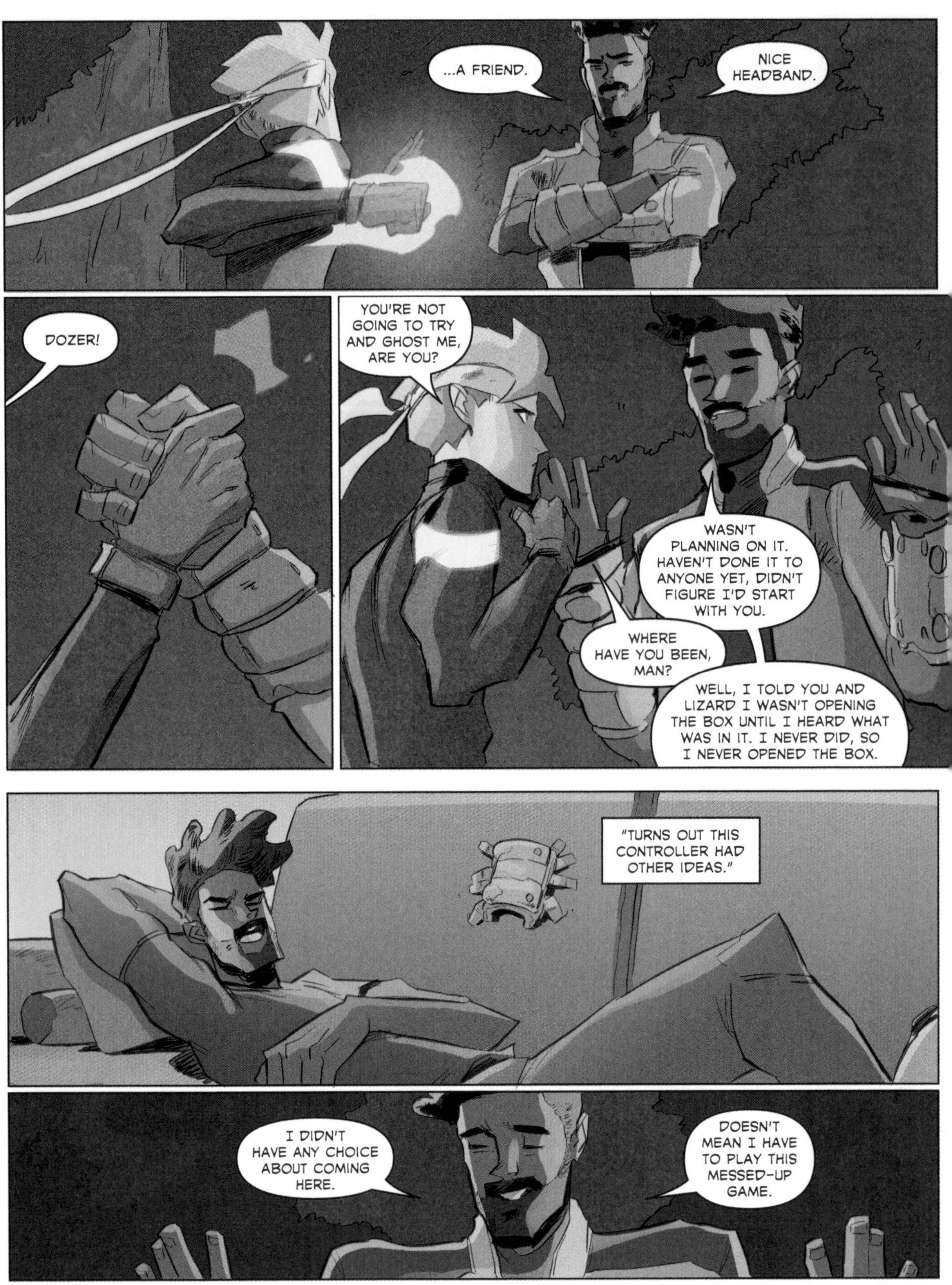
...A FRIEND.
NICE HEADBAND.
DOZER!
YOU'RE NOT GOING TO TRY AND GHOST ME, ARE YOU?
WASN'T PLANNING ON IT. HAVEN'T DONE IT TO ANYONE YET, DIDN'T FIGURE I'D START WITH YOU.
WHERE HAVE YOU BEEN, MAN?
WELL, I TOLD YOU AND LIZARD I WASN'T OPENING THE BOX UNTIL I HEARD WHAT WAS IN IT. I NEVER DID, SO I NEVER OPENED THE BOX.
"TURNS OUT THIS CONTROLLER HAD OTHER IDEAS."
I DIDN'T HAVE ANY CHOICE ABOUT COMING HERE.
DOESN'T MEAN I HAVE TO PLAY THIS MESSED-UP GAME.

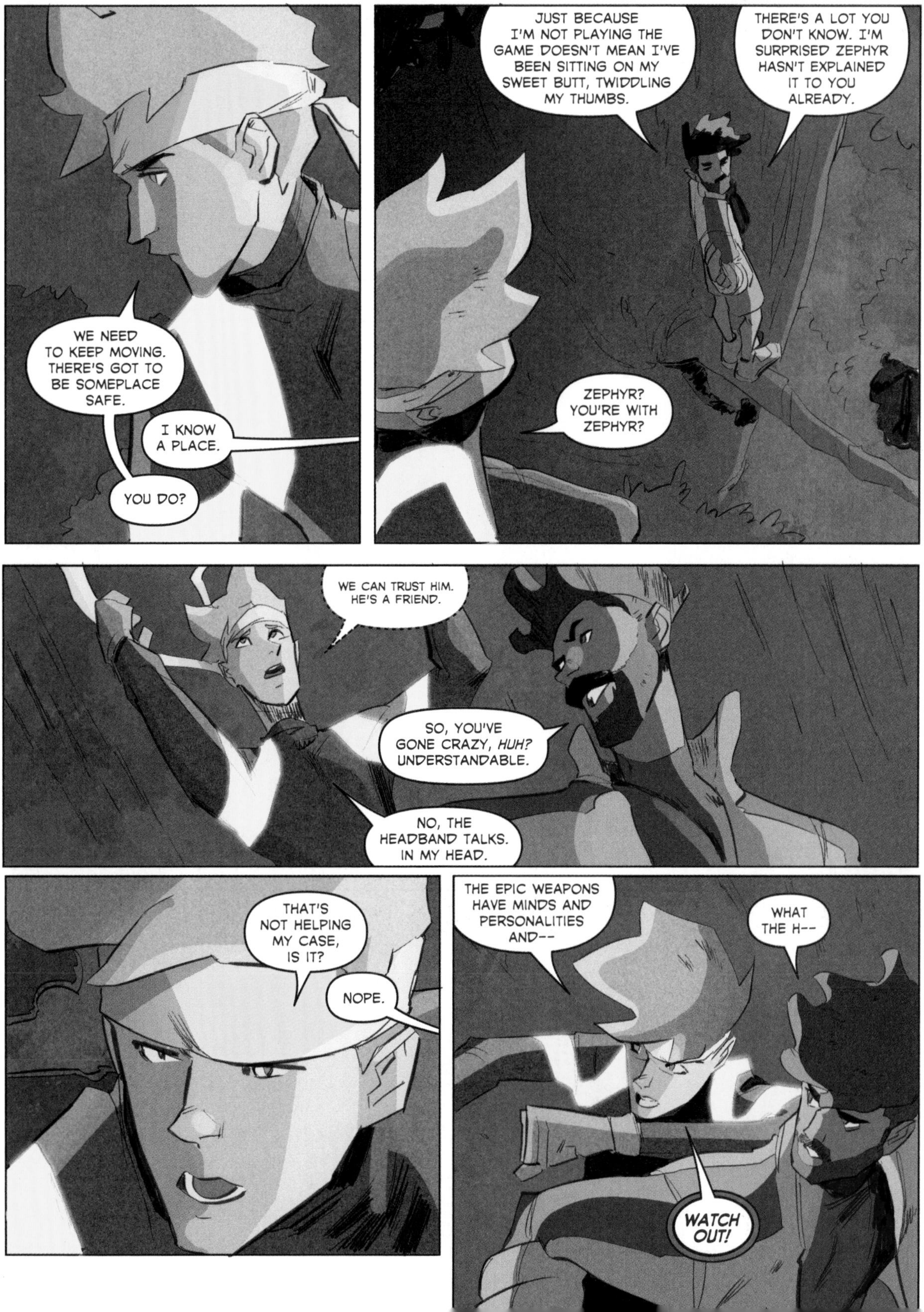
WE NEED TO KEEP MOVING. THERE'S GOT TO BE SOMEPLACE SAFE.
I KNOW A PLACE.
YOU DO?
JUST BECAUSE I'M NOT PLAYING THE GAME DOESN'T MEAN I'VE BEEN SITTING ON MY SWEET BUTT, TWIDDLING MY THUMBS.
THERE'S A LOT YOU DON'T KNOW. I'M SURPRISED ZEPHYR HASN'T EXPLAINED IT TO YOU ALREADY.
ZEPHYR? YOU'RE WITH ZEPHYR?
WE CAN TRUST HIM. HE'S A FRIEND.
SO, YOU'VE GONE CRAZY, *HUH?* UNDERSTANDABLE.
NO, THE HEADBAND TALKS. IN MY HEAD.
THAT'S NOT HELPING MY CASE, IS IT?
NOPE.
THE EPIC WEAPONS HAVE MINDS AND PERSONALITIES AND--
WHAT THE H--
WATCH OUT!

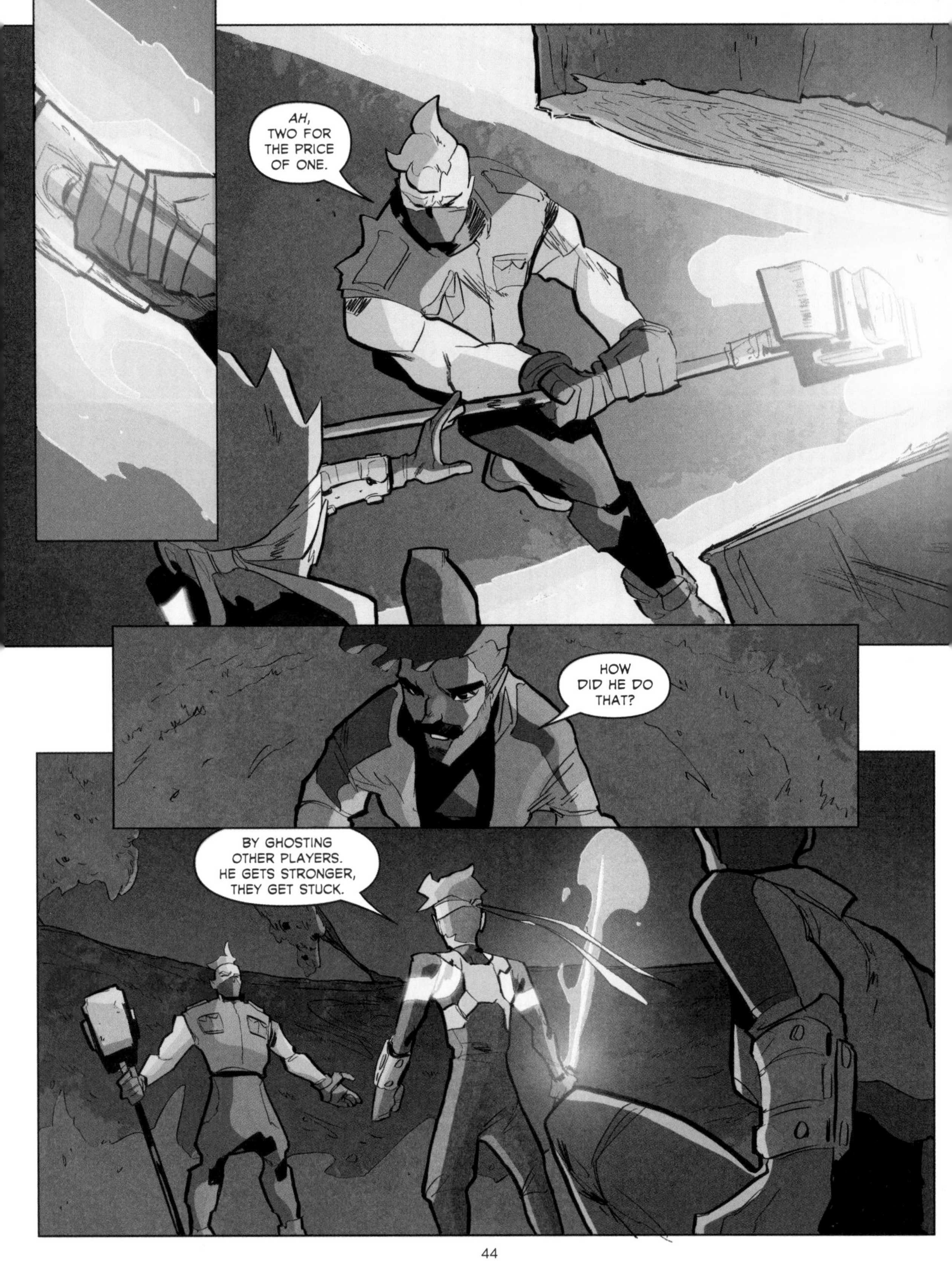
AH, TWO FOR THE PRICE OF ONE.
HOW DID HE DO THAT?
BY GHOSTING OTHER PLAYERS. HE GETS STRONGER, THEY GET STUCK.

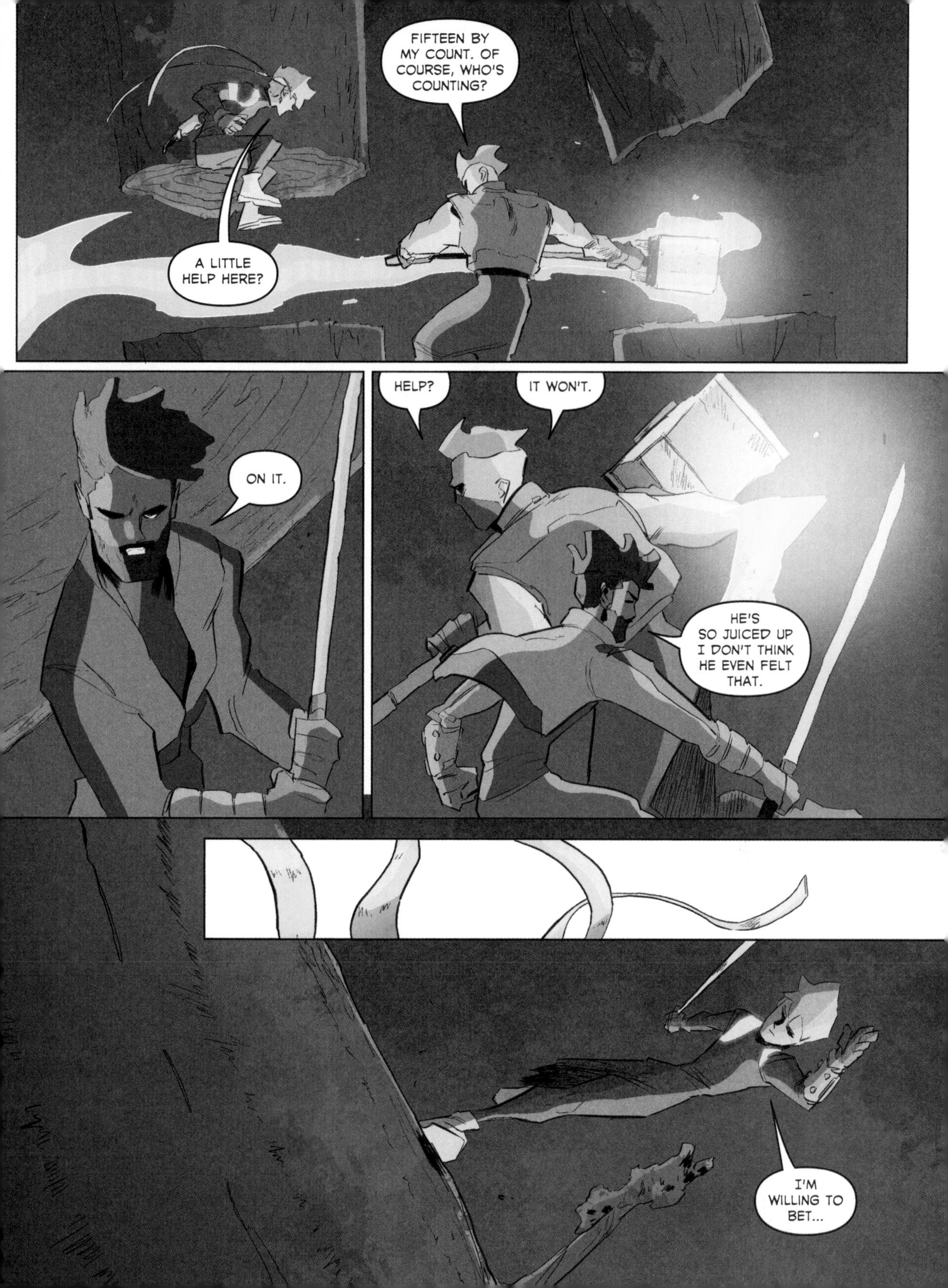
A LITTLE HELP HERE?
FIFTEEN BY MY COUNT. OF COURSE, WHO'S COUNTING?
ON IT.
HELP?
IT WON'T.
HE'S SO JUICED UP I DON'T THINK HE EVEN FELT THAT.
I'M WILLING TO BET...

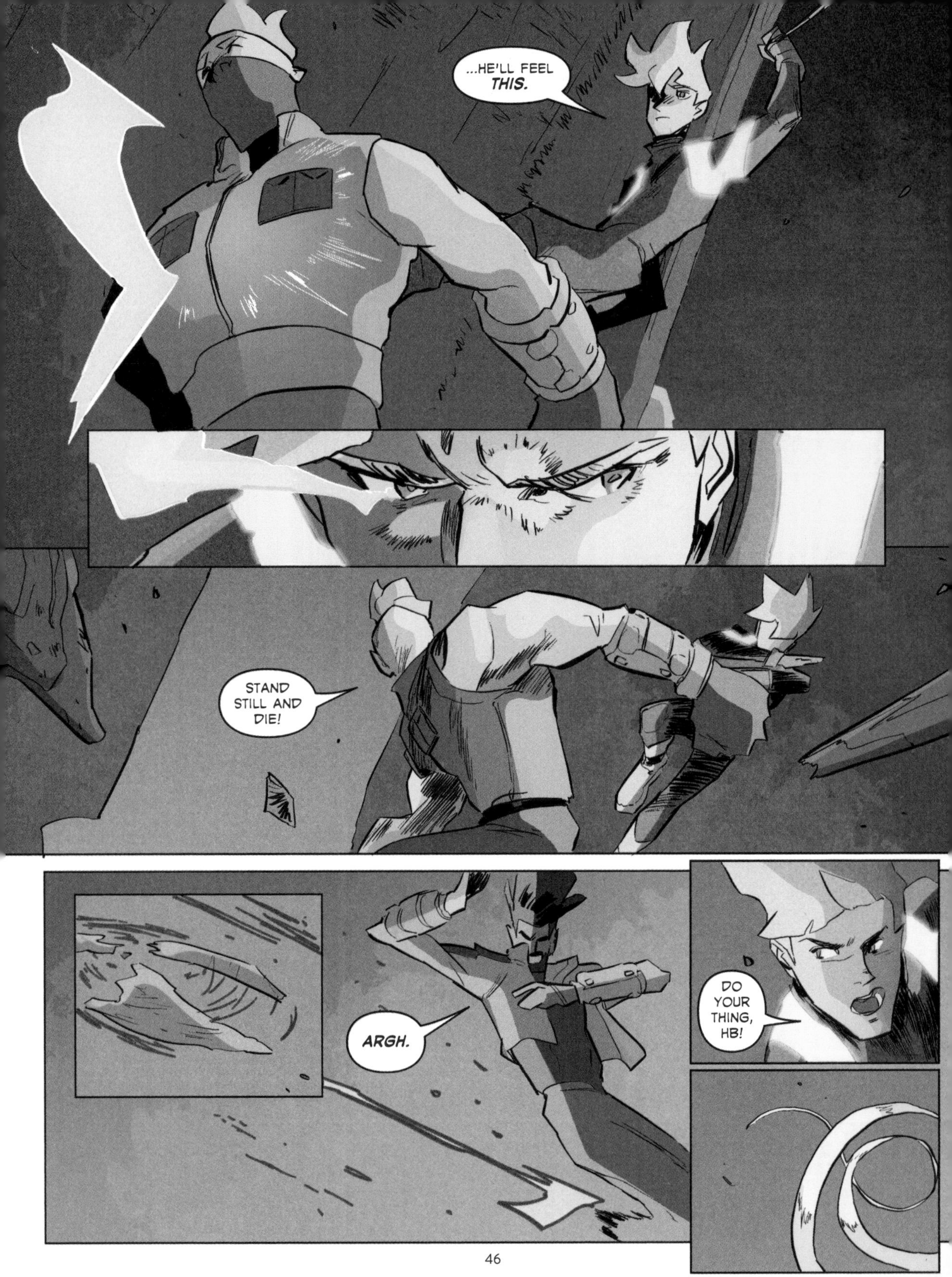
...HE'LL FEEL THIS.
STAND STILL AND DIE!
ARGH.
DO YOUR THING, HB!

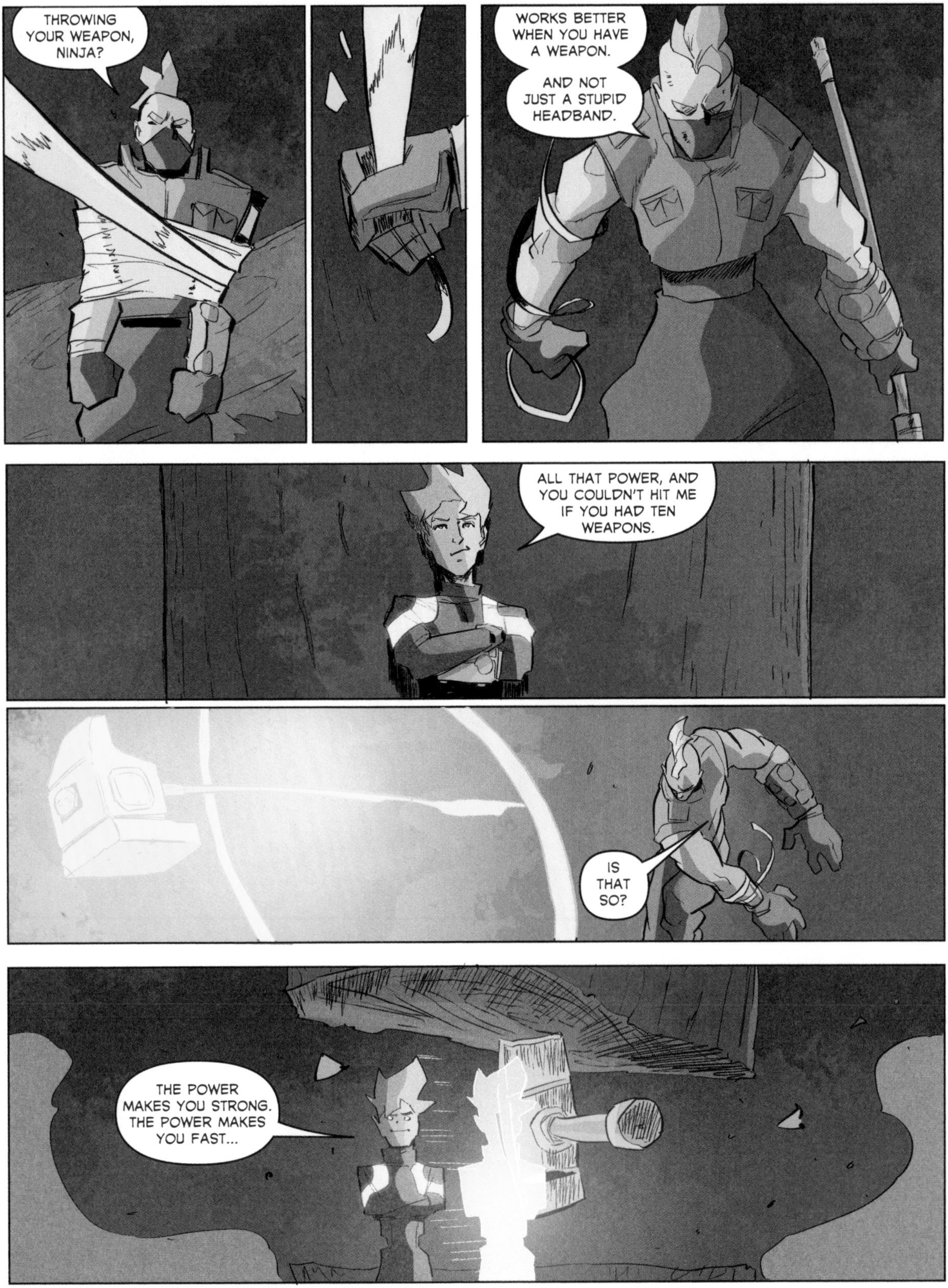
THROWING YOUR WEAPON, NINJA?
WORKS BETTER WHEN YOU HAVE A WEAPON.
AND NOT JUST A STUPID HEADBAND.
ALL THAT POWER, AND YOU COULDN'T HIT ME IF YOU HAD TEN WEAPONS.
IS THAT SO?
THE POWER MAKES YOU STRONG. THE POWER MAKES YOU FAST...

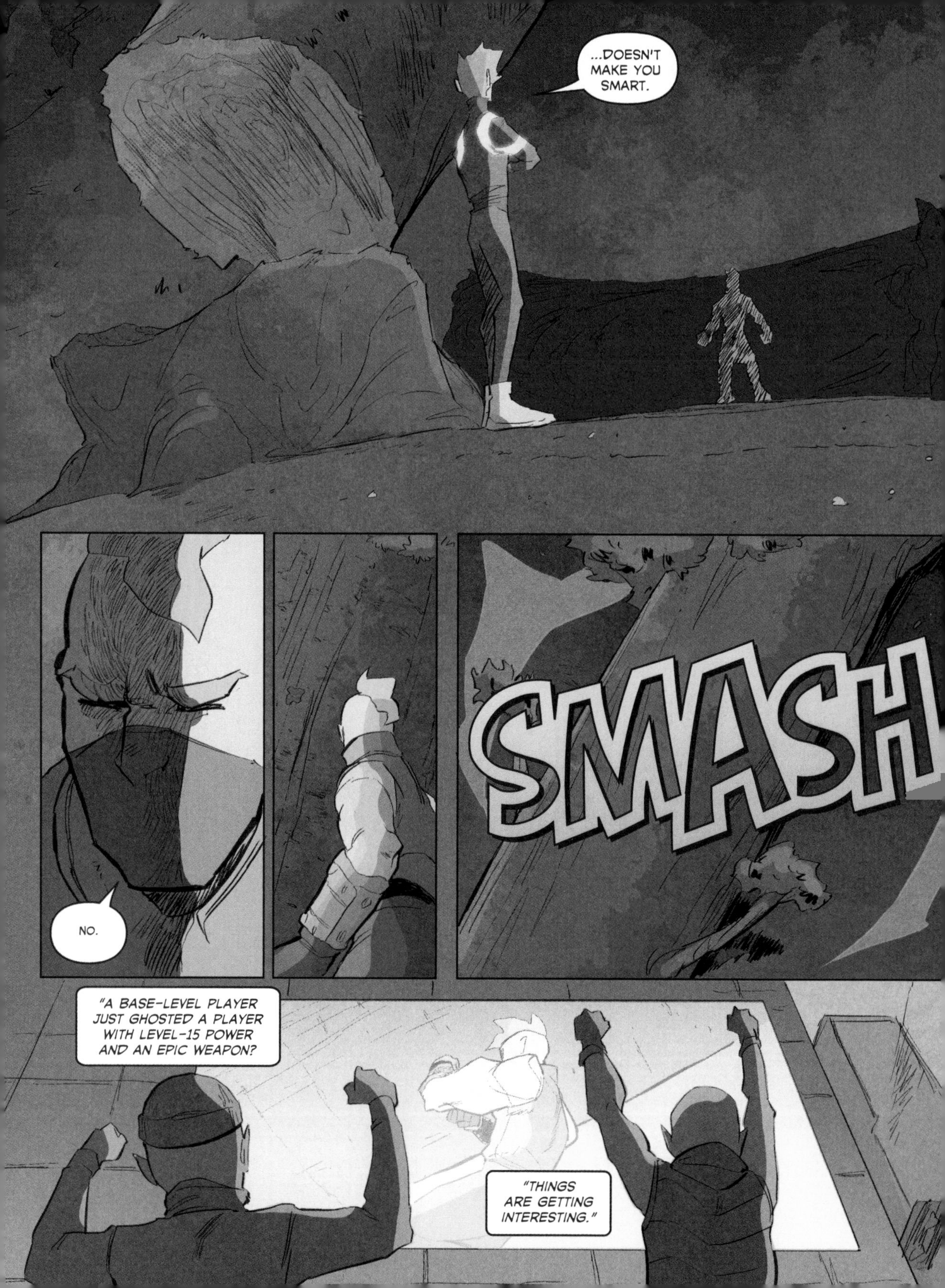
...DOESN'T MAKE YOU SMART.
NO.
SMASH
"A BASE-LEVEL PLAYER JUST GHOSTED A PLAYER WITH LEVEL-15 POWER AND AN EPIC WEAPON?
"THINGS ARE GETTING INTERESTING."

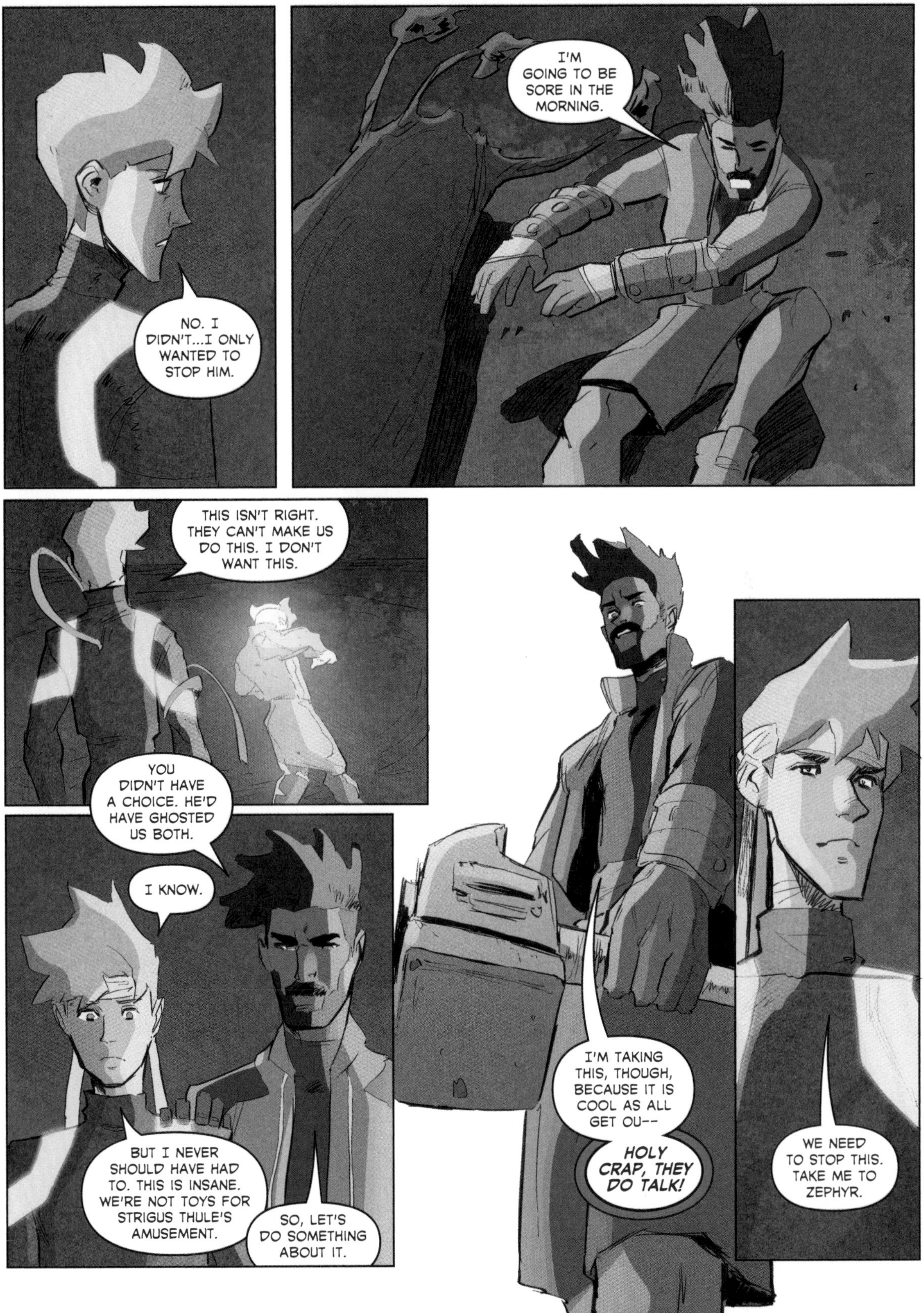
NO. I DIDN'T...I ONLY WANTED TO STOP HIM.
I'M GOING TO BE SORE IN THE MORNING.
THIS ISN'T RIGHT. THEY CAN'T MAKE US DO THIS. I DON'T WANT THIS.
YOU DIDN'T HAVE A CHOICE. HE'D HAVE GHOSTED US BOTH.
I KNOW.
BUT I NEVER SHOULD HAVE HAD TO. THIS IS INSANE. WE'RE NOT TOYS FOR STRIGUS THULE'S AMUSEMENT.
SO, LET'S DO SOMETHING ABOUT IT.
I'M TAKING THIS, THOUGH, BECAUSE IT IS COOL AS ALL GET OU--
HOLY CRAP, THEY DO TALK!
WE NEED TO STOP THIS. TAKE ME TO ZEPHYR.

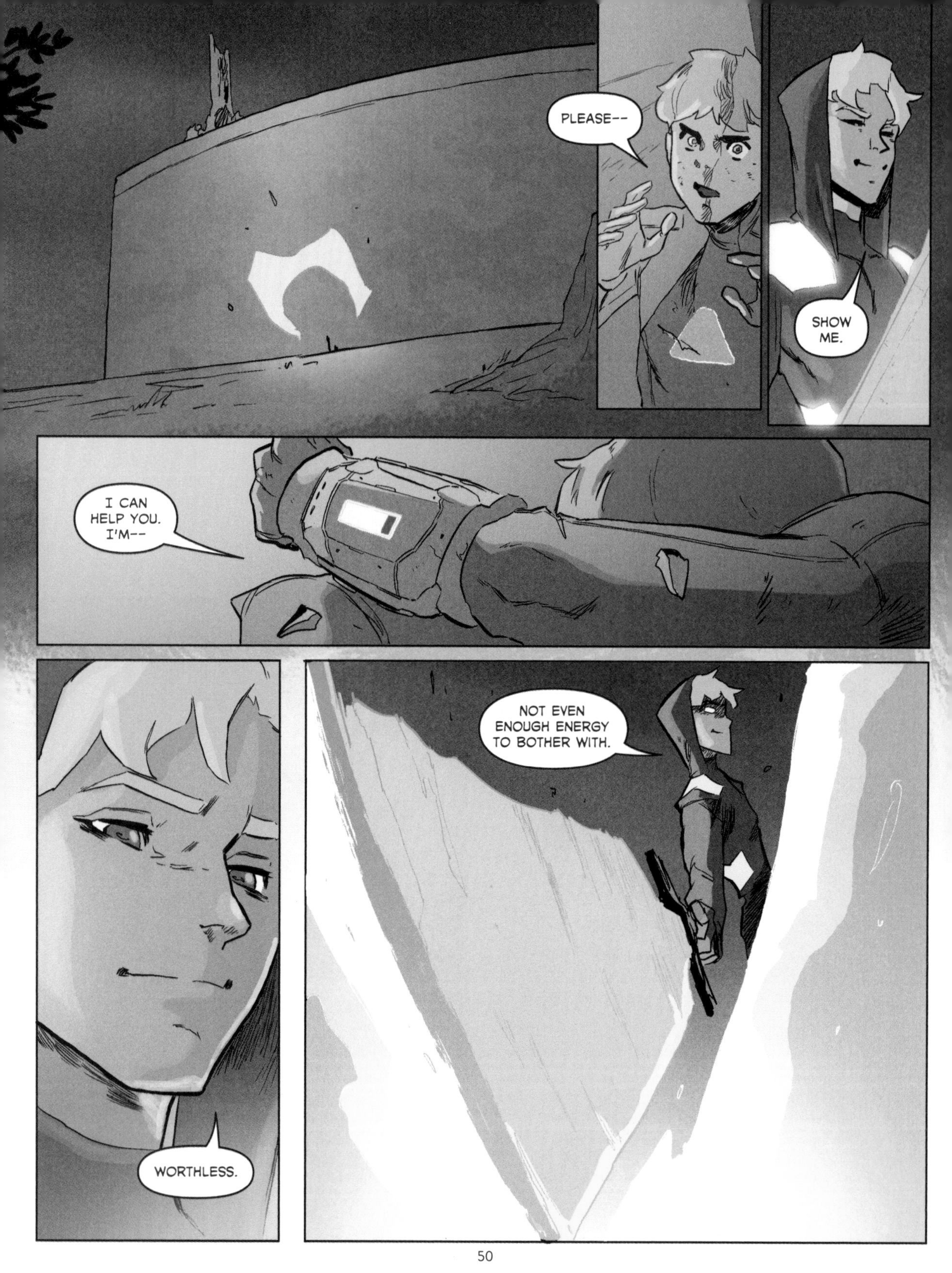
PLEASE--
SHOW ME.
I CAN HELP YOU. I'M--
WORTHLESS.
NOT EVEN ENOUGH ENERGY TO BOTHER WITH.

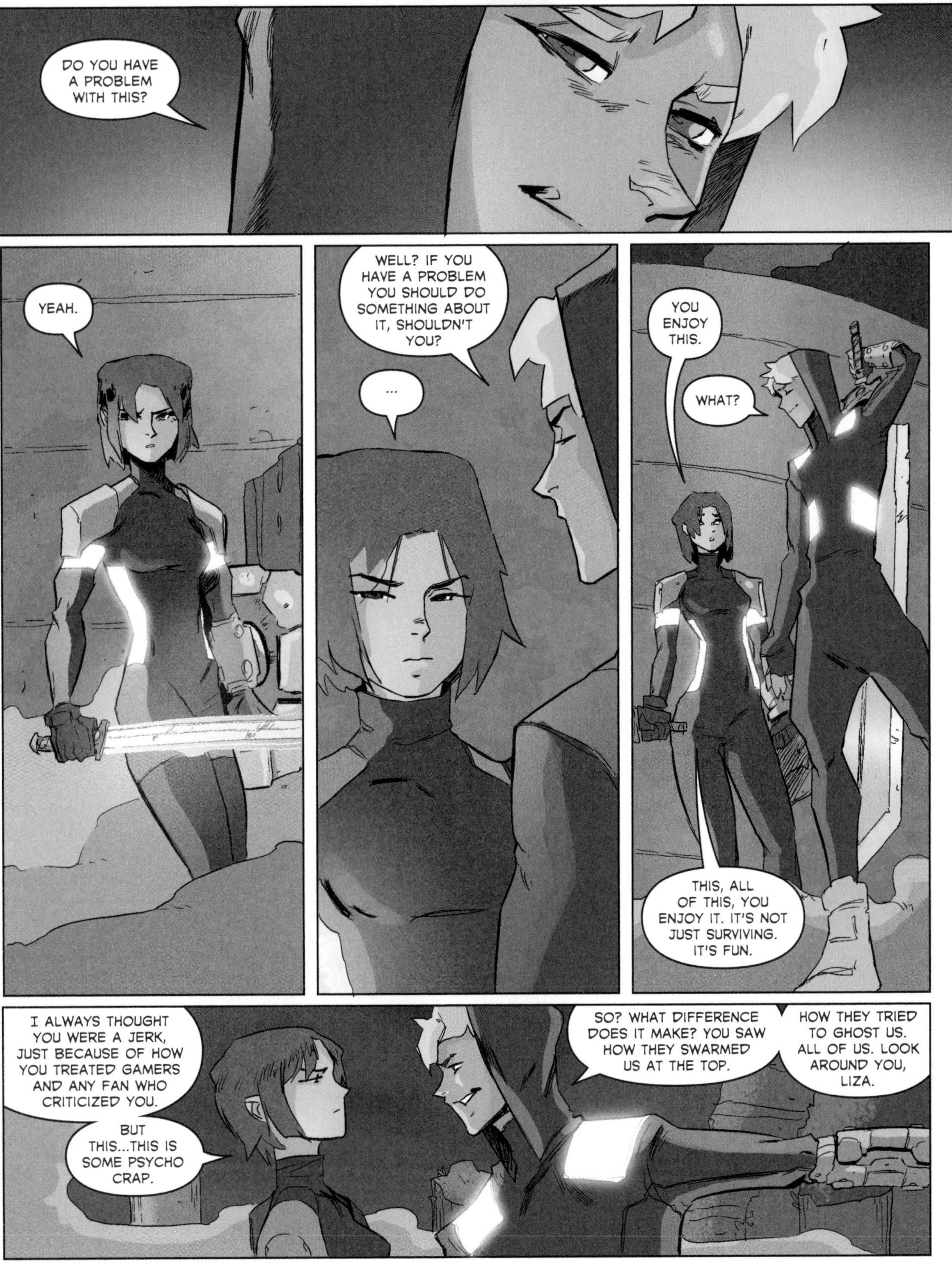
DO YOU HAVE A PROBLEM WITH THIS?
YEAH.
WELL? IF YOU HAVE A PROBLEM YOU SHOULD DO SOMETHING ABOUT IT, SHOULDN'T YOU?
...
YOU ENJOY THIS.
WHAT?
THIS, ALL OF THIS, YOU ENJOY IT. IT'S NOT JUST SURVIVING. IT'S FUN.
I ALWAYS THOUGHT YOU WERE A JERK, JUST BECAUSE OF HOW YOU TREATED GAMERS AND ANY FAN WHO CRITICIZED YOU.
BUT THIS...THIS IS SOME PSYCHO CRAP.
SO? WHAT DIFFERENCE DOES IT MAKE? YOU SAW HOW THEY SWARMED US AT THE TOP.
HOW THEY TRIED TO GHOST US. ALL OF US. LOOK AROUND YOU, LIZA.

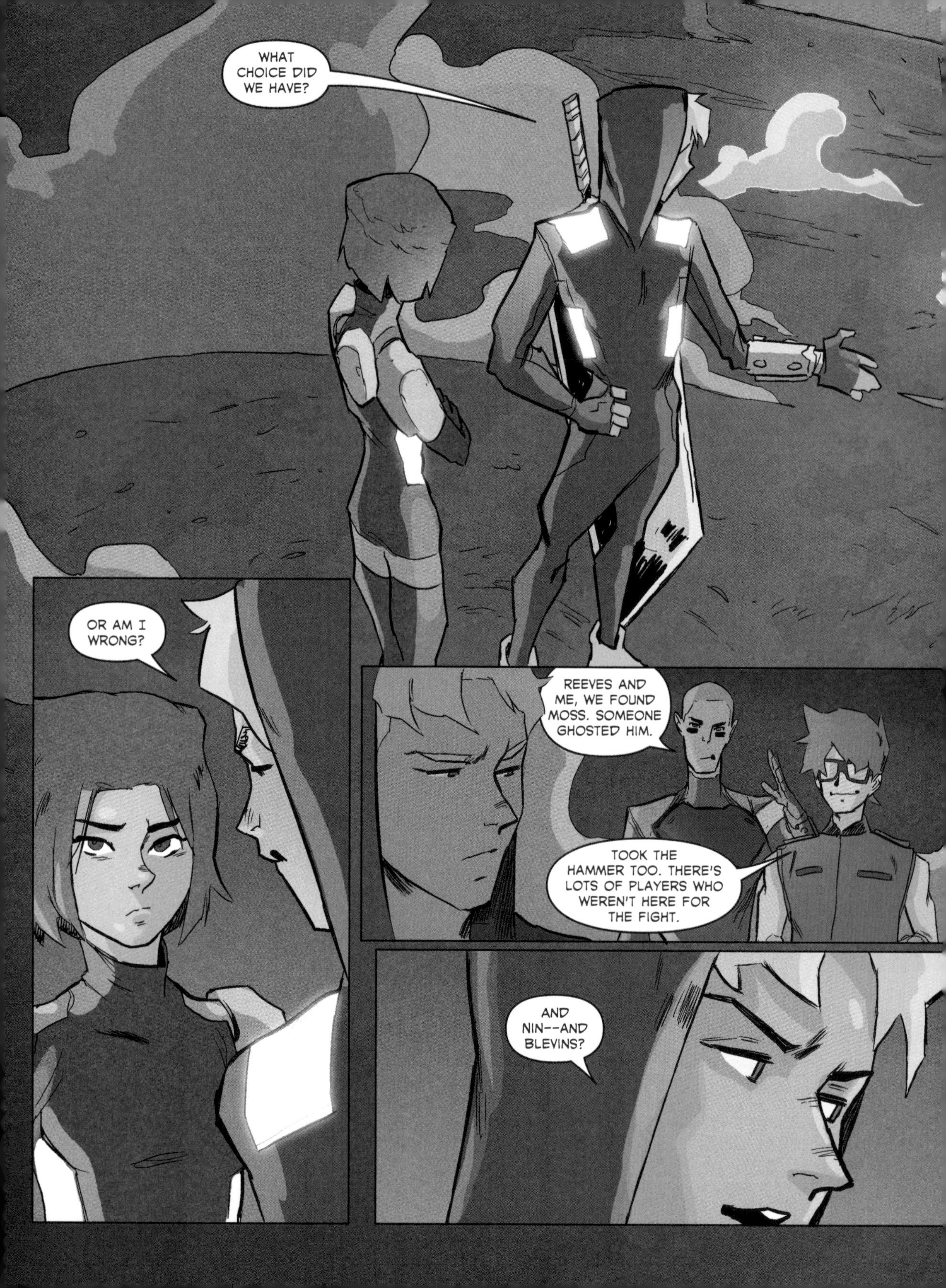
WHAT CHOICE DID WE HAVE?
OR AM I WRONG?
REEVES AND ME, WE FOUND MOSS. SOMEONE GHOSTED HIM.
TOOK THE HAMMER TOO. THERE'S LOTS OF PLAYERS WHO WEREN'T HERE FOR THE FIGHT.
AND NIN--AND BLEVINS?

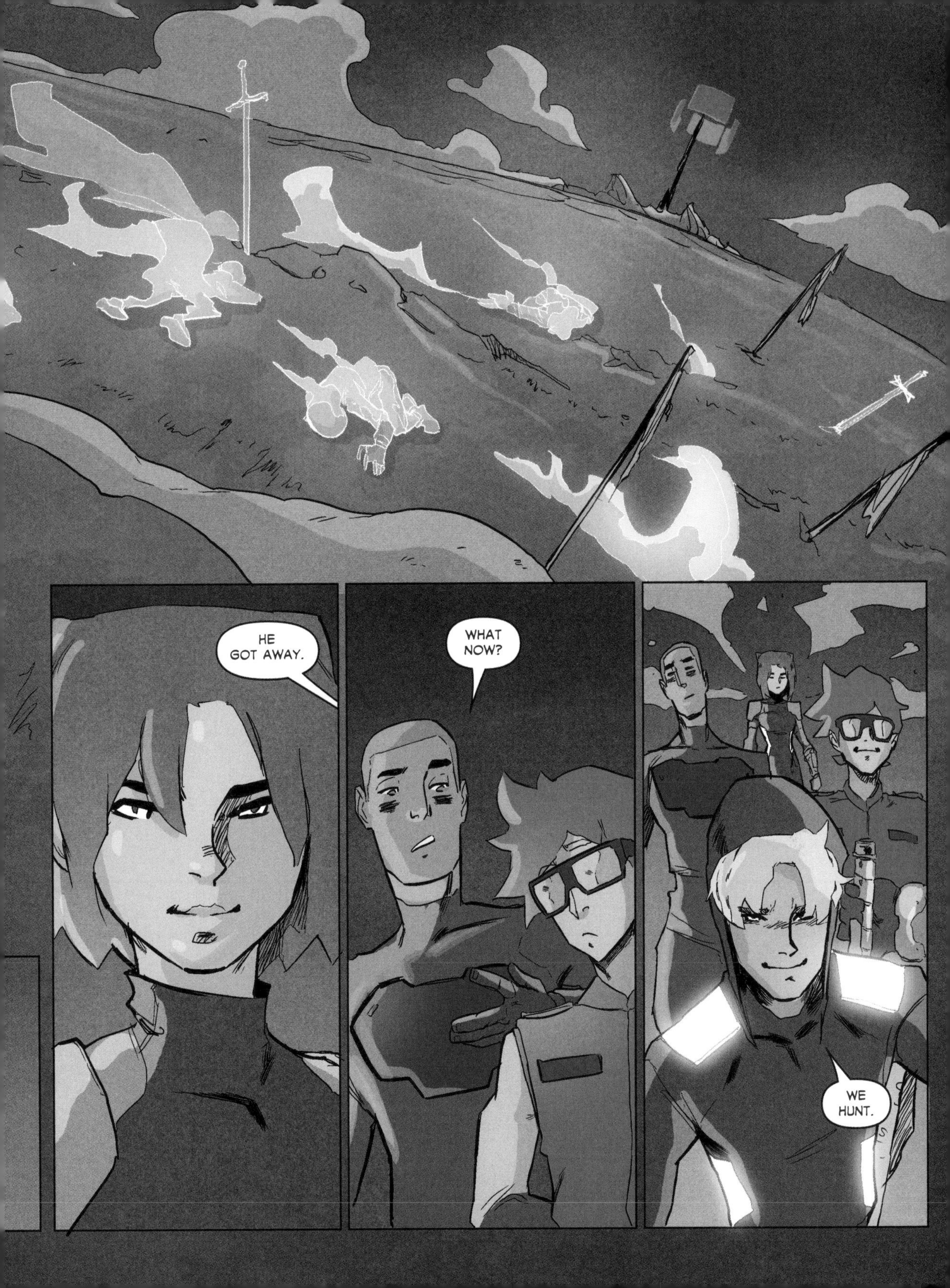
HE GOT AWAY.
WHAT NOW?
WE HUNT.

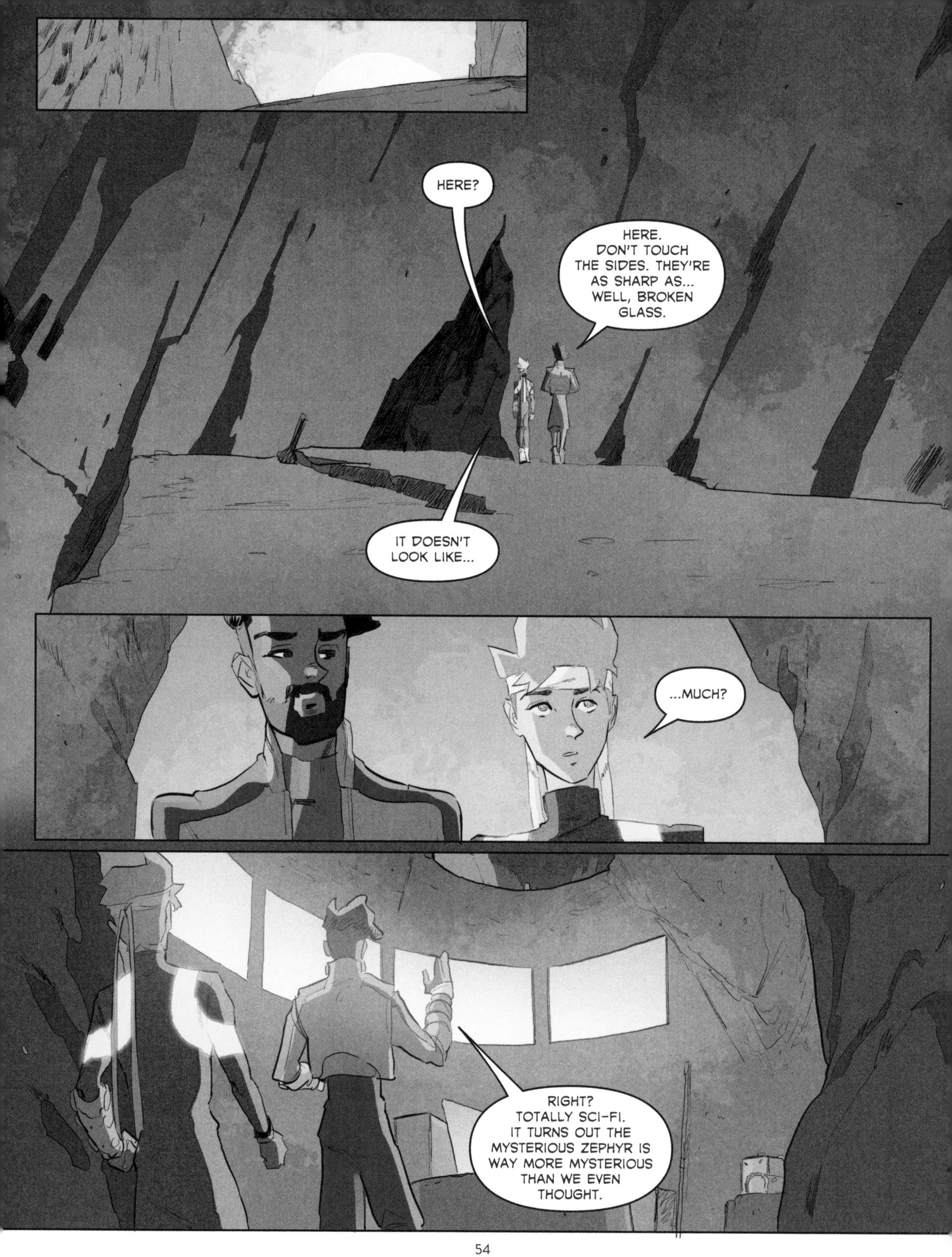
HERE?
HERE. DON'T TOUCH THE SIDES. THEY'RE AS SHARP AS... WELL, BROKEN GLASS.
IT DOESN'T LOOK LIKE...
...MUCH?
RIGHT? TOTALLY SCI-FI. IT TURNS OUT THE MYSTERIOUS ZEPHYR IS WAY MORE MYSTERIOUS THAN WE EVEN THOUGHT.

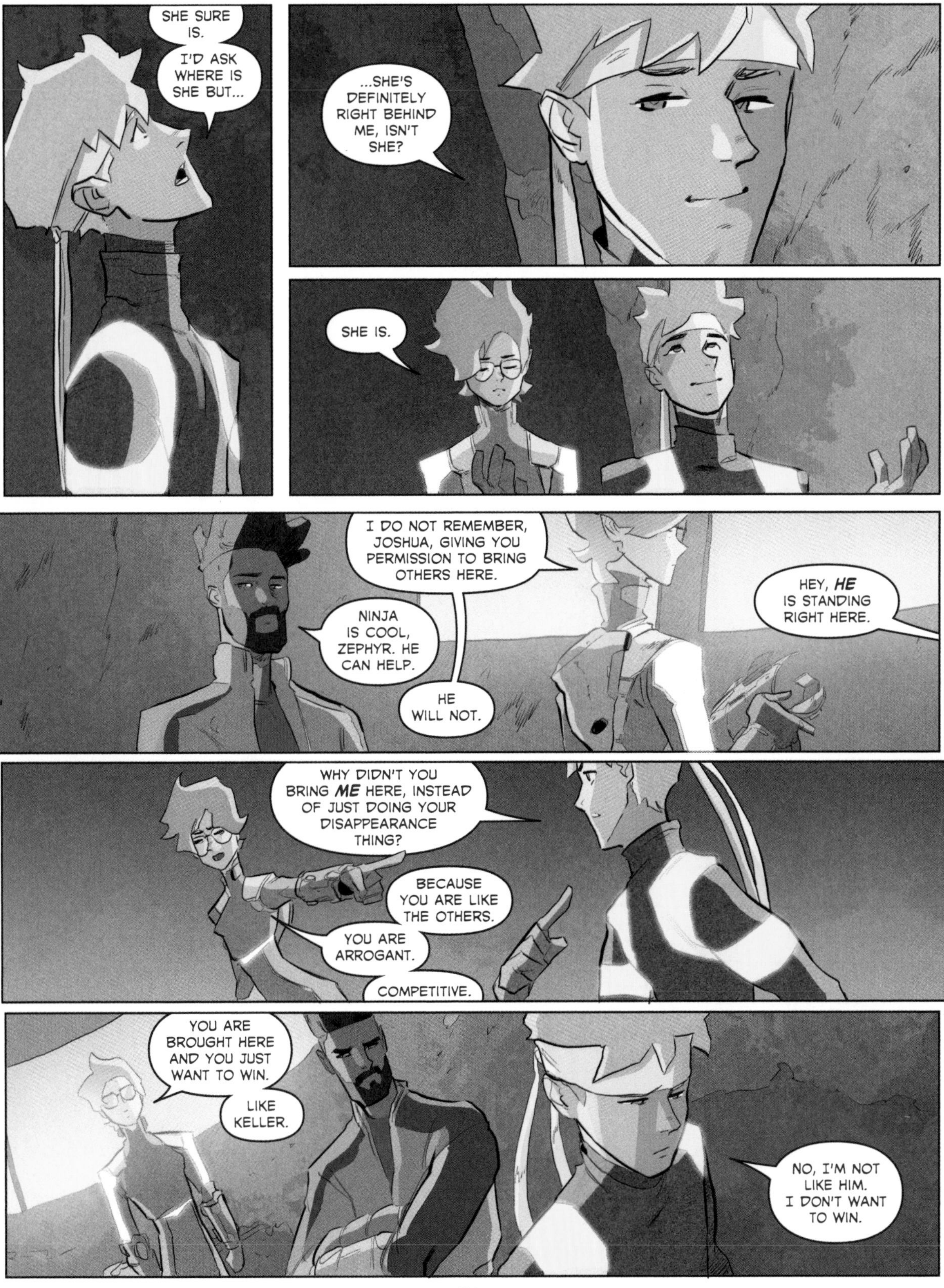

SHE SURE IS.
I'D ASK WHERE IS SHE BUT...
...SHE'S DEFINITELY RIGHT BEHIND ME, ISN'T SHE?
SHE IS.
I DO NOT REMEMBER, JOSHUA, GIVING YOU PERMISSION TO BRING OTHERS HERE.
NINJA IS COOL, ZEPHYR. HE CAN HELP.
HE WILL NOT.
HEY, *HE* IS STANDING RIGHT HERE.
WHY DIDN'T YOU BRING *ME* HERE, INSTEAD OF JUST DOING YOUR DISAPPEARANCE THING?
BECAUSE YOU ARE LIKE THE OTHERS.
YOU ARE ARROGANT.
COMPETITIVE.
YOU ARE BROUGHT HERE AND YOU JUST WANT TO WIN.
LIKE KELLER.
NO, I'M NOT LIKE HIM. I DON'T WANT TO WIN.

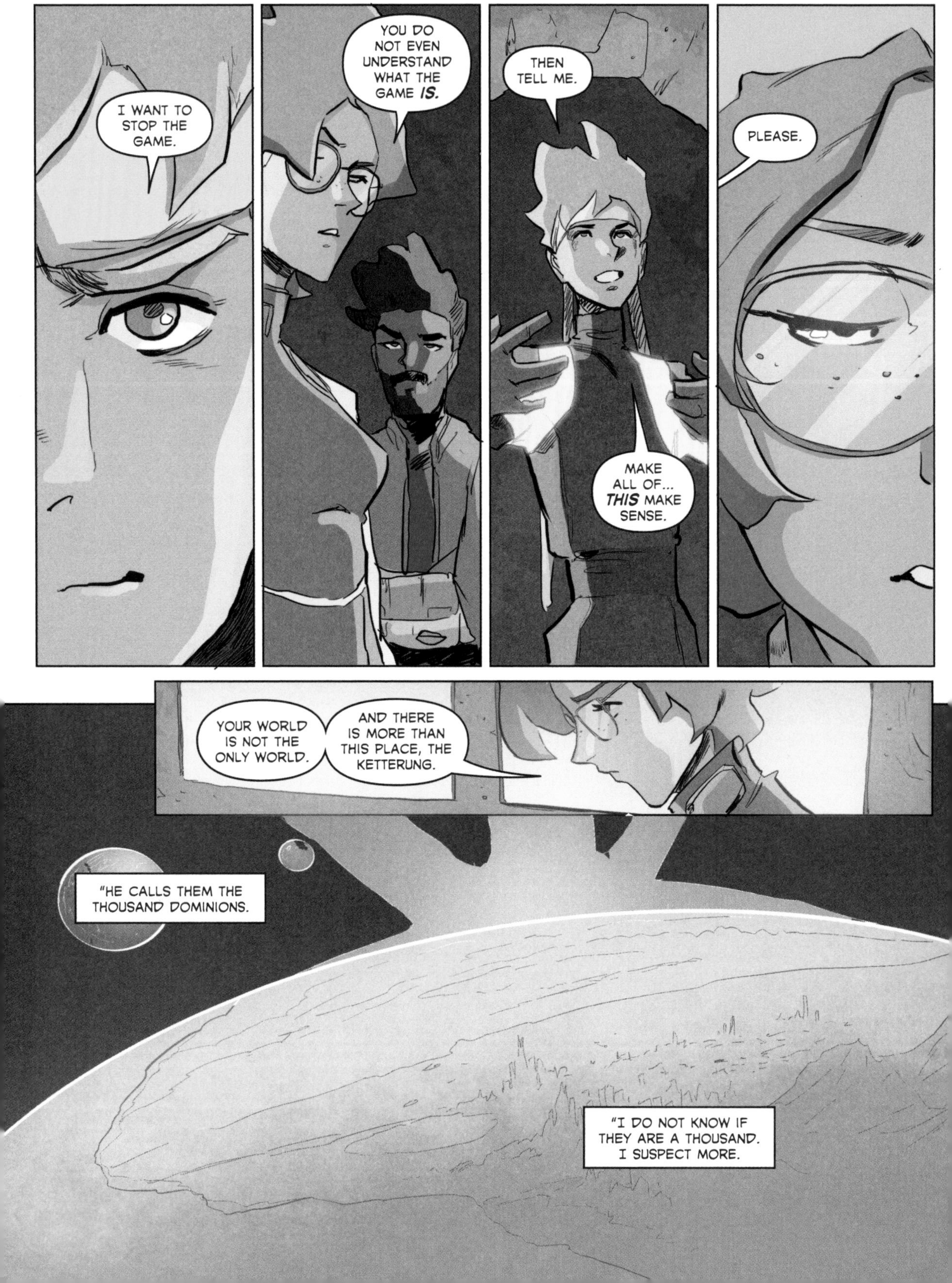
I WANT TO STOP THE GAME.
YOU DO NOT EVEN UNDERSTAND WHAT THE GAME *IS.*
THEN TELL ME.
MAKE ALL OF... *THIS* MAKE SENSE.
PLEASE.
YOUR WORLD IS NOT THE ONLY WORLD.
AND THERE IS MORE THAN THIS PLACE, THE KETTERUNG.
"HE CALLS THEM THE THOUSAND DOMINIONS.
"I DO NOT KNOW IF THEY ARE A THOUSAND. I SUSPECT MORE.

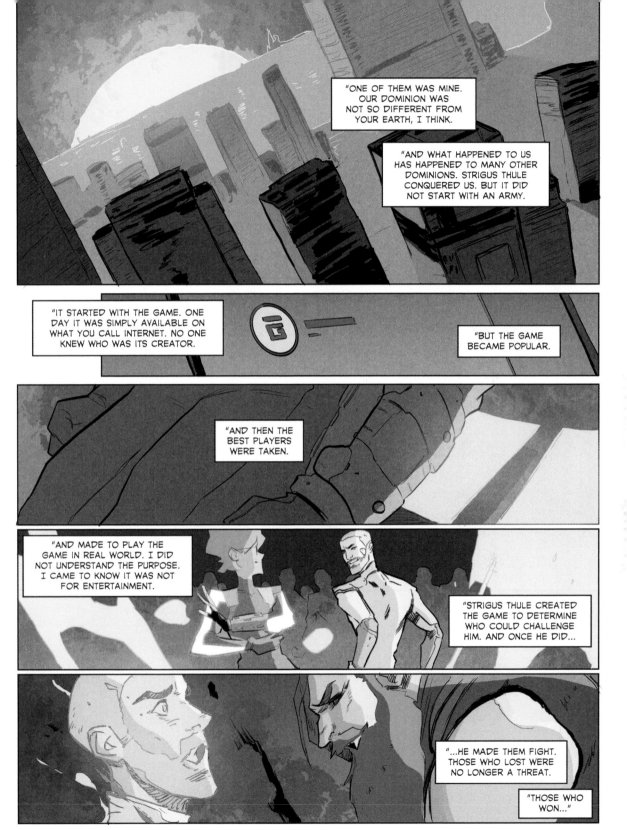

"ONE OF THEM WAS MINE. OUR DOMINION WAS NOT SO DIFFERENT FROM YOUR EARTH, I THINK.

"AND WHAT HAPPENED TO US HAS HAPPENED TO MANY OTHER DOMINIONS. STRIGUS THULE CONQUERED US. BUT IT DID NOT START WITH AN ARMY.

"IT STARTED WITH THE GAME. ONE DAY IT WAS SIMPLY AVAILABLE ON WHAT YOU CALL INTERNET. NO ONE KNEW WHO WAS ITS CREATOR.

"BUT THE GAME BECAME POPULAR.

"AND THEN THE BEST PLAYERS WERE TAKEN.

"AND MADE TO PLAY THE GAME IN REAL WORLD. I DID NOT UNDERSTAND THE PURPOSE. I CAME TO KNOW IT WAS NOT FOR ENTERTAINMENT.

"STRIGUS THULE CREATED THE GAME TO DETERMINE WHO COULD CHALLENGE HIM. AND ONCE HE DID...

"...HE MADE THEM FIGHT. THOSE WHO LOST WERE NO LONGER A THREAT.

"THOSE WHO WON..."

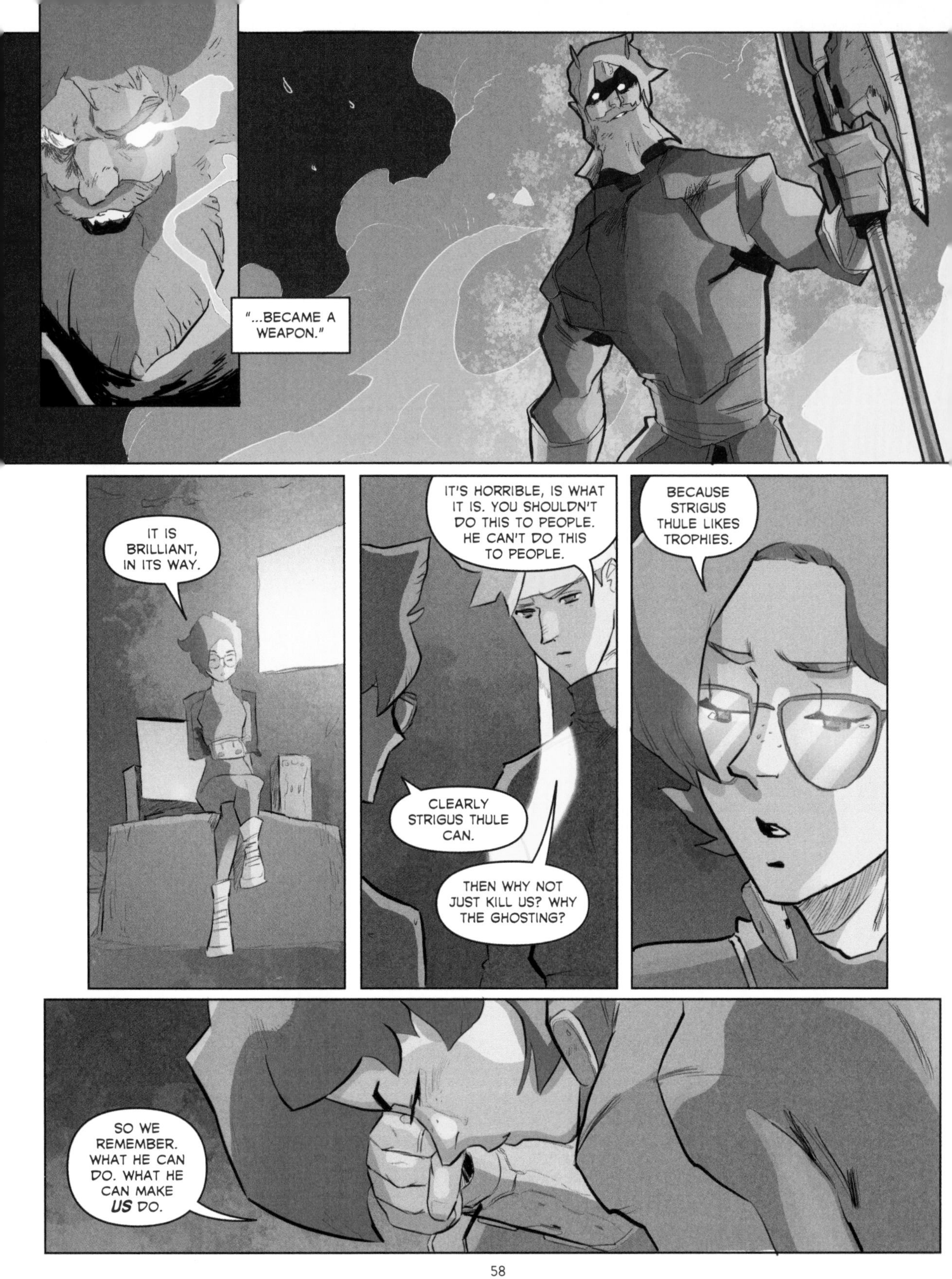
"...BECAME A WEAPON."
IT IS BRILLIANT, IN ITS WAY.
IT'S HORRIBLE, IS WHAT IT IS. YOU SHOULDN'T DO THIS TO PEOPLE. HE CAN'T DO THIS TO PEOPLE.
CLEARLY STRIGUS THULE CAN.
THEN WHY NOT JUST KILL US? WHY THE GHOSTING?
BECAUSE STRIGUS THULE LIKES TROPHIES.
SO WE REMEMBER. WHAT HE CAN DO. WHAT HE CAN MAKE US DO.

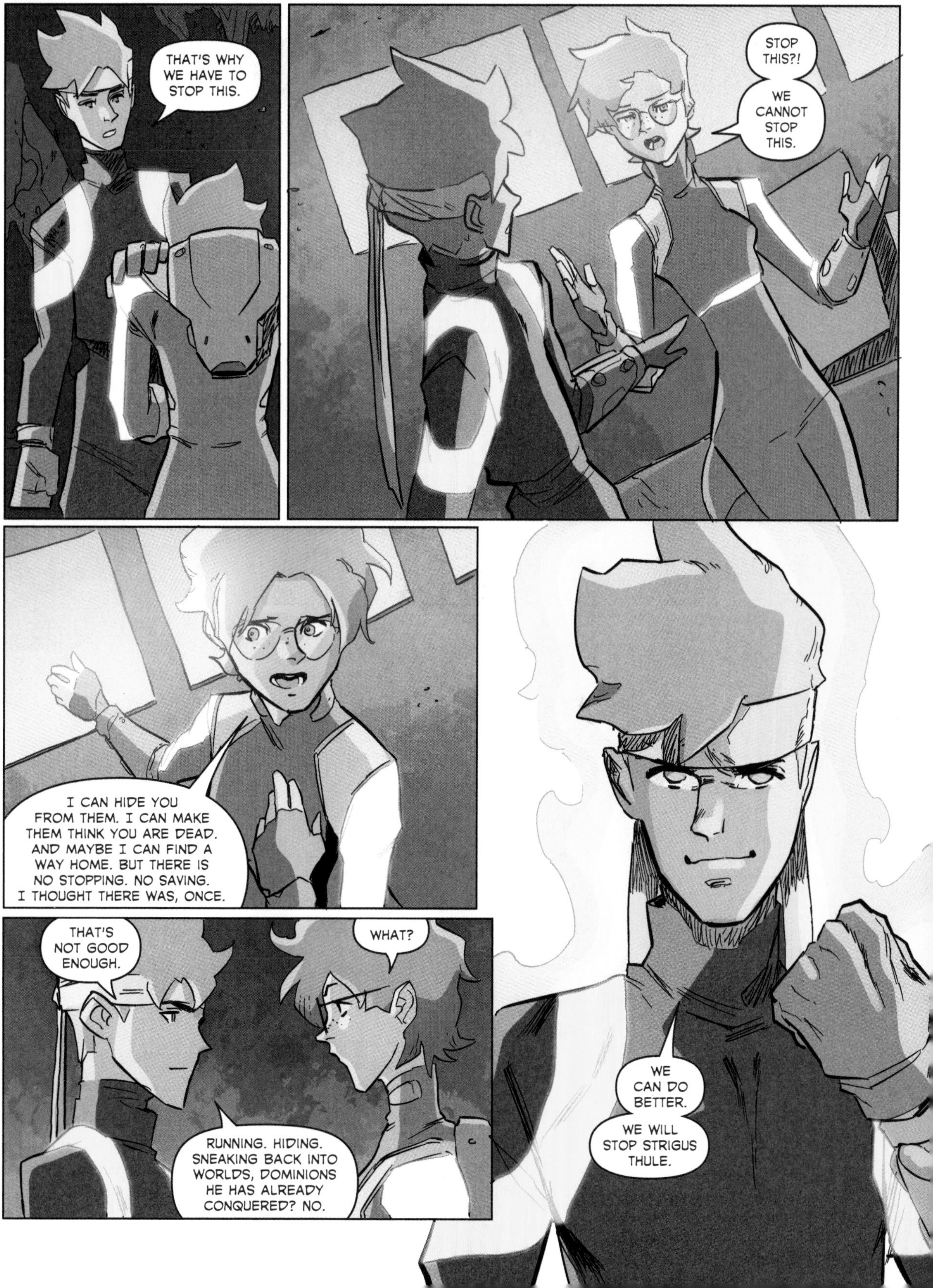
THAT'S WHY WE HAVE TO STOP THIS.
STOP THIS?!
WE CANNOT STOP THIS.
I CAN HIDE YOU FROM THEM. I CAN MAKE THEM THINK YOU ARE DEAD. AND MAYBE I CAN FIND A WAY HOME. BUT THERE IS NO STOPPING. NO SAVING. I THOUGHT THERE WAS, ONCE.
THAT'S NOT GOOD ENOUGH.
WHAT?
RUNNING. HIDING. SNEAKING BACK INTO WORLDS, DOMINIONS HE HAS ALREADY CONQUERED? NO.
WE CAN DO BETTER.
WE WILL STOP STRIGUS THULE.

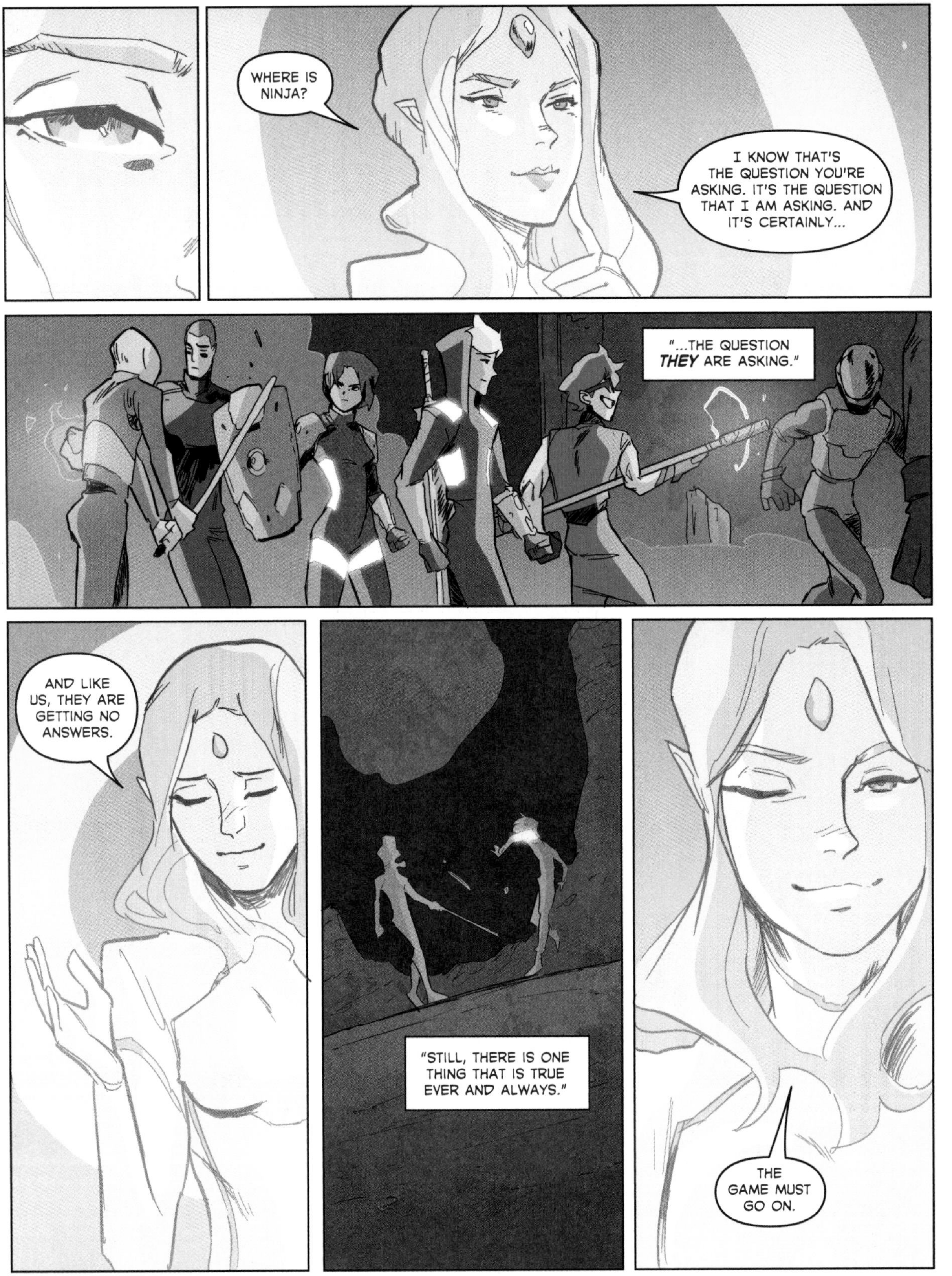
WHERE IS NINJA?
I KNOW THAT'S THE QUESTION YOU'RE ASKING. IT'S THE QUESTION THAT I AM ASKING. AND IT'S CERTAINLY...
"...THE QUESTION *THEY* ARE ASKING."
AND LIKE US, THEY ARE GETTING NO ANSWERS.
"STILL, THERE IS ONE THING THAT IS TRUE EVER AND ALWAYS."
THE GAME MUST GO ON.

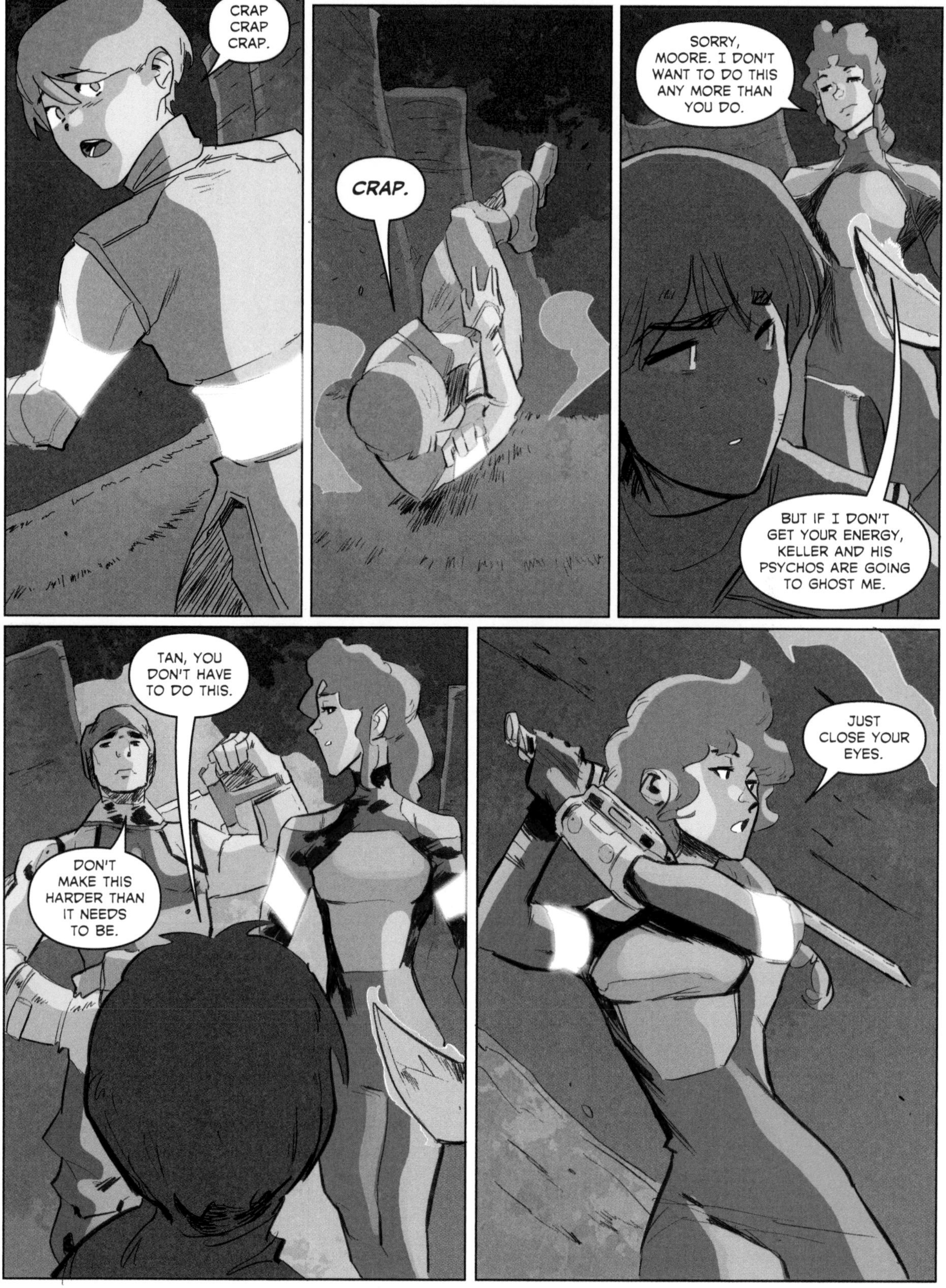
CRAP CRAP CRAP.
CRAP.
SORRY, MOORE. I DON'T WANT TO DO THIS ANY MORE THAN YOU DO.
BUT IF I DON'T GET YOUR ENERGY, KELLER AND HIS PSYCHOS ARE GOING TO GHOST ME.
TAN, YOU DON'T HAVE TO DO THIS.
DON'T MAKE THIS HARDER THAN IT NEEDS TO BE.
JUST CLOSE YOUR EYES.

YOINK!

HI THERE.

THANK YOU.

DON'T THANK HIM Y--

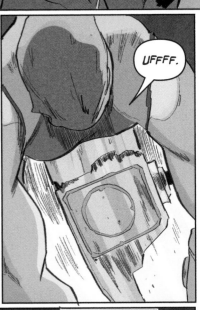

UFFFF.

SORRY ABOUT THAT. YOU DIDN'T LOOK LIKE YOU WERE IN A "LISTEN TO REASON" MODE.

I DON'T WANT TO FIGHT YOU.

THEN I GUESS THIS WILL BE EASY.

I SAID I DIDN'T WANT TO FIGHT.

I DID NOT SAY I WAS JUST GOING TO LET YOU GHOST ME.

I'M NOT GOING TO LET YOU GHOST ME EITHER.

STOP THAT.

THAT'S EXACTLY WHAT I'M TRYING TO DO.

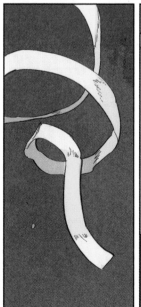

YOU'RE NOT MAKING IT EASY THOUGH.

GOOD.

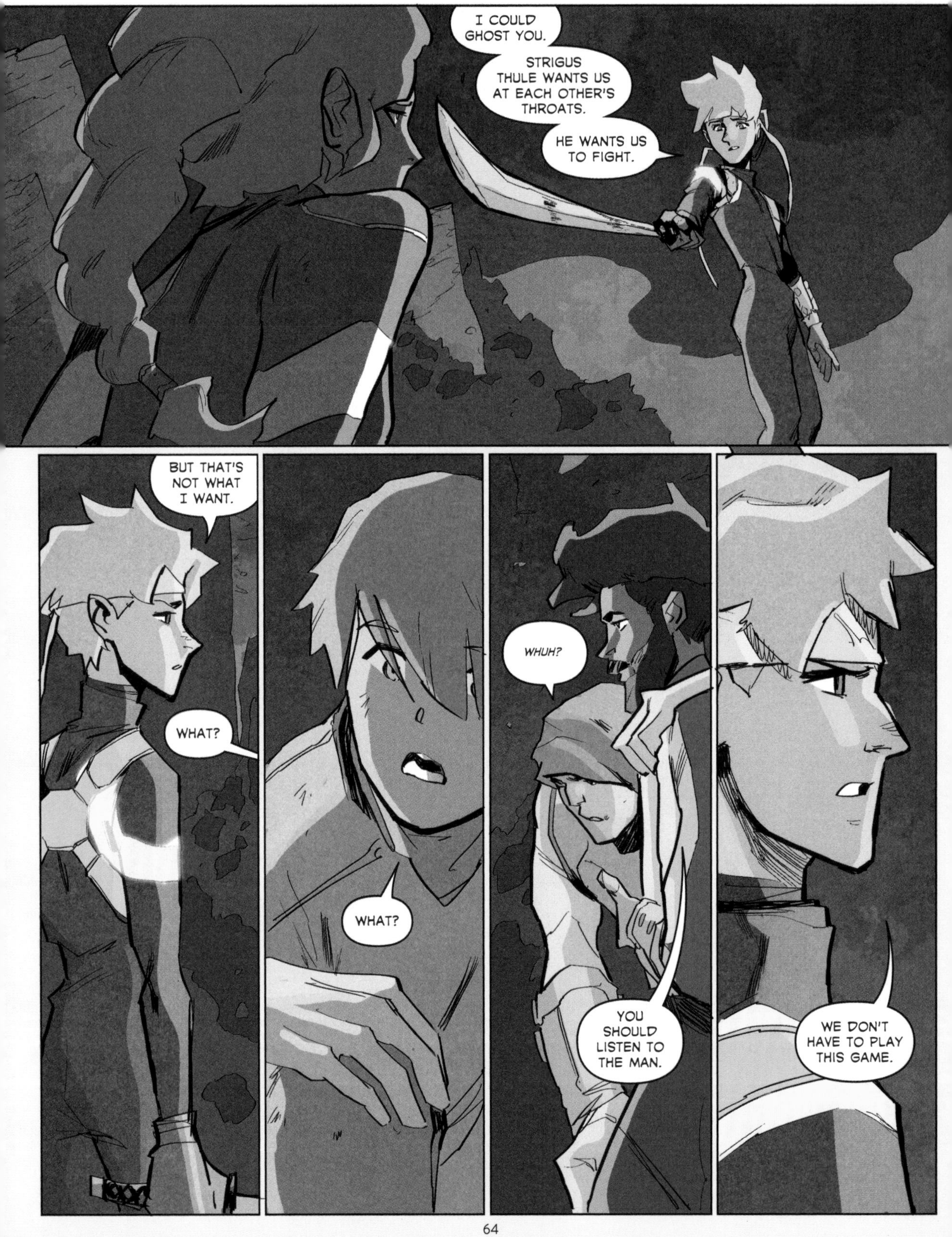
I COULD GHOST YOU.
STRIGUS THULE WANTS US AT EACH OTHER'S THROATS.
HE WANTS US TO FIGHT.
BUT THAT'S NOT WHAT I WANT.
WHAT?
WHAT?
WHUH?
YOU SHOULD LISTEN TO THE MAN.
WE DON'T HAVE TO PLAY THIS GAME.

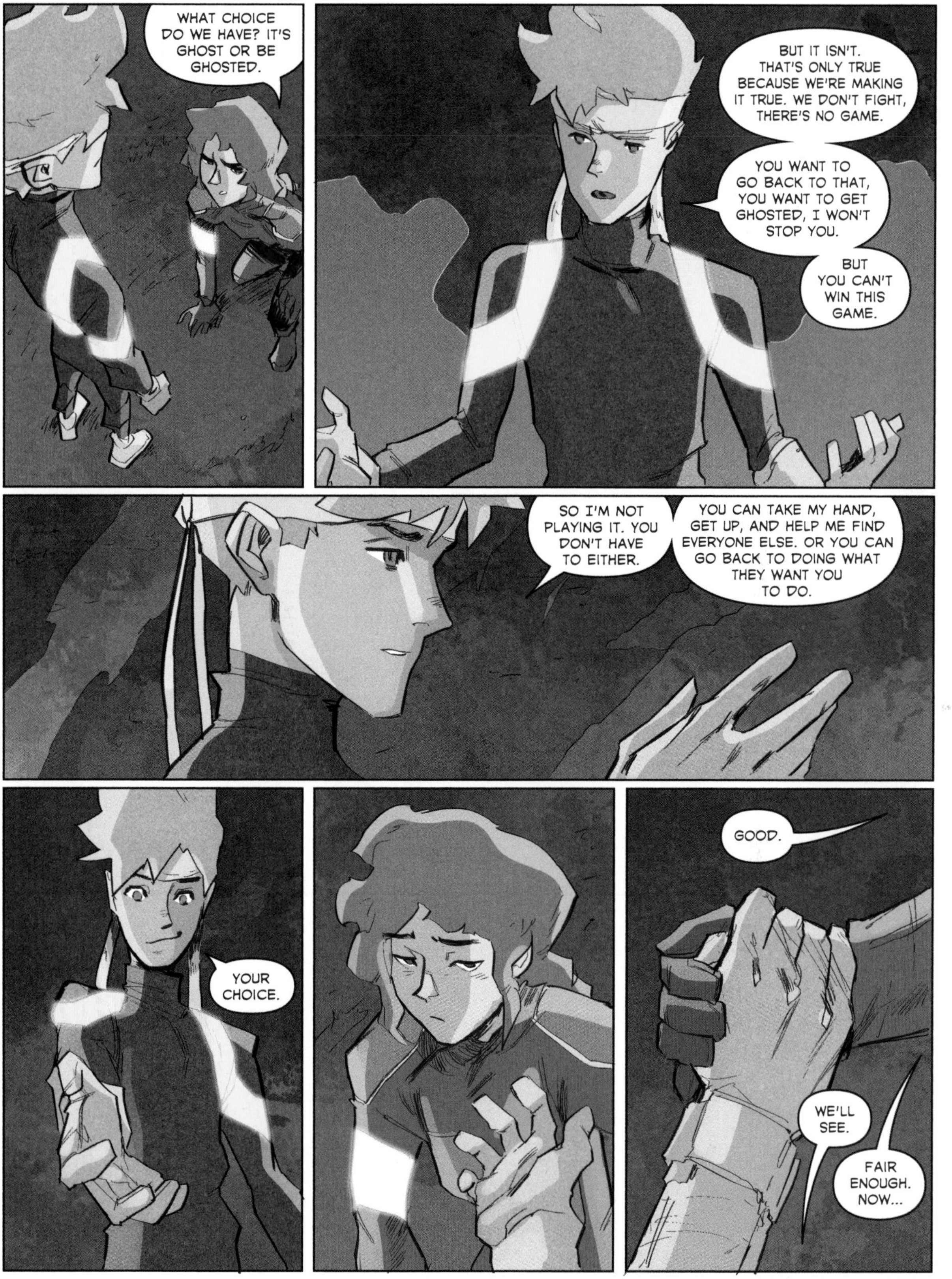
WHAT CHOICE DO WE HAVE? IT'S GHOST OR BE GHOSTED.
BUT IT ISN'T. THAT'S ONLY TRUE BECAUSE WE'RE MAKING IT TRUE. WE DON'T FIGHT, THERE'S NO GAME.
YOU WANT TO GO BACK TO THAT, YOU WANT TO GET GHOSTED, I WON'T STOP YOU.
BUT YOU CAN'T WIN THIS GAME.
SO I'M NOT PLAYING IT. YOU DON'T HAVE TO EITHER.
YOU CAN TAKE MY HAND, GET UP, AND HELP ME FIND EVERYONE ELSE. OR YOU CAN GO BACK TO DOING WHAT THEY WANT YOU TO DO.
YOUR CHOICE.
GOOD.
WE'LL SEE.
FAIR ENOUGH. NOW...

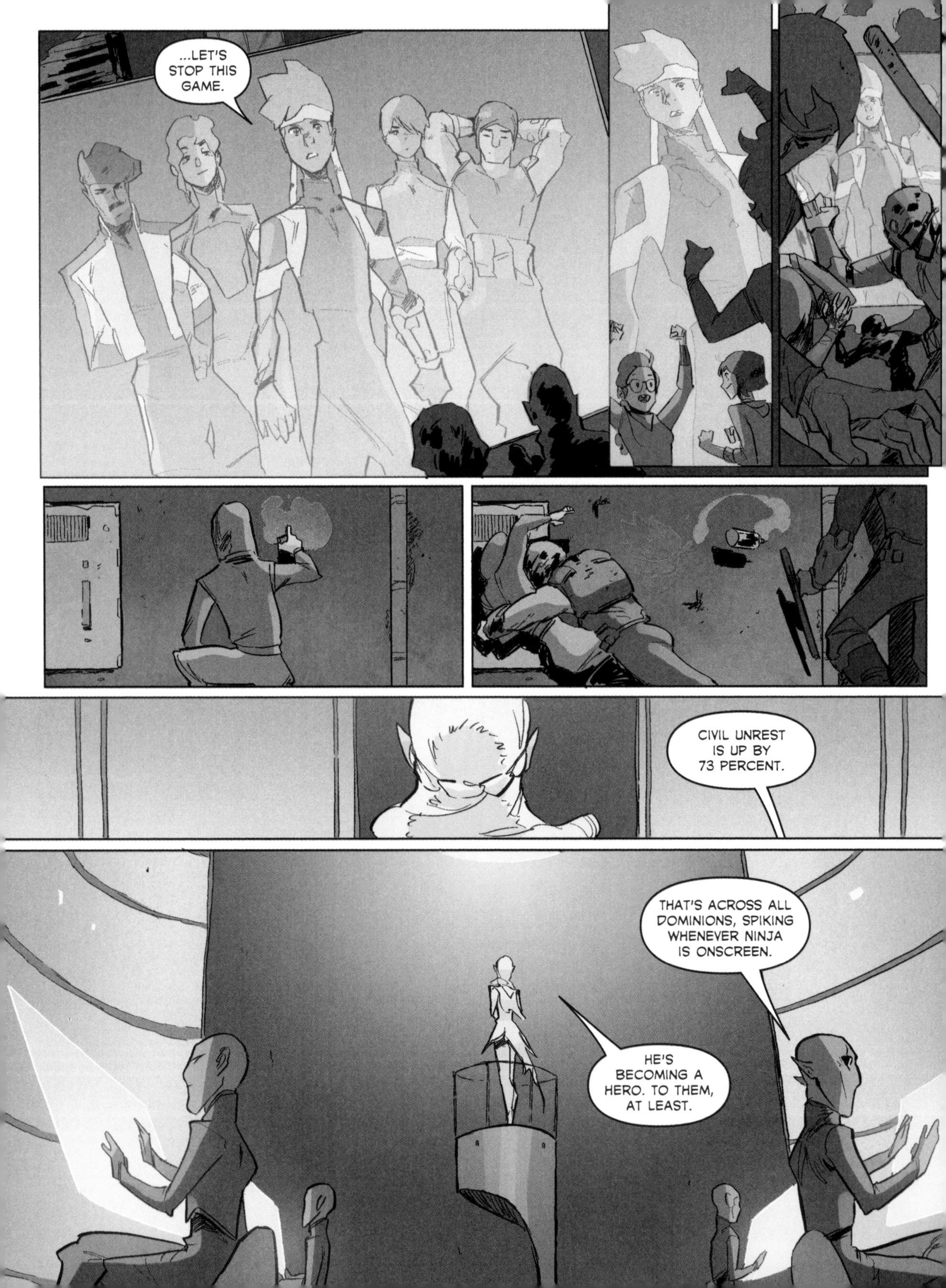
...LET'S STOP THIS GAME.
CIVIL UNREST IS UP BY 73 PERCENT.
THAT'S ACROSS ALL DOMINIONS, SPIKING WHENEVER NINJA IS ONSCREEN.
HE'S BECOMING A HERO. TO THEM, AT LEAST.

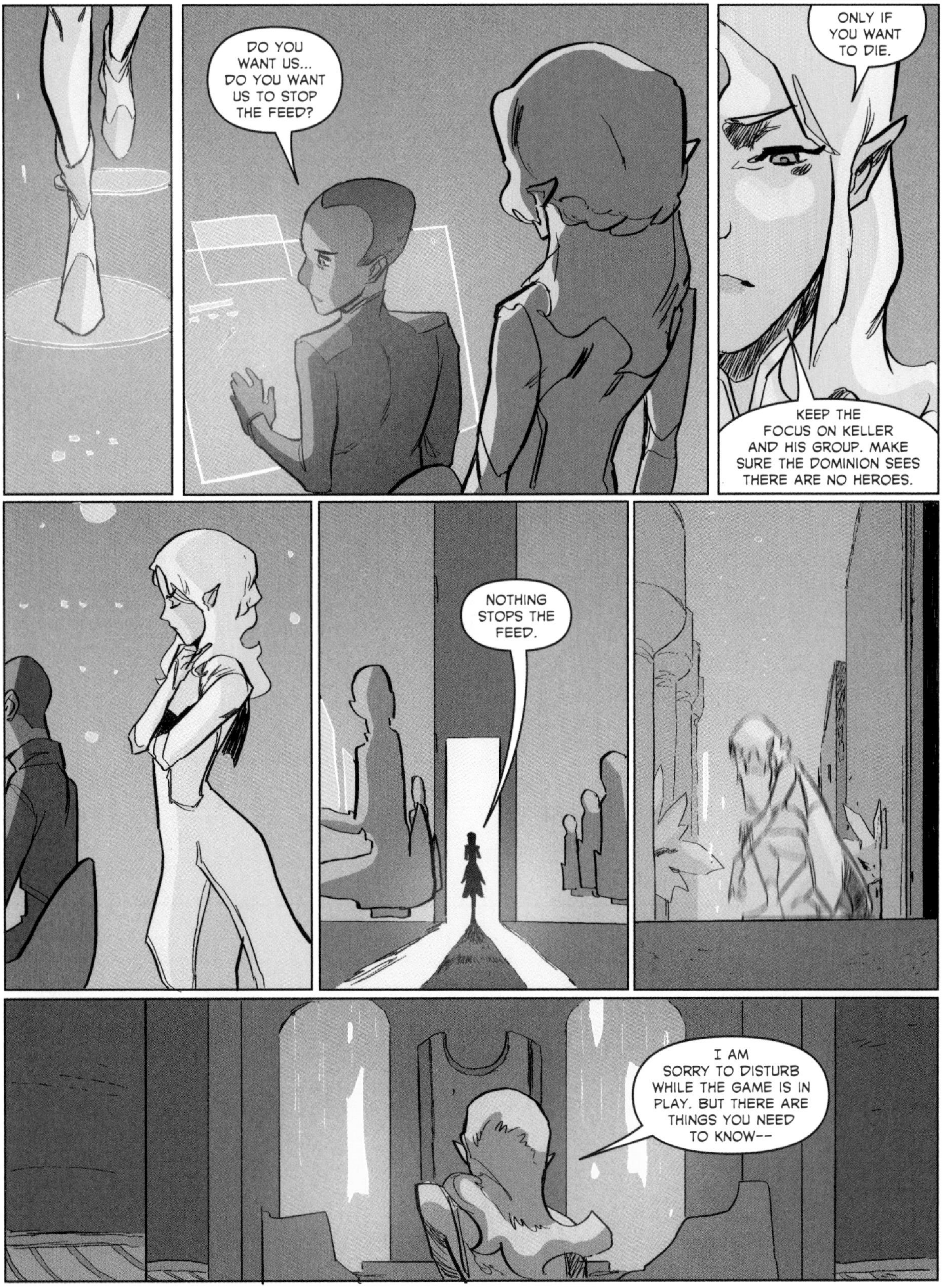

DO YOU WANT US... DO YOU WANT US TO STOP THE FEED?
ONLY IF YOU WANT TO DIE.
KEEP THE FOCUS ON KELLER AND HIS GROUP. MAKE SURE THE DOMINION SEES THERE ARE NO HEROES.
NOTHING STOPS THE FEED.
I AM SORRY TO DISTURB WHILE THE GAME IS IN PLAY. BUT THERE ARE THINGS YOU NEED TO KNOW--

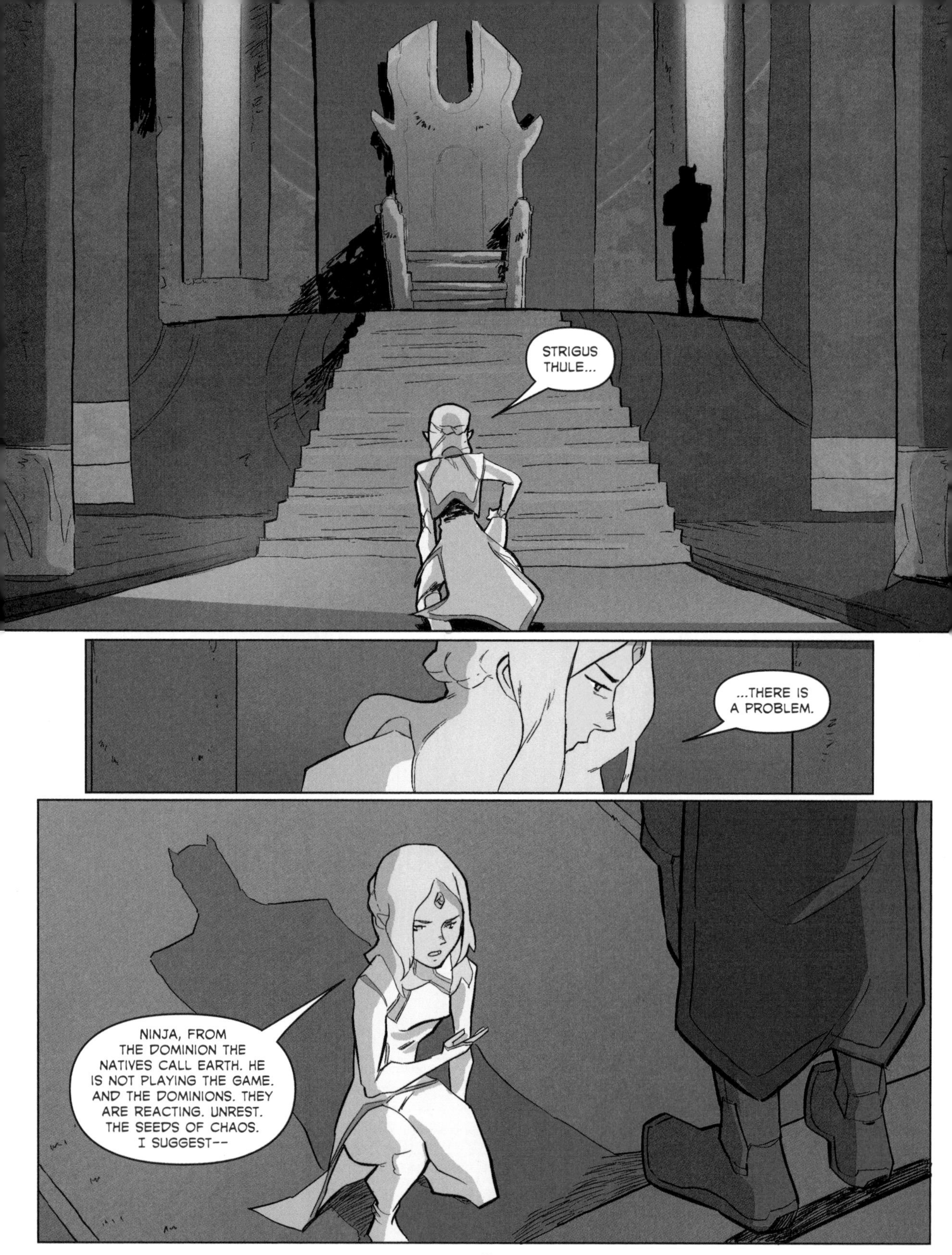
STRIGUS THULE...
...THERE IS A PROBLEM.
NINJA, FROM THE DOMINION THE NATIVES CALL EARTH. HE IS NOT PLAYING THE GAME. AND THE DOMINIONS. THEY ARE REACTING. UNREST. THE SEEDS OF CHAOS. I SUGGEST--

YOU SUGGEST?

URK.

I...I ADVISE THAT...THAT WE STOP THE FEED. THIS ONE FEELS DIFFERENT.

THE PLAYERS ARE REACTING TO HIM. THE DOMINIONS ARE REACTING TO HIM.

IF THEY SEE THE GAME CAN BE BEATEN...IF THEY REALIZE THAT TOGETHER THEY ARE STRONGER THAN THEY ARE APART...THEY COULD TEAR DOWN WHAT YOU'VE BUILT.

WE NEED TO STOP THE FEED. WE NEED TO STOP THE GAME.

NO, SISTER...

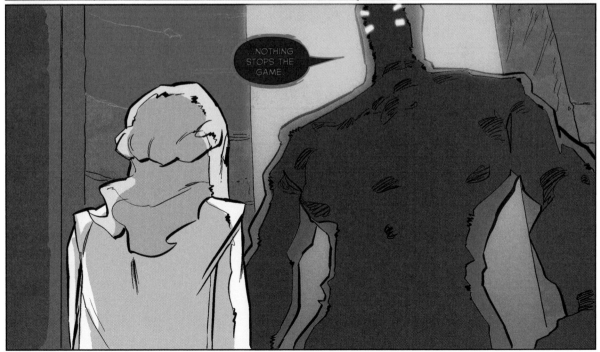

...NOTHING STOPS THE GAME.

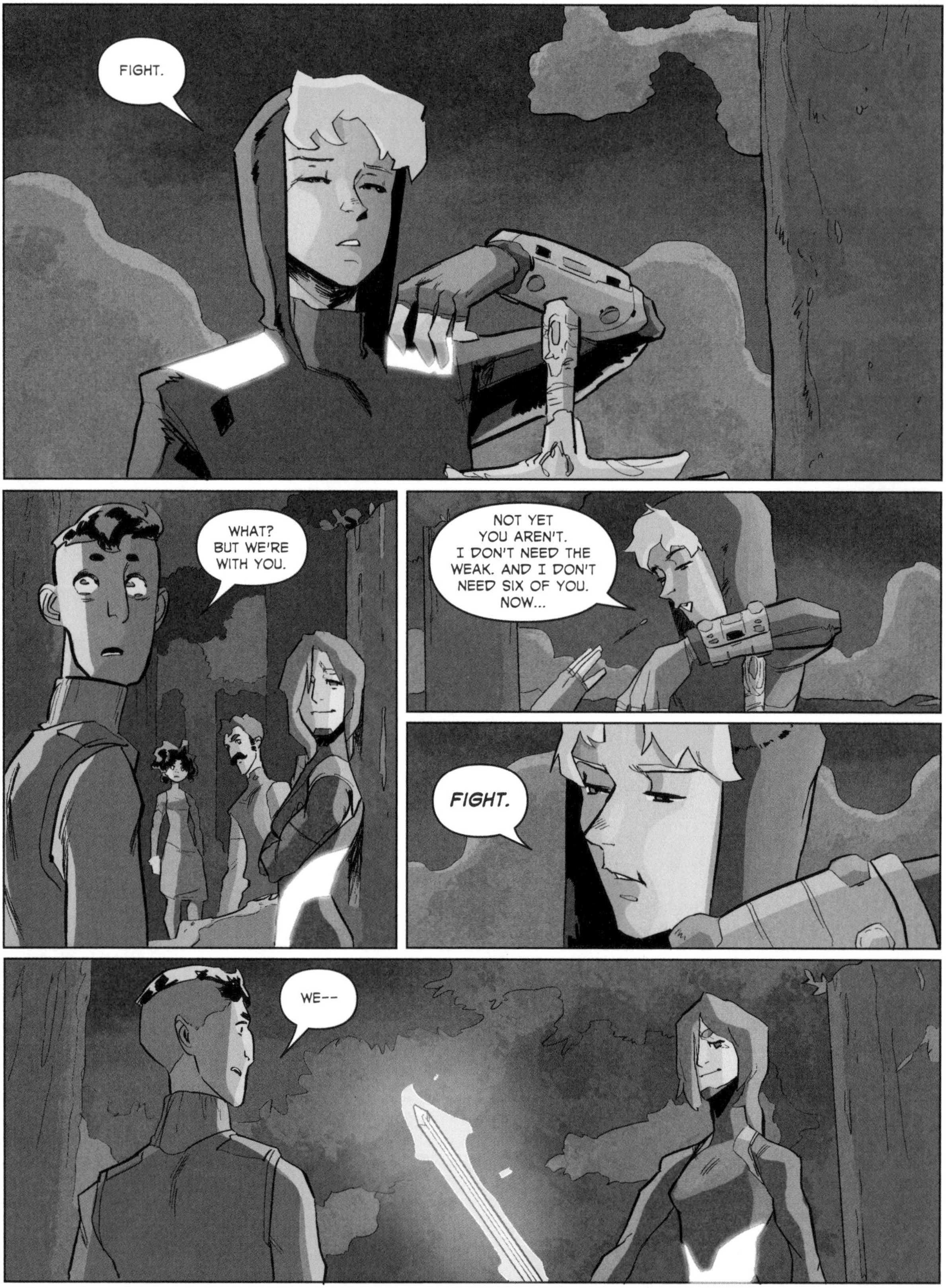
FIGHT.
WHAT? BUT WE'RE WITH YOU.
NOT YET YOU AREN'T. I DON'T NEED THE WEAK. AND I DON'T NEED SIX OF YOU. NOW...
FIGHT.
WE--

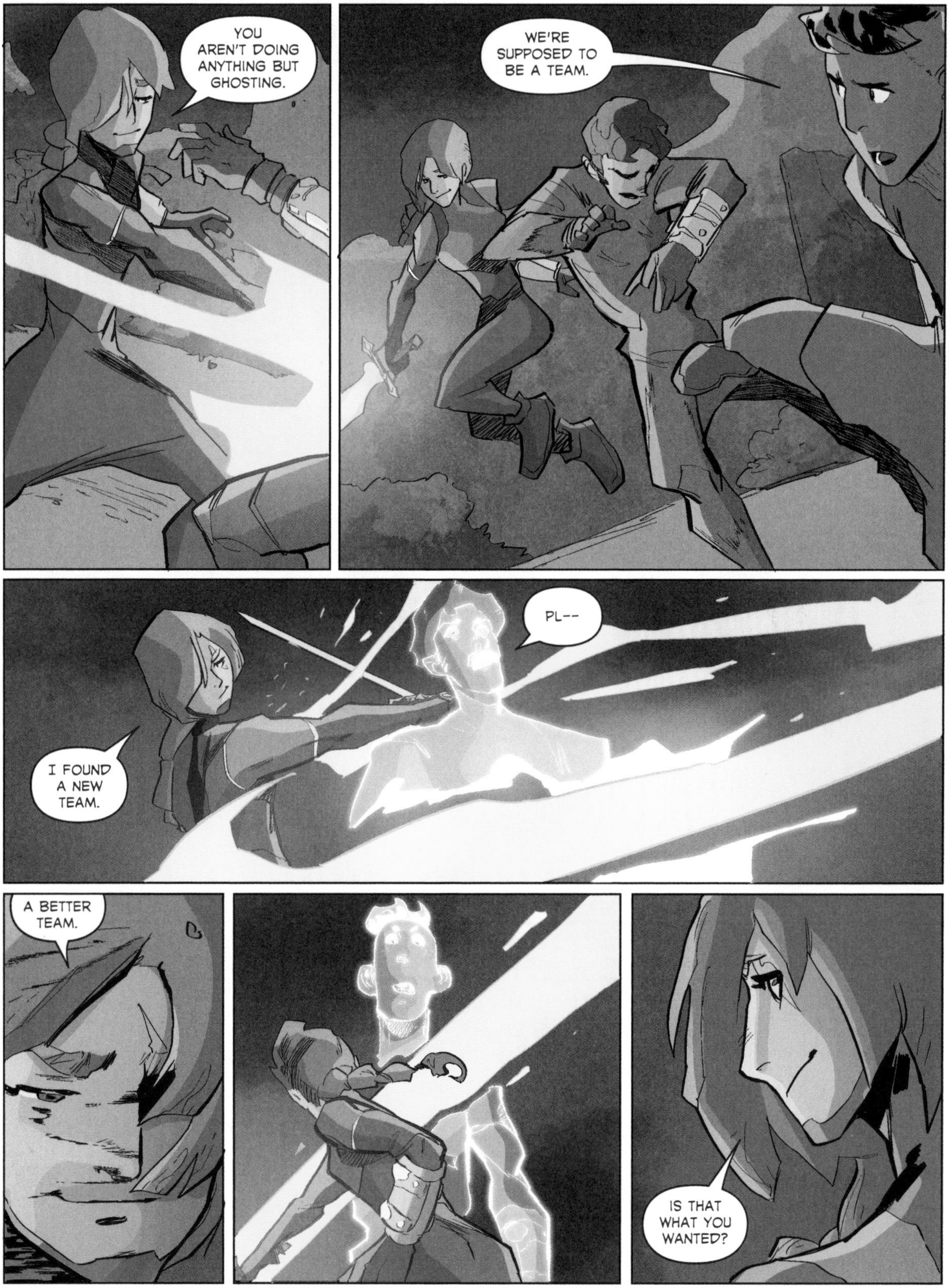
YOU AREN'T DOING ANYTHING BUT GHOSTING.
WE'RE SUPPOSED TO BE A TEAM.
PL--
I FOUND A NEW TEAM.
A BETTER TEAM.
IS THAT WHAT YOU WANTED?

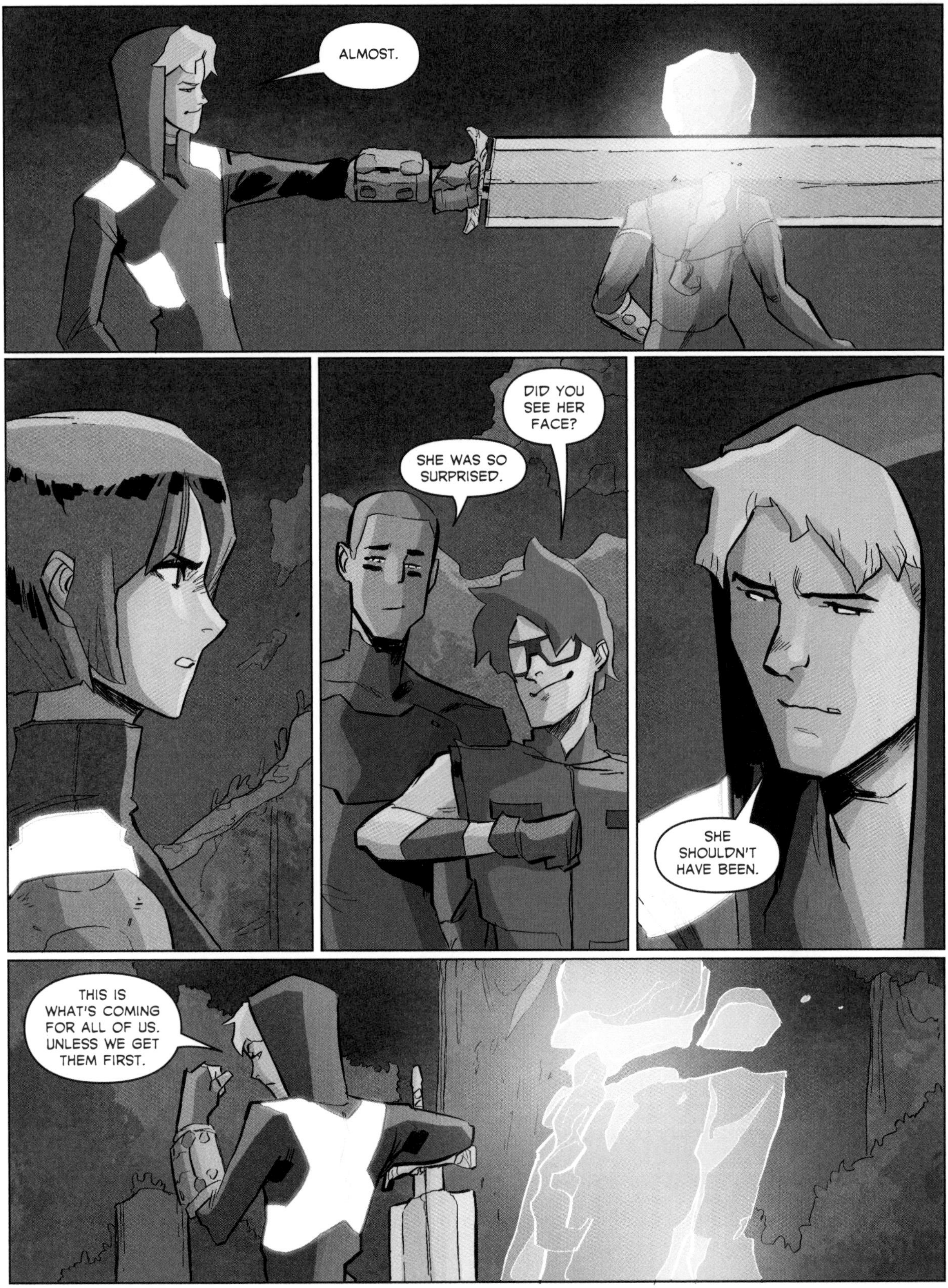
ALMOST.
SHE WAS SO SURPRISED.
DID YOU SEE HER FACE?
SHE SHOULDN'T HAVE BEEN.
THIS IS WHAT'S COMING FOR ALL OF US. UNLESS WE GET THEM FIRST.

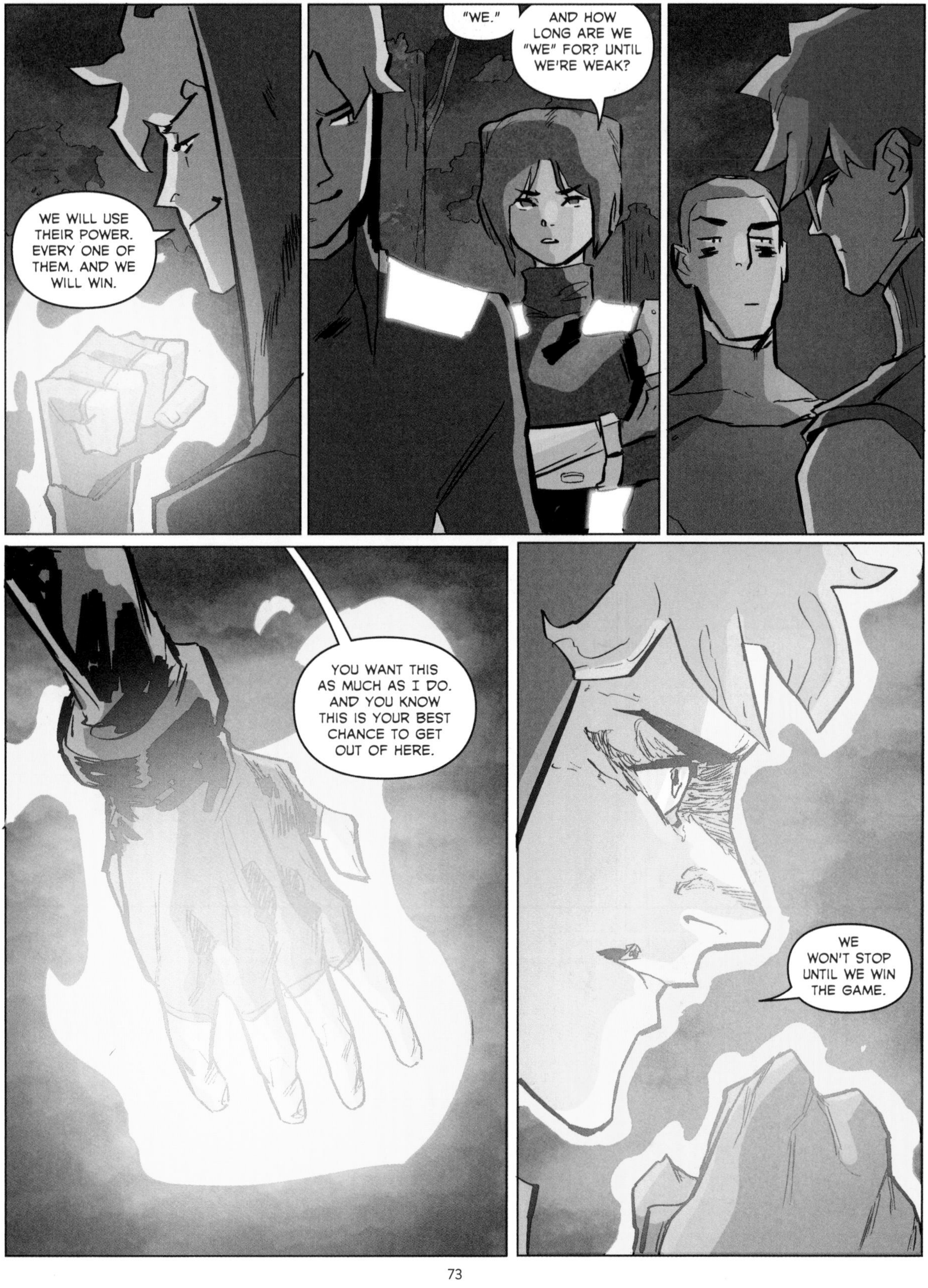
WE WILL USE THEIR POWER. EVERY ONE OF THEM. AND WE WILL WIN.
"WE."
AND HOW LONG ARE WE "WE" FOR? UNTIL WE'RE WEAK?
YOU WANT THIS AS MUCH AS I DO. AND YOU KNOW THIS IS YOUR BEST CHANCE TO GET OUT OF HERE.
WE WON'T STOP UNTIL WE WIN THE GAME.

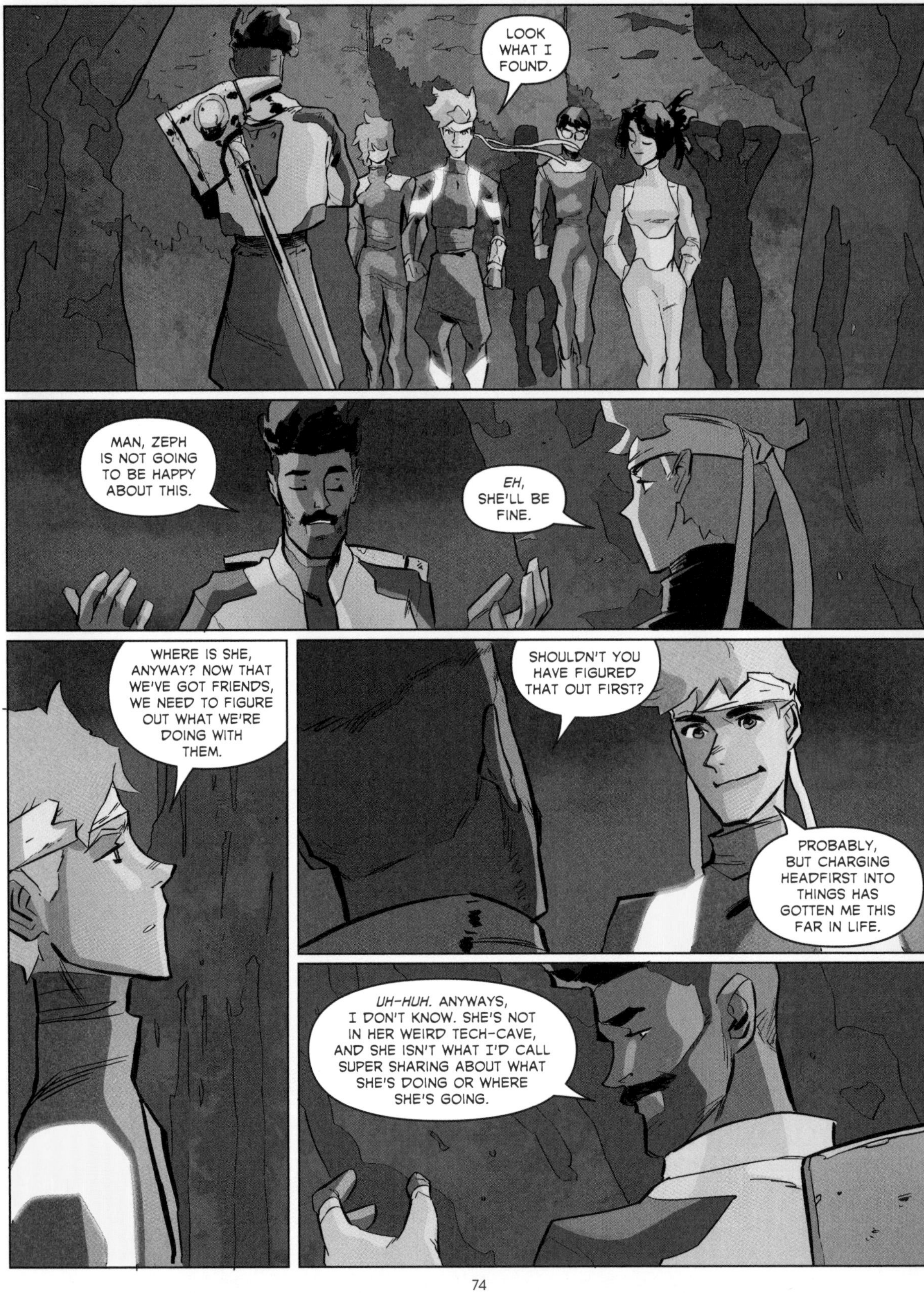
LOOK WHAT I FOUND.
MAN, ZEPH IS NOT GOING TO BE HAPPY ABOUT THIS.
EH, SHE'LL BE FINE.
WHERE IS SHE, ANYWAY? NOW THAT WE'VE GOT FRIENDS, WE NEED TO FIGURE OUT WHAT WE'RE DOING WITH THEM.
SHOULDN'T YOU HAVE FIGURED THAT OUT FIRST?
PROBABLY, BUT CHARGING HEADFIRST INTO THINGS HAS GOTTEN ME THIS FAR IN LIFE.
UH-HUH. ANYWAYS, I DON'T KNOW. SHE'S NOT IN HER WEIRD TECH-CAVE, AND SHE ISN'T WHAT I'D CALL SUPER SHARING ABOUT WHAT SHE'S DOING OR WHERE SHE'S GOING.

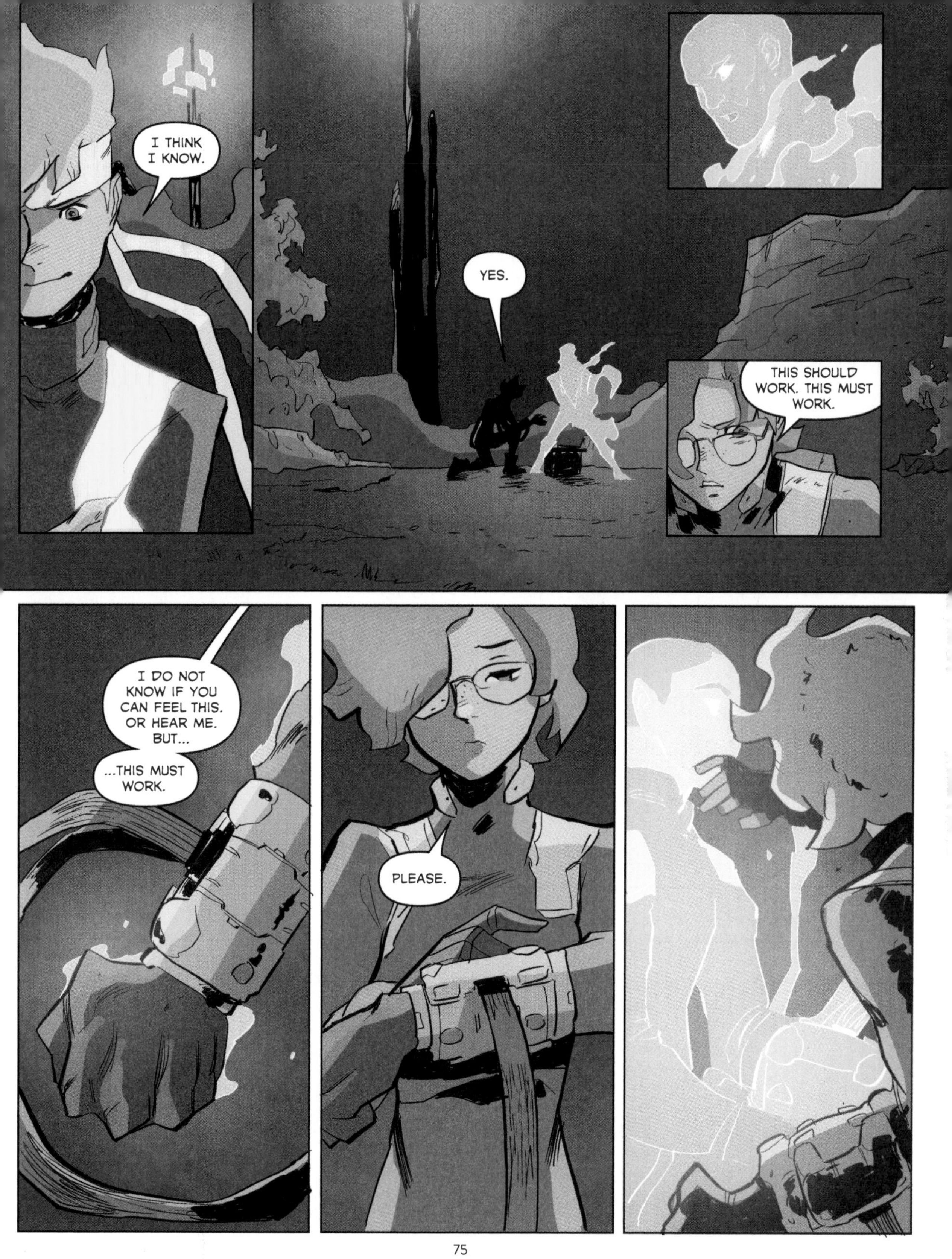
I THINK I KNOW.
YES.
THIS SHOULD WORK. THIS MUST WORK.
I DO NOT KNOW IF YOU CAN FEEL THIS. OR HEAR ME. BUT...
...THIS MUST WORK.
PLEASE.

NO, NO, *NO!* STUPID, STUPID GIRL.

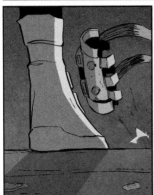

WHAT DO YOU WANT?

JUST TO TALK.

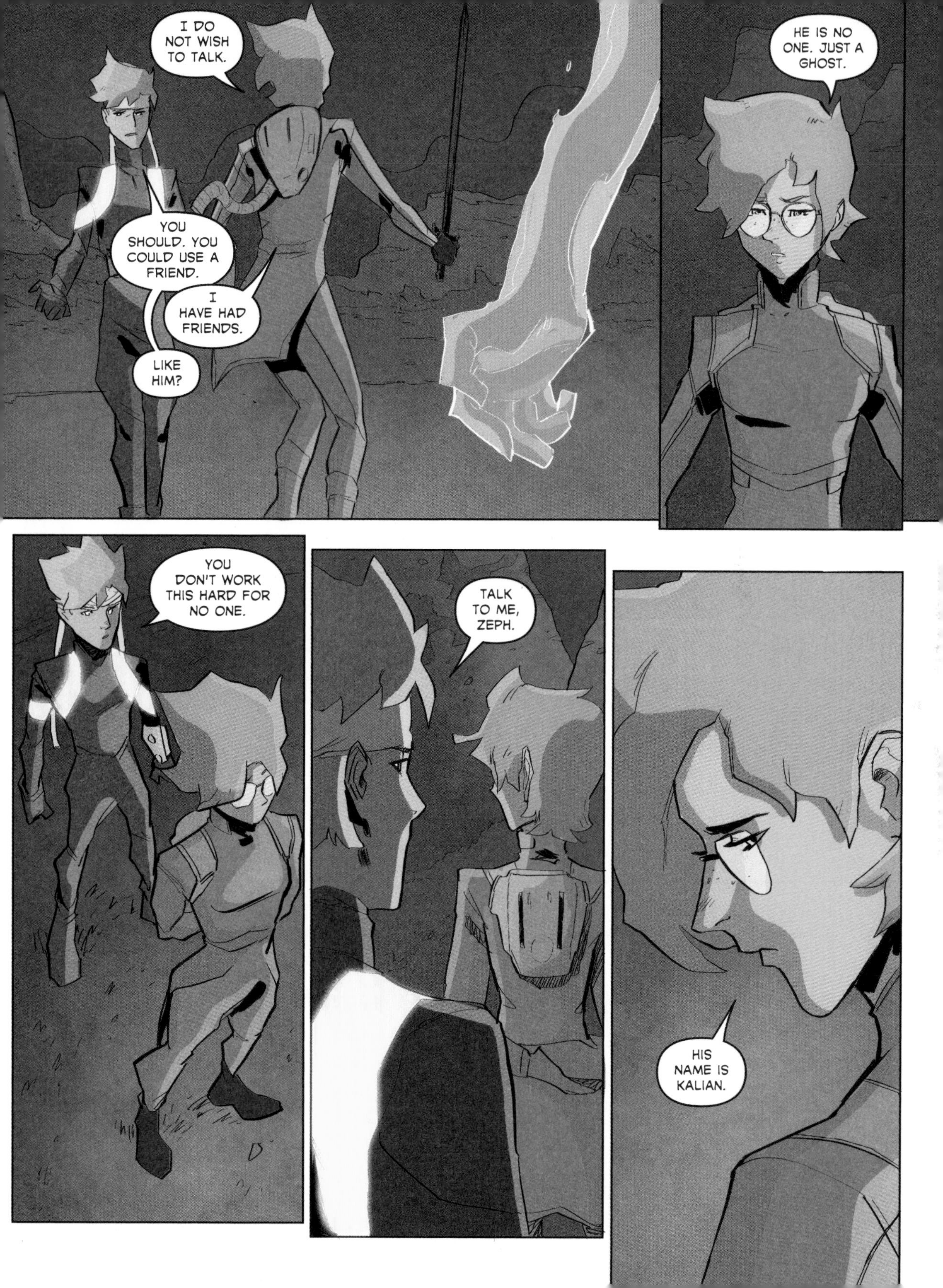
I DO NOT WISH TO TALK.
YOU SHOULD. YOU COULD USE A FRIEND.
I HAVE HAD FRIENDS.
LIKE HIM?
HE IS NO ONE. JUST A GHOST.
YOU DON'T WORK THIS HARD FOR NO ONE.
TALK TO ME, ZEPH.
HIS NAME IS KALIAN.

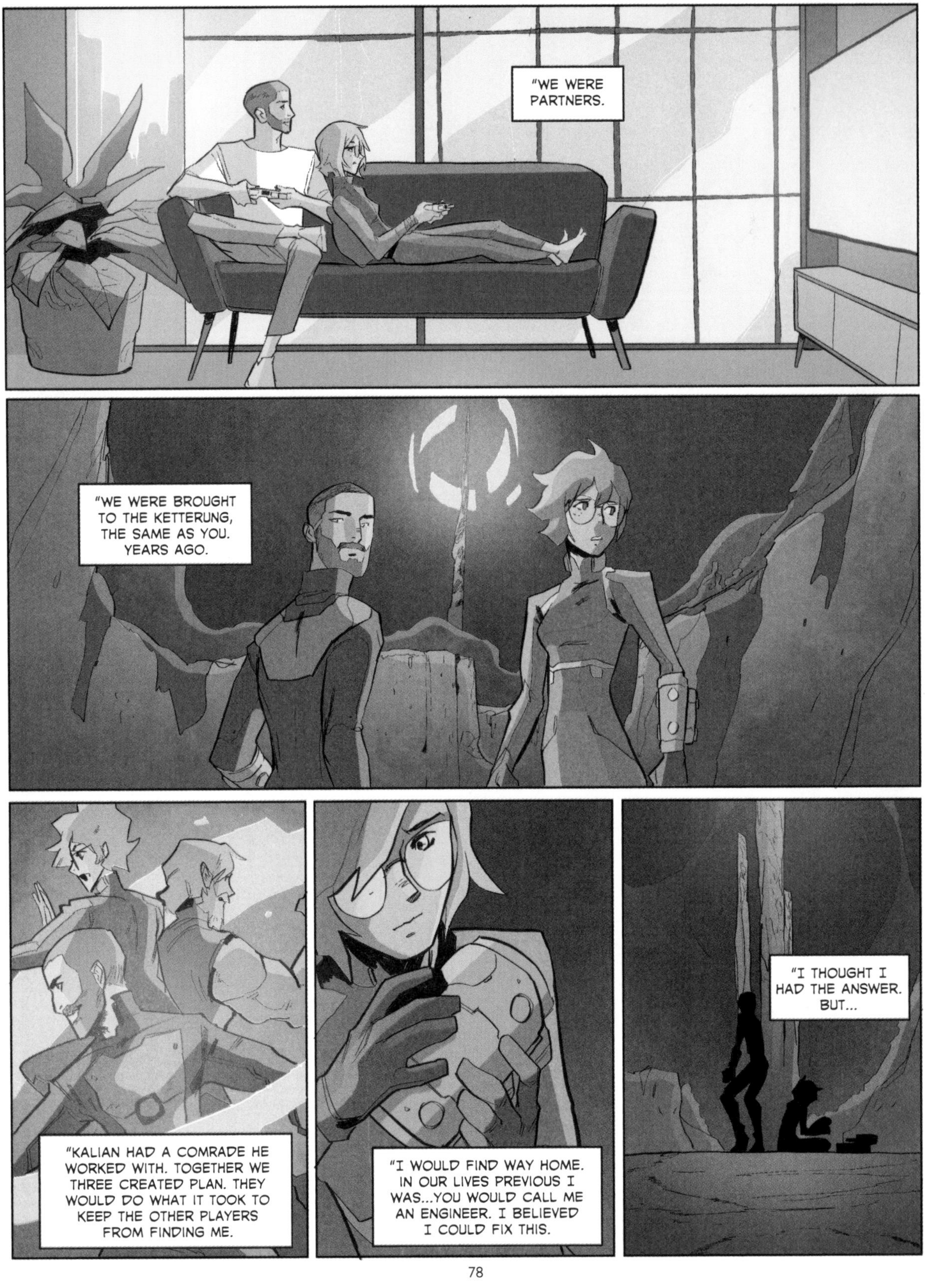
"WE WERE PARTNERS.
"WE WERE BROUGHT TO THE KETTERUNG, THE SAME AS YOU. YEARS AGO.
"KALIAN HAD A COMRADE HE WORKED WITH. TOGETHER WE THREE CREATED PLAN. THEY WOULD DO WHAT IT TOOK TO KEEP THE OTHER PLAYERS FROM FINDING ME.
"I WOULD FIND WAY HOME. IN OUR LIVES PREVIOUS I WAS...YOU WOULD CALL ME AN ENGINEER. I BELIEVED I COULD FIX THIS.
"I THOUGHT I HAD THE ANSWER. BUT...

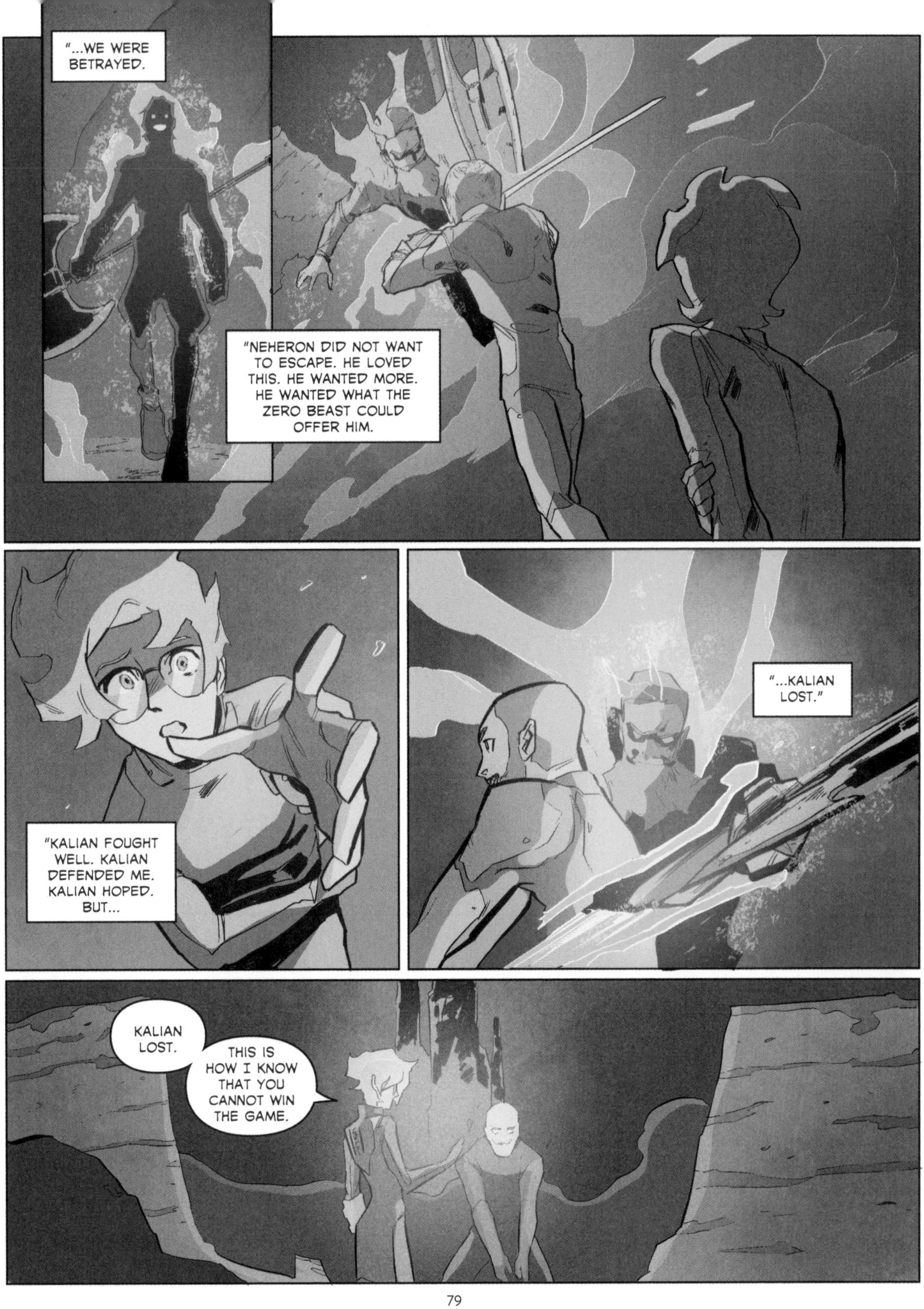
"...WE WERE BETRAYED.
"NEHERON DID NOT WANT TO ESCAPE. HE LOVED THIS. HE WANTED MORE. HE WANTED WHAT THE ZERO BEAST COULD OFFER HIM.
"KALIAN FOUGHT WELL. KALIAN DEFENDED ME. KALIAN HOPED. BUT...
"...KALIAN LOST."
KALIAN LOST.
THIS IS HOW I KNOW THAT YOU CANNOT WIN THE GAME.

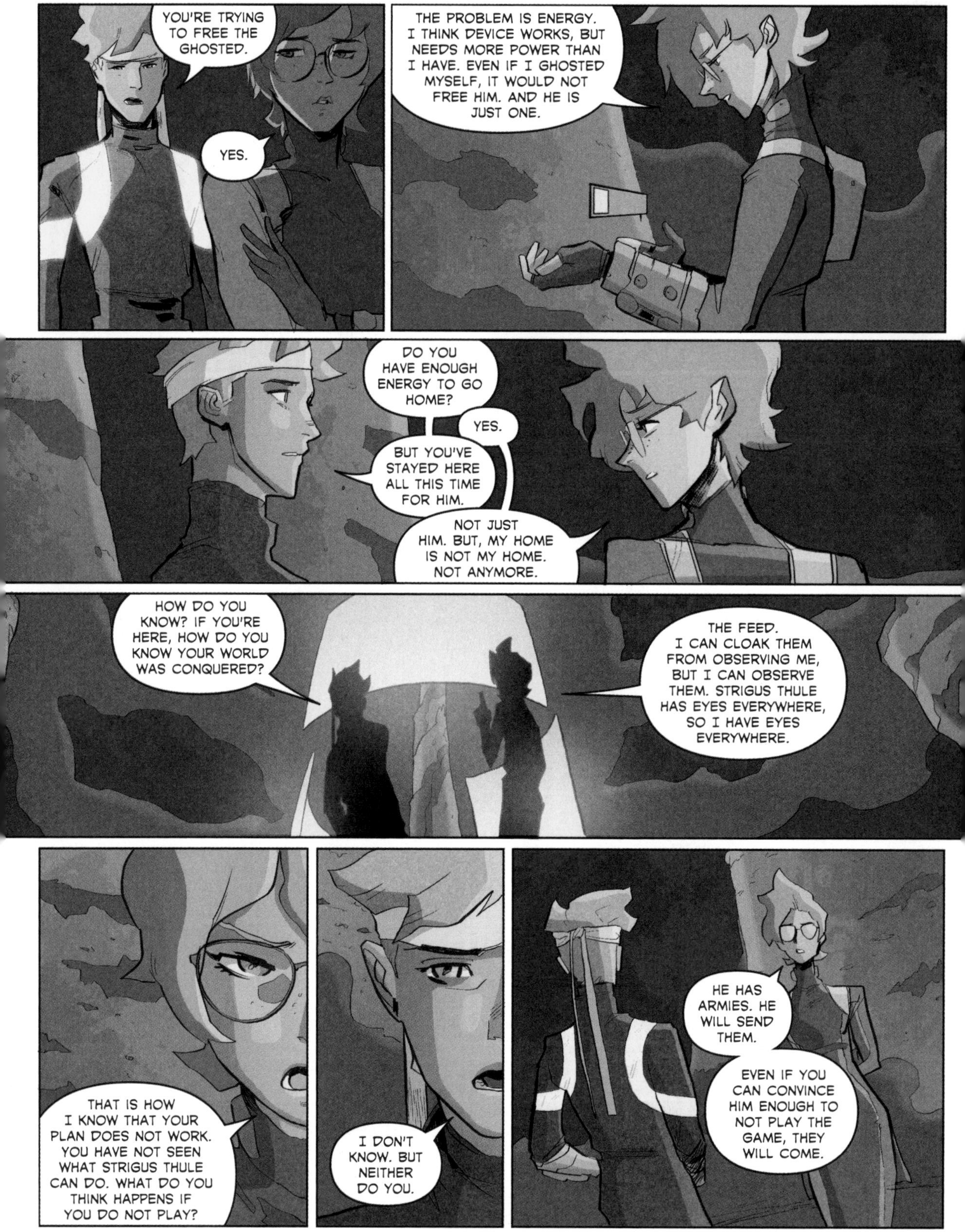
YOU'RE TRYING TO FREE THE GHOSTED.
YES.
THE PROBLEM IS ENERGY. I THINK DEVICE WORKS, BUT NEEDS MORE POWER THAN I HAVE. EVEN IF I GHOSTED MYSELF, IT WOULD NOT FREE HIM. AND HE IS JUST ONE.
DO YOU HAVE ENOUGH ENERGY TO GO HOME?
YES.
BUT YOU'VE STAYED HERE ALL THIS TIME FOR HIM.
NOT JUST HIM. BUT, MY HOME IS NOT MY HOME. NOT ANYMORE.
HOW DO YOU KNOW? IF YOU'RE HERE, HOW DO YOU KNOW YOUR WORLD WAS CONQUERED?
THE FEED. I CAN CLOAK THEM FROM OBSERVING ME, BUT I CAN OBSERVE THEM. STRIGUS THULE HAS EYES EVERYWHERE, SO I HAVE EYES EVERYWHERE.
THAT IS HOW I KNOW THAT YOUR PLAN DOES NOT WORK. YOU HAVE NOT SEEN WHAT STRIGUS THULE CAN DO. WHAT DO YOU THINK HAPPENS IF YOU DO NOT PLAY?
I DON'T KNOW. BUT NEITHER DO YOU.
HE HAS ARMIES. HE WILL SEND THEM.
EVEN IF YOU CAN CONVINCE HIM ENOUGH TO NOT PLAY THE GAME, THEY WILL COME.

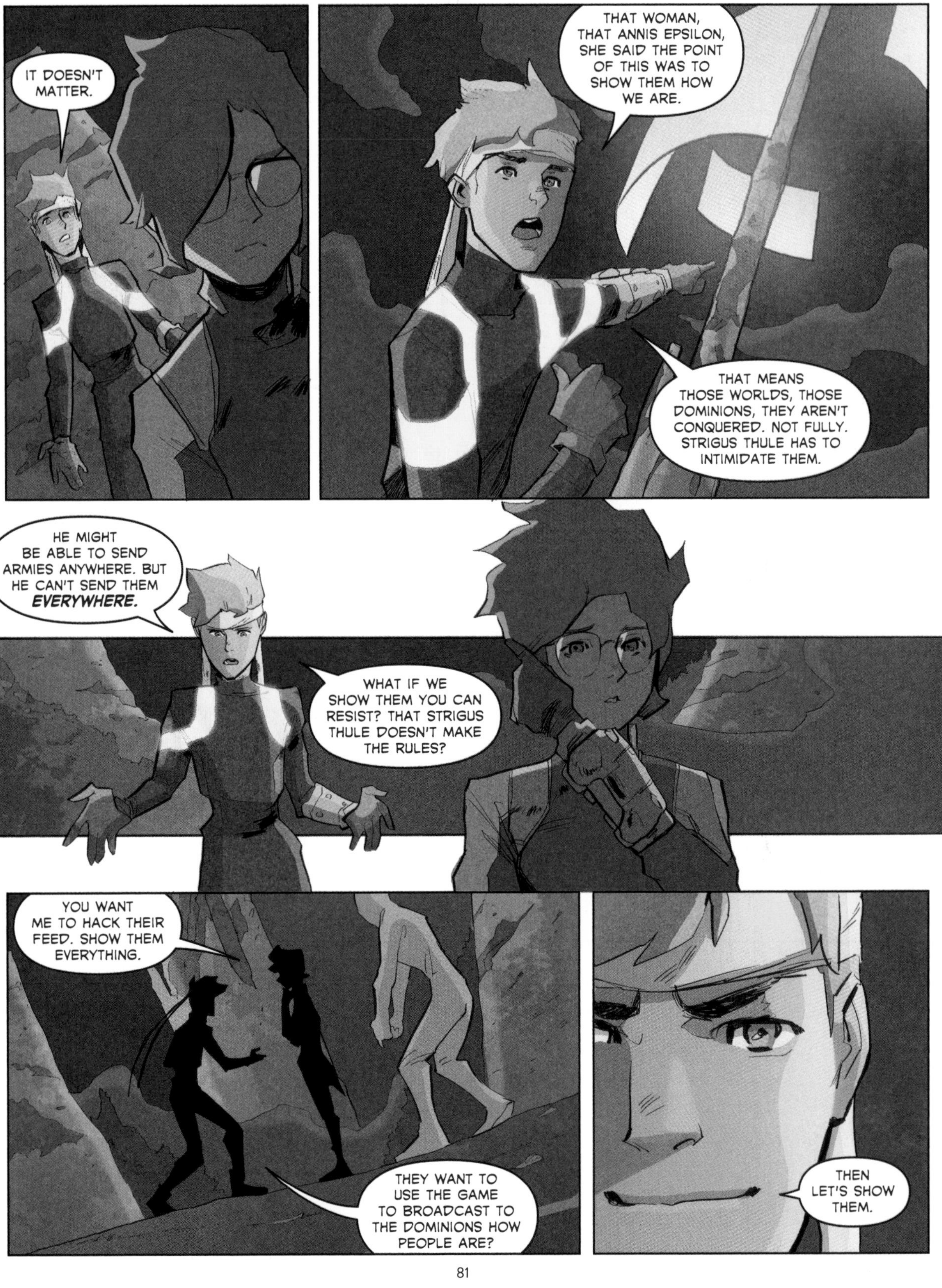
IT DOESN'T MATTER.
THAT WOMAN, THAT ANNIS EPSILON, SHE SAID THE POINT OF THIS WAS TO SHOW THEM HOW WE ARE.
THAT MEANS THOSE WORLDS, THOSE DOMINIONS, THEY AREN'T CONQUERED. NOT FULLY. STRIGUS THULE HAS TO INTIMIDATE THEM.
HE MIGHT BE ABLE TO SEND ARMIES ANYWHERE. BUT HE CAN'T SEND THEM ***EVERYWHERE.***
WHAT IF WE SHOW THEM YOU CAN RESIST? THAT STRIGUS THULE DOESN'T MAKE THE RULES?
YOU WANT ME TO HACK THEIR FEED. SHOW THEM EVERYTHING.
THEY WANT TO USE THE GAME TO BROADCAST TO THE DOMINIONS HOW PEOPLE ARE?
THEN LET'S SHOW THEM.

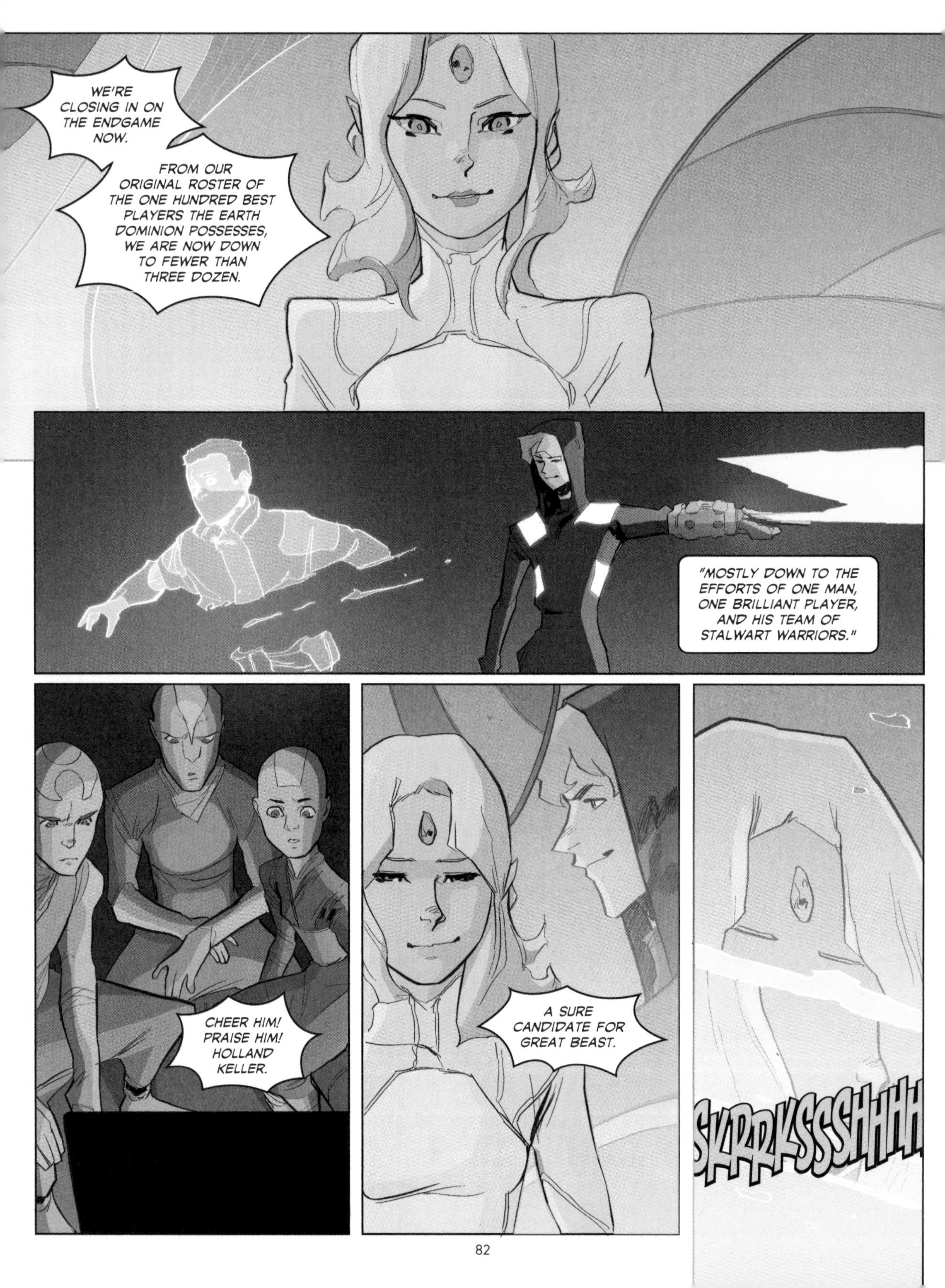
WE'RE CLOSING IN ON THE ENDGAME NOW.
FROM OUR ORIGINAL ROSTER OF THE ONE HUNDRED BEST PLAYERS THE EARTH DOMINION POSSESSES, WE ARE NOW DOWN TO FEWER THAN THREE DOZEN.
"MOSTLY DOWN TO THE EFFORTS OF ONE MAN, ONE BRILLIANT PLAYER, AND HIS TEAM OF STALWART WARRIORS."
CHEER HIM! PRAISE HIM! HOLLAND KELLER.
A SURE CANDIDATE FOR GREAT BEAST.
SKRRKSSSHHH

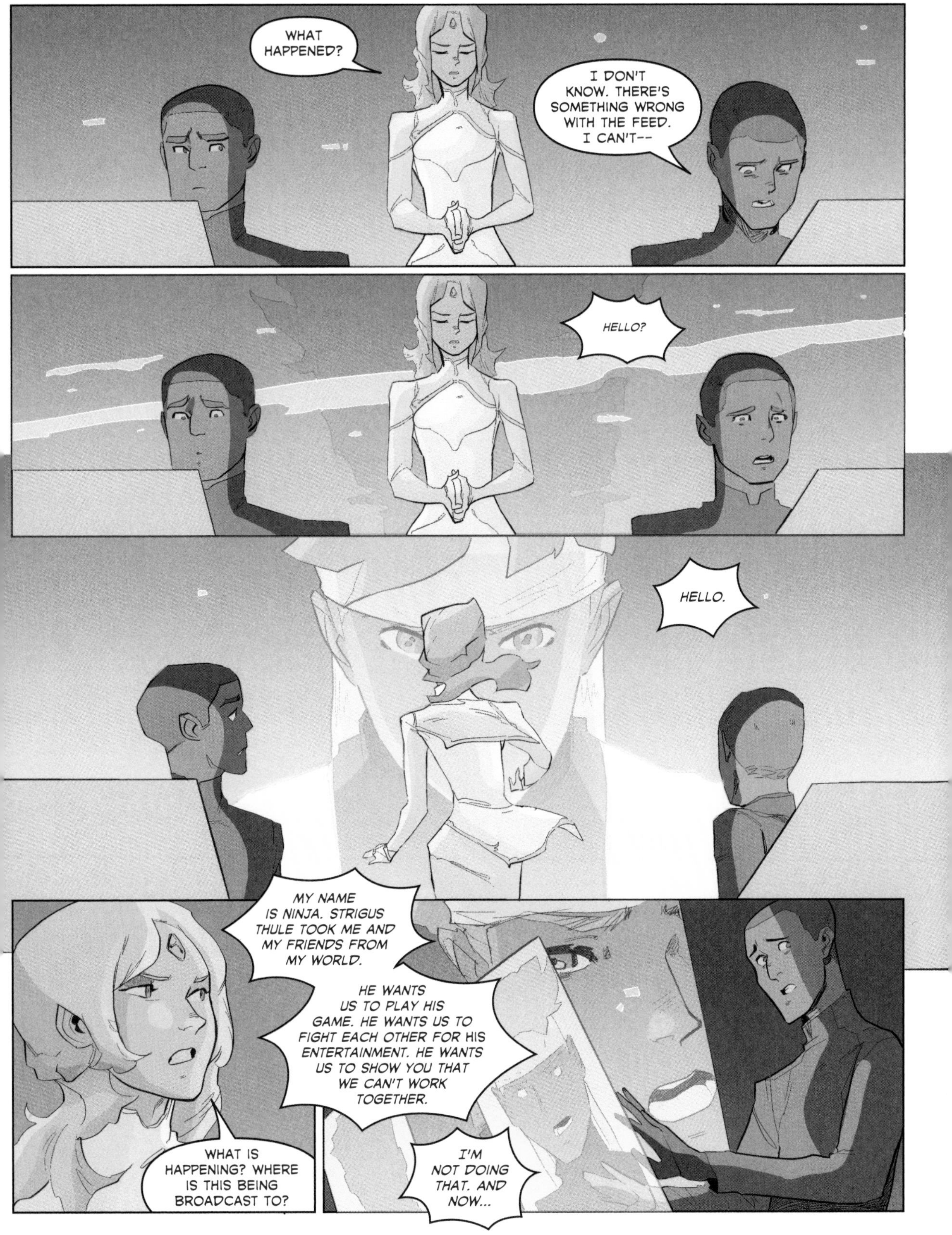
WHAT HAPPENED?
I DON'T KNOW. THERE'S SOMETHING WRONG WITH THE FEED. I CAN'T--
HELLO?
HELLO.
MY NAME IS NINJA. STRIGUS THULE TOOK ME AND MY FRIENDS FROM MY WORLD.
HE WANTS US TO PLAY HIS GAME. HE WANTS US TO FIGHT EACH OTHER FOR HIS ENTERTAINMENT. HE WANTS US TO SHOW YOU THAT WE CAN'T WORK TOGETHER.
WHAT IS HAPPENING? WHERE IS THIS BEING BROADCAST TO?
I'M NOT DOING THAT. AND NOW...

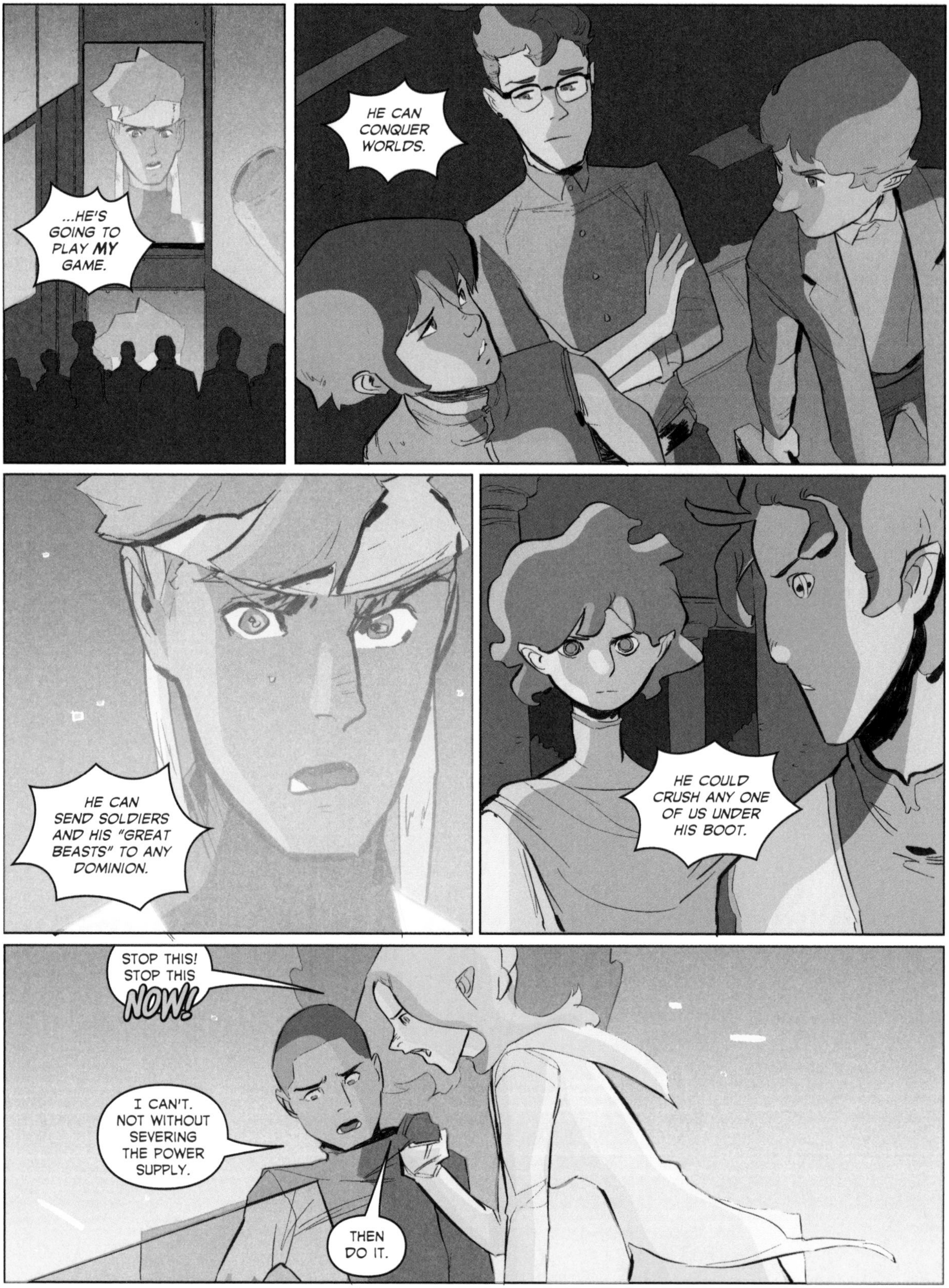
...HE'S GOING TO PLAY MY GAME.
HE CAN CONQUER WORLDS.
HE CAN SEND SOLDIERS AND HIS "GREAT BEASTS" TO ANY DOMINION.
HE COULD CRUSH ANY ONE OF US UNDER HIS BOOT.
STOP THIS! STOP THIS NOW!
I CAN'T. NOT WITHOUT SEVERING THE POWER SUPPLY.
THEN DO IT.

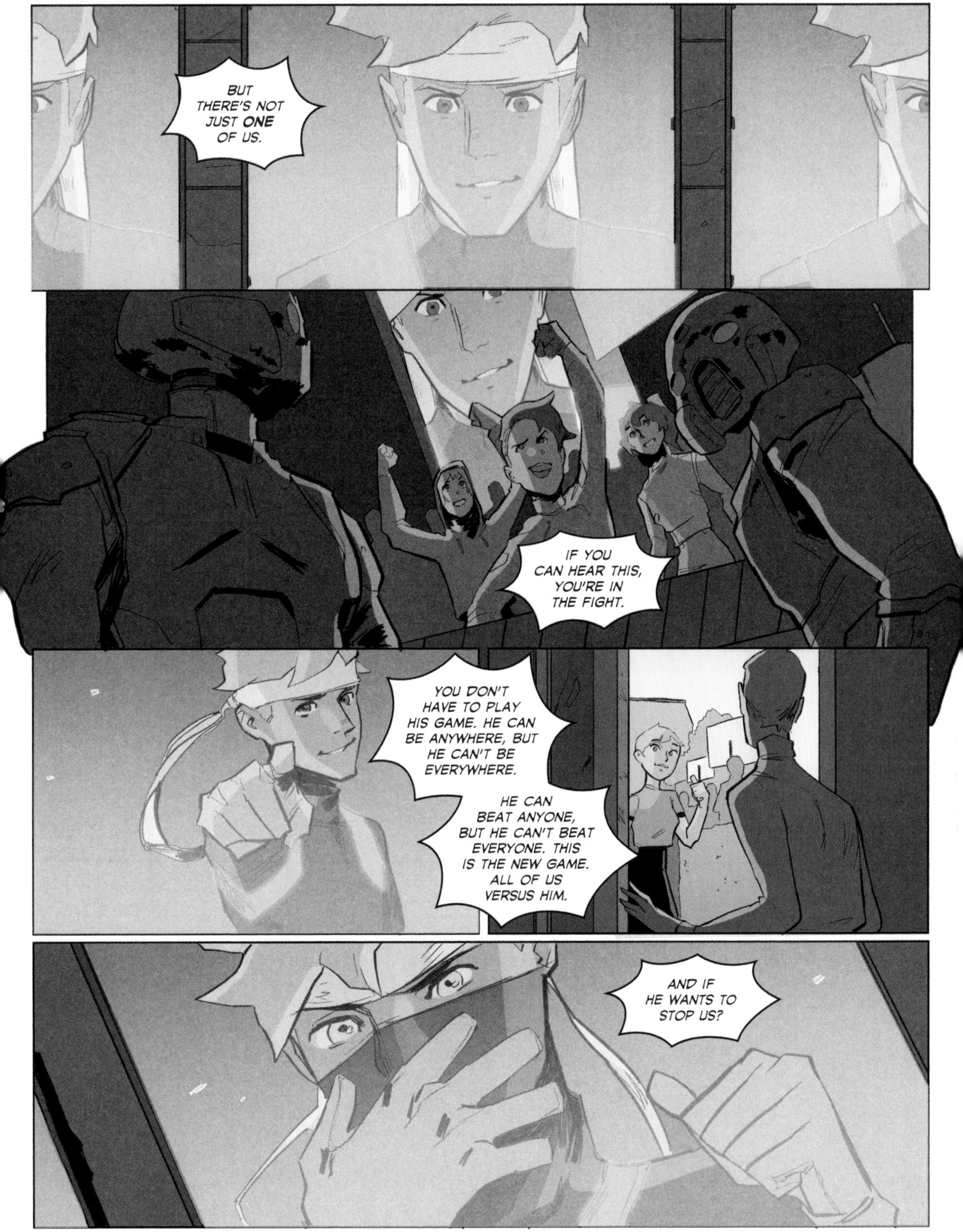
BUT THERE'S NOT JUST **ONE** OF US.
IF YOU CAN HEAR THIS, YOU'RE IN THE FIGHT.
YOU DON'T HAVE TO PLAY HIS GAME. HE CAN BE ANYWHERE, BUT HE CAN'T BE EVERYWHERE.
HE CAN BEAT ANYONE, BUT HE CAN'T BEAT EVERYONE. THIS IS THE NEW GAME. ALL OF US VERSUS HIM.
AND IF HE WANTS TO STOP US?

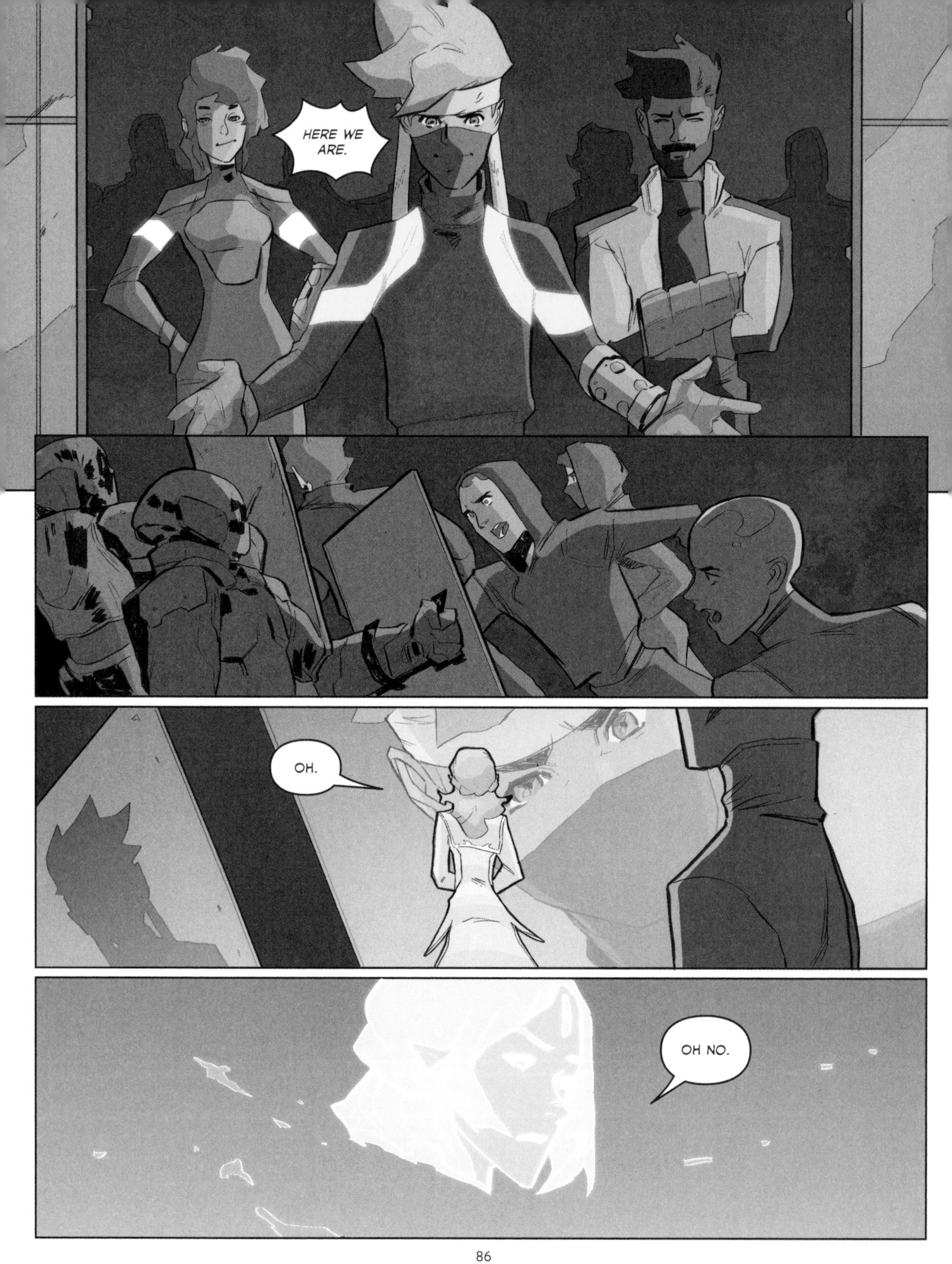
HERE WE ARE.
OH.
OH NO.

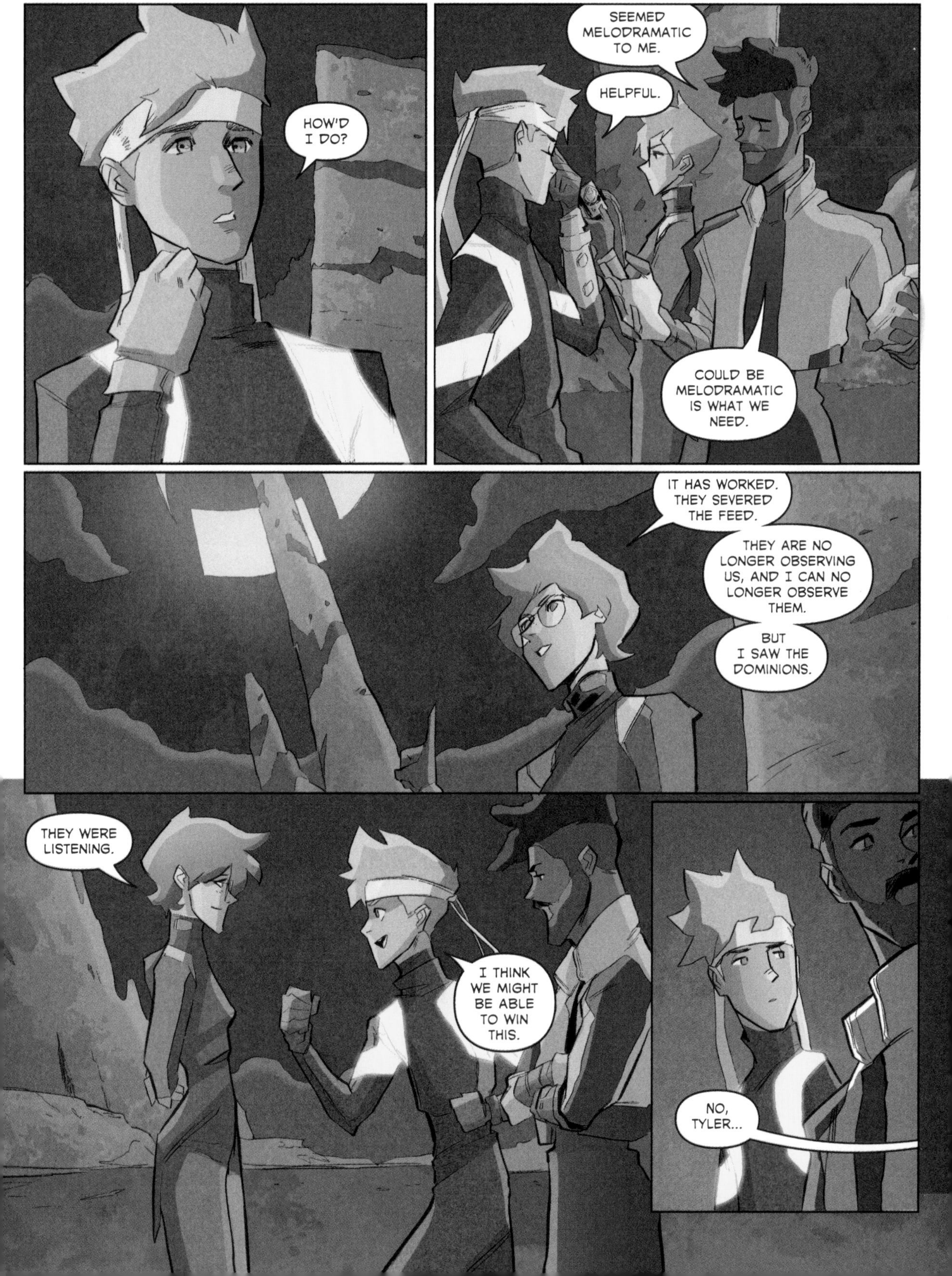
HOW'D I DO?
SEEMED MELODRAMATIC TO ME.
HELPFUL.
COULD BE MELODRAMATIC IS WHAT WE NEED.
IT HAS WORKED. THEY SEVERED THE FEED.
THEY ARE NO LONGER OBSERVING US, AND I CAN NO LONGER OBSERVE THEM.
BUT I SAW THE DOMINIONS.
THEY WERE LISTENING.
I THINK WE MIGHT BE ABLE TO WIN THIS.
NO, TYLER...

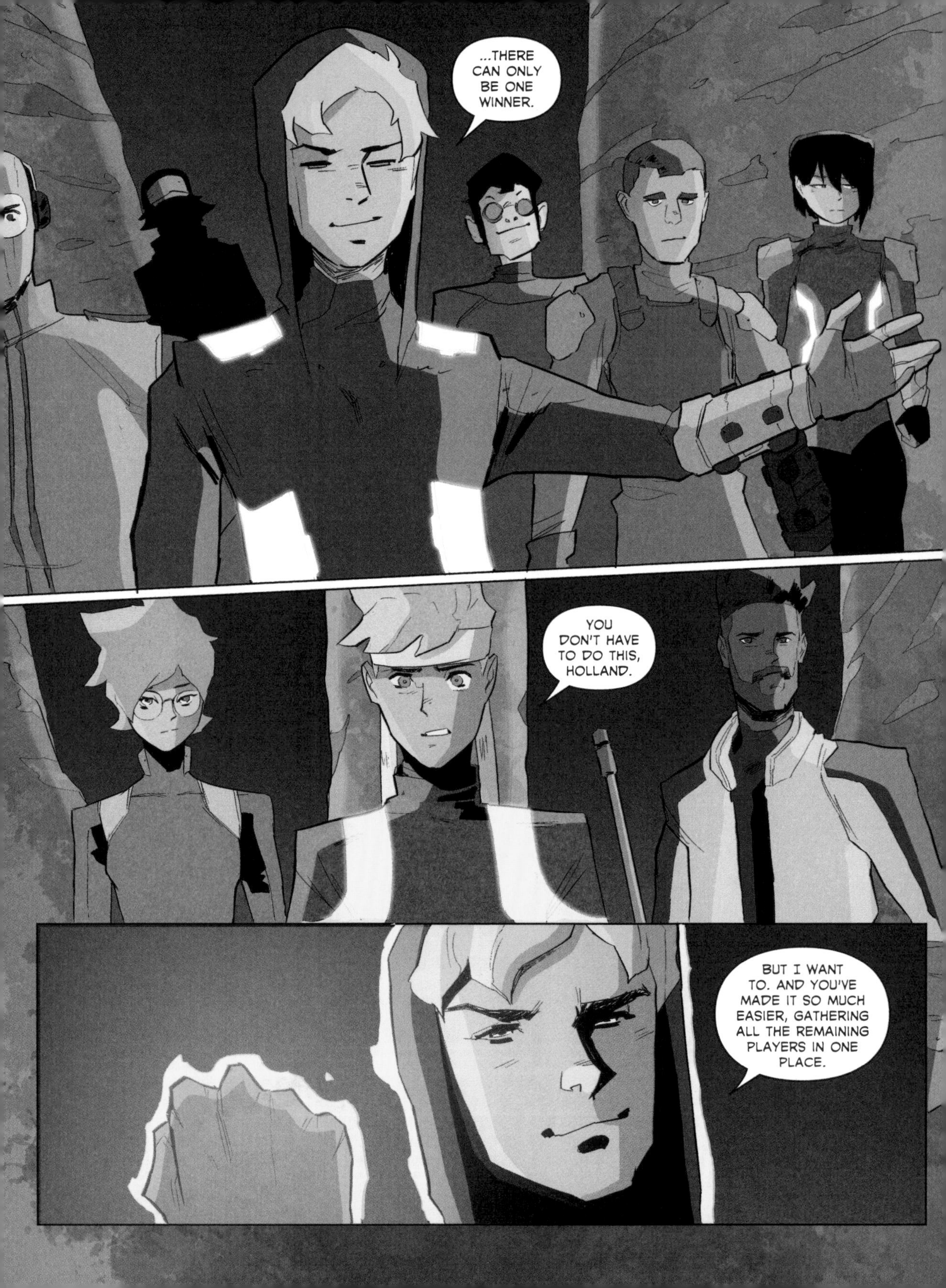
...THERE CAN ONLY BE ONE WINNER.
YOU DON'T HAVE TO DO THIS, HOLLAND.
BUT I WANT TO. AND YOU'VE MADE IT SO MUCH EASIER, GATHERING ALL THE REMAINING PLAYERS IN ONE PLACE.

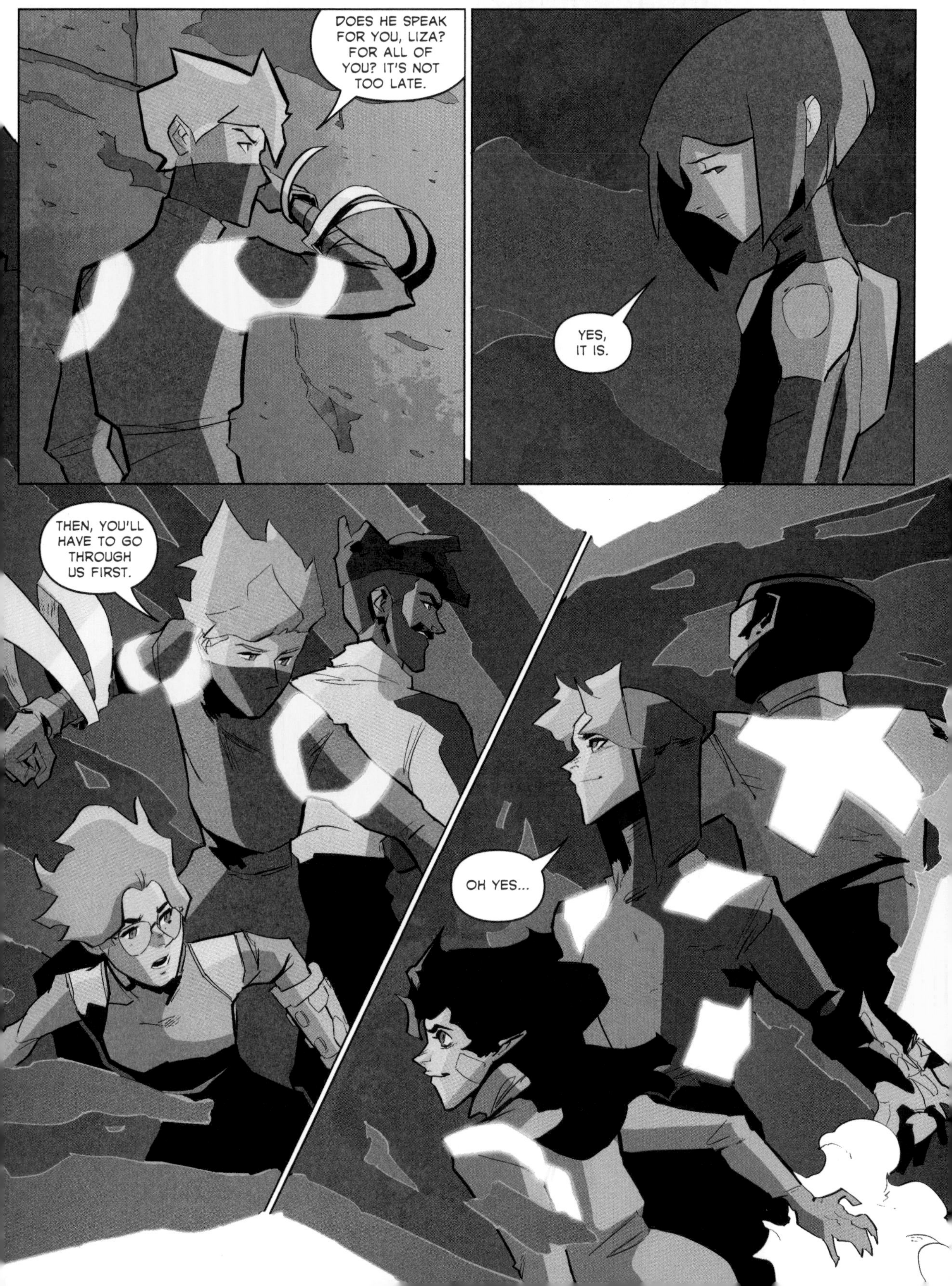
DOES HE SPEAK FOR YOU, LIZA? FOR ALL OF YOU? IT'S NOT TOO LATE.
YES, IT IS.
THEN, YOU'LL HAVE TO GO THROUGH US FIRST.
OH YES...

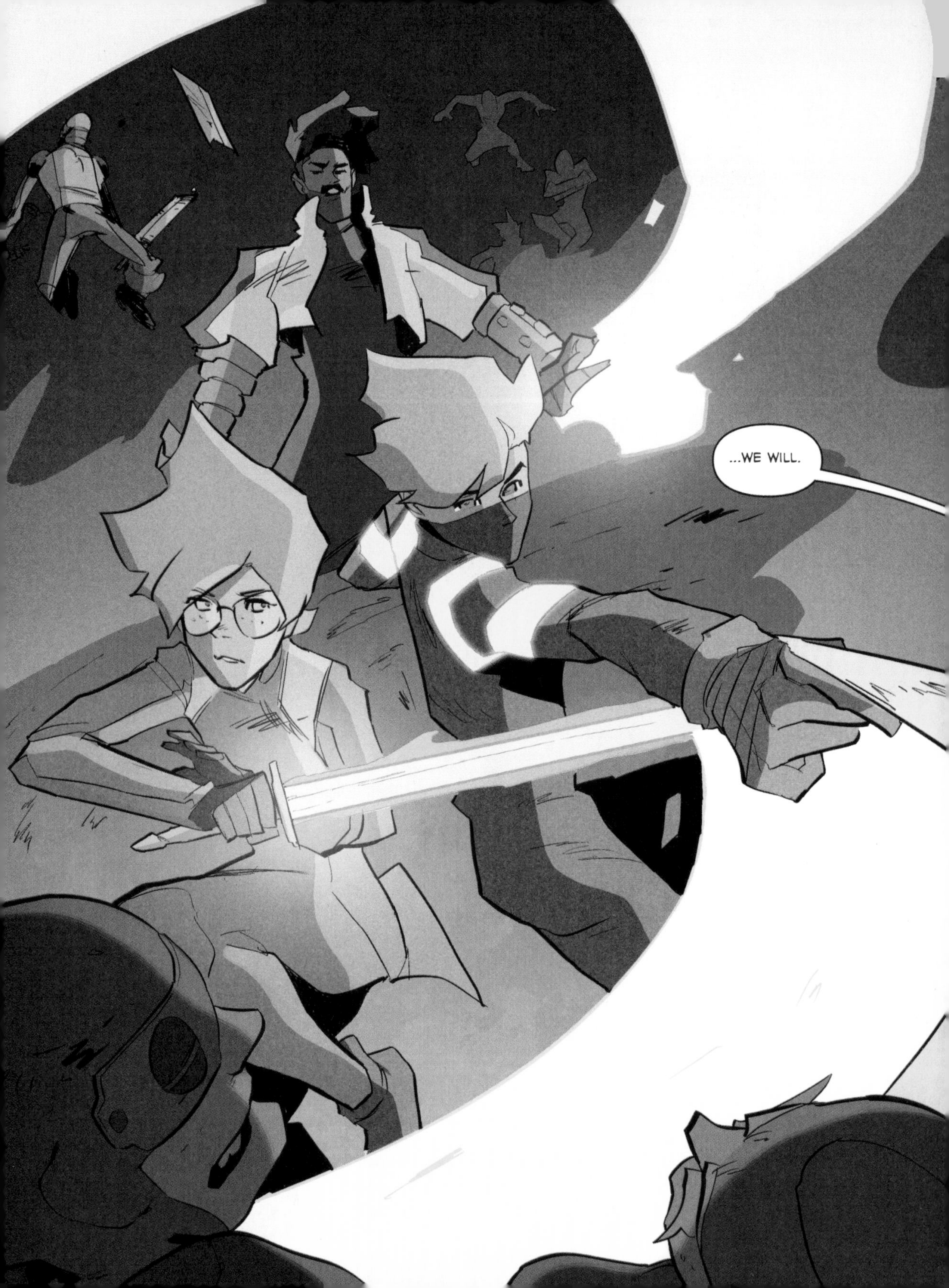
...WE WILL.

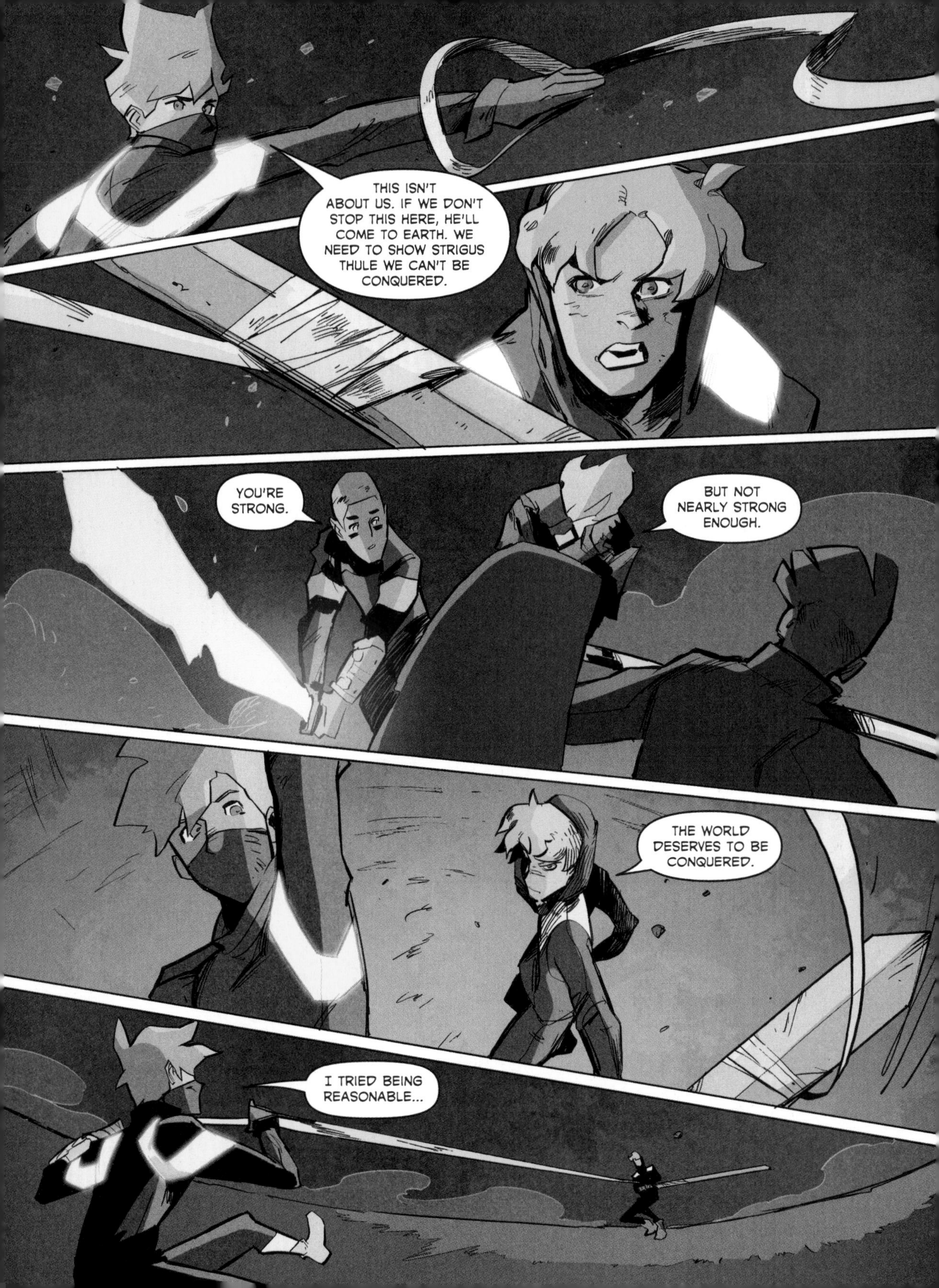
THIS ISN'T ABOUT US. IF WE DON'T STOP THIS HERE, HE'LL COME TO EARTH. WE NEED TO SHOW STRIGUS THULE WE CAN'T BE CONQUERED.
YOU'RE STRONG.
BUT NOT NEARLY STRONG ENOUGH.
THE WORLD DESERVES TO BE CONQUERED.
I TRIED BEING REASONABLE...

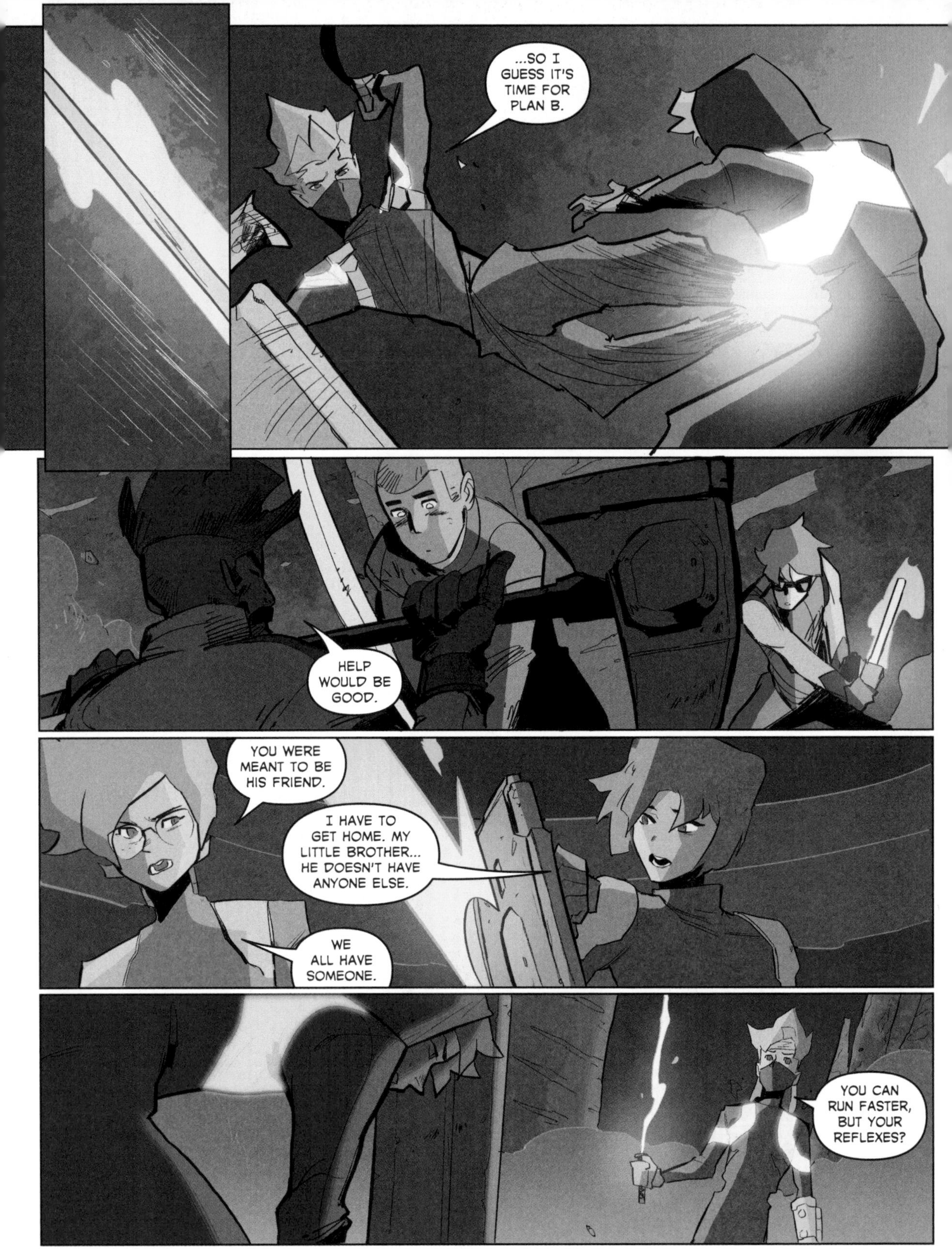
...SO I GUESS IT'S TIME FOR PLAN B.
HELP WOULD BE GOOD.
YOU WERE MEANT TO BE HIS FRIEND.
I HAVE TO GET HOME. MY LITTLE BROTHER... HE DOESN'T HAVE ANYONE ELSE.
WE ALL HAVE SOMEONE.
YOU CAN RUN FASTER, BUT YOUR REFLEXES?

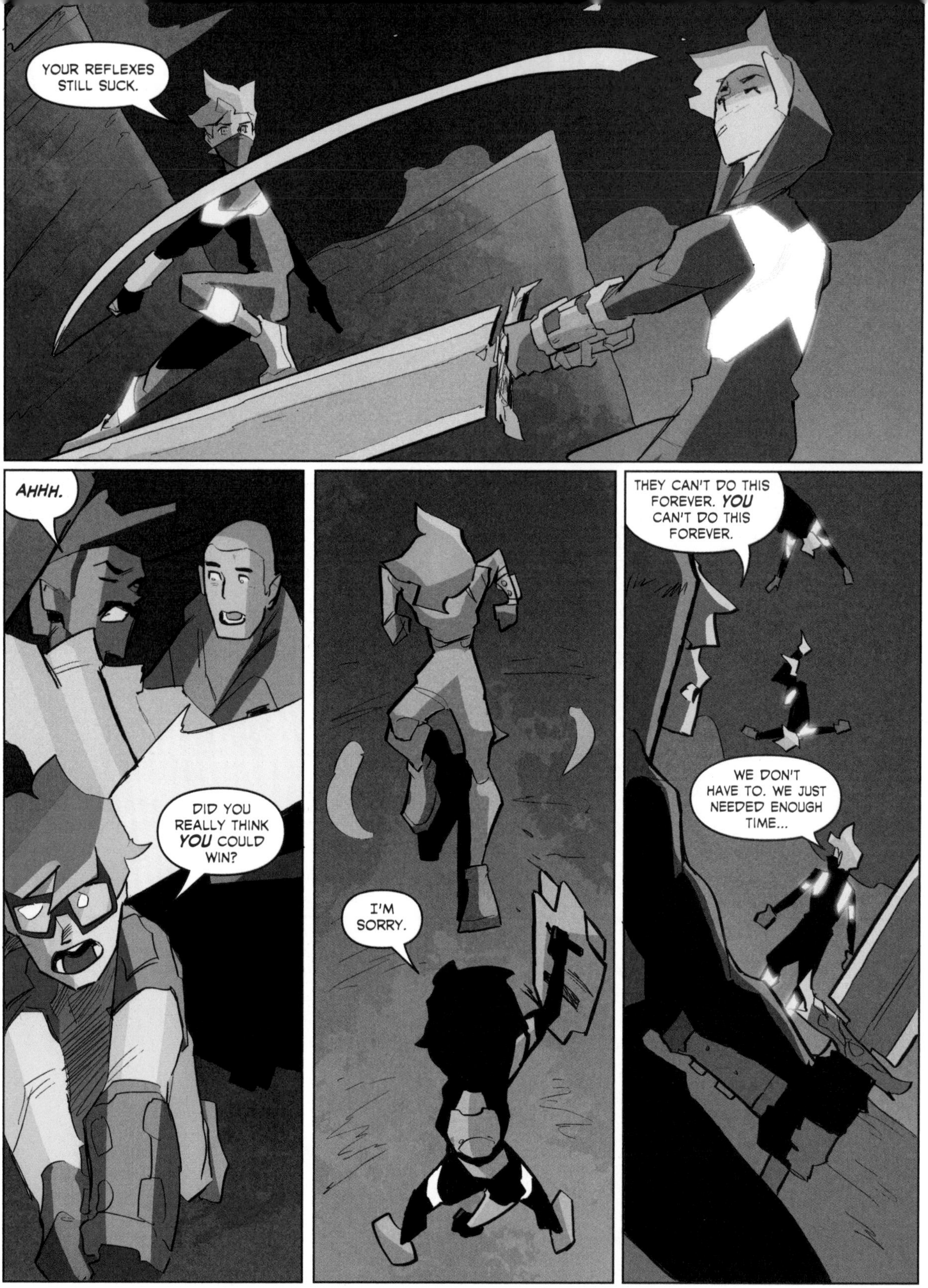
YOUR REFLEXES STILL SUCK.
AHHH.
DID YOU REALLY THINK *YOU* COULD WIN?
I'M SORRY.
THEY CAN'T DO THIS FOREVER. *YOU* CAN'T DO THIS FOREVER.
WE DON'T HAVE TO. WE JUST NEEDED ENOUGH TIME...

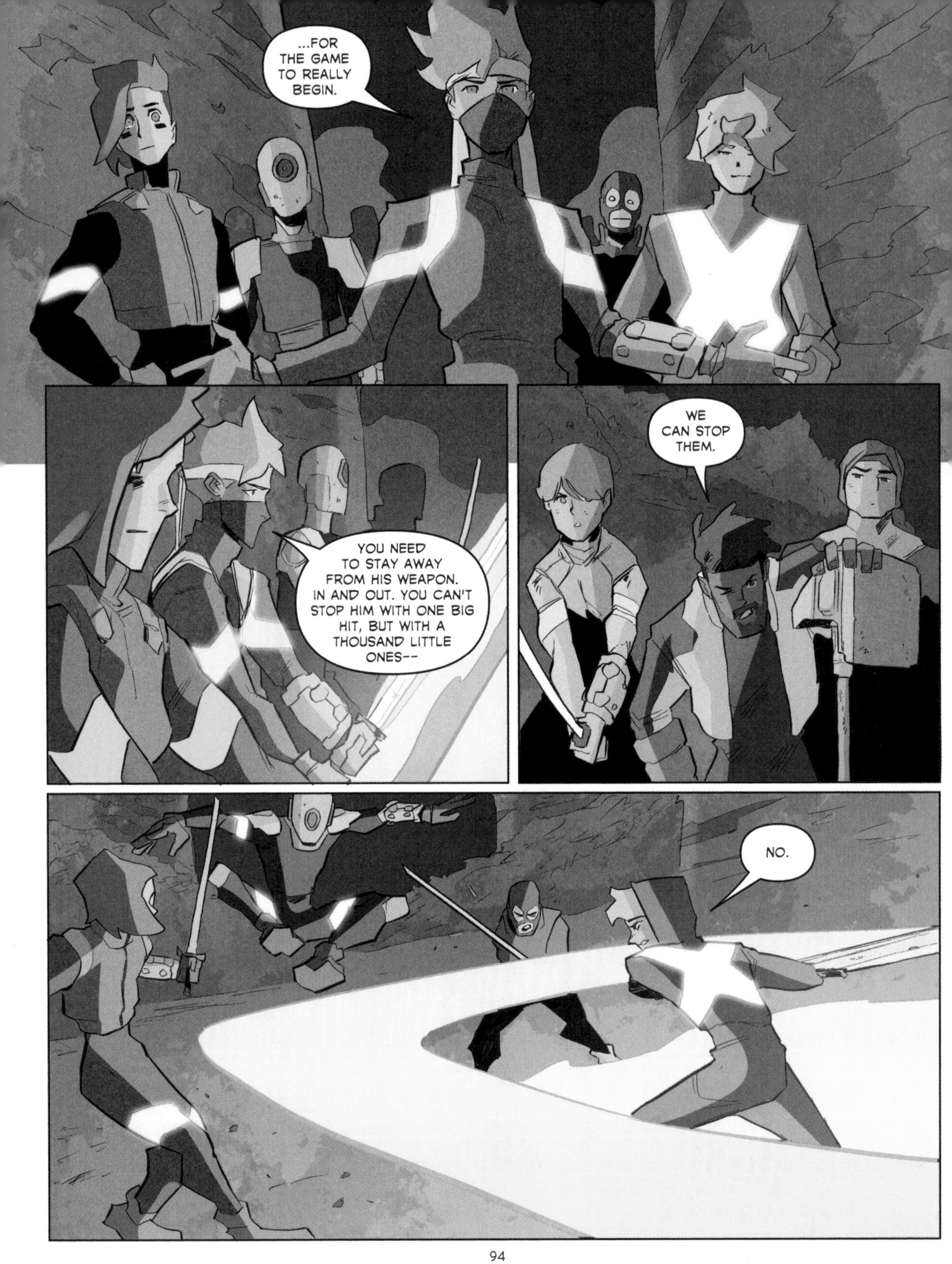
...FOR THE GAME TO REALLY BEGIN.
YOU NEED TO STAY AWAY FROM HIS WEAPON. IN AND OUT. YOU CAN'T STOP HIM WITH ONE BIG HIT, BUT WITH A THOUSAND LITTLE ONES--
WE CAN STOP THEM.
NO.

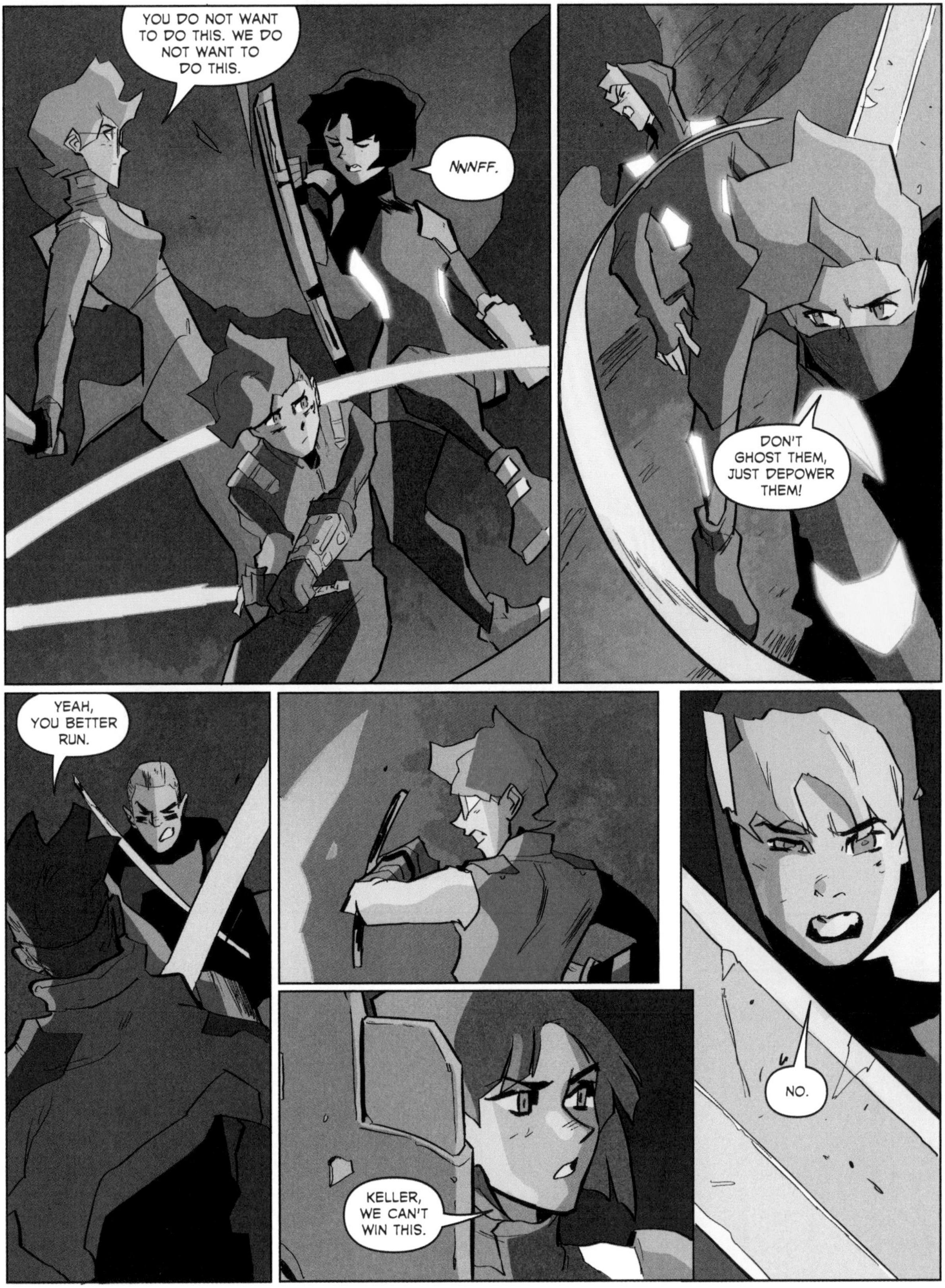
YOU DO NOT WANT TO DO THIS. WE DO NOT WANT TO DO THIS.
NNNFF.
DON'T GHOST THEM, JUST DEPOWER THEM!
YEAH, YOU BETTER RUN.
NO.
KELLER, WE CAN'T WIN THIS.

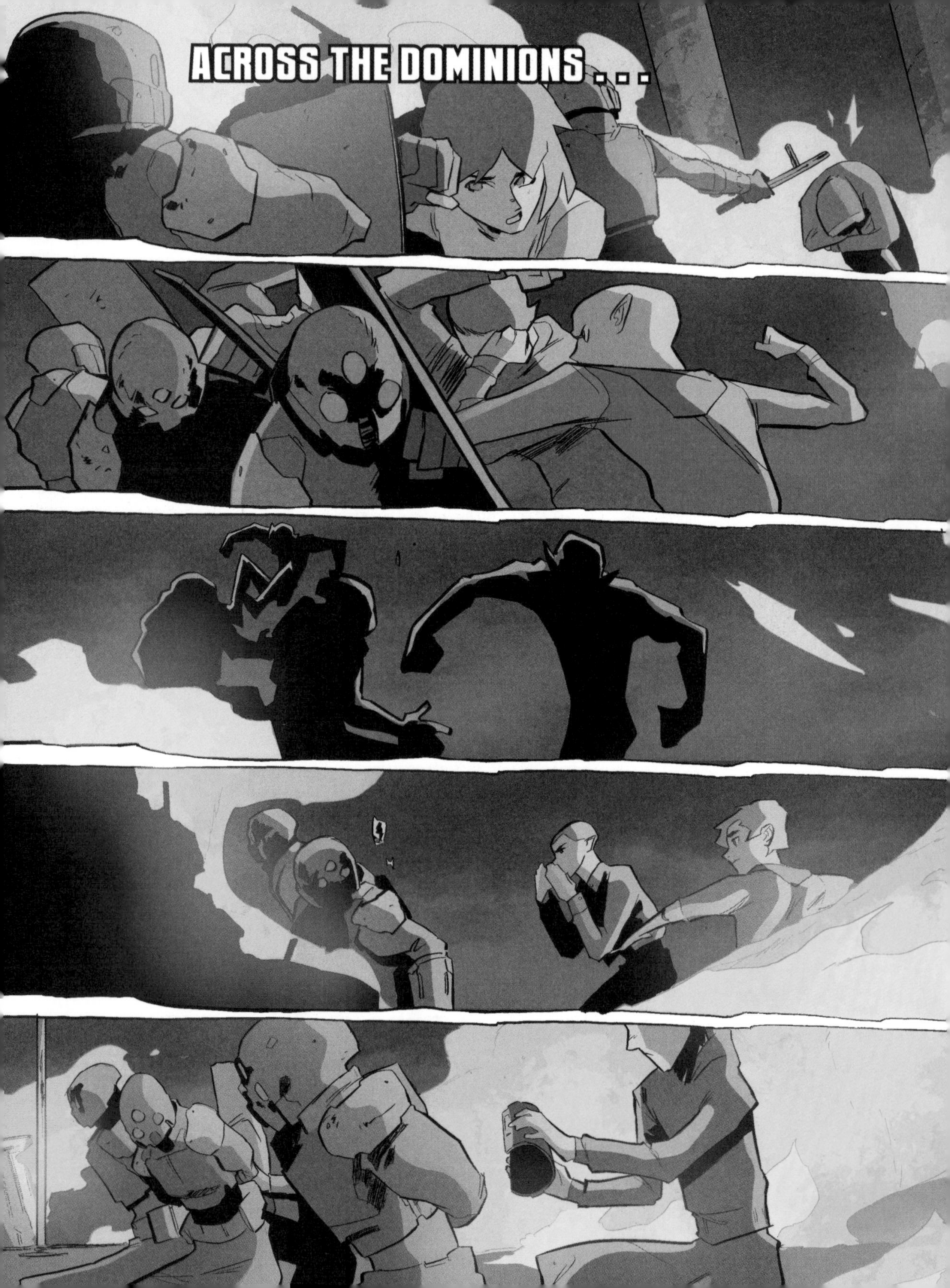
ACROSS THE DOMINIONS . . .

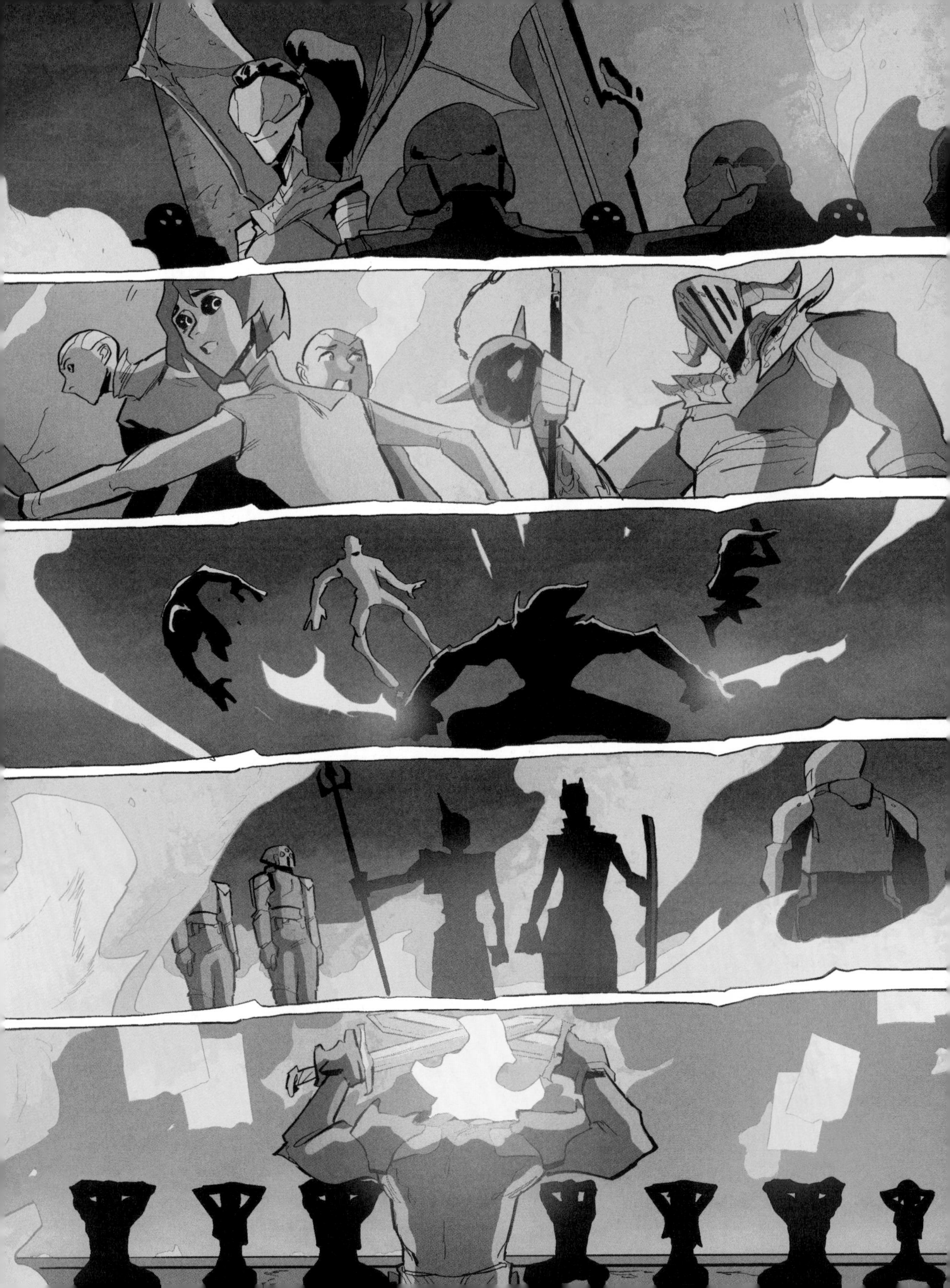

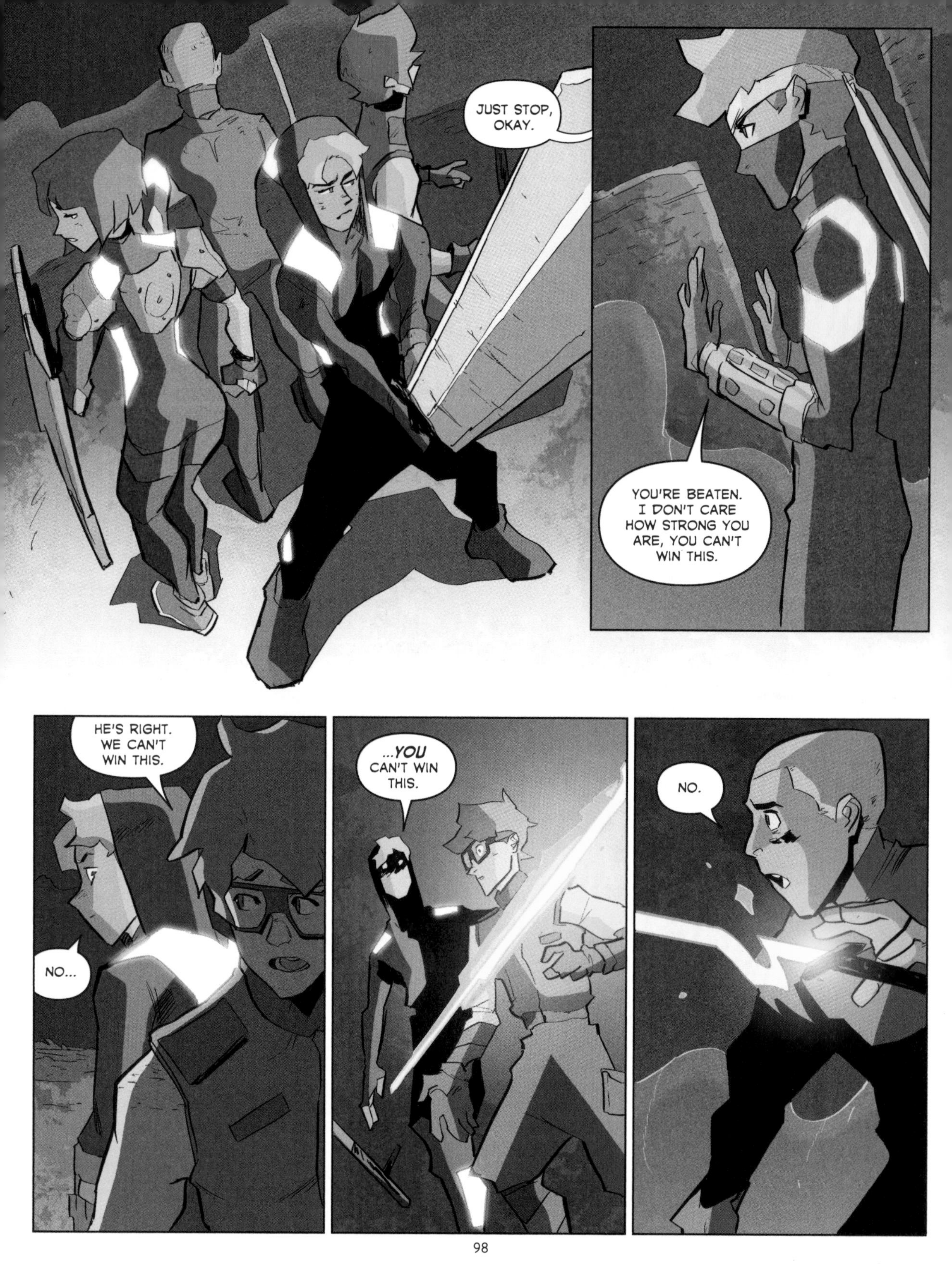
JUST STOP, OKAY.
YOU'RE BEATEN. I DON'T CARE HOW STRONG YOU ARE, YOU CAN'T WIN THIS.
HE'S RIGHT. WE CAN'T WIN THIS.
NO...
...YOU CAN'T WIN THIS.
NO.

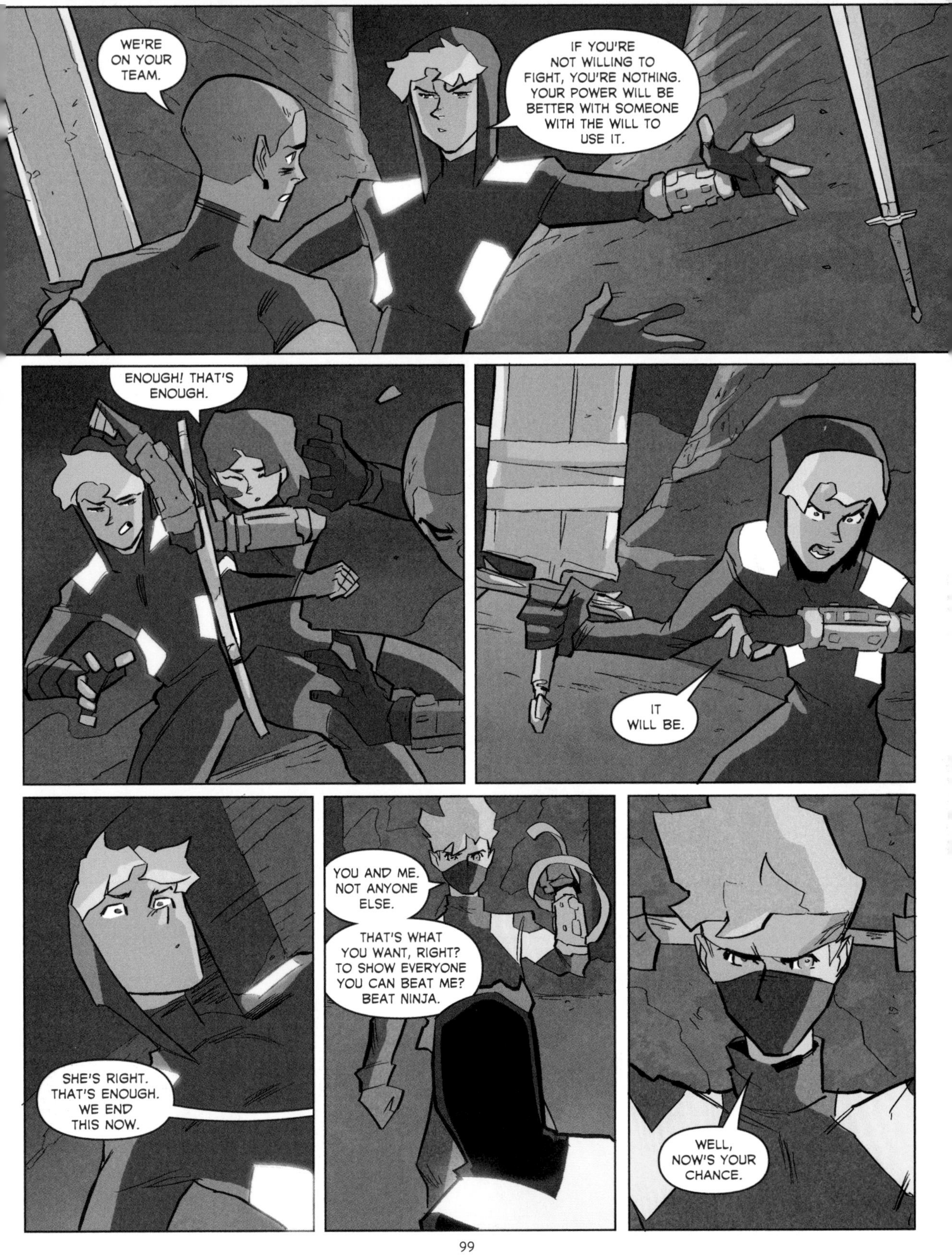
WE'RE ON YOUR TEAM.
IF YOU'RE NOT WILLING TO FIGHT, YOU'RE NOTHING. YOUR POWER WILL BE BETTER WITH SOMEONE WITH THE WILL TO USE IT.
ENOUGH! THAT'S ENOUGH.
IT WILL BE.
SHE'S RIGHT. THAT'S ENOUGH. WE END THIS NOW.
YOU AND ME. NOT ANYONE ELSE.
THAT'S WHAT YOU WANT, RIGHT? TO SHOW EVERYONE YOU CAN BEAT ME? BEAT NINJA.
WELL, NOW'S YOUR CHANCE.

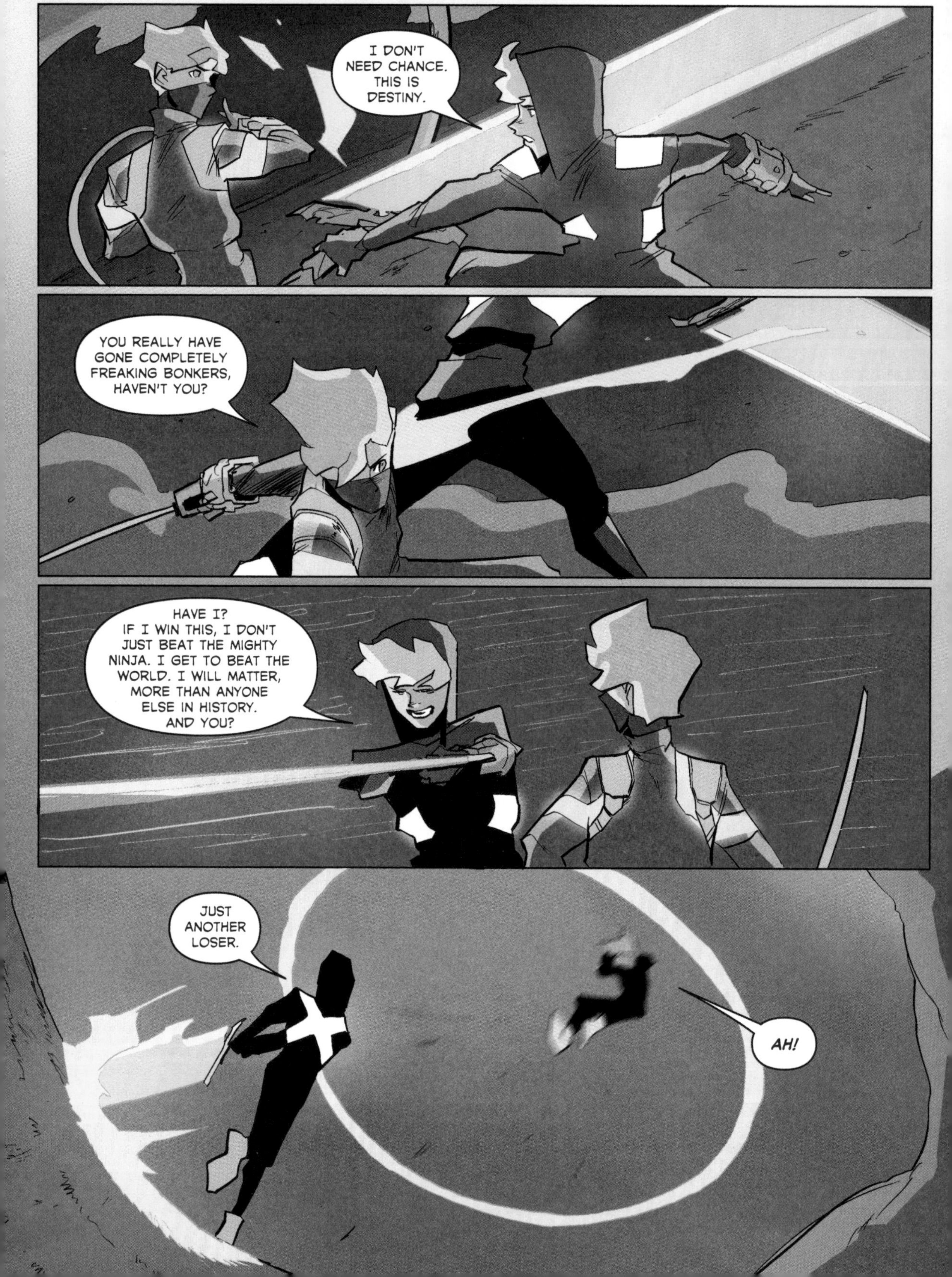
I DON'T NEED CHANCE. THIS IS DESTINY.
YOU REALLY HAVE GONE COMPLETELY FREAKING BONKERS, HAVEN'T YOU?
HAVE I? IF I WIN THIS, I DON'T JUST BEAT THE MIGHTY NINJA. I GET TO BEAT THE WORLD. I WILL MATTER, MORE THAN ANYONE ELSE IN HISTORY. AND YOU?
JUST ANOTHER LOSER.
AH!

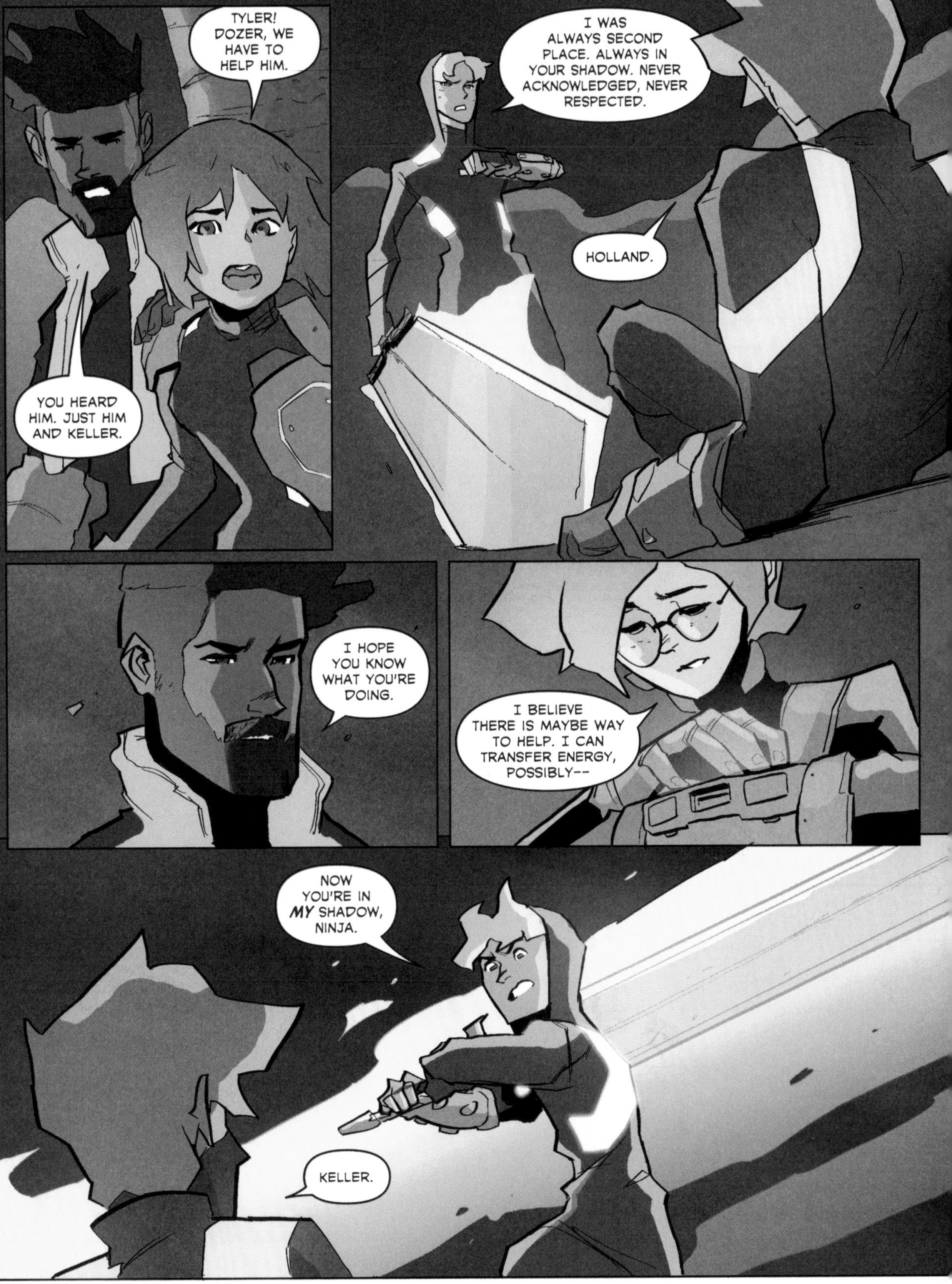
TYLER! DOZER, WE HAVE TO HELP HIM.
YOU HEARD HIM. JUST HIM AND KELLER.
I WAS ALWAYS SECOND PLACE. ALWAYS IN YOUR SHADOW. NEVER ACKNOWLEDGED, NEVER RESPECTED.
HOLLAND.
I HOPE YOU KNOW WHAT YOU'RE DOING.
I BELIEVE THERE IS MAYBE WAY TO HELP. I CAN TRANSFER ENERGY, POSSIBLY--
NOW YOU'RE IN *MY* SHADOW, NINJA.
KELLER.

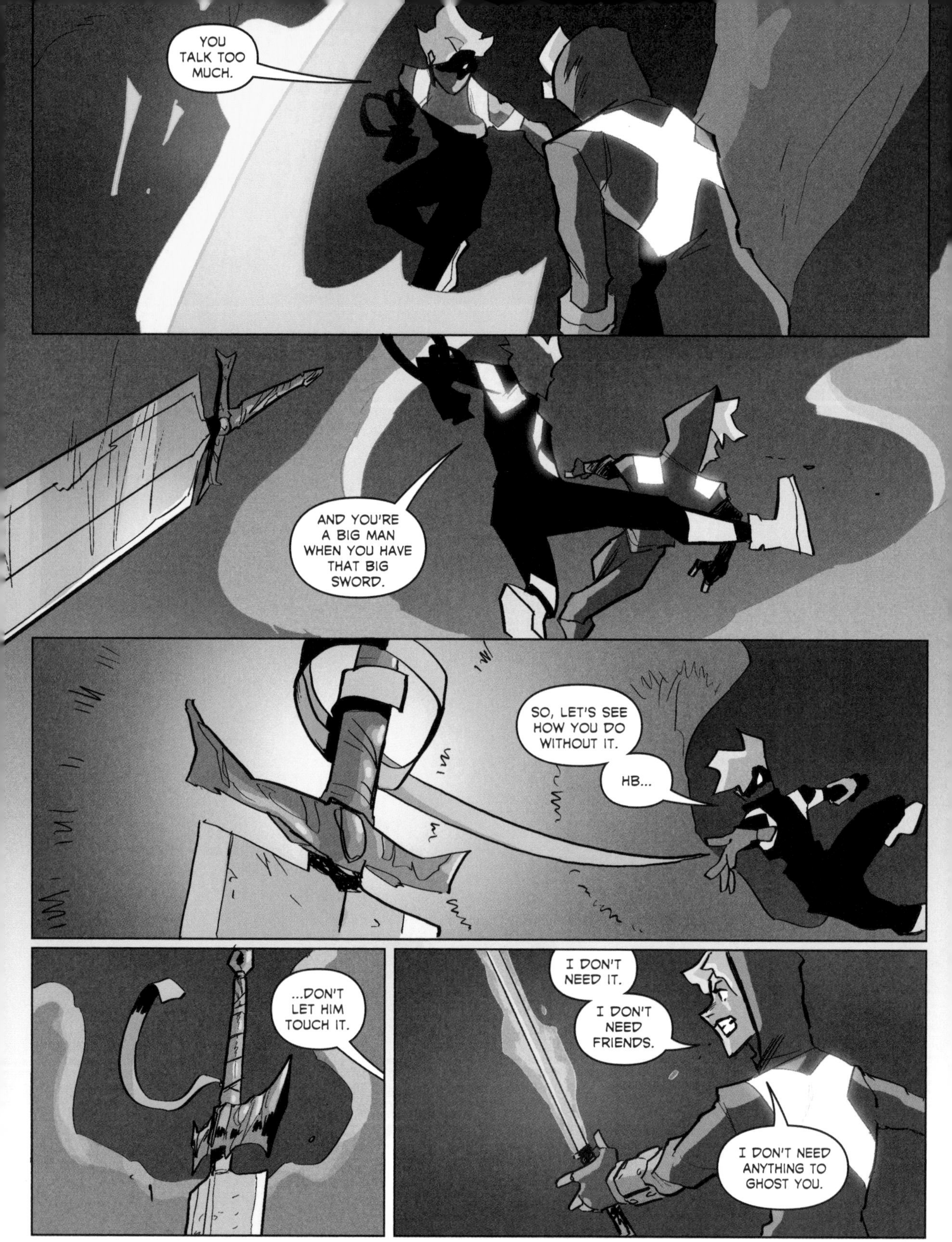
YOU TALK TOO MUCH.
AND YOU'RE A BIG MAN WHEN YOU HAVE THAT BIG SWORD.
SO, LET'S SEE HOW YOU DO WITHOUT IT.
HB...
...DON'T LET HIM TOUCH IT.
I DON'T NEED IT.
I DON'T NEED FRIENDS.
I DON'T NEED ANYTHING TO GHOST YOU.

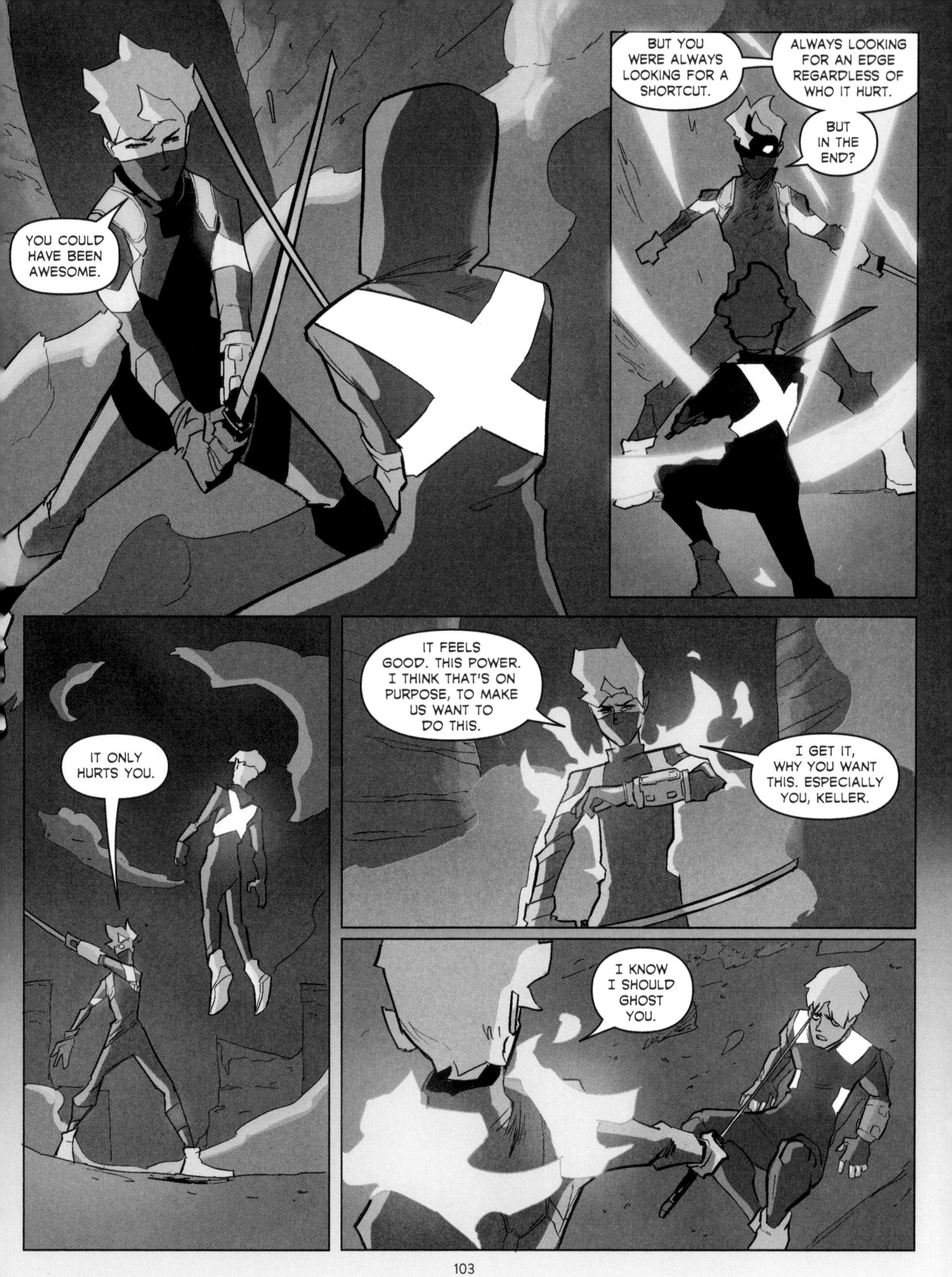
YOU COULD HAVE BEEN AWESOME.
BUT YOU WERE ALWAYS LOOKING FOR A SHORTCUT.
ALWAYS LOOKING FOR AN EDGE REGARDLESS OF WHO IT HURT.
BUT IN THE END?
IT ONLY HURTS YOU.
IT FEELS GOOD. THIS POWER. I THINK THAT'S ON PURPOSE, TO MAKE US WANT TO DO THIS.
I GET IT, WHY YOU WANT THIS. ESPECIALLY YOU, KELLER.
I KNOW I SHOULD GHOST YOU.

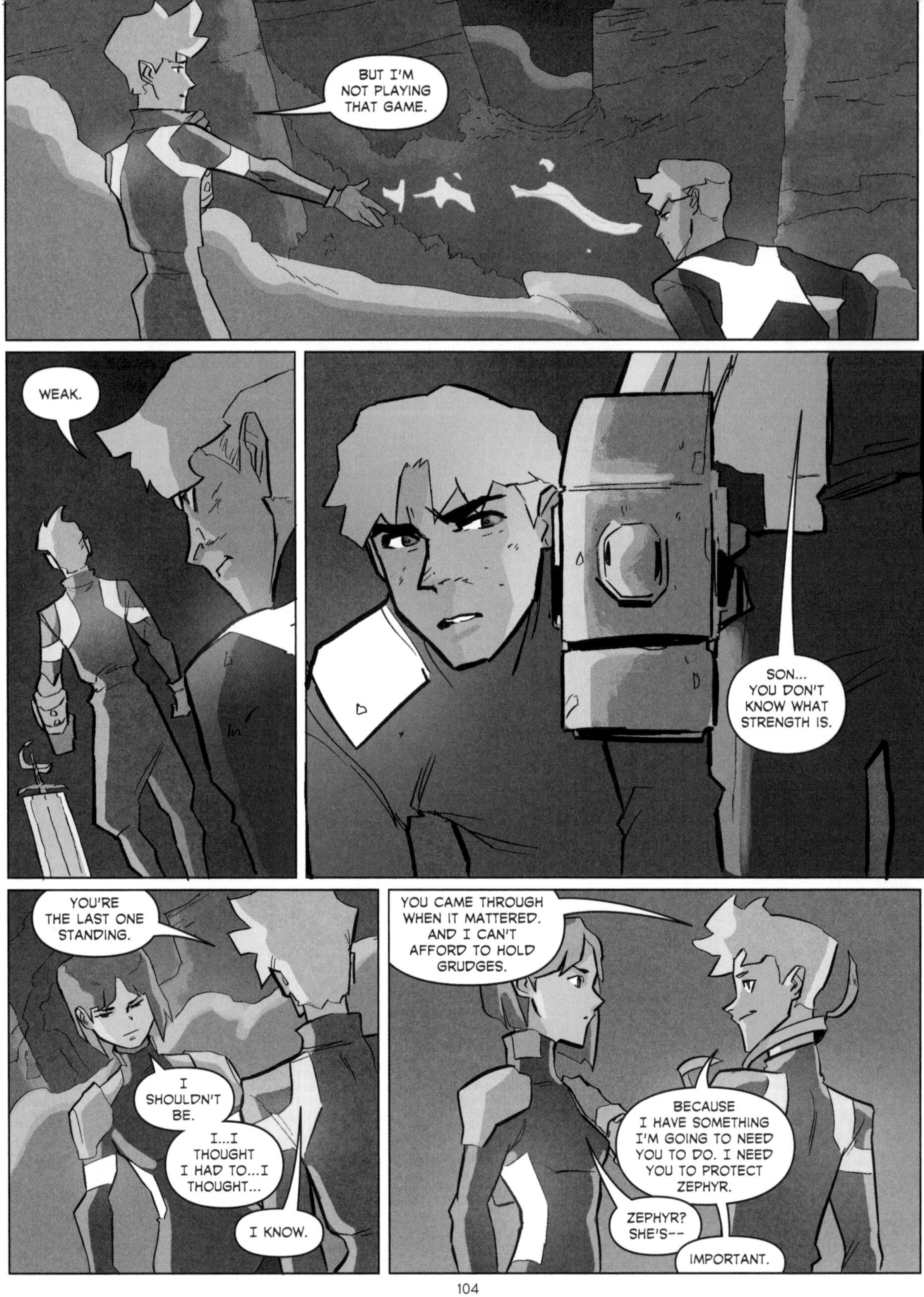
BUT I'M NOT PLAYING THAT GAME.
WEAK.
SON... YOU DON'T KNOW WHAT STRENGTH IS.
YOU'RE THE LAST ONE STANDING.
I SHOULDN'T BE.
I...I THOUGHT I HAD TO...I THOUGHT...
I KNOW.
YOU CAME THROUGH WHEN IT MATTERED. AND I CAN'T AFFORD TO HOLD GRUDGES.
BECAUSE I HAVE SOMETHING I'M GOING TO NEED YOU TO DO. I NEED YOU TO PROTECT ZEPHYR.
ZEPHYR? SHE'S--
IMPORTANT.

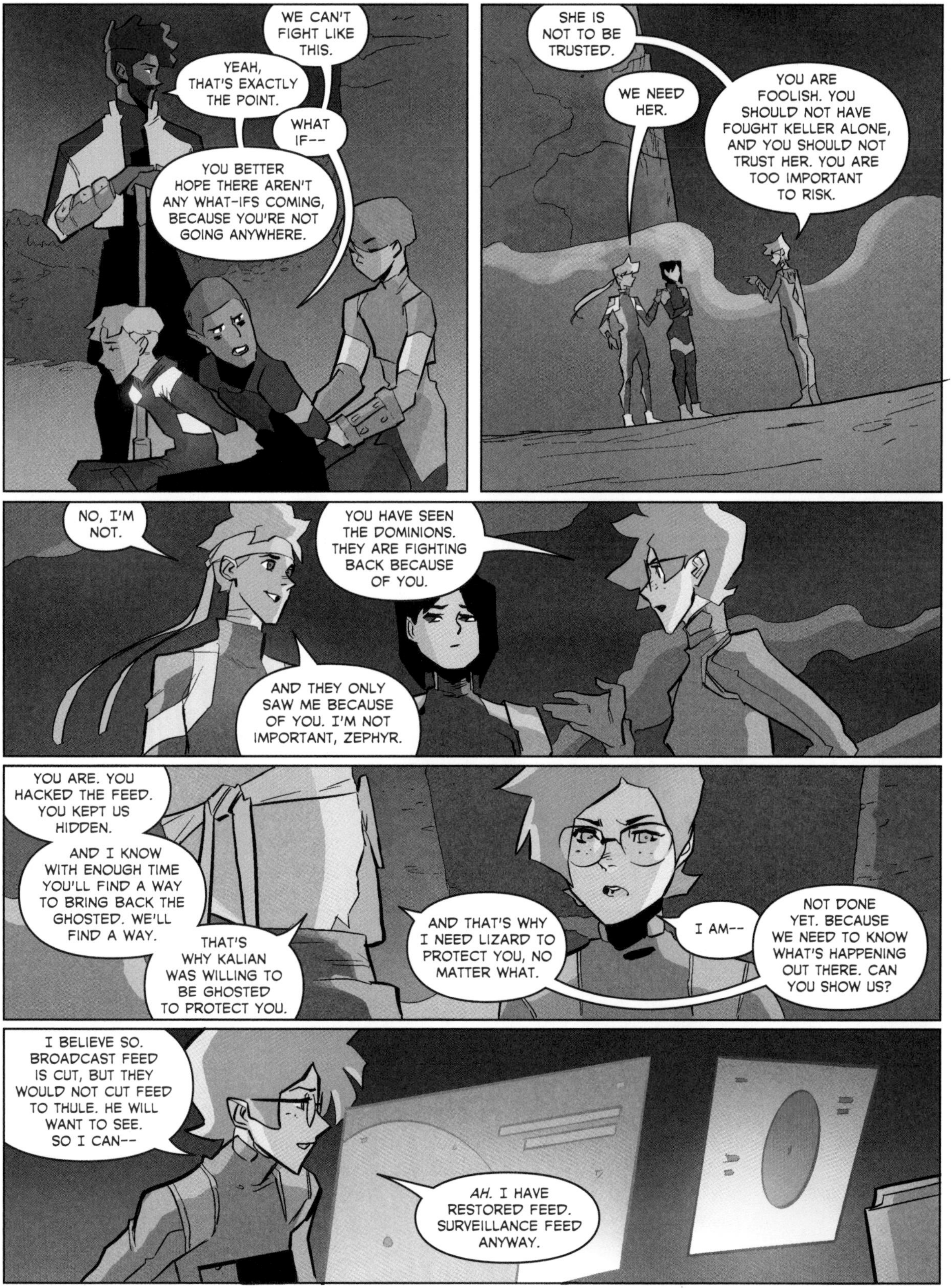
WE CAN'T FIGHT LIKE THIS.
YEAH, THAT'S EXACTLY THE POINT.
WHAT IF--
YOU BETTER HOPE THERE AREN'T ANY WHAT-IFS COMING, BECAUSE YOU'RE NOT GOING ANYWHERE.
SHE IS NOT TO BE TRUSTED.
WE NEED HER.
YOU ARE FOOLISH. YOU SHOULD NOT HAVE FOUGHT KELLER ALONE, AND YOU SHOULD NOT TRUST HER. YOU ARE TOO IMPORTANT TO RISK.
NO, I'M NOT.
YOU HAVE SEEN THE DOMINIONS. THEY ARE FIGHTING BACK BECAUSE OF YOU.
AND THEY ONLY SAW ME BECAUSE OF YOU. I'M NOT IMPORTANT, ZEPHYR.
YOU ARE. YOU HACKED THE FEED. YOU KEPT US HIDDEN.
AND I KNOW WITH ENOUGH TIME YOU'LL FIND A WAY TO BRING BACK THE GHOSTED. WE'LL FIND A WAY.
THAT'S WHY KALIAN WAS WILLING TO BE GHOSTED TO PROTECT YOU.
AND THAT'S WHY I NEED LIZARD TO PROTECT YOU, NO MATTER WHAT.
I AM--
NOT DONE YET. BECAUSE WE NEED TO KNOW WHAT'S HAPPENING OUT THERE. CAN YOU SHOW US?
I BELIEVE SO. BROADCAST FEED IS CUT, BUT THEY WOULD NOT CUT FEED TO THULE. HE WILL WANT TO SEE. SO I CAN--
AH. I HAVE RESTORED FEED. SURVEILLANCE FEED ANYWAY.

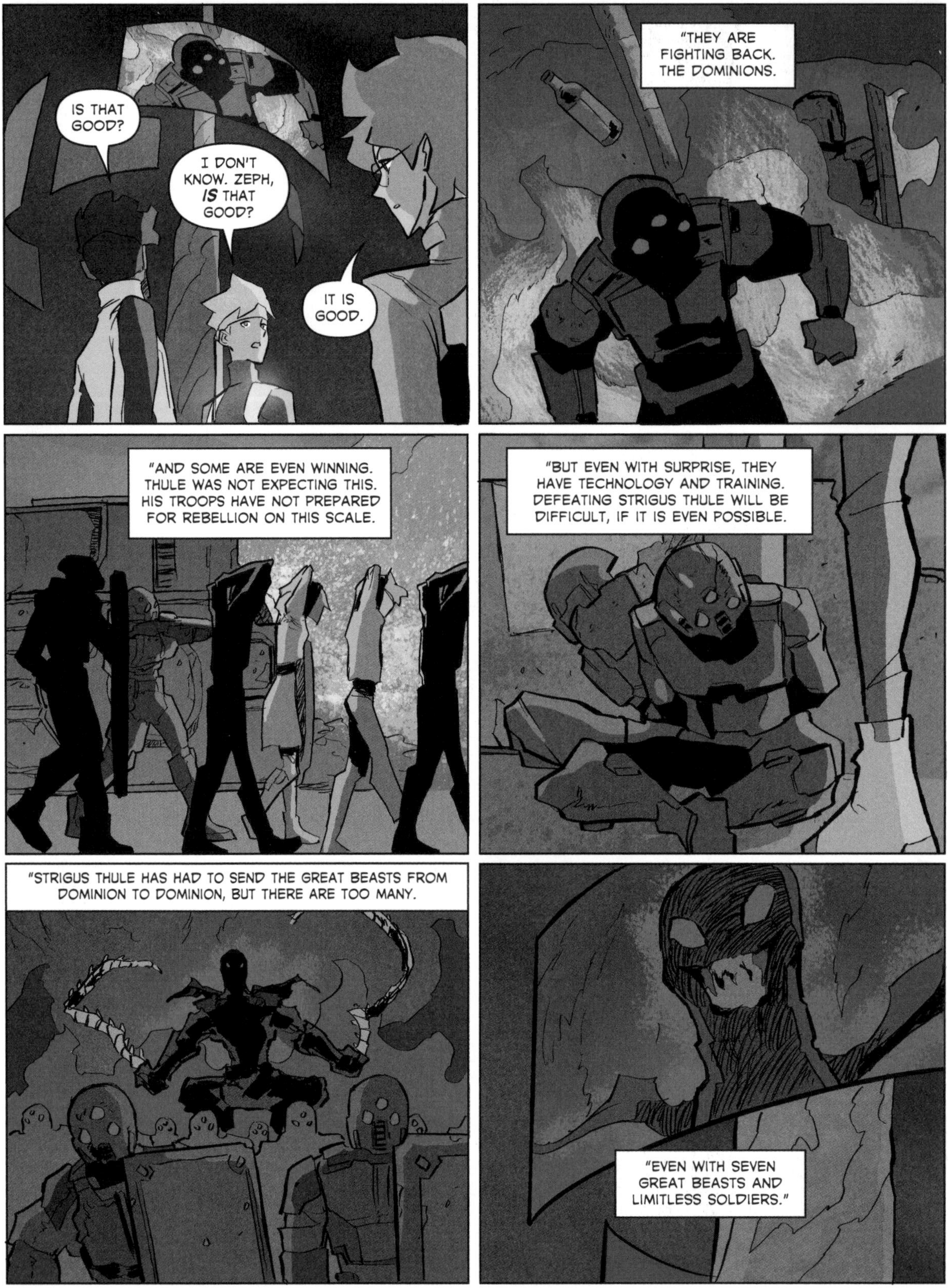
IS THAT GOOD?
I DON'T KNOW. ZEPH, *IS* THAT GOOD?
IT IS GOOD.
"THEY ARE FIGHTING BACK. THE DOMINIONS.
"AND SOME ARE EVEN WINNING. THULE WAS NOT EXPECTING THIS. HIS TROOPS HAVE NOT PREPARED FOR REBELLION ON THIS SCALE.
"BUT EVEN WITH SURPRISE, THEY HAVE TECHNOLOGY AND TRAINING. DEFEATING STRIGUS THULE WILL BE DIFFICULT, IF IT IS EVEN POSSIBLE.
"STRIGUS THULE HAS HAD TO SEND THE GREAT BEASTS FROM DOMINION TO DOMINION, BUT THERE ARE TOO MANY.
"EVEN WITH SEVEN GREAT BEASTS AND LIMITLESS SOLDIERS."

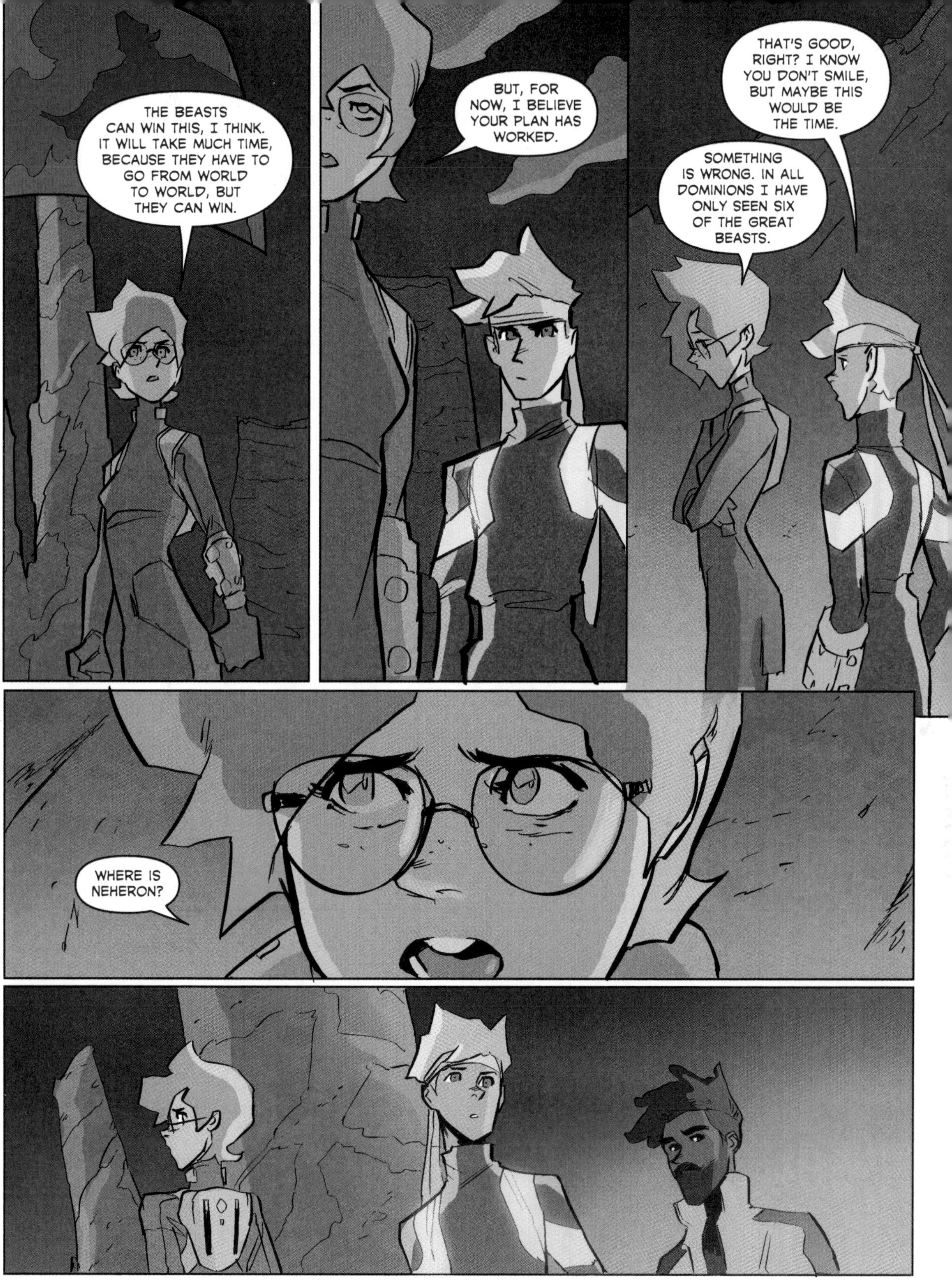
THE BEASTS CAN WIN THIS, I THINK. IT WILL TAKE MUCH TIME, BECAUSE THEY HAVE TO GO FROM WORLD TO WORLD, BUT THEY CAN WIN.
BUT, FOR NOW, I BELIEVE YOUR PLAN HAS WORKED.
THAT'S GOOD, RIGHT? I KNOW YOU DON'T SMILE, BUT MAYBE THIS WOULD BE THE TIME.
SOMETHING IS WRONG. IN ALL DOMINIONS I HAVE ONLY SEEN SIX OF THE GREAT BEASTS.
WHERE IS NEHERON?

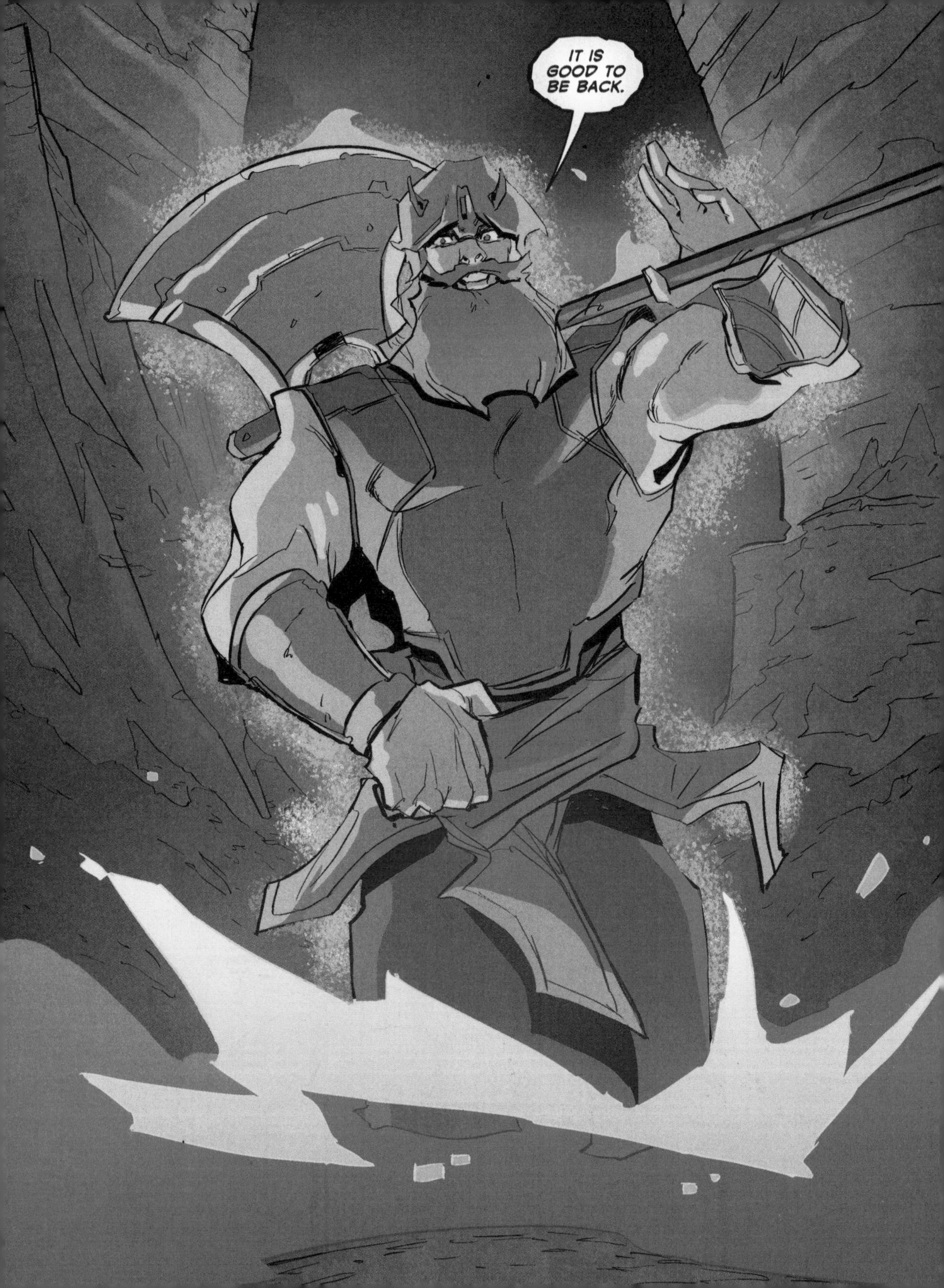
IT IS GOOD TO BE BACK.

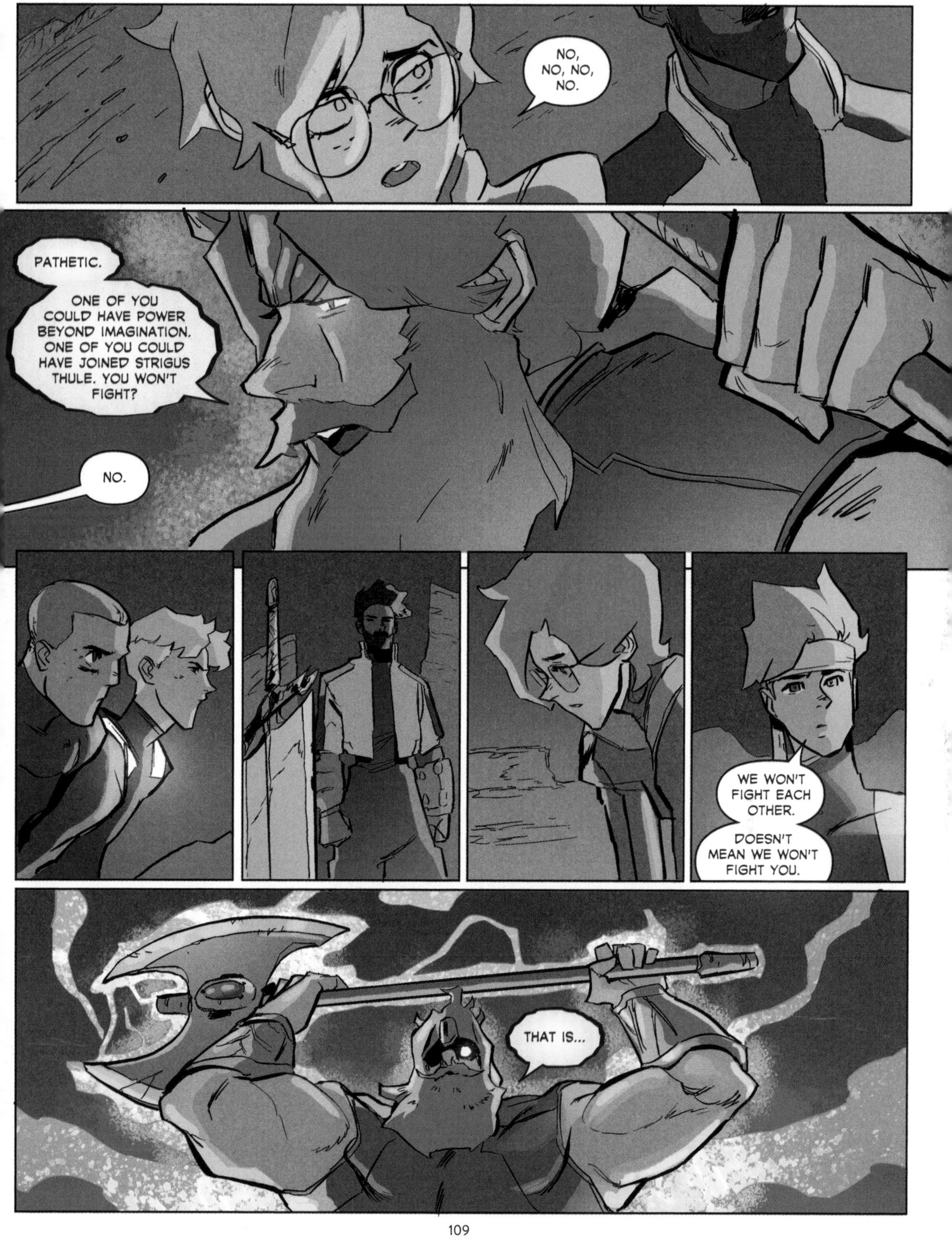
NO, NO, NO, NO.
PATHETIC.
ONE OF YOU COULD HAVE POWER BEYOND IMAGINATION. ONE OF YOU COULD HAVE JOINED STRIGUS THULE. YOU WON'T FIGHT?
NO.
WE WON'T FIGHT EACH OTHER.
DOESN'T MEAN WE WON'T FIGHT YOU.
THAT IS...

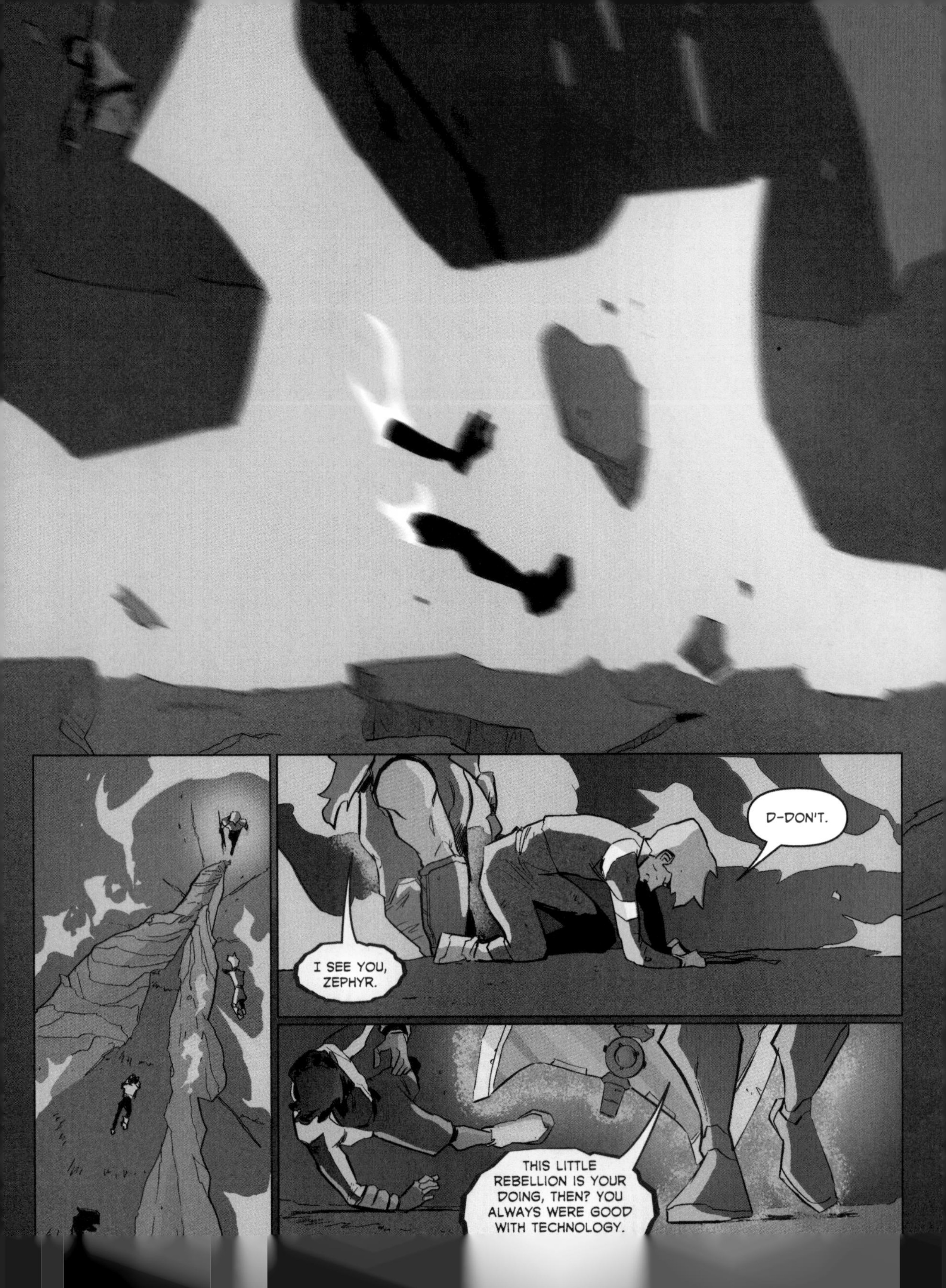

D-DON'T.
I SEE YOU, ZEPHYR.
THIS LITTLE REBELLION IS YOUR DOING, THEN? YOU ALWAYS WERE GOOD WITH TECHNOLOGY.

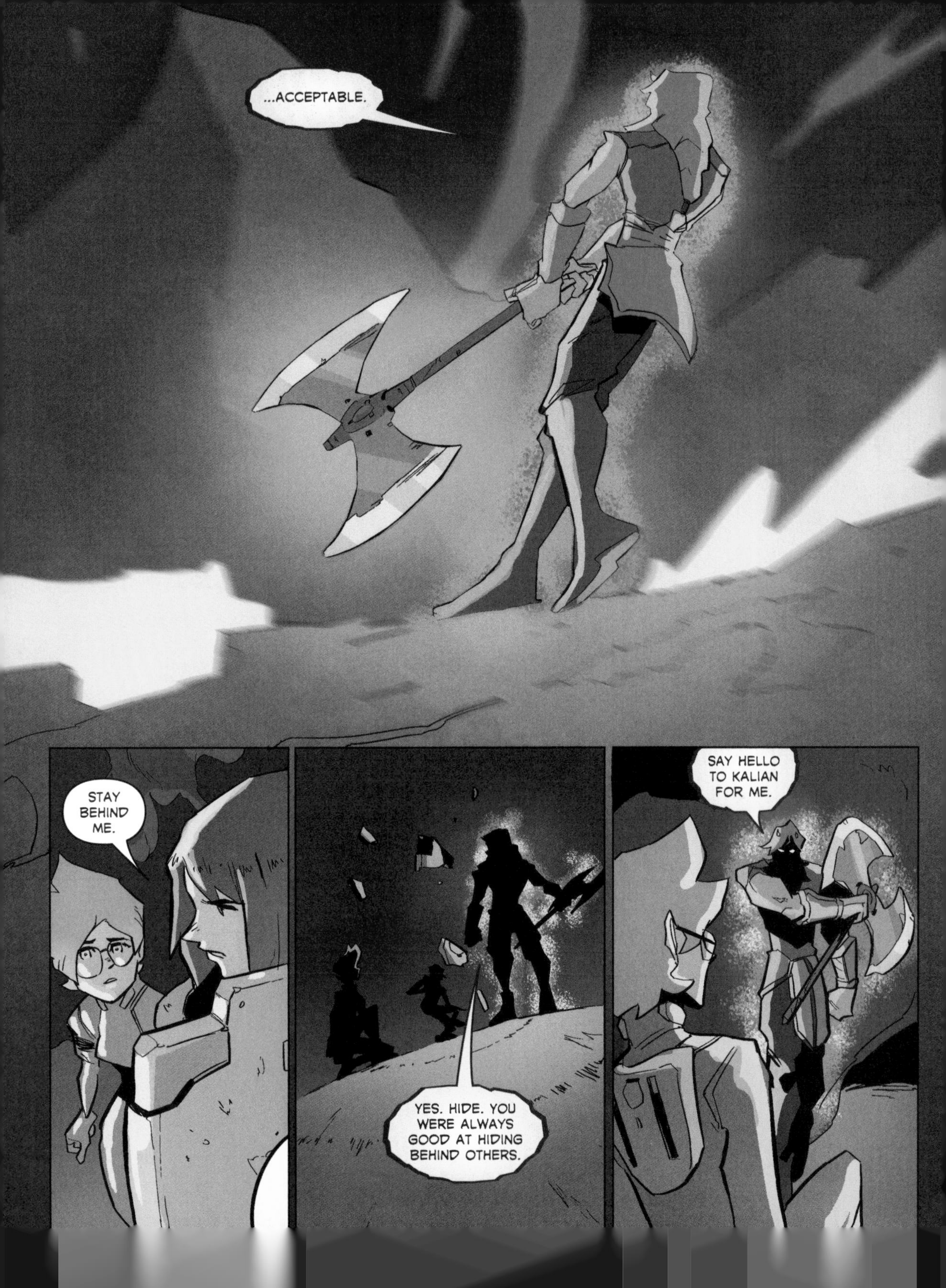
...ACCEPTABLE.
STAY BEHIND ME.
YES. HIDE. YOU WERE ALWAYS GOOD AT HIDING BEHIND OTHERS.
SAY HELLO TO KALIAN FOR ME.

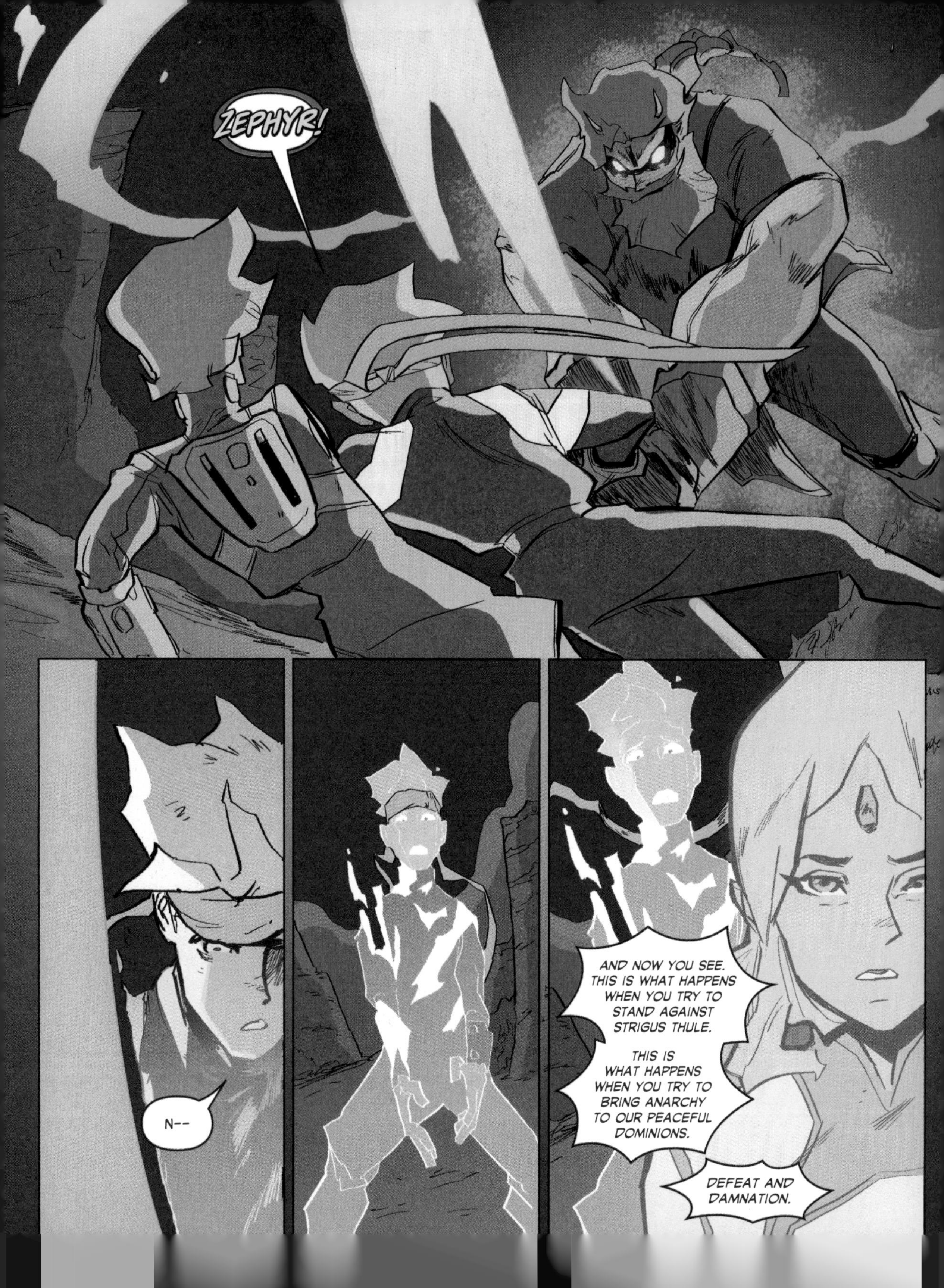
ZEPHYR!
N--
AND NOW YOU SEE. THIS IS WHAT HAPPENS WHEN YOU TRY TO STAND AGAINST STRIGUS THULE.
THIS IS WHAT HAPPENS WHEN YOU TRY TO BRING ANARCHY TO OUR PEACEFUL DOMINIONS.
DEFEAT AND DAMNATION.

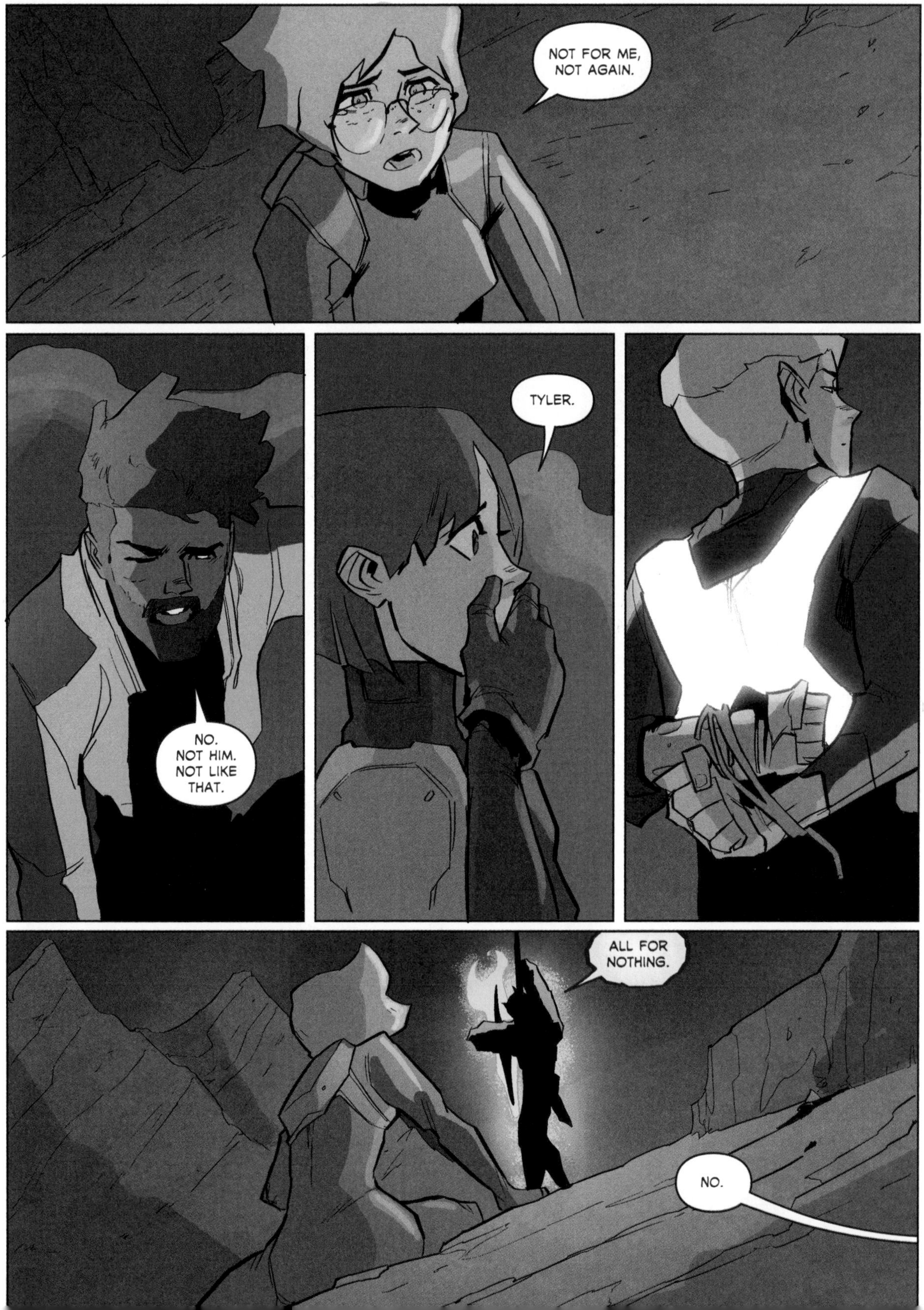
NOT FOR ME, NOT AGAIN.
NO. NOT HIM. NOT LIKE THAT.
TYLER.
ALL FOR NOTHING.
NO.

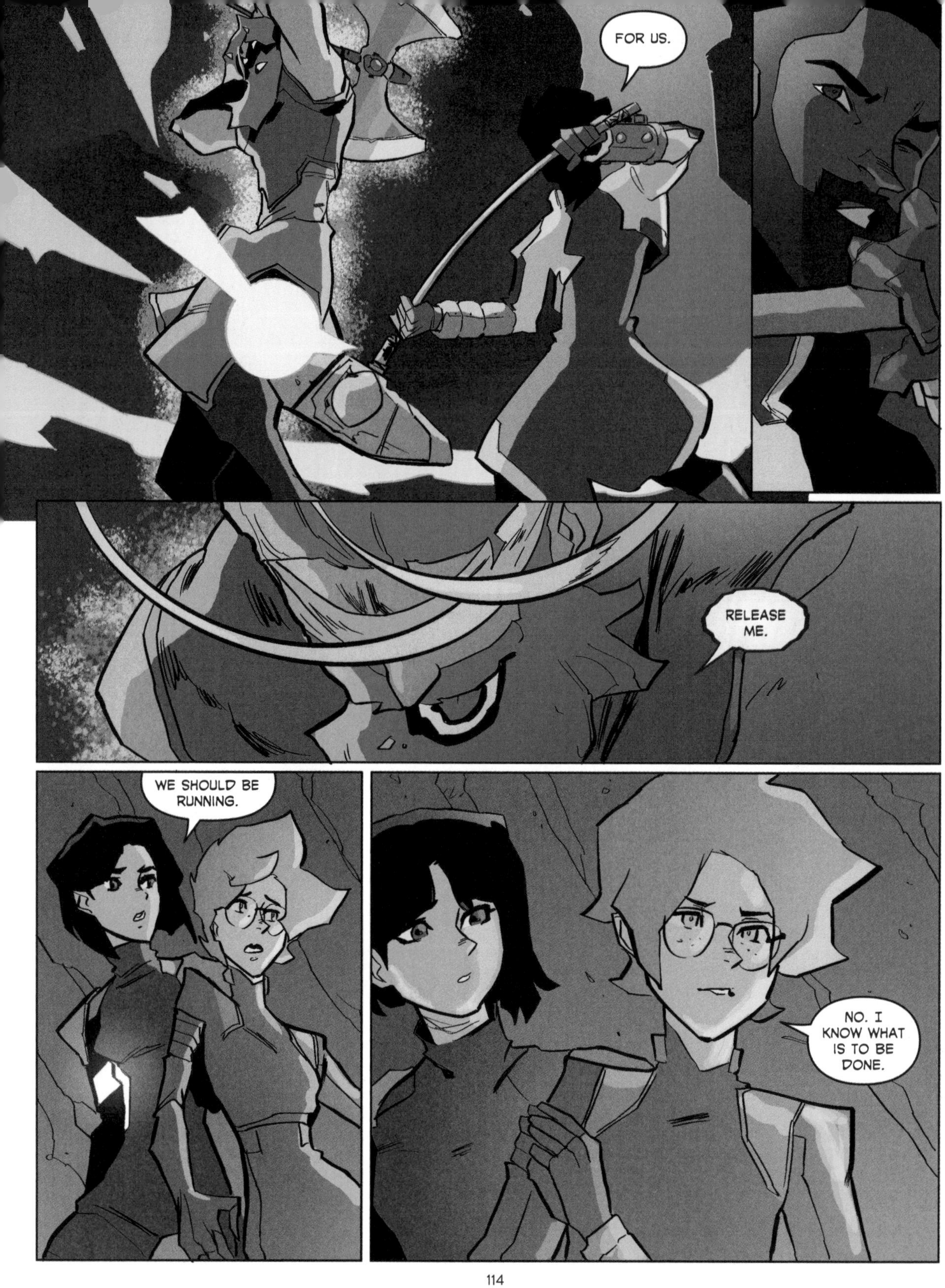
FOR US.
RELEASE ME.
WE SHOULD BE RUNNING.
NO. I KNOW WHAT IS TO BE DONE.

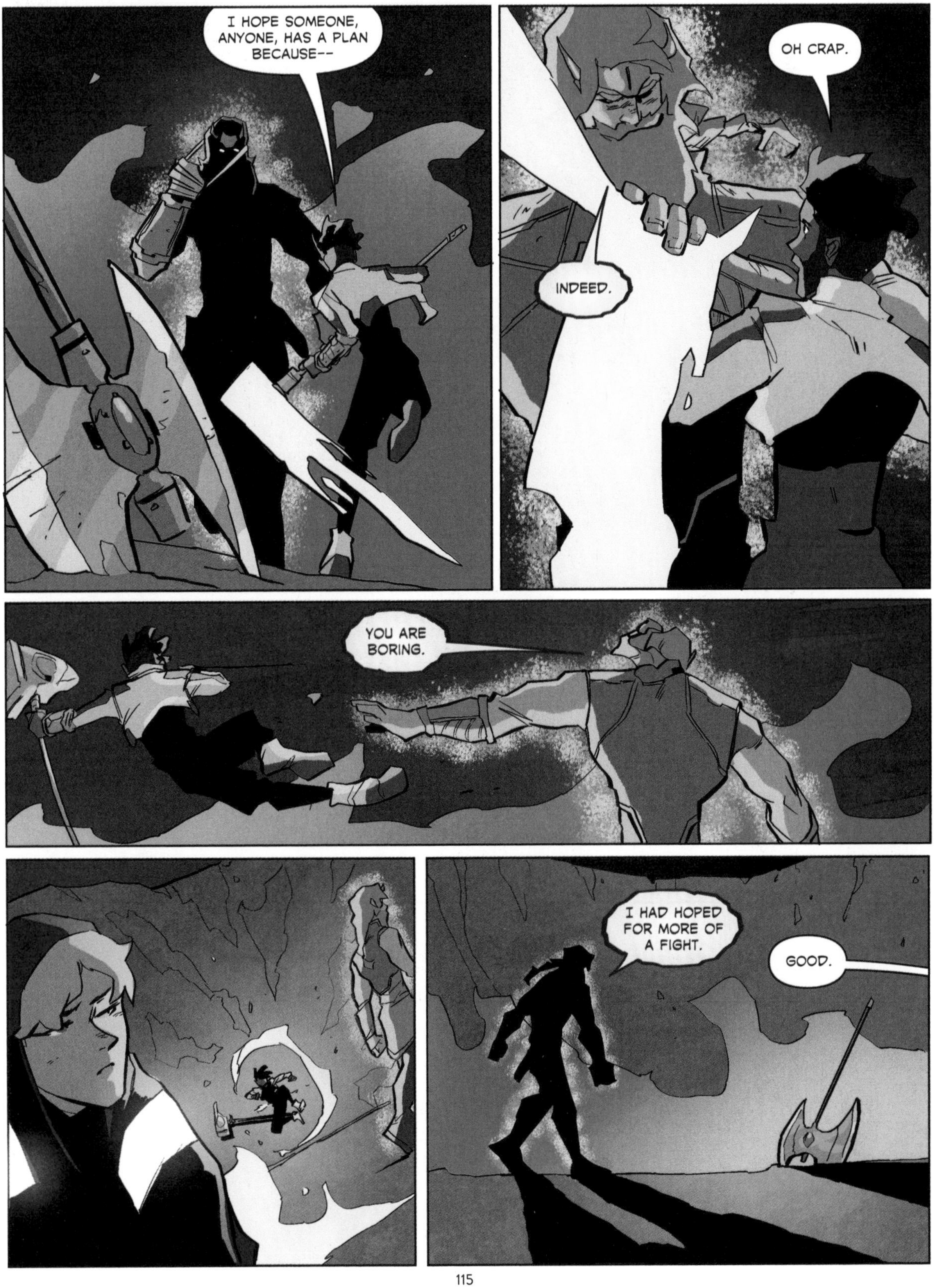

I HOPE SOMEONE, ANYONE, HAS A PLAN BECAUSE--
OH CRAP.
INDEED.
YOU ARE BORING.
I HAD HOPED FOR MORE OF A FIGHT.
GOOD.

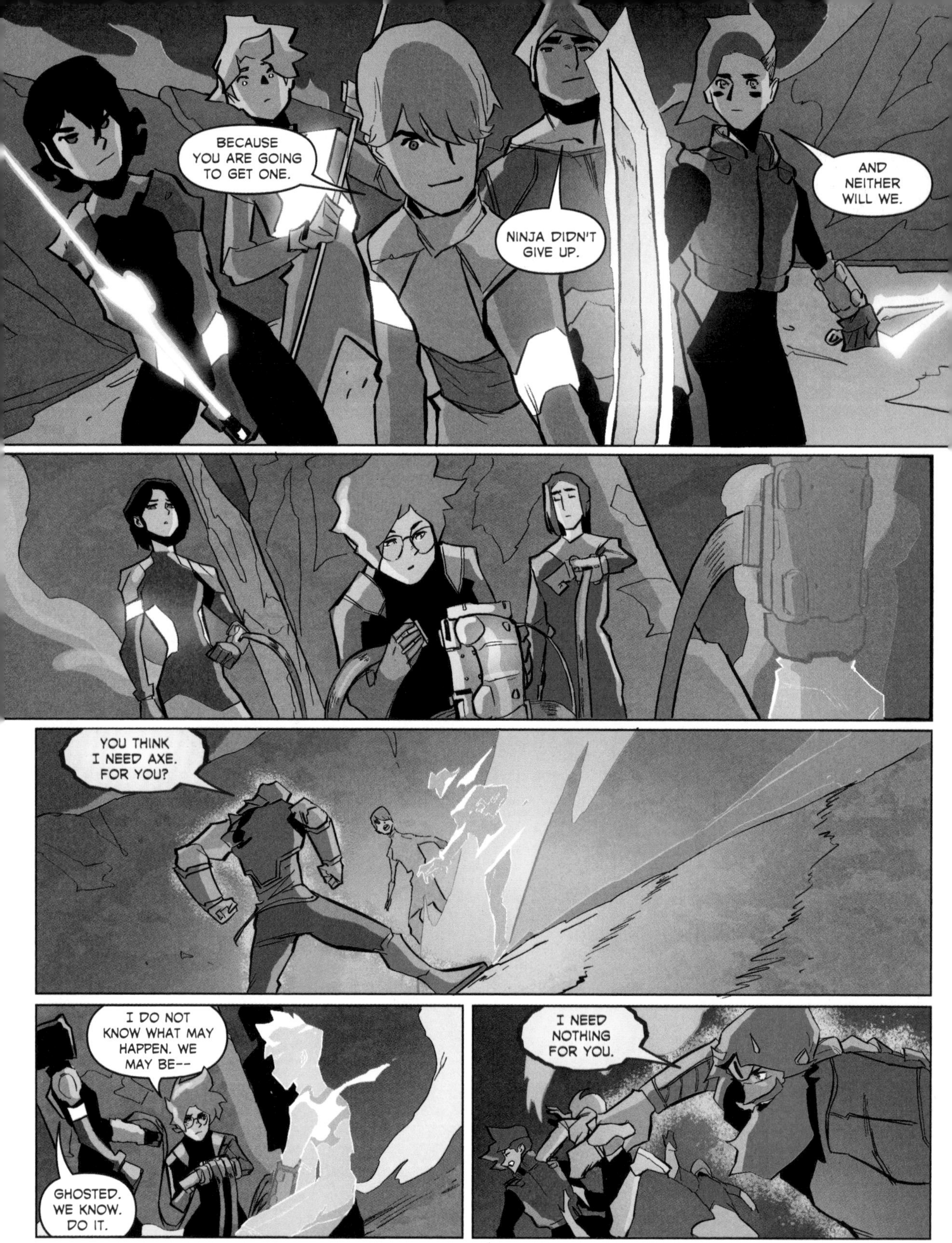
BECAUSE YOU ARE GOING TO GET ONE.
NINJA DIDN'T GIVE UP.
AND NEITHER WILL WE.
YOU THINK I NEED AXE. FOR YOU?
I DO NOT KNOW WHAT MAY HAPPEN. WE MAY BE--
GHOSTED. WE KNOW. DO IT.
I NEED NOTHING FOR YOU.

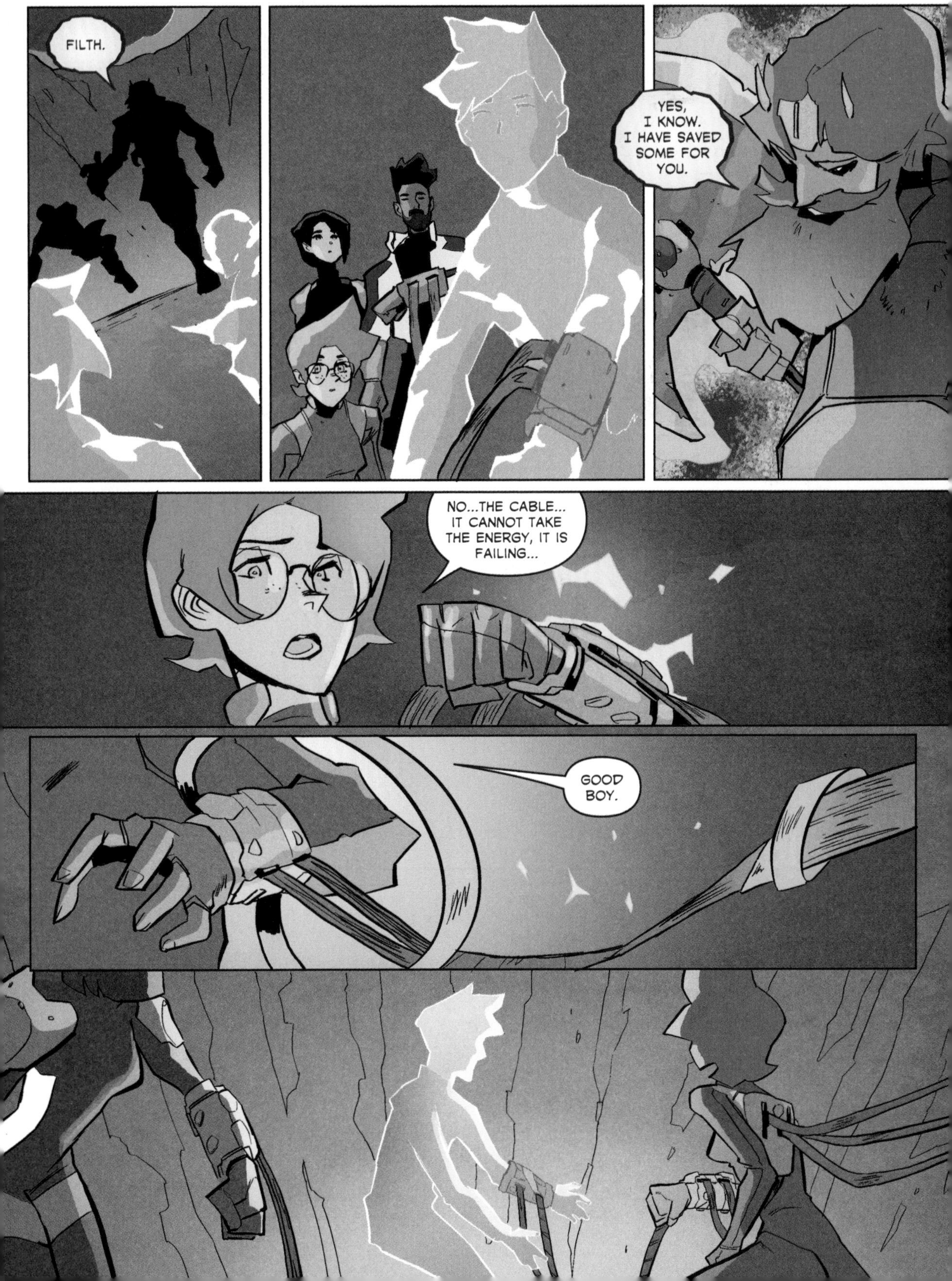
FILTH.
YES, I KNOW. I HAVE SAVED SOME FOR YOU.
NO...THE CABLE... IT CANNOT TAKE THE ENERGY, IT IS FAILING...
GOOD BOY.

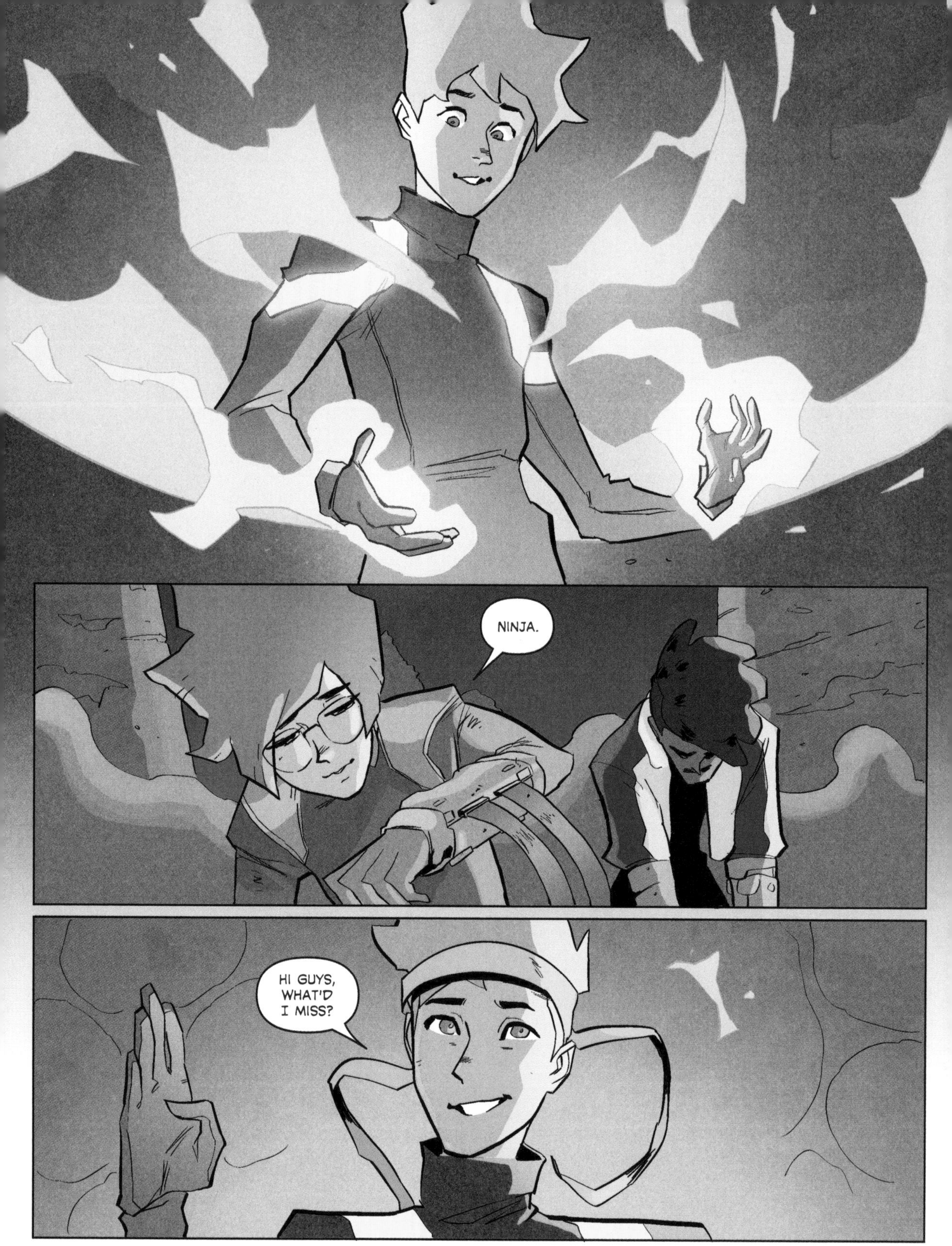
NINJA.
HI GUYS, WHAT'D I MISS?

DOOM.

NNNFF.

SO MUCH EFFORT, WHEN YOU ONLY WILL BE GHOSTED AGAIN.

NINJA!

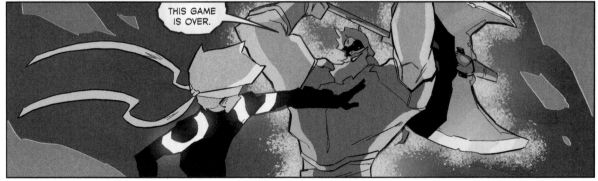

THIS GAME IS OVER.

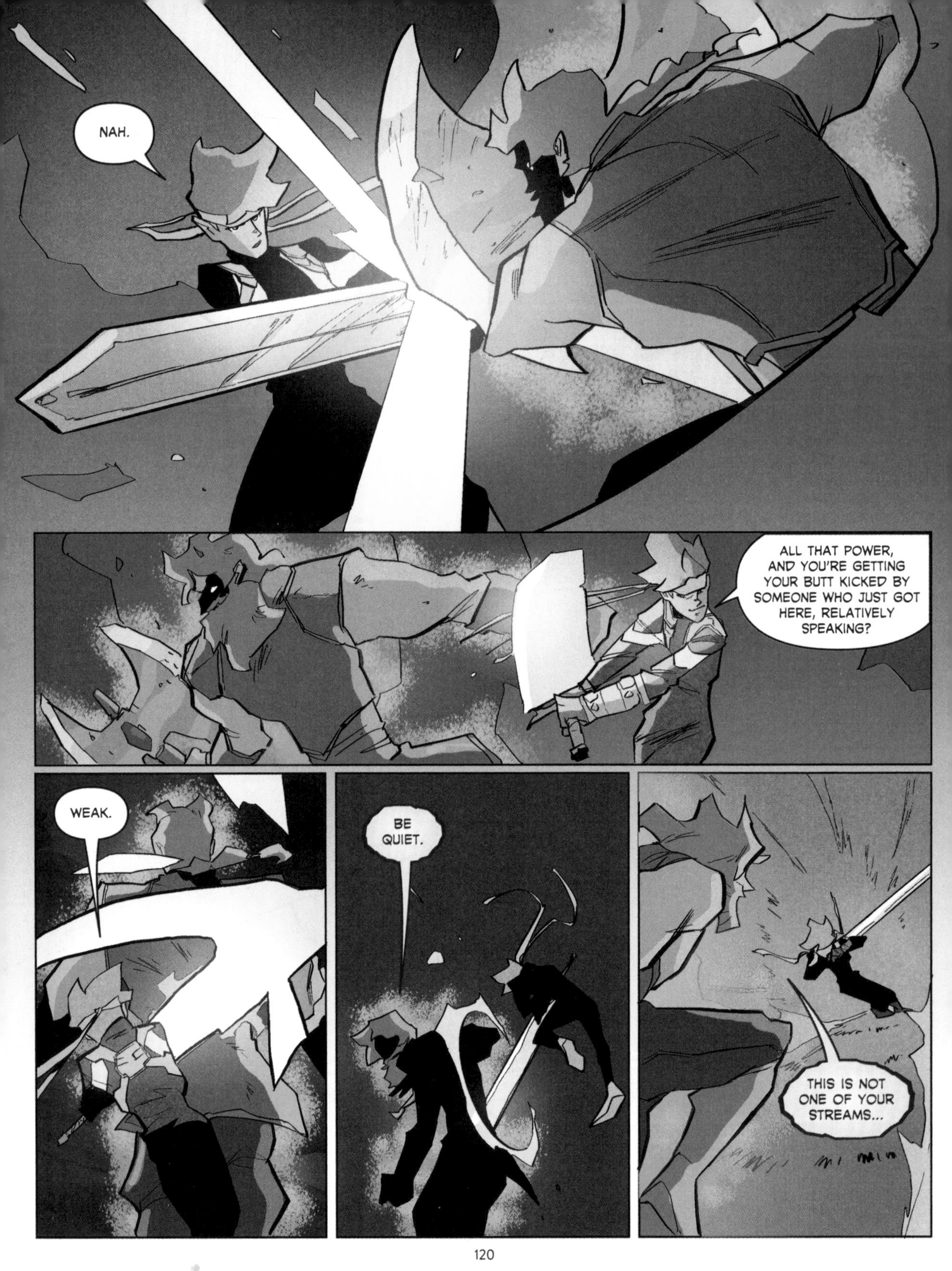
NAH.
ALL THAT POWER, AND YOU'RE GETTING YOUR BUTT KICKED BY SOMEONE WHO JUST GOT HERE, RELATIVELY SPEAKING?
WEAK.
BE QUIET.
THIS IS NOT ONE OF YOUR STREAMS...

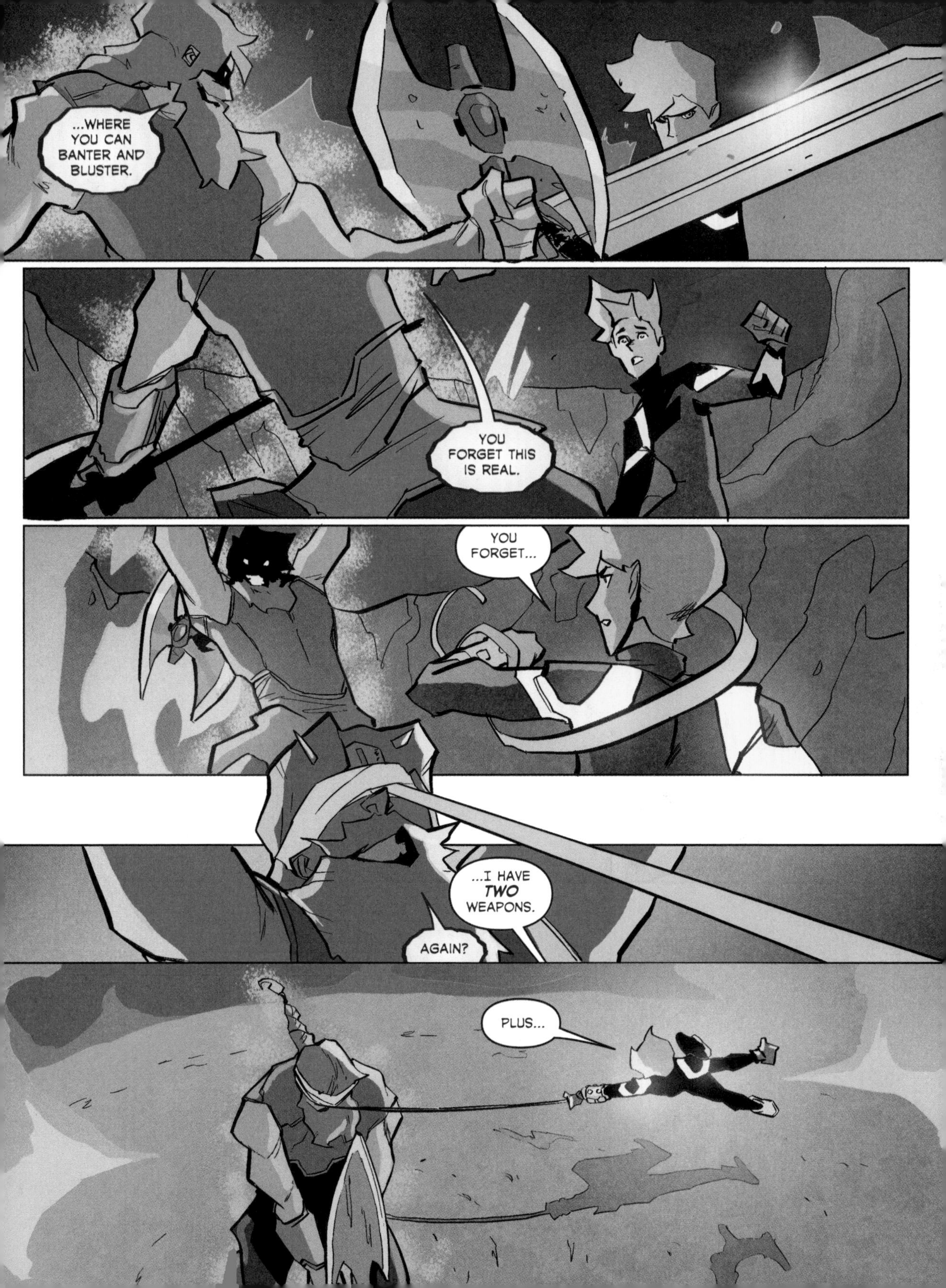
...WHERE YOU CAN BANTER AND BLUSTER.
YOU FORGET THIS IS REAL.
YOU FORGET...
...I HAVE *TWO* WEAPONS.
AGAIN?
PLUS...

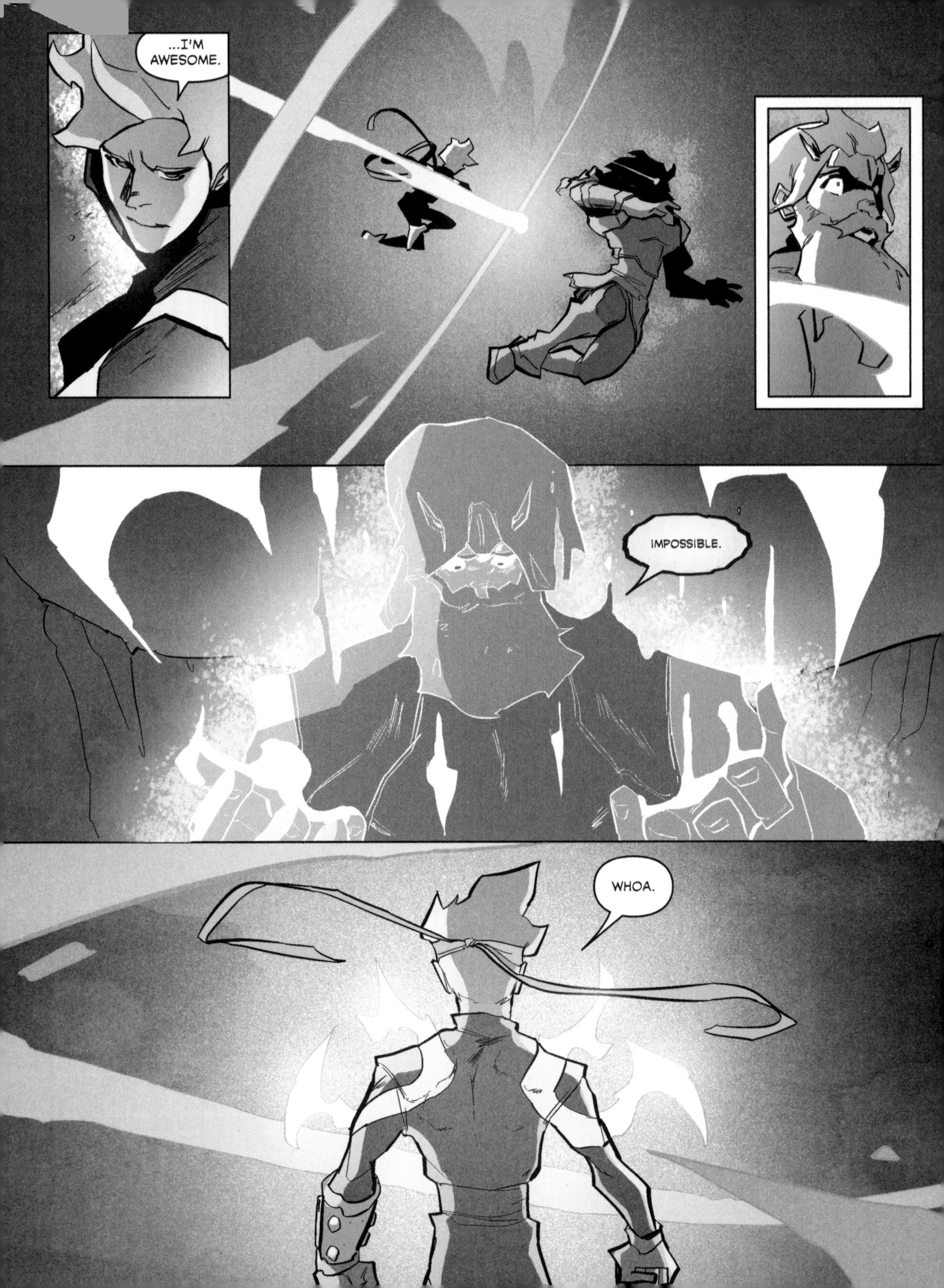
...I'M AWESOME.
IMPOSSIBLE.
WHOA.

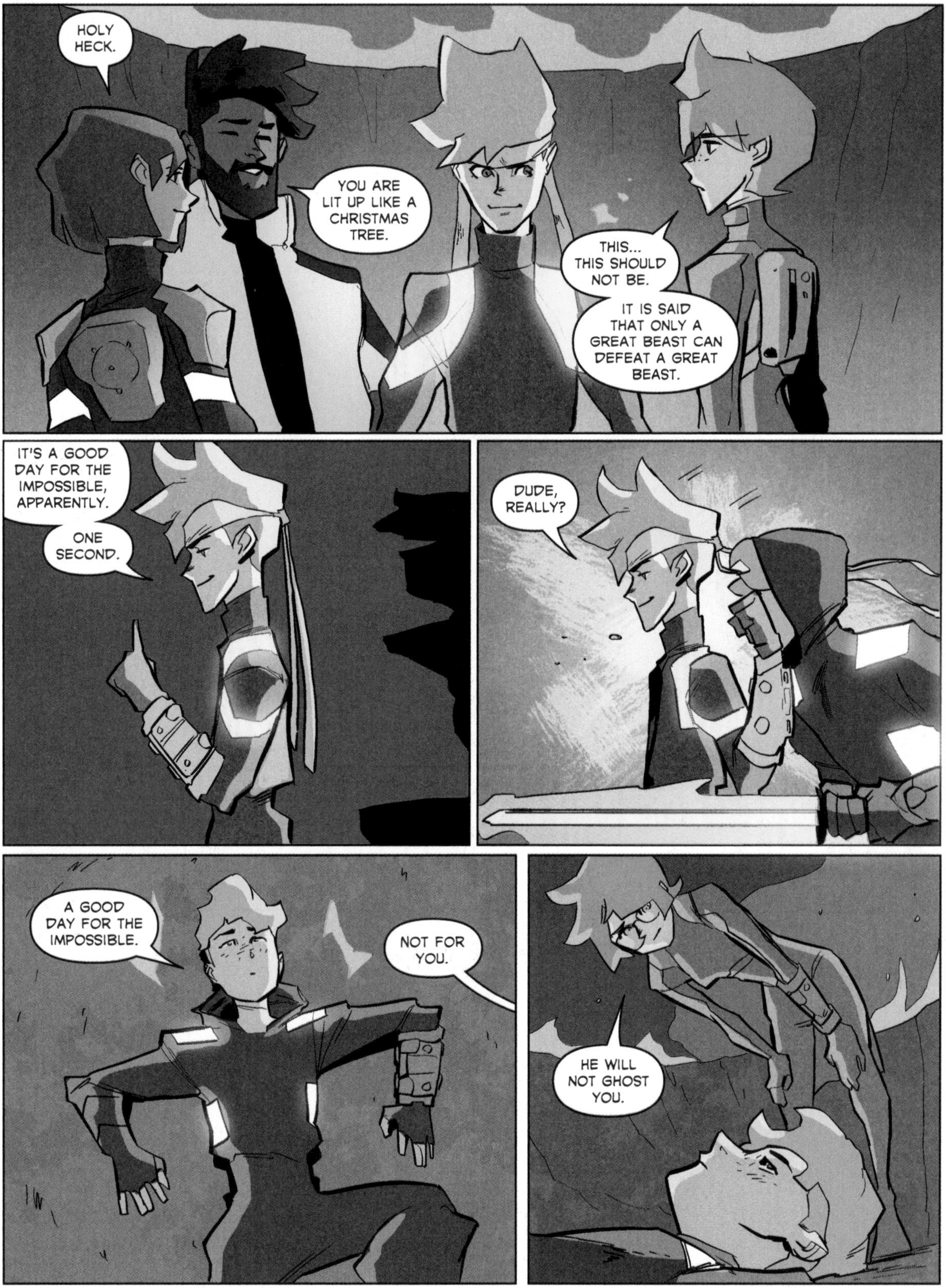
HOLY HECK.
YOU ARE LIT UP LIKE A CHRISTMAS TREE.
THIS... THIS SHOULD NOT BE.
IT IS SAID THAT ONLY A GREAT BEAST CAN DEFEAT A GREAT BEAST.
IT'S A GOOD DAY FOR THE IMPOSSIBLE, APPARENTLY.
ONE SECOND.
DUDE, REALLY?
A GOOD DAY FOR THE IMPOSSIBLE.
NOT FOR YOU.
HE WILL NOT GHOST YOU.

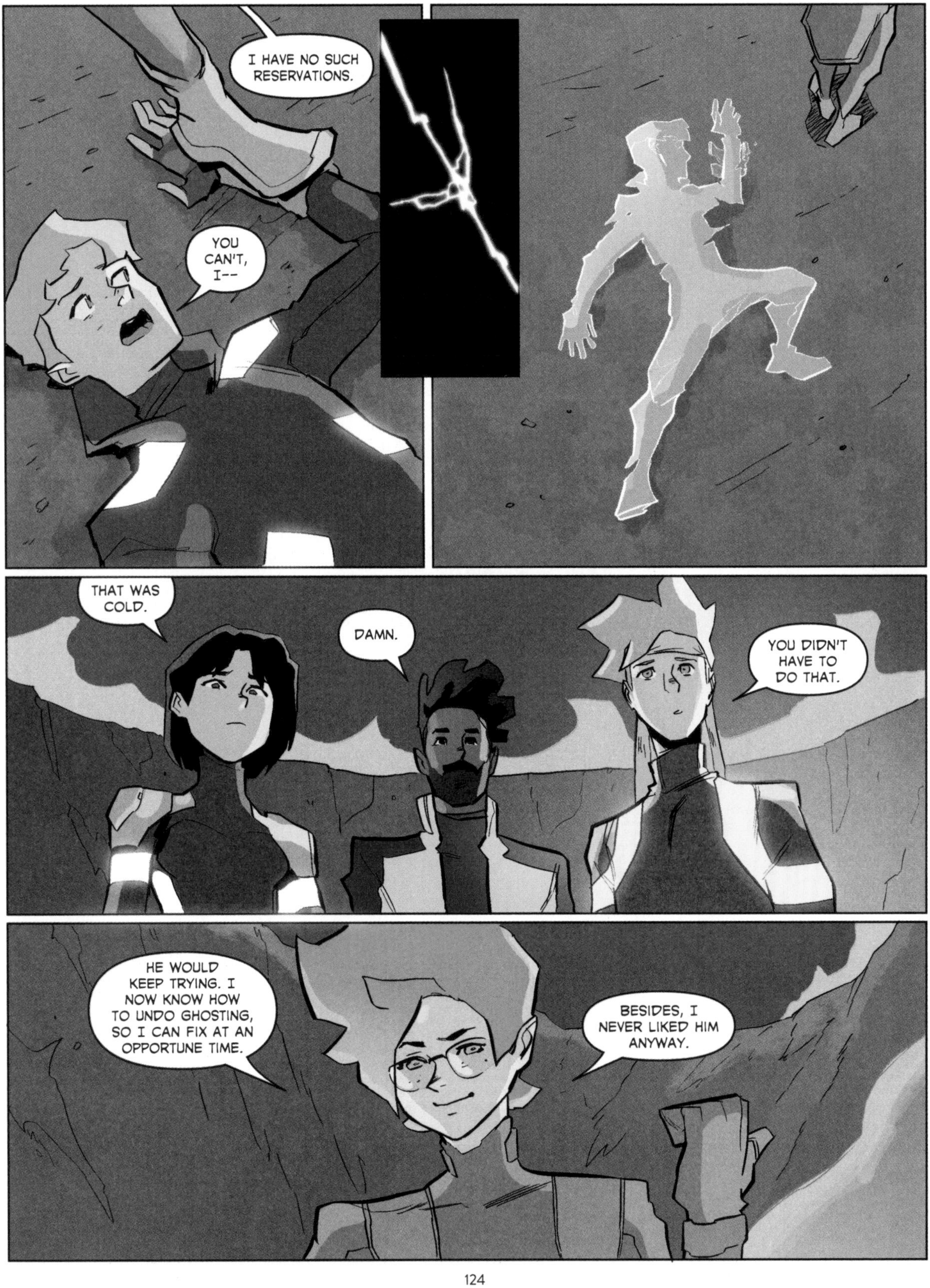
I HAVE NO SUCH RESERVATIONS.
YOU CAN'T, I--
THAT WAS COLD.
DAMN.
YOU DIDN'T HAVE TO DO THAT.
HE WOULD KEEP TRYING. I NOW KNOW HOW TO UNDO GHOSTING, SO I CAN FIX AT AN OPPORTUNE TIME.
BESIDES, I NEVER LIKED HIM ANYWAY.

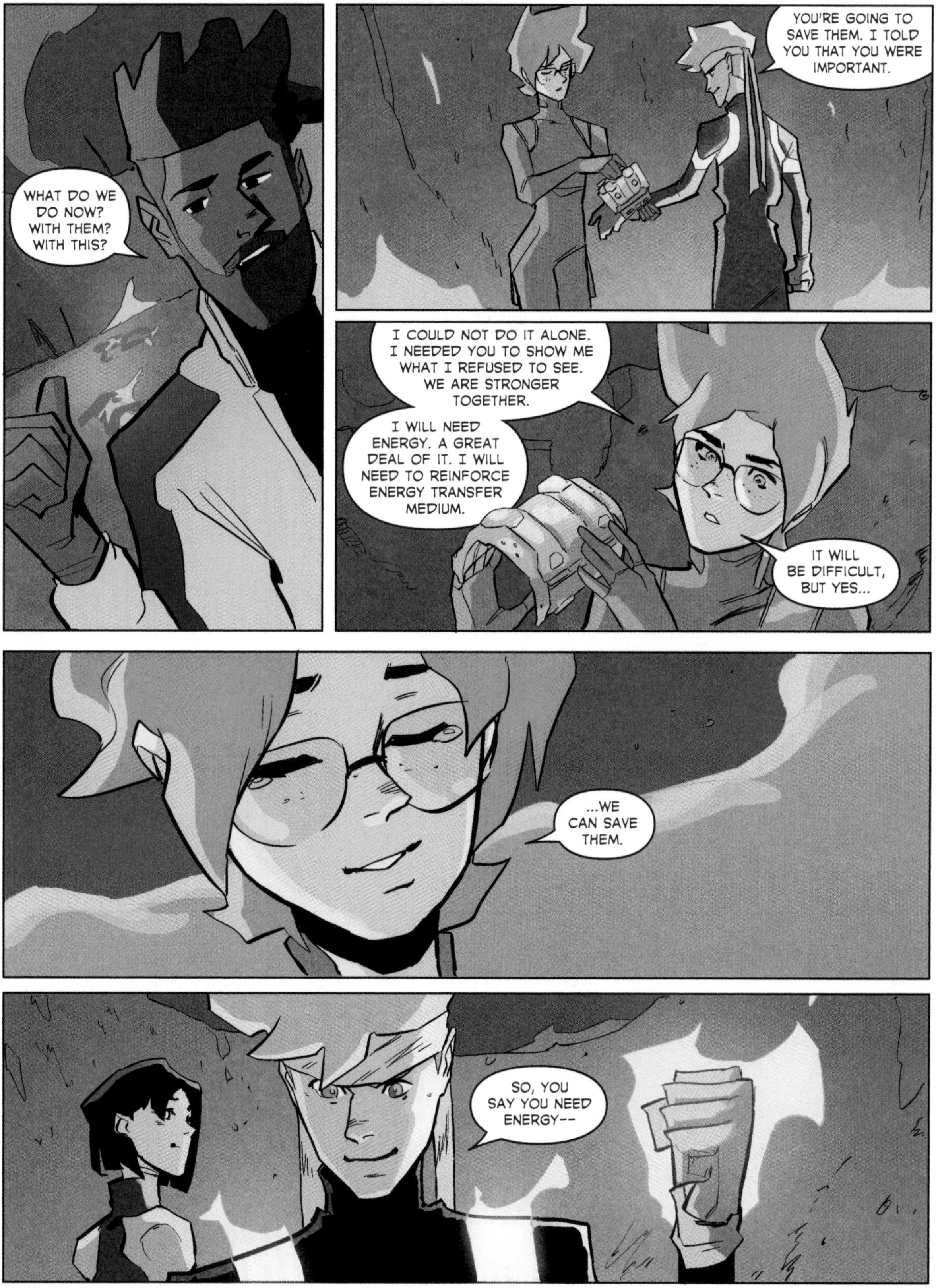
WHAT DO WE DO NOW? WITH THEM? WITH THIS?
YOU'RE GOING TO SAVE THEM. I TOLD YOU THAT YOU WERE IMPORTANT.
I COULD NOT DO IT ALONE. I NEEDED YOU TO SHOW ME WHAT I REFUSED TO SEE. WE ARE STRONGER TOGETHER.
I WILL NEED ENERGY. A GREAT DEAL OF IT. I WILL NEED TO REINFORCE ENERGY TRANSFER MEDIUM.
IT WILL BE DIFFICULT, BUT YES...
...WE CAN SAVE THEM.
SO, YOU SAY YOU NEED ENERGY--

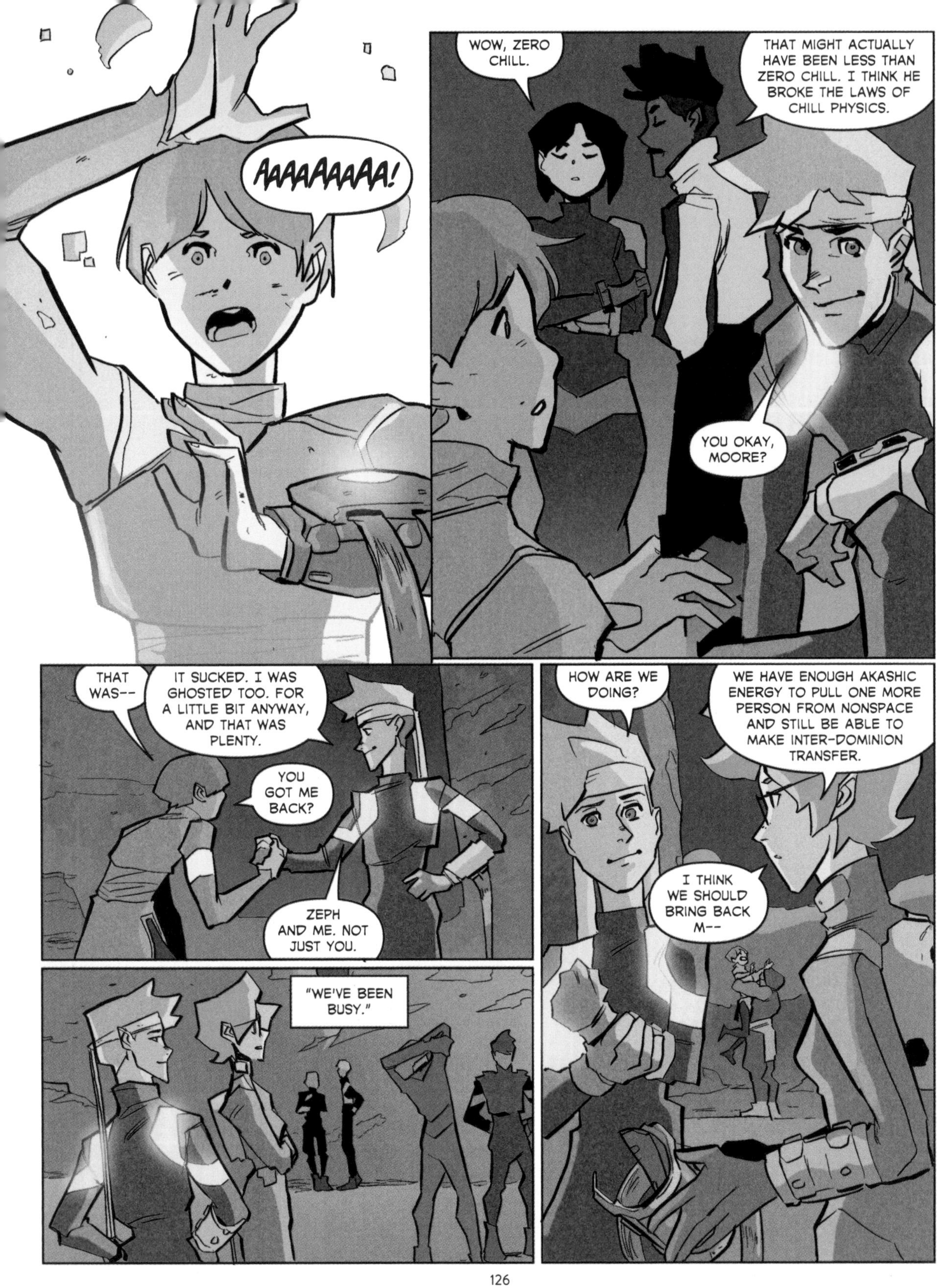
AAAAAAAAA!
WOW, ZERO CHILL.
THAT MIGHT ACTUALLY HAVE BEEN LESS THAN ZERO CHILL. I THINK HE BROKE THE LAWS OF CHILL PHYSICS.
YOU OKAY, MOORE?
THAT WAS--
IT SUCKED. I WAS GHOSTED TOO. FOR A LITTLE BIT ANYWAY, AND THAT WAS PLENTY.
YOU GOT ME BACK?
ZEPH AND ME. NOT JUST YOU.
"WE'VE BEEN BUSY."
HOW ARE WE DOING?
WE HAVE ENOUGH AKASHIC ENERGY TO PULL ONE MORE PERSON FROM NONSPACE AND STILL BE ABLE TO MAKE INTER-DOMINION TRANSFER.
I THINK WE SHOULD BRING BACK M--

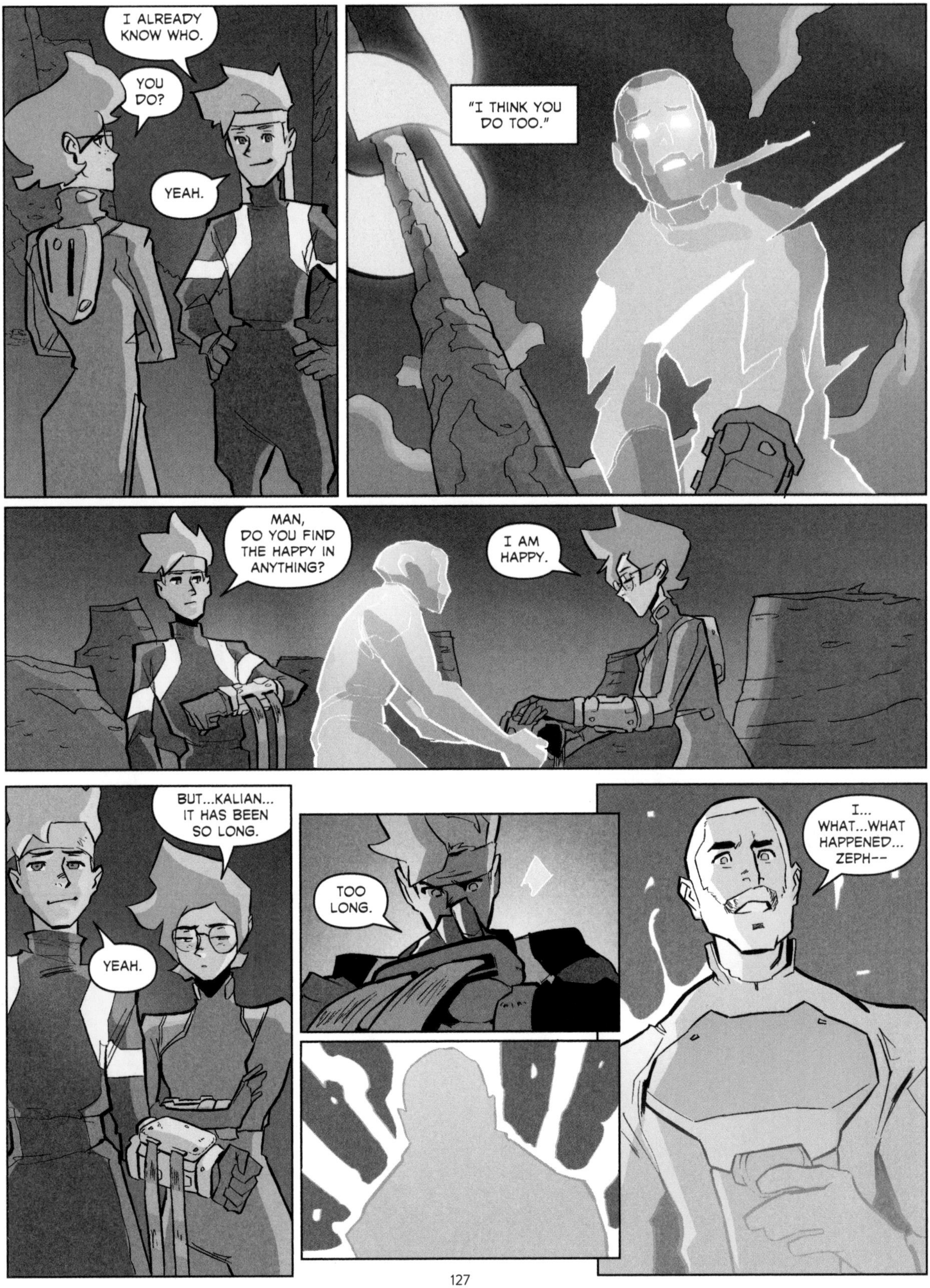
I ALREADY KNOW WHO.
YOU DO?
YEAH.
"I THINK YOU DO TOO."
MAN, DO YOU FIND THE HAPPY IN ANYTHING?
I AM HAPPY.
BUT...KALIAN... IT HAS BEEN SO LONG.
YEAH.
TOO LONG.
I... WHAT...WHAT HAPPENED... ZEPH--

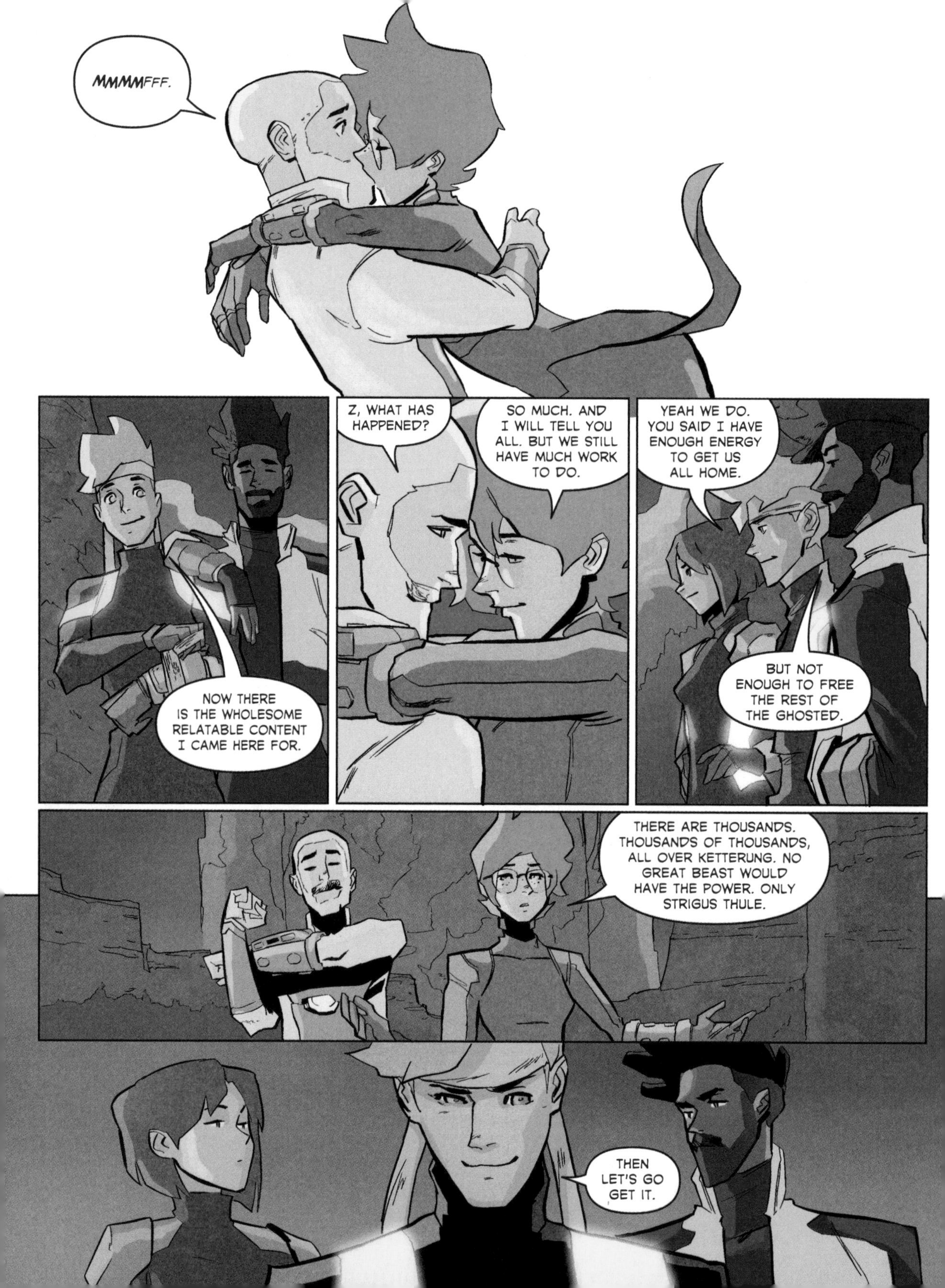
MMMMFFF.
NOW THERE IS THE WHOLESOME RELATABLE CONTENT I CAME HERE FOR.
Z, WHAT HAS HAPPENED?
SO MUCH. AND I WILL TELL YOU ALL. BUT WE STILL HAVE MUCH WORK TO DO.
YEAH WE DO. YOU SAID I HAVE ENOUGH ENERGY TO GET US ALL HOME.
BUT NOT ENOUGH TO FREE THE REST OF THE GHOSTED.
THERE ARE THOUSANDS. THOUSANDS OF THOUSANDS, ALL OVER KETTERUNG. NO GREAT BEAST WOULD HAVE THE POWER. ONLY STRIGUS THULE.
THEN LET'S GO GET IT.

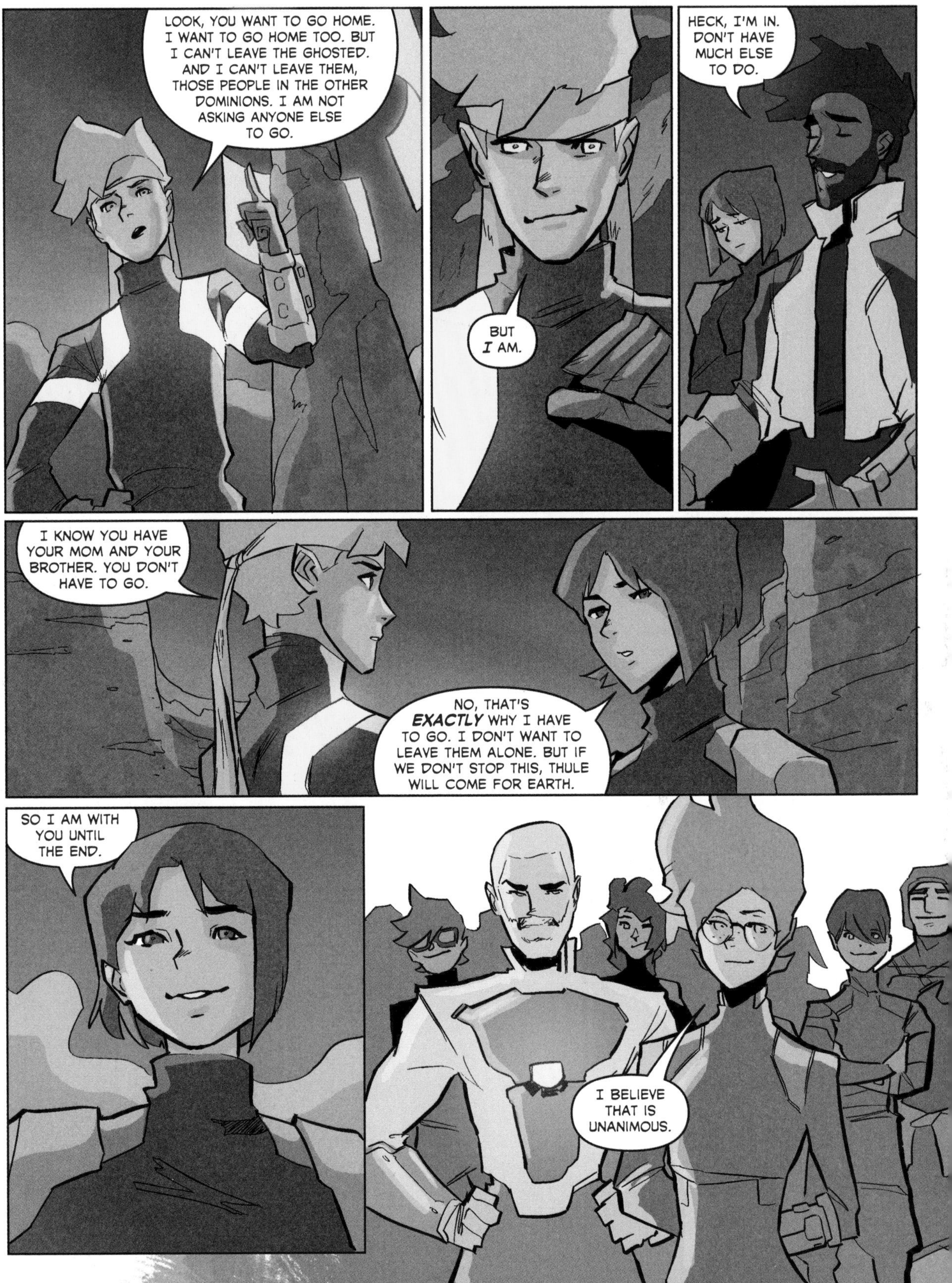
LOOK, YOU WANT TO GO HOME. I WANT TO GO HOME TOO. BUT I CAN'T LEAVE THE GHOSTED. AND I CAN'T LEAVE THEM, THOSE PEOPLE IN THE OTHER DOMINIONS. I AM NOT ASKING ANYONE ELSE TO GO.
BUT *I* AM.
HECK, I'M IN. DON'T HAVE MUCH ELSE TO DO.
I KNOW YOU HAVE YOUR MOM AND YOUR BROTHER. YOU DON'T HAVE TO GO.
NO, THAT'S ***EXACTLY*** WHY I HAVE TO GO. I DON'T WANT TO LEAVE THEM ALONE. BUT IF WE DON'T STOP THIS, THULE WILL COME FOR EARTH.
SO I AM WITH YOU UNTIL THE END.
I BELIEVE THAT IS UNANIMOUS.

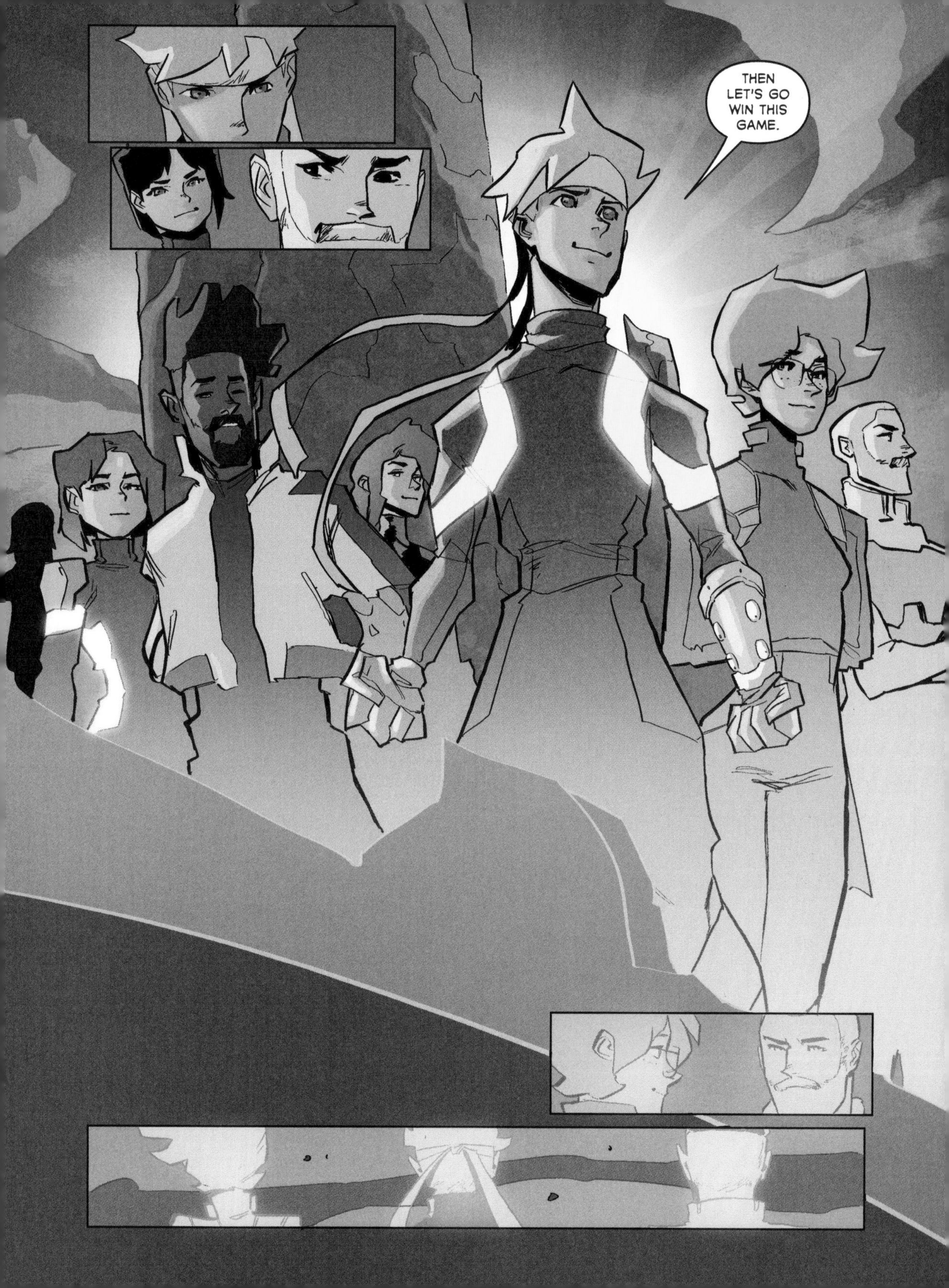
THEN LET'S GO WIN THIS GAME.

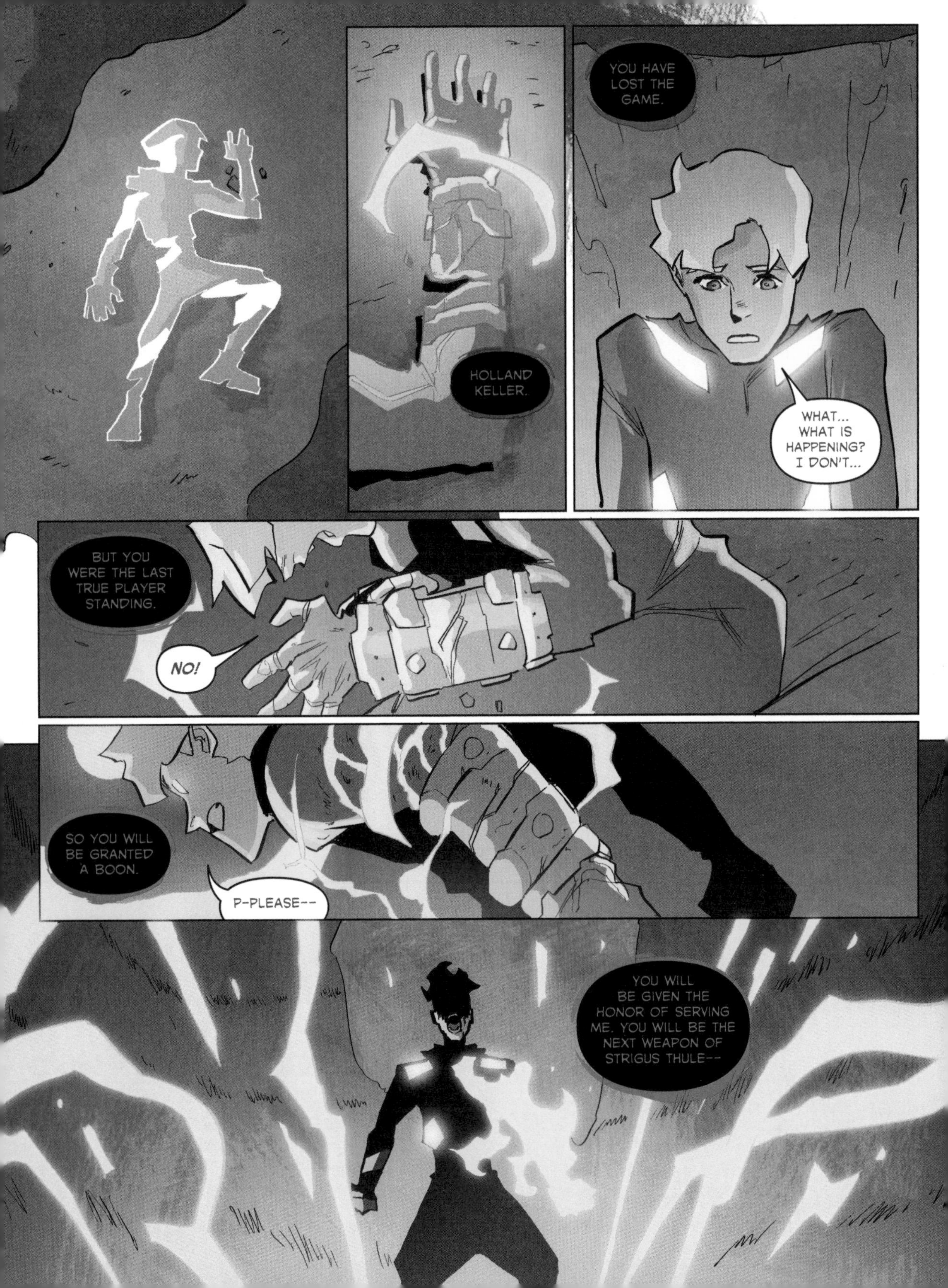
HOLLAND KELLER.
YOU HAVE LOST THE GAME.
WHAT... WHAT IS HAPPENING? I DON'T...
BUT YOU WERE THE LAST TRUE PLAYER STANDING.
NO!
SO YOU WILL BE GRANTED A BOON.
P-PLEASE--
YOU WILL BE GIVEN THE HONOR OF SERVING ME. YOU WILL BE THE NEXT WEAPON OF STRIGUS THULE--

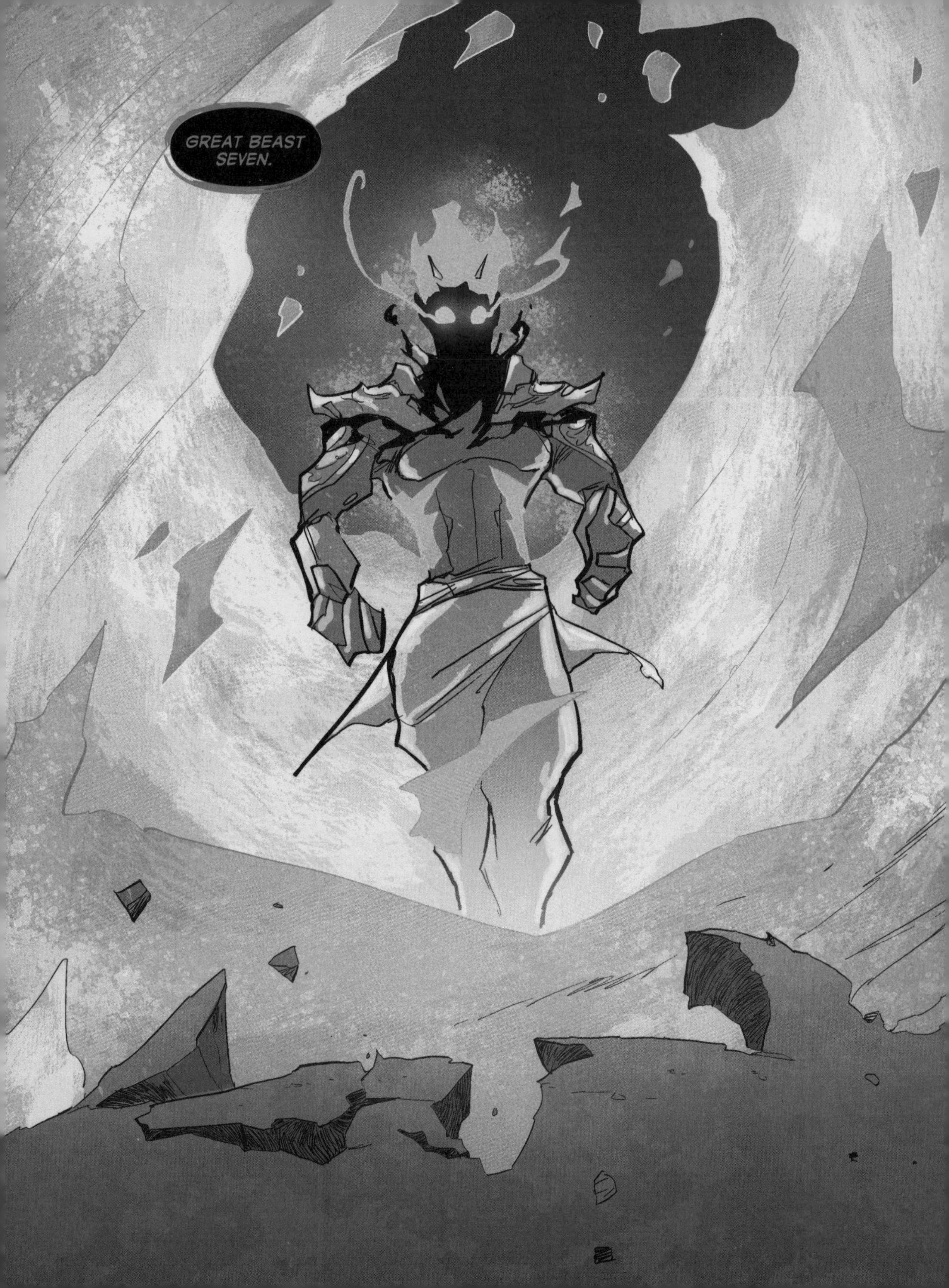
GREAT BEAST SEVEN.

TYLER "NINJA" BLEVINS is a professional gamer, streamer, and content creator. He is massively popular for playing *Fortnite* (which boasts forty million players per month), though he initially gained his fanbase by competing in professional *HALO* tournaments. After quitting esports to become a streamer, he played various "First-Person Shooter Battle Royale"games (such as *H1Z1* and *PUBG*), but found his big break with *Fortnite*. His energetic, entertaining persona and unmatched gaming prestige have garnered him tens of millions of followers worldwide.

JUSTIN JORDAN has penned comics for Image, DC, and Marvel Comics, as well as the "Call of Duty: Zombies" graphic novels for Dark Horse and *Urban Animal* on Webtoon. In 2012, he was nominated for the Harvey Award for Most Promising New Talent and is one of the writers of the Eisner-nominated *In the Dark: A Horror Anthology* and *Where We Live: A Benefit for the Survivors in Las Vegas*.

FELIPE MAGAÑA is a character designer and concept artist for comics and videogames. He has worked with Team Ninja on a number of projects, including concept art and apparel design. His clients include esports organization Team Liquid, DeviantArt, and BOOM! Studios.

Published in the United States by Ten Speed Press, an imprint of
Random House, a division of Penguin Random House LLC, New York.
www.tenspeed.com

Ten Speed Press and the Ten Speed Press colophon are
registered trademarks of Penguin Random House LLC.

Library of Congress Cataloging-in-Publication Data
Names: Blevins, Tyler, 1991- author. | Jordan, Justin, author. |
    Magaña, Felipe, illustrator.
Title: Ninja : the most dangerous game : a graphic novel / Tyler Blevins
    and Justin Jordan ; art by Felipe Magaña.
Description: California : Ten Speed Press, [2019] | Summary: Ninja, the
    undisputed champion of the world's most popular online battle royale,
    accepts a mysterious challenge and finds himself, along with dozens of
    other players, in the battle royale's universe, where they must start
    from scratch, avoid being ghosted, and maybe save the world.
Identifiers: LCCN 2019019906 | ISBN 9781984857446 (trade pbk.)
Subjects: LCSH: Graphic novels. | CYAC: Graphic novels. |
    Video games—Fiction. | Contests—Fiction.
Classification: LCC PZ7.7.B567 Ni 2019 | DDC 741.5/973—dc23
    LC record available at https://lccn.loc.gov/2019019906

Trade Paperback ISBN: 978-1-9848-5744-6
eBook ISBN: 978-1-9848-5745-3

Printed in the United States of America

Design by Chloe Rawlins
Art by Felipe Magaña
Colors by Brad Simpson
Lettering by Carlos M. Mangual

10 9 8 7 6 5 4 3 2 1

First Edition